Collected Stories

The Dalkey Archive Edition of
ARNO SCHMIDT
Collected Early Fiction, 1949-1964
Translated by John E. Woods

Volume 1: *Collected Novellas*

Enthymesis (1949) – *Leviathan* (1949) – *Gadir* (1949)
Alexander (1953) – *The Displaced* (1953)
Lake Scenery with Pocahontas (1955) – *Cosmas* (1955) – *Tina* (1956)
Goethe (1957) – *Republica Intelligentsia* (1957)

Volume 2: *Nobodaddy's Children*

Scenes from the Life of a Faun (1953) – *Brand's Heath* (1951)
Dark Mirrors (1951)

Volume 3: *Collected Stories*

Tales from Island Street (16 stories, 1955-1962)
Stürenburg Stories (9 stories, 1955-1959) – *Country Matters*
(10 stories, 1960-1964)

The Collected Stories of Arno Schmidt

Translated by John E. Woods

Dalkey Archive Press

"Great Cain" and "Tall Grete" first appeared in John E. Woods's translation in *Partisan Review*.

Library of Congress Cataloging-in-Publication Data

Schmidt, Arno, 1914-1979
    [Short stories. English]
    The collected stories of Arno Schmidt / translated by John E. Woods. — 1st ed.
        p.   cm. — (Collected early fiction, 1949-1964 / Arno Schmidt ; v. 3)
    Contains 35 stories grouped under the headings Tales from Island Street, Stürenburg stories, and Country matters.
    1. Schmidt, Arno, 1914-1979. —Translations into English. I. Woods, John E. (John Edwin) II. Title. III. Series: Schmidt, Arno, 1914-1979. Selections. English. 1994 ; v. 3.
PT2638.M453A15   1994 vol. 3   833'.914—dc20   96-2316
ISBN 1-56478-135-6 (cloth)
ISBN 1-56478-134-8 (paper)

Partially funded by a grant from the Arno Schmidt Stiftung.

Dalkey Archive Press
Illinois State University
Campus Box 4241
Normal, IL 61790-4241

CONTENTS

TRANSLATOR'S INTRODUCTION

You have before you a book that resembles nothing so much as the fabled beast with two heads or two tails – or better, perhaps, of two aesthetic minds. For Schmidt readers who have happily explored the first two volumes of the Dalkey Archive edition of his early fiction, both minds represented here will come as something of a surprise; for them, the seemingly simple *Tales from Island Street* and *Stürenburg Stories* will probably read like Schmidt Lite, a charming echo of the obstreperous fiction they have come to expect. New readers of Schmidt, however – and I can only hope this volume brings those as well – will find this a perfect place to dip their toes in Schmidtian waters. For both beginner and seasoned veteran, however, the ten stories included in *Country Matters* are sure to seem unusual, if not outlandish – explosions of the conventions of fictional prose, brain-curdling blows even for devoted fans of early experimental works like *Brand's Heath* and *Scenes from the Life of a Faun* (Dalkey Archive edition, volume 2). How these diverse elements come to be united in one book, how it is that both kinds of tales are part of Arno Schmidt's body of "stories," requires some explanation. And, as unfashionable as it has become to use biography as a referent for critical literary understanding, it seems to me that a biographical context may help the reader grasp how it is that two such very different bodies of material come to be found in a volume entitled *Collected Stories of Arno Schmidt.*

All these stories were written between 1955 and 1963. The first four years of that period battered Schmidt about, left him bruised but still writing; in the late fall of 1958, however, he would land at last in Bargfeld, his retreat on the heath, where writing virtually swallowed up his life. The year 1955 found him, at age forty-one, still eking out a living in Kastel, an obscure village in the Saarland, to which he and his wife Alice had moved in 1951 as displaced persons. Thus far, three slender volumes had brought him little money and only marginal literary acclaim. Three novellas ("The Displaced," 1952; "Lake Scenery with Pocahontas," 1953; and "Cosmas," 1954 – all Dalkey Archive edition, volume 1) had also been published, but only in small literary magazines or in minieditions by minipresses. He could find no publisher for his recently completed novel, *The Stony Heart* (Dalkey Archive edition, volume 4). In the autumn of 1954, casting about for some source of income, Schmidt had begun sending newspapers short essays on literary and historical (later, also political and popular-scientific) topics – at this early stage, often no more than facile reworkings of material lifted from his novellas and novels. But over time, by diligently passing them around to various small-town papers, Schmidt earned some meager income from them – "necessity makes everyone the muse's pimp," he had written four years before. These same straitened circumstances are the genesis of the tales collected here as *Stürenburg Stories*. During just one week in May 1955, he wrote six of them in one furious burst. Over the next four years, Schmidt returned frequently to this means for quick petty cash, writing a total of thirty-one stories. Twenty-five of them are presented here in translation – the ones that he himself selected to include in *Trommler beim Zaren*, the volume of collected early stories published in 1966, and that he arranged in the same order in which you find them here.

Another opportunity for earning money with his pen opened up for Schmidt in the spring of 1955 when his friend Alfred Andersch became editor of the Radio-Essay Department at *Süddeutsche Rundfunk* (South German Broadcasting) in Stuttgart. By July, Schmidt had turned out the first of his "evening programs" – essays shaped as hour-long dialogues about the sung (Herder, Wieland, Tieck) and unsung (Brockes, Pape, Schnabel) heroes of German literature. Over the next ten years, these evening programs would be a semi-steady source of income for Schmidt and, just as importantly, an arena for personal literary exploration. Also in August of that same year, again through Andersch's mediation, a publisher for *The Stony Heart* was found: Ernst Krawehl, who would remain Schmidt's publisher and editor until Schmidt's death.

But 1955 also brought a threat perhaps more serious than slow death as a starving artist. In March a suit was brought against Schmidt, in which it was charged that his novella "Lake Scenery with Pocahontas" was both blasphemous and pornographic. Because certain circles within the Catholic Church and its political ally, the Christian Democratic Union, were among the prime movers behind the suit, Schmidt felt he had to get out of the Saarland, a predominantly Catholic region.

By September he had taken refuge in Darmstadt, a city near Frankfurt, with about 130,000 inhabitants and a quite lively colony of artists and writers, who welcomed him. Ever the loner, Schmidt called the town "New Weimar" (not a flattering sobriquet in his mouth) and its lively literary scene a "repulsive, clique-ridden operation." By some quirky turn of fate (but as was only proper for a solipsist), Schmidt's address in Darmstadt was Insel Strasse 42 – Island Street. Alone on his urban atoll, he produced (by my best count) over the next three years: one short novel (*Republica*

Intelligentsia, Dalkey Archive edition, volume 1); two novellas; fourteen radio dialogues; forty essays; nineteen stories; and four translations of novels from the English.

All the while, however, he was desperately searching for a home that he hoped would be more conducive to his art. He put Heinrich Böll to the task of investigating possible emigration to Ireland – could one bring one's cats? He applied for a job as the sexton of a small rural parish church near Bremen – what was this rabid atheist thinking? In the fall of 1958, with borrowed money he bought a tiny frame cottage he had located with the help of friends in the village of Bargfeld, thirteen miles from Celle, the nearest town of any size, and as remote a spot on the Lüneburg Heath as one can imagine. Arno Schmidt had found his home among birches, junipers, and fog – his spiritual island. Within a year, the last two of the *Island* tales ("Drummer for the Czar" and "Moondog and Pink Eyes") were written, but these two latecomers are already moving in a new direction, are obviously on a different plane from the earlier, more modest newspaper stories. Something momentous had happened – Arno Schmidt had invited James Joyce and Sigmund Freud into his cottage on the heath.

The literary eruption that had begun in Darmstadt continued apace. In the three and a half years between November 1958 when he arrived in Bargfeld and the spring of 1963, he produced: one novel ($\frac{B}{M}$*oondocks,* Dalkey Archive edition, volume 4); a full-length psychosexual literary analysis of the works of Karl May; twelve radio dialogues; thirty-seven essays; six translations (including Stanislaus Joyce's *My Brother's Keeper,* James Fenimore Cooper's *The Wept of Wish-Ton-Wish,* and William Faulkner's *New Orleans Sketches,* which then plays a significant role in the story "Piporakemes !"); the two transitional stories mentioned above; and, finally, the ten stories that became *Country Matters* – beginning with "Windmills" in August 1960 and ending with "Caliban upon Setebos," completed in May 1963.

By December of that same year, Schmidt had begun to translate Edgar Allan Poe (together with Hans Wollschläger, the two men acting in tandem as the primary translators for a new complete German edition) and to gather materials for the single project that would consume almost all his massive energies for the next five years, his magnum opus, *Zettels Traum* (Bottom's Dream).

In Schmidt's case, short stories did not "come natural" – to use the cryptic phrase that frames "Drummer for the Czar." Only three months before that first burst of *Stürenburg Stories,* he had written a brief essay that espoused the cause of the longer tale and novella and in which he called short stories "little poisonous weeds." He was quite explicit – these were "bread-and-butter jobs." Why, then, do even the earliest ones, even those that are obviously hasty puddings, have such a deft charm about them? Their accessibility makes them among the most frequently anthologized works of Arno Schmidt – but, surely, more than accessibility is at work here. One factor, I would suggest, is the reader's immediate sense that she is cozying up to a storyteller in the best nineteenth-century tradition – your immediate response to the tone of most of these stories is to throw another log on the fire, tuck the blanket tighter around your legs, and listen wide-eyed. There is a good reason for that response, too – not only was Schmidt adept at striking that tone, but he also pilfered the narrative core of most of these tales from obscurer corners of the literary past. Can anyone doubt that the horseplay at the heart of "Hurrah for the Gypsy Life" has not been lifted from some older author's work?

The scholarly response to these stories has pretty much been confined to chasing down those purloined originals. A noble pursuit, to be sure. But little has been written to explain why these tales are also such favorites with even the most serious of Schmidt readers. The *Stürenburg Stories* sparkle with their cast of memorable caricatures – Frau Dr. Waring and Captain von Dieskau are immediately real. You sense that the series could easily be extended into a veritable Thousand and One Nights, and Schmidt once remarked that he would like to write more of these fables in his old age. I am tempted to think that it was his own ambivalence toward the short-story form that helped enliven these tales. Schmidt was, as usual, playing hide-and-seek not only with his readers but with himself as well.

You also find a gentleness here that Schmidt the Jacobin seldom willingly lets peek through. In *Brand's Heath* Lore admonishes the hero: " 'You'll have to write a story about it : but a sweet one ! Not one from your rabid box !' (Because she had read my Leviathan). A sweet one then; and I was softhearted and promised." But in writing stories that are less rabid (and less bawdy and less obstreperous), Schmidt also bathed almost all of them in an eerie whimsy, with the accent on the eerie – which suddenly lands you smack in the middle of the German Romantics he so loved. A train ride, a home screening of slides taken on vacation, a blooming cactus, a lost key, a humming electric meter – and you are off into a slippery world where nothing seems to be quite what you expected, a highly sophisticated "Twilight Zone" if you will.

Stories open with lines like: "There are strange days : when the sun rises in its own odd way; tepid clouds draw low; the wind rasps suspiciously from all regions of this world," or "Walk to the window : the streets marched forlornly here and there. Into the hard-frozen courtyard came an

aproned man who shouted : 'Ashes ! Ashes !' " And they can also close
with startling puzzlements like: "Baconberkeleylockeandhume : why *do*
we live like this ?" and "From then on, we leaned in our windows rather
regularly; sluggishly told each other about ourselves; and went on waiting
for death."

Now those are heady sentiments to find in your morning newspaper!

And so, I repeat, these are *seemingly* simple stories, and in their seeming,
then, not quite so distant from *Country Matters* as they would first appear.
After all, the military anecdote that concludes "Cows in Half Mourning"
could easily be taken from a Stürenburg story. Vice versa, the banter about
favorite animals in "Little Gray Mouse" has more than just Freud in common with another "dream" story, "Tools by Kunde." Further evidence that
these series of stories are related, however different the audience and the
occasion, is found in the fact that "Drummer for the Tsar" and "Windmills"
– written only one year apart (and both in the sultry heat of August) – are
obviously "transitional" in tone and in theme. The homoerotic elements
hidden in the former become hilariously explicit in the latter.

These late stories are presented here in the order in which they were
written, a somewhat different order from that of the first German edition,
which took its title, *Kühe in Halbtrauer,* from the story "Cows in Half
Mourning." Schmidt later came to call the collection his *Ländliche
Geschichten* – the best literal translation of which would probably be
"Rural Stories." And indeed, most of them are set in the rustic village of
Bargfeld and its environs. But, of course, as always Schmidt was playing
games, because German *ländlich* (rural) is a homophone of *lendlich,* a
nonce word that is immediately recognizable as meaning "of the loins."
Hamlet's pun seemed a natural here (did it "come natural" perhaps?) –
hence my English title of *Country Matters.*

It quickly becomes apparent as you make your way through them that
the stories' ordering is more than simply chronological. One after the
other, they meander down ever more tortuous psychosexual paths overgrown with the tangles and brambles of literary and linguistic complexity.
No doubt of it – Joyce and Freud are constant companions. And yet, every
page of every story raises the cry and flaunts the artistry of Arno Schmidt.
Here they are, all ten of them: the idyllic summer's day of "Windmills,"
when a lifeguard learns he is being reassigned to Buggersdorf; the geodetic
conundrum of "Sunward . . ."; the high silliness of "Tails," ending in pages
of "nonsense" poetry; a hard day of sawing wood in "Cows in Half Mourning"; the phallic TV tower that somehow gets "inverted" into a tube in
"Great Cain"; those Dutch dolls at the end of the dream-laden "Tools by

Kunde"; the wild burlesque of "Piporakemes !," whose title is the first in a myriad of riddles that demand and seem to defy solution; the upstream traipse of "The Waterway," ending in MURDER!; the chilled dialogue of "New Year's Eve Adventures"; and, finally, the mythic, Orphean madness of "Caliban," about which Schmidt wrote to his publisher Ernst Krawehl, "Screw myth! People should amuse themselves."

Indeed they should, and I know of no writer who can amuse on such a high level of intellectual ribaldry and ribald intellectuality – and simultaneously expose the pain that haunts our human enterprise.

Given Arno Schmidt's reputation as an experimental modernist, a reputation that surely precedes him, I probably do not need to note that particularly with *Country Matters* the reader will be entering a most unconventional world, where Joycean ploys do somersaults across the page. The spoken language cavorts, and its dialects are meticulously transcribed – and here my translating skills are indeed overtaxed. (Where absolutely necessary and, to be sure, with only limited success, I have attempted to reproduce something like a New England farmer's clipped vowels to represent the rural tones of Lower Saxony.) And, most importantly, in order to explode meaning, to supply it with the multiple valences he called "etyms," Schmidt was willing to try more or less anything. When it comes to spelling, then, the reader had best just relax:

> *Faithfully following new regulations* to use the smallest possible phormat for every letter (looks cute with a "ph," doesn't it ?), I wrote practically nothing but postcards, or used 4 x 6 index cards for frasing in-house memos (the "f" in exchange for the above; for pedants).

That is a quote from *Scenes from the Life of a Faun*, written in 1953 – Schmidt was ready to cast convention aside very early on. By the time you get to *Country Matters* a decade later, all bets are off. Capitalization? – you'll find pronouns with and without capital letters in haphazard abandon, but not, at least as far as I can discover, in any schematically thought-out pattern. Perhaps the best way to explain all this is for me to repeat the note with which I concluded the introductions to both volumes 1 and 2.

The unusual punctuation of these texts, which is sure to look strange to the American eye, reproduces that found in the German original (i.e., the "Bargfeld Edition" [Haffmans Verlag], the most accurate to date). But why such slavish faithfulness in a translation? Perhaps Schmidt's own "Calculations III" may help explain:

We are not dealing with a mania for originality or love of the grand gesture, but with . . . the necessary refinement of the writer's tool. I shall begin with punctuation. – It can be used as stenografy ! When I write : ‹She looked around : ?›, the out=come (with an "=", I despise Websterian rules for compound words : it's not an oútcome, but an oút=cóme !) is that the *colon* becomes the inquiring opened face, the *question mark* the torsion of the body turned to ask, and the *whole* of "The Question" retains its validity – no : is far better ! : the reader is intentionally not force-fed a stale salad of words, à la ‹and she asked : "What is it ?"› . . . Let us retain the lovely=essential freedom to reproduce a hesitation precisely : "well – hm – : Idunno – – : can we *do* that . . . ." (Instead of the rigidly=prescribed : "Well, I don't know . . ." . . . Perhaps many will wonder why I sometimes place the period *before* the parenthesis; sometimes after; sometimes use none at all : I have my reasons – in almost every case (and with a little thought, anyone could discover them.)

That "almost every" is a hedge – yes, Schmidt usually had his reasons, but sometimes he was careless. Despite his avowals of meticulously orchestrated punctuation, I must admit I often find no real consistency; usage varies from text to text and can even seem out of sync within a given text. But rather than attempt to correct this or that usage or rigorously substitute American conventions, I thought it best simply to preserve the original visual *text*uality.

With that, my introduction is at an end, but please do not skip these final words of gratitude (the same ones, I admit, that are to be found in the first two volumes of this series – but then my gratitude is abiding), for any pleasure you may find in reading this English translation of Arno Schmidt is due to the constant support and advice of many people. My thanks, then, to the Arno Schmidt Foundation, to Jan Philipp Reemtsma, Bernd and Petra Rauschenbach, Erika Knop. And especially to Hans Wollschläger, whose spirited, wise, and kindly counsel lives in every word of this translation.

—JOHN E. WOODS

TALES FROM
ISLAND STREET

DRUMMER FOR THE CZAR

I've never had any grand experiences myself – which doesn't bother me at
all by the way; I'm not fool enough to envy some world-traveler, I've read
too much in Seydlitz or the unabridged Brehm for that. And what's New
York after all ? Big city is big city; I've been to Hanover often enough; I
know what it's like of a morning when a thousand lunch-boxers with their
thermoses double-time it out of Grand Central, in fan formation, and into
the Gilded Age. One of them walks as if a dachshund were on his tail.
Brick-hued creatures intermingle, umbrellarrows in their bloody hands, (or
in hands black as death, too; soon their typewriters will ring out brightly
like bobwhites. All those aroused by alarms. And the car next to me now
clears its chastising throat; even though just looking at me it's obvious I'm
really no longer at an age for anyone to entertain the suspicion that I might
still make a fool of myself at the sight of two lactic glands !).

So, none of that. But of an evening or at night, I'm glad to get out and go
for a walk – please note the triple glottal ‹g›, it just struck me how unpleasant it is, too (‹why›, however, is something I don't care to know; I no
longer set any store by ‹psychological evidence›, not since I made an inquiry on the qt about the meaning of these nocturnal strolls of mine. One
expert said point-blank that I was cowardly as a hyena and a potential
criminal; most of us are, sure. Another maintained I was man of phenomenal courage – good God ! It all quickly became too much for me, and too
expensive. I then gave it some extended thought myself; the real reason
may well be that my eyesight is so poor, and that it's too bright and too hot
for me by day).

In any case my stroll always lasts a wholish hour – I should have written
the more customary ‹whole›, I know; but that would have rhymed with
stroll, and I don't like poems – and you see all sorts of things, and don't
have to feel you're a ‹voyeur›, I mean ‹guilty› or even ‹sinful› : most-of-us
spend our lives painfully readjusting the inverted standards inculcated in
our youth.

The time of year plays no role – I'm quite capable of appreciating a
wintery construction site, at 5 in the morning; when the workers are melt-
ing the frozen pump of the finished job next door by setting fag ends of
wallpaper ablaze. It can be a summer meteor drawing its nylon thread

through Camelopardus, and bursting above the GDR; (I live that close to the zone crossing. And so have granted recognition to the GDR just to be on the safe side.) It can be an evening in late autumn, when you stand there and listen : what was that noise just now ? A nearby cricket; or a tractor miles away ? (Nothing occurs to me for spring at the moment, and I'm not pedant enough to force something just for that; autumn is my favorite among the seasons in any case.)

Afterwards I make it a practice to go to the truck stop; and that can sometimes last a while; because the only people there are the kind who have had ‹experiences›, that is to say, are all still in the midst of experiencing, and with a vengeance.

Just the whole atmosfere of the place : the hyperoptical fusion of naked artificial light and shadows minced small & stubby. The stained tabletops (only 2 tables have cloths, those to the left of the entrance, where the closely monitored high-class customers sit, slender spiral of fingers around glass sundae goblets, in which bow ties of lemon rind are swimming : HE with that dignified insipidity and vacant gravity so invaluable for civil servants, (and so stupid that if he ever had to be self-supporting, he couldn't sell ice cream in hell !); SHE, the sort who immediately plants flowers in front of the camp-ground tent and sets out a pinecone beside them.)

The ones to take seriously are of course the others, both males and females. Broad faces mostly, draped with energetic flesh, the drivers; to a man capable of using a smallish piece of abstract sculpture as a can-opener; (I'm not much for modern stuff; maybe that's already apparent). The women mostly ‹Dollys›, with slightly strained defensor virginitatis, but stalwart : the breast up-front is no Bluff & Tare, nor at the rear is the Porta Nigra.

I had often seen the woman in question, a broad-shouldered fifty-year-old, in here before by the way; always slightly be-toddied, so that her voice had taken on a charming high hoarse bass. She was just declaring by means of the same : "My father was drummer to the czar : It all comes natural to me !". (A logic that frankly I found rather bold, but which apparently seemed quite legitimate to her partner for today, for he nodded eagerly. I realized what his profession was when he then promptly drove off alone : he was out for his weekend jaunt in a hearse. And for 1 whole minute I vividly pictured that to myself. Until I had to giggle.)

My 2 neighbors on the other side first ordered "a packa cig'rettes," (one of them some "peppahmints" as well); and then they did as follows : each put 2 heaping teaspoonfuls of Nescafé in his empty glass, and then poured fresh Coca-Cola over that : it foamed up; thick & yellowbrown; it all seemed to dissolve; they slurped and smiled technoidally. (That must work you up into a wild lather ! Give it a try sometime.) With a draught like that in their bellies they were ready for some good apostasy calumny & history :

told by the laryngectomee, whose silver cannula the Russians had pilfered right out of his throat; (and here his name was ‹Wilke›, and everybody knows that comes from the Slavic ‹vlk›, which means ‹wolf› : but none of that had helped !).

"What d' y' think a live-in maid desuhrves aftah wuhkin' foah the same fam'ly foah 60 yeahs ?" : "A cehtificate from the county commiss'nah ?" the other fellow declared unctuously. / They also wanted, relata refero, to neutralize & disarm Germany; and then some sorta solid-loose confederation ‹between Bonn and the GDR›; and their argument, as always with truckers, wasn't all that stupid. Their premise, you see, was the 5% clause and some future world government : ‹Bonn› wouldn't even be represented in that parliament ! " 'cause five puhcent o' three billion, when y' reckon it out, comes to a hunduht fifty million !".". (And the other one nodded, thrusting out his lower labiation, à la ‹Yep, things ain't all that hunky-dory round heah›.) / "Hell, you still readin' Kahl May ? ! Theah ain't so much as a single cah in his stuff ! They'ah all still ridin' round on hohses, like they did in Fritz the Great's day – no futuah in *that* whatevah !" / (And finally he began to tell about his ‹'speriences› – which was what I was waiting for; which is what I always wait for; there's nothing else I do wait for. I felt like I was at Homer's place : come on : skin the goat !)

: the man in question – (for the mystery of it, I want to call him ‹The Man in Question›. That fits a lot of people : drought in Lower Saxony; while floods ravish Salzburg ? : ‹The Man in Question has once again messed up the arrangements !›) – had been visiting ‹in the West›, goodtimehadbyall; and, being a bus owner by trade, had frequented our local gas stations and auto dealers. Enviously inspected the best-preserved used vehicles – all of a sudden, his blue eye flashed : wasn't that bus there just like ‹his own› ? Naturally, a good deal spiffier and almost like new. – : "Gotta have it !"

They came to terms relatively fast; because the man in question also managed a ComOrg branch on the side, and as everyone knows there's always some cream to be skimmed off that. Except that ‹his› had 2 extra oval windows at the rear : ? "We'll jist cut 'em in !"

"Fifteen thousand ? Okay ?". – "Yep. But due only on receipt o' the goods !" (And how to get the thing across the various zone boundaries; it was after all an object that you couldn't just slip up your sleeve !).

: "So it was me that got it crosst the bohdah !" (Now the offspring of the czar's drummer was showing interest too and leaned her mighty charms closer. Well, at least a portion was definitely natural.)

: " 'Cept that fuhst they'd buhned the whole inside o' the roof"; when cutting out the two new back windows so indispensable for camouflage. They had to go clear to Lüneburg to fetch a saddler : " 'nd me sittin' on the anxious seat ! Nine o'clock came 'nd went" (that's P.M.; it's been 30 years now, but the average joe still doesn't tell time by the 24-hour clock); "ten o'clock came 'nd went; fin'ly, round eleven, I could head out !"

And had been a dark night : the rain poured in torrents; the weathercocks up on the steeples screeched down at him as he, leviathan in tow, spurted his way through the sleeping villages; Paul Revere couldn't hold a torch; on to Helmstedt.

: "I know one o' the customs boys, 'nd he says : ‹Get a load o' them two; they been waitin' now foah three days foah somebody t' pick 'em up. Betcha they skedaddled togethah 'nd now 're tuhnin' tail back to mommy.› They looked pretty grim to me." (No trick to it : waiting 3 days; probably never washing up; with no money; and in that weather. At any rate, the bus was completely empty, so for chrissake he'd taken them along as far as Lehnin. But as might be expected, had adjusted the rearview mirror so that he could keep an eye on the crumpled pair just to play it safe. Also described their more intimate evolutions; to which our oldish listener, her expert's lips pressed tight, gave several approving nods. Though at one point she gave a thrust of disdainful air through her nose : beginners !).

: "Othahsida Braunschweig I now had a white mouse on my tail," (among this sort of people, that's the irreverent name given to a lone traffic cop on his motorcycle); in West Berlin it had been a "prowl car" (one whole carfull) that had pulled him over to the curb and checked his papers : they had been issued for the FRG & West Berlin via the Zone, and therefore unassailable; so there was no difficulty at all there; but

: "theah I stood in Buhlin-Chahlottenbuhg, and the man in question shows up : with a briefcase *that big* ! All of it fifties 'nd hunduhts." And so the money from the sale was transferred to a neutral and trusted third party known to them both; he stood there and by the sweat of his brow wrote out 15 postal money orders at a thousand marks a piece, and mailed 7 of them right there in the post office – nothing surprises people in Berlin anymore.

: "Y' got the license plates ? !" The ones, that is, from the man in question's "old East-zone jalopy" : they first had to be made to fit; which meant aligning the screw holes exactly, oiling all the nuts. And then came the first real risky part

: "through the Brandenbuhg Gate : 'nd was *that* evah tight, like a vuhgin's : ‹You watch the left side; I'll take the right.›"; and that's how they steered their way, almost scraping the sides, through that non-marble symbol of Germany; and on the far side the People's Policeman was waiting.

Now for driving around inside Berlin no extra papers are necessary – but for someone to choose, of all things, an empty bus for seeing the East-sector sights, that did indeed disconcert Mr. Spit & Polish a little, and rightly so. But the plump fellow, who'd had a bellyful of stony looks by now, just kept on pointing to his own sight-seeing corpulence, and to his 1 friend, until the officer finally said with a shrug : "*You*'ah payin' for the gas." And let him drive on.

: "but now came the real problem"; and that was the crossing from East Berlin into the ‹Zone›, that is, disons le mot, the GDR : "Now I'd already mobilized all my buddies befoahand : ‹Find yoahself a real lonely bordah crossin'›" – he held his index finger to great effect an inch away from his thick caesarian lips, and glinted majestically at us listeners (and flattered too. The gesticulations of narrators here are manifold.)

: " 'nd best head in the direction of Ludwigslust. – So I jist keep drivin' right along the canal. Nobody ahead of us, nobody behind; it's really not much mohn'n a tractuh path." Up on the starboard the guardhouse came into view : just a plank shanty, quite nondescript. They pulled up to within 1000 feet :

: "then we climbed down. I say : ‹Git the plates : me up front, you at the reah !› And jist screwed on the nuts with our bahr finguhs. The old plates into the canal; and still not a lousy soul in sight. 'nd now I stand up. 'nd now I tuhn around. 'nd all I say is : ‹Heah's youah bus.›" (And we all nodded in envious rhythm : there are still some real men !).

: "He couldn't believe it neithah ! That he had a new vehicle." Just kept beaming at the shiny lacquer of his Western prodigy, the man in question did. And then at his bold-plump pal. Had swung himself up blissfully behind the wheel; pressed an extra "East c=note : foah a good lunch !" in his hand; and then had rumbled off.

: " 'nd I go on watchin' till he cruised up to that guahdhouse. And one fella peeks out, jist his head. And then jist a wave o' his hand" – and gave a limp and drowsy imitation wave of his own such as I, in a long and mis-spent life, had never seen before – "and he gives anothah wave – : and then he's through. No papahs checked. Nothin' . . .". And, shaking his head slightly, spread his hands; and let them fall back down onto the tabletop : home run.

We were obliged to nod yet again. And did it gladly. The other fellow offered him a butt in recognition.

"Now that's somethin' I didn't know neithah, that that Brandenbuhg Gate ain't all that massive. I al'ays figuhed granite at the least, or

whatevah." But the narrator just dismissed this with a shake of his knowledgeable head : no; not at all : "Whitewash 's flakin' off it everywheah."

"It all comes natural to *me*," said the valkyrie, and leaned back more
amply : "My father was drummer to the czar !"

TRADING KEYS

It's very lonely way out here on the Saar. Ravines with vertical walls of variegated Triassic sandstone; blocking your path are boulder boys, tall as houses and in rust-red bushrangers outfits, the giant tottering wacke for skulls; (‹then come mountains where it is said people with goatfeet dwell; and when you have crossed them, others who sleep for six months long› – I have always loved to read passages like that in Herodotus. (My first epos, ‹SATASPES›.))

In that sleepy village where I lived in those days, I had just returned from a walk in the woods; the usual invisible cobwebs had rustled and glued themselves across my bit of brow as I twisted my way through brush and hardwood. Above, to both sides of the road, the meadows stormed toward me, sabered tufts atop the giddy heads; wind dodged in here and out there; it looked as if the weather would turn round.

Afterward I sat, tired and content, in my one room, rather devoid of furniture, but if need be I can use my typewriter case for a pillow, and the parlor door for my blanket. Besides which, you think better with less gear : my ideal would be an empty room with no door; two naked windows, with no curtains, in each of which the gaunt crossbar wrenches – invaluable for trimmed skies like those at four in the morning; or evenings, when spindly red serpents' tongues hiss in search of the sun, (and already my fingers were twisting congruently).

(Plus this, by way of explanation : I live from the revenues of my typewriter. Mostly sweet trifles : newspaper articles; small talk; in the unabridged Brehm you'll find the concept of the ‹menagerie scene› – where ten or so species stand around informally in a paradisiacal landscape – which was the method I used for my little productions, ‹Concerning Learned Men with Scoldes for Wives›. At most, a serious evening radio program on occasion. ‹Fouqué and Several of His Contemporaries›. Not an attractive profession !).

So sit there, and with eyes wide gaze across the garden beds of thought. (Up ahead, in front of me, the pocket watch ticked; I'm old-fashioned, and prize these crude clock clumps, in miner's case, on steel chain). The white wall gazed, as always, sedately down upon me, sedately down; – sedately. Down. – – (The thick shiny dot in the doorlock, that was the end of the key shaft; very shiny. Disturbingly shiny in fact; I decided to glue a paper circlet over it tomorrow.).

Silence. Far off in the village fields, a puny tractor kicked up a rumpus. Had a nose like a duckbill. And the wall was patient as ary a stone; Baron von und zum Stein. – But something was wrong here ! I puckered up my face : ? : Ah ! There !

Very softly, noticeable only in the altered flash, the thick shiny dot in the doorlock turned. Turned : and disappeared !

Now I'm always slow at shifting gears. I'm usually immersed up to my chest in the jungle of thought, and first have to set my palms in place and prop my way out – : the key was gone !

I leapt to the door; I hit the handle and scrambled through; my head to the right : nothing ! My head to the left ? : hadn't the bolt of the front door just slipped into place ? ! I took three steps (I'm six foot one and have long legs !) – and saw something brown vanishing over in the orchard. An overpowering hand gave me a shove : follow it !

Hunting the brown : the branches gave me a full share of their swordsmanship, carte, tierce, indirect seconde. A dubious yellow sun splotched everywhere.

Chivy down farmers' lanes. After a hundred yards we were at the rocky ledge, and my brown one tumbled headlong into hazel bushes. I trundled down a wall; let all my joints go soft – mygod, I was still picking up speed ! – was sloshed through a brooklet, slammed against a fir trunk; and stood up with arms spread wide : something was sliding overhead; the bushes thrashed more savagely; I ducked, and caught the large brown ball with my whole body; attached to it, a girl's face with sandy head : and we held each other like that for a while, and first caught some breath.

Sitting next to each other. "Yes, I've got it," she confessed to my key with a gasp. Wind suddenly gave a surprised moan; then silence before the thunderstorm returned : medium height; slim legs; abstracted face. "You see I collect keys – famous keys. Of statesmen; or professors." (Meanwhile we both let out yet another gasp, ‹todos : juntos› as the Spaniards say for ‹Yo-Heave-Ho !›). "Or of poets."

"Where do you live then ?" it struck me to ask; and she pointed her head toward the little house up the slope. And her coat, too, was as frazzled as my own, and her shoes worn disreputably awry. "Don't believe it; have to see it first !". And so we walked peaceably side by side to her place : one room; white walls; refugee from Silesia.

She turned around in embarrassment amid her shabby furniture; but first bolted the door; then she pulled open a drawer : "Here." And I gazed in amazement at the huge bundles of keys, some already partly rusted; on each of them a handwritten tag : ‹Greta Garbo's Bedroom Key›; ‹This One's Eisenhower's›; ‹Key to the Studio of Prof. Max Bense›. She cradled mine indecisively in her pale brown hand; she inquired in a high, hoarse witching voice : "May I ?"

A quick dash outside; I furtively asked the farmer's wife : "Who is this renter of yours actually ?" The robust fat woman nodded with all her red-marbled flesh and laughed : "She lost everything in the east, and 's come unhinged. Lives all alone; harmless. But you have to watch out for your keys !" – With some hesitation, I went back in; if there's one sort of person I have a weakness for, it's collectors : passionate and ruthless; tender and bloodthirsty.

So I walked up to the pale brown girl : her head fit my chest. A thick nest of hair that you could hide diamonds in (and keys ! She was promptly enthusiastic about the notion !) Early forties : that fit too. We looked at one another for a while.

"Alright, I'll let you keep my key – if you'll give me yours !". She lifted her smooth face : "Ooh," she said innocently, "mine's just a very simple lock – it's not worth it." Silence. I took one deep breath, so that my shoulders grew invitingly broad (‹bushrangers in rust-red outfits› was how I put it before I think) : "All the same; I'd like to have it !" I said softly.

She first looked at the key, then at me; up at me; then back at the simple key. Slowly a gentle flush covered her face. "Oh I see" she said hesitantly. Glances to and fro. "I'm probably crazy you know," she protested feebly. I dismissed this curtly with my head; and promised besides : "I'll get you lots of poets' keys : I know 'em all !".

She lowered her brow against me in surrender; her shoulders doubted a bit yet. Then she routined her way slowly to the door; extracted it; came toward me; bored self-consciously at my belly with the key; looked up and smiled : at first doubtful; then beaming more and more. Her hands began to nestle upon me : chest, shoulders, higher, – neck ! And I too angled my elbows, and laid my hands around her slender shoulder blades.

"Oh yes !" she said, reassured. To our trading keys.

THE DAY THE CACTUS BLOOMED

Within the space of a week, the protuberance had grown longer and thicker than your finger, swollen full of promise, the soft slime-green scales splendidly pregnant and distended – : and this morning the blossom had opened, an old-fashioned gramophone horn, and violet, naturally : made you think you heard melodies coming from it, ipecacuanha; I angrily drove off a bumblebee that, car tel est notre plaisir, was about to make himself sprawlingly at home, and amid the clattering of my typewriter, tasted, faint and bitter, a serving of its little bouquet.

Doorbell : I took proper fright at the uniform; and went down with him to where the mysterious mailbox was to be opened at last. Herr Bank-treasurer Meissner from the fourth floor had been able to endure it no longer and had filed a written report with the post office : how correspondence was mysteriously piling up in the twelfth of the built-in mail boxes. (There were only eleven rentals, yet for the sake of symmetry the landlord had used two times six, etcetera, etcetera). In any case, it had been the talk of the building, well before my cactus began to bud.

All the same, excluding the civil servant, there were only five of us witnesses; for it was morning and most people were at work. To wit : the old man of a thousand moons, gushing his customary verbal castings; the house-painter's little boy; Frau Findeisen, well into her forties and with recently renovated bronze hair; Gudrun Lauenstein (age seventeen); and I, moi même. With my left eye, I greeted the beaming lady of fresh coiffure; with my right, I gave Gudrun a wink (I'm a bachelor and may do this !) : she stood there solemnly on legs like black pins, portraying a Fate. A red-hooded child, a scrawny branch in its hand, galloped past the open house door, screaming gently, all the while bouncing up off the asphalt, bouncing up, bouncing up.

The civil servant tried keys and picklocks (‹And from the top : it's no go, it's no go !›) : Aahh the plethora of polychromatic print ! (Quick as lightning, Gudrun slipped a note into my hand : ‹The sun is gone !›. – I understood at once : she had decided to become a writer, and was in the habit of presenting me from time to time with themes for my consideration. She read anything in print, at madcap speed, and identified with the heroine; once a detective story, with the faithless husband an object of conscientious loathing : three days later and her behavior toward me was still strangely loutish, and her frigidity, ominous in any case, glacial. I gave a disapproving shake of the mouth : too violent an invention, this pereat mundus fiat poesia : no go !).

So then, the junk mail : the grand opening of a self-service market; the total-electric household; buy Dairy=Maidenform margarine : barbaric names, I entertained no hope of retaining them. Ah, here, some printed matter with an address : "C'mon Holofernes !" (the Saxon house-painter had once sent the lad off to the bakery, "Whole loaf, Ernie !", and the poor thing, previously just ‹Ernst›, now bore the full title for all time).

Peep to the left : what a bosom Frau Findeisen had, a 42 at least ! Outside a police squad=(prowl= ??)car came yowling down the street; we cozily watched it drive on, and hazarded our guesses : size 42 ?

(Gudrun had been carefully observing my touch-typing eyes; scribbled, and shoved the note between my fingers : ‹Outbreak of a plague that cuts down everyone over seventeen !›. I concentrated on my right eye; I flirtatiously whispinquired : "Me too ? !". Propped icily on thin legs, she wrote : "You too ! !").

Meanwhile more printed matter gushed forth : old newspapers; a company in Essen was offering A-bomb-proof coats, 10% extra with hood; remodel with an all-gas household. There ! : a letter for the widow Margarete Selbner, Herrenweg 3 (and a half dozen question marks all over it; the mailmen, at their wit's end, poor bastards, had blindly stuffed the thing in the nameless slot). But things were getting serious now; the civil servant made a note of the matter, grim and with lips layered tight. I also pretended to be taking notes : I'm a journalist, I made haste to explain. And he groaned through his nose : spared nothing !

A lottery ticket; the ‹Alliance of Germans› was active; I decided I preferred Gudrun today after all. "Religion is based more on the fear of the devil than on love of God," I said, driving Frau Findeisen off. "The wise man keeps his superior knowledge as secret as he would a hernia" I acceded to the cautious civil servant. On the stairs, I instructed Gudrun in an unfailing method for getting acquainted with the domestic life of poets : dress up as a chimney sweep; blacken the face; check the ovens and fireplaces : "You'll have to lay a metal plate there across the front; twelve by eighteen, new regulation !"

Then, up in my place, I also explained to her about the cactus blossom – she, however, heard a quite different melody, (something like ‹Apoxyomenus›, most remarkable !) – and her second-shift instructions didn't begin until 2:45.

NEIGHBOR, DEATH AND SOLIDUS

Wan green face, with mouth tied in a loose black bow – at least that's how it looked by moonlight, at five in the morning. Once again, I hadn't been able to sleep, and had gone to the window : and right-angled, too, in her oriel, there my neighbor stood, a war widow, we hadn't spoken yet.

(Ingebartels, Ingebartels, Ingebartels, the clock behind me repeated the name several times over, and broke into Flemish laughter : ho ho ho ! : so it's 4:45 A.M. A black car on a black street; its front paws shoveling away untiringly. An invisible motorcycle bubbled up as well, and then pulled the diminishing beads of sound behind it).

I opened my window; and her hand, too, began to nestle formally before her, and we each shuffled into his or her aperture : did she have heart trouble as well ? (I had just moved in, true; but I am very direct on such occasions – and why not ? Life is so short !).

"We two can't sleep," I observed, soft as pajamas (and with what sly grammar : We ! Two ! : now if *that* isn't suggestive ? !). But she was strong too; she nodded her head briefly, and then went on busying herself with the frazzled moon stuck above the old cemetery. Unfortunately, there were also several morning clouds there in the east, thin as stripes (although too undulatory for me; straight ones are tidier). "I like that cloud !" she declared with bold jaw.

May one contradict after such brief acquaintance ? I decided ‹no›; and was mercifully spared any reply by the whistle of the train from the East Station : thus does a wandering animal-spirit howl from the alone to the alone ! It moaned, diligent and cold, like those alien voices in the chimney (you can hear them sometimes in our building : do the architects actually include them in their calculations, or is it pure chance ? A clever landlord could place an add : ‹Special romantic howling from the stove : 5 marks extra rent !› – but thankgod, no landlord *is* that clever !). Once again the ebony disk of the whistle floated our way, now edge, now plate (while beneath, it was probably storming off with black lowered brow, through the forests in the direction of Aschaffenburg. Blind).

"I find the thought of death much more comforting than that of eternal life" I said, and she nodded, profoundly convinced : once you've been through two wars, plus refugee, plus inflation – – the long mouth glided disdainfully about in her face : No sir ! Eternal life ain't for anybody born in aught fourteen.

The moon ? : The heavenly dust around it had taken on a soft rosy hue in the meantime; and it, faithfully obeying color theory, an insipid white-green – I turned away, counterclockwise to the left, and by way of illustration fetched the coin :

"No ! A gold piece !" : an Emperor Justinian solidus (527–65; the ninny couldn't even write his own name : he signed things with the aid of a stencil, and they had to guide his hand *besides* : ‹authority› !). Where had I got it ? : From my grandfather, for my confirmation. She leaned further forward, eyes opened with interest, and our faces floated high above the evacuated street (: ‹reciprocal›).

"My grandfather was a collector. Enthusiastic, passionate, ruthless, the way that sort of people are. Physician in Fiume, 1860. One windy and cool evening, there is a knock at his door : a sturdily built stranger enters moaning, his hand to his stomach. ‹How can I be of service ?›. And the helpless fellow admits : after a long journey through the Orient, he arrived safely in Greece; his hoard of ancient gold coins endangered by strict customs control : in the harbor of Hagion Oros, he swallowed twenty of his rarest pieces. Since then, he has been traveling for three days, and nights, without a stop. But the pain has overwhelmed him : help ! ! – My grandfather, himself a numismatist of high rank, palpated with expertise and cunning, muttering and greedily eyeing the frightened man's stomach – another ghastly grab ! – then implacable : without an operation, death was inevitable inside of three hours ! The Frenchman rolled his eyes. My grandfather passed the massive laxative off as a compassionate dose of morphine, and decoratively whetted scalpel against scalpel – for the ‹operation› ! And casually inquired whether among those ancient coins there might be some from the Byzantine Empire ? The traveler, horrified amid deadly white sheets and menacing tongues of metal, consented to all terms : after a successful ‹operation› my grandfather would be allowed to choose ten of the rare specimens."

Languid neighborly laughter, emerging from rounded shoulders, while she gradually pictured the situation to herself. Another glance to the moon penny : "And then ?".

"My grandfather administered a cup of opium to the stranger as well; once narcosis had ensued, emptied out the man's gastrointestinal tract, and joyfully gleaned among the coinage – plus, there was *the* alternative of opening one of the traveler's veins and allowing him to expire ‹during the operation› : twenty rare coins ? ! My grandfather struggled long and hard; finally an unexpected remnant of humanity triumphed; he let the stranger awaken, and shared the plunder with him. – *One* piece, however, he took for himself in advance : a coin from the Thracian city of Bizye, one of a kind : Artemis in archaic-stiff style, a torch in one hand, before her a stag. – Upon his departure, and well aware of his boundless loss, the stranger summoned him with many a curse before God's Judgment Seat – but collectors don't believe in that. Pointless."

"And you inherited this gold piece then from that grandfather ?". Not inherited; for my confirmation. "And the coin with Artemis ?". No one ever saw it again; presumably he took it with him to his grave. Yes. Collectors.

Yes. We then briefly compared the sinking moon with an eggshell; with a baseball of goat-leather; with an aspirin tablet. From then on, we leaned in our windows rather regularly; sluggishly told each other about ourselves; and went on waiting for death.

Hurrah for the Gypsy Life

"Between birth and the grave, there are only two forms of bliss a man can know : that of a conscience that gives no offense; and that of a conscience that takes no offense !"

He broke off, took a lithe leap into the tiny ring, and presented the troop's female tightrope walker with the modest bouquet he had been holding at the ready; his cloak, ablaze in red and black, impressively underscored the salient old face; he told a few stale folksy jokes, announced the next act, and ambled back to us; the black pits of his eyes slid restlessly about in his face, missing nothing : the circumsilhouette of the little town, the smudgeography of the trees, the excited commonplace audience. I know now that he must have been a wise man and a misanthrope, who took malicious pleasure in bewildering us children. And so he continued telling of his youth among Gypsies :

"I stayed among these very special and wonderful people for almost three years, and was initiated into all their wicked ways. No chains could hold them fast; no prisons shut them in; neither bolts nor locks could secure the treasures of the well-to-do from them. With foods and odors, they made animals submissive to them : the wildest horse had to stand still before them; the fiercest mastiff dared not bark at them; all courtyards, gardens and bleachfields were as open to them as the public streets. They could assume all forms and almost any size; they could make themselves visible or invisible as they pleased; for every disguise they had a different face, so that even their daily companions could not recognize them except by passwords and signs. In this fashion, they ruled, without violence or apparent fraud, without commotion, incrimination or accusation."

His glance swept once in haste over us youngsters, we who listened, spellbound by his lawless words : He was more silver-tongued than our old spindle-legged teachers.

"Nonetheless" – he spoke as imperturbably as fate itself – "while I was among them, one of them got caught stealing a young chestnut stallion. They put him in irons and kept him under stringent watch."

(Cornelia, the dancer, here lifted her leg almost perpendicularly, leading our instincts not inappreciably astray; he tolerated this for one understanding moment, and then went on compellingly) :

"At first we attempted to scare off the guards. A large coffin was slapped together, covered with a white cloth, and borne on the shoulders of four fiery devils; torches were lit and held in the right hand. Ringing trumpets along with other instruments of penetrating clangor were set to many a mouth, and off we went in our infernal procession. Some bellowed like bulls, others howled and barked like dogs at the midnight moon : in short, we created such an assemblage of cacophony that no human ear could bear it. Unfortunately, among the guards there were both a good Catholic and a determined atheist, who immediately crept right for us : and so we doused our torches in the pond when the word was given, and everywhere and all at once it was night again."

(In our own minds, we stole the fat brown horse of Farmer Weiner, were locked up inside black soft walls, and expectantly awaited the verdict : the wrong *had* to win out, did it not ? !)

"On the day of the trial, the thief was found guilty without further ado; and the jury was standing up to leave when the wretch begged for one last word. I am innocent as a child, he cried; and : have them lead that horse in here just once ! The judge acceded, and the witnesses swore once again in the presence of the horse, that it was indeed the three-year-old stallion they were missing. The thief asked that the animal's mouth be examined by veteran experts; at once three or four reliable horse-traders stepped up – who were immediately taken aback, and cried out in chorus : why this horse is at least fifteen years old; there are hardly any marks left in its mouth ! The malefactor spoke up once more, still more pitifully : could these gentlemen perhaps look to see if the horse was even a stallion ? This was carried out posthaste, and the experts shouted as one voice : a mare, your honor, a mare ! The jury gazed at the floor in dismay; the witnesses slunk away in shame and confusion; and the judge reluctantly ordered the prisoner be released at once, and the mare in question be given to him as his own property."

He looked at us in triumph, we at him in dazed expectation, ready to believe any kind of sorcery. He continued compassionately :

"The secret was that several of our fraternity had caught another animal; scissors and other tools were produced, along with glasses full of dying liquids; twenty hands set to work simultaneously – and in less than five minutes, the owner himself would not have recognized his own horse. In the night before the sentence was to be passed, we silently broke open the stable and, in place of the stallion, led in the mare made to look exactly like it."

We nodded, completely convinced; the music came to a boom of a conclusion; we ran home in a crouch along bumpy lanes, and in our thoughts broke open many a door.

CAUTIOUS PEOPLE

Walk to the window : the streets marched forlornly here and there. Into the hard-frozen courtyard came an aproned man who shouted : "Ashes ! Ashes !".

I had just finished my daily work – lord, what do I mean work ? : I get a disability pension, and manage to keep busy. I'm setting up a giant index, of two to three hundred thousand tiny cards, to include if possible all the persons who lived during the days of the old Duchy of Verden (I come from the area, from Rotenburg; and – particularly now, having landed in southern Germany – have taken a special fancy to do it).

And so my quota was finished. I had also lain on my studio couch for half an hour : how I've learned to despise that Indian-red skeleton ! At the time I bought it, I hoped to lend my two rooms a fashionable ambience : the tiny one became the midget kitchen; the other was meant to feign a kind of ‹studio›. How I have repented sacrificing my old honest bed ! Ah well; too late. – –

A bicycler in fuzzy cap, red, pumped by in a crouch; two girls in black diving gear, their hands in all their pants pockets, strode schoolward. Then the antarctic river of tar froze empty again.

Implacable, I indulged in my customary reflection : what would be the most unpleasant thing you could do right now ? ! And promptly answered me : put on your coat and go for a walk. – So I did just that; flung on the heavy scarf; the mittens : I am cautious.

At one time, it was little train stations that drew me irresistibly. There I would sit before a beer in the dusty light of the yellow waiting rooms; the strong gold and red of the packs of Salems; illumined train windows pearled into the night; the fat and skinny travelers – lovely days, the days of youth ! Nowadays (it's always so drafty in train stations; I am cautious !) it's department stores. It's a gaudy spectral-analytic world; heads roll by; elbows jostle; clothing jungles, coated forests; hands are yapping bright-dyed fabrics; eyeballs rummage; mouths start stumbling; yarn-balls cower, motley helots. Usually I pick out a girl for myself.

She was stepping, short and skinny, very cautiously through the cocomats on sale cheap today; on past carpet-stretchers; (whenever Some-one brushed against her, I noticed, she would pat at her right coat pocket afterwards. Ah, of course : she bought a very skimpy brassiere, and paid out of that right coat pocket : meaning her wallet was in there; and every ten seconds she would feel if it was still there. Very good !).

Well then, nothing for it but unobtrusive pursuit ! Through bovine leather; dunes of cocoa; butt-end eyeballs and teeth agaping, word prostheses; rosy gristled earfuls; ah, the escalator ! (I picked up a cheap new edition of the immortal ‹Shock-headed Peter› and continued to watch. (Meanwhile, who would be watching *me,* ah woe ! And then who was watching *him* ? : ‹We watchers watch the watchers who watch the daughter of the king.›)).

The escalator, solemnly trimmed with statues, glided ceaselessly to the top (across and behind, belts looped adders, socks in mountains). She waited inconspicuously; hesitated – there : now ten stairsteps were empty in front of her – and she set a firm foot onto the rilled tin treads. (Assumes then, that an overloaded escalator could collapse ? And always waits until the thing is moving with almost no load : very good ! A practical, cautious creature).

I followed her at a distance to the third floor as well, where the furniture rests; armchairs settle. Black-smocked girl trainees dragged around cardboard boulders. We barely escaped the lazy vulturing salesmen; and so back down !

And out. Outside the air clotted like black glass; immobile, and so cold that you were sure to roll up your collar with one hand. She held her ground, wise and still, on the sidewalk – from the left, here came another gaudy, spitting tin mandrill of a DKW – let it pass – wait another ten yards (and I nodded with satisfaction : that's how you have to be nowadays !).

She followed almost the identical way home, short and skinny; there wasn't much to her (but nowadays who *does* have much to them when you come down to it ? –). As is the nature of objects, her shopping net trolled along beside her, indifferent and disciplined. I decided I would pickle myself (alone in my little chamber; I am cautious !) in Dujardin this evening.

Sure enough : she was still walking ahead of me. Gervinus Street, Island Street. Down the sidewalk adorned with crusted snow a little man sailed toward her; in black coat, wide cut, with flat cap à la bohème : "Wherrre eez numbaahrr twinti naeeen ?". She vainly tried to dodge him. He swore supplications, with body splayed wide : "O : Wherre ? !". And, disappointed : "You nut professorr : *I* professorr !" And flowed toward where I was following. I stepped up tall and broad in between (between my short quarry and this offspring of Rasputin – though I'm the sort you can knock over with one finger !) : "Back !" I commanded; "Here forty-two : you me understand ?". He gazed at me with white head atilt; he yielded round to the right and back; as he moved away you could still hear him muttering : "Pisantsss ! All Pisantsss ! : Eat onions and podadoes. Drrink gasoline : Oh ! : Gezzoline !"

I turned to the nondescript soul behind me; I said : "Don't pay any attention to that. The man was apparently drunk : foreigner." She muttered, straight into the night; her headgear nodded; and vanished, down Rossdörfer Street (which leads to Aschaffenburg; I leaned against the drugstore wall, and just stared a bit : alright, she had vanished.).

Upstairs : I regarded my studio couch full of loathing : would never be big enough for two ! Automatically pulled the curtains shut; amid furniture stumps : always be cautious !

STRANGE DAYS

: "There are strange days : when the sun rises in its own odd way; tepid clouds draw low; the wind rasps suspiciously from all regions of this world. Jet fighters loop witches' snares in the sky; all creditors take a notion to demand payments due; you hear from people who once made a sudden exit."

On days like these, it is wise not to undertake anything – although, of course, that can be precisely the wrong thing to do ! For who knows if it's the right thing to disconnect the doorbell, drape the windows, and play dead on the couch in the corner of the room ? Reading is not recommended : out of that obscure novel from 1800, there suddenly falls a letter written in an antique, yellowed hand, plus a silhouette of a young girl in the fashion of the Napoleonic wars, and you can only thank your stars if your own name isn't on the envelope – there are peculiar days !

Well, the current one had happily come and gone yet again. To be sure, a gentleman in a black suit had been here, and had wanted to convert me to Mormonism. A long letter from a total stranger had arrived from Spain – and, as became clear in the last paragraph, was not intended for me at all. The usual ice-gray tramp had rung my bell too : said he was a student; and offered razor blades, guaranteed used only once.

On the telephone, a strange Englishwoman had reported, amid accusations and assignations, the following anecdote from her trip around the world : on the island of Tristan da Cunha – 120 inhabitants, no clergy, no magistrate – two people had wanted to wed. The only person who could read fluently disapproved of the marriage, so he had refused to read the wedding vows on this occasion. There was nothing for it but to fetch the next best learned personage : who had then spelled it out, letter by letter ! (Which among illiterates probably only served to heighten the solemn atmosphere – but then I just had to keep picturing it ever so vividly to myself : how the fellow stands there at the desk, his finger pressed to each line and focusing; at the difficult spots he picks his nose in desperation.)

Well, as noted, I had survived all that. Even the sassy red-and-blue checked sunset had been scrolled down : surely one could venture an evening walk ? –

In the black crags of the neighboring building, the door to the brightly lit groundfloor balcony stood wide open; they were tenaciously record-playing; girls stamped and squalled to hit-paradings, shook their colorful locks, and slapped away at the soles of their feet : just get by quick ! (And up on the sidewalk a bicycler was heading straight for me, as if my spot were vacant and I no longer present on this earth !)

At the edge of town, where the gas lanterns have not yet been replaced by arc lamps, it was almost silent and lonely. Moon buoy, anchored aslant in the cloud current. Cats went about their obscure businesses, diligent and self-confident. But all at once, the green Isetta beside me braked to a halt : 2 policemen climbed right out, and compared me with a typed list. Now, of course, every human being is in some sense ‹guilty› (according to Schopenhauer worthy of hanging just on principle); and so I stood patiently quiet, and a few items from the past did occur to me (not ‹rape and murder› or the like – just trifles; it's not important). "Left hand ? !" – only when it turned out I had the regulation 5 fingers on it did it appear I was saved this time round. They apologized military-fashion; and I walked on past the new buildings, heading back – it was probably better to turn around today after all.

Around the lawn the U-shaped front lines, tall as houses; and across the street, too, the same cement Siegfried Line, except for little yellow squares in it. The gigantic bronze duck next to me tried to spit in my face.

And stopped stock-still, dumbfounded – : way up in the wall, there sat the blue giantess ! Immobile at the table; she must have been at least 12 feet tall ! And now I noticed the window framing her, right, just like those on the lower floors : so you were merely looking into a room : relieved.

(But that really was quite impossible ! A female being, as large as . . . . . I closed my eyes; shook my head blindly; who knows what it was I had seen; maybe she'd be gone if I . . . . .)

: Yes ! She was gone ! – Peaceful and gray, with no posters and so, almost beautiful, the building's wall stood there in the night. Accordingly, I ought to be able to breath easy – but what was wrong with my brain then ? ! Certainly, I'll grant you, I am one of those people who tend to introspection, and had long suspected myself. I made a hasty decision to pull my hat further down over my face (which is to say, in the absence of such, to lower my brow), and simply blame it all on this remarkable day : what I had seen I had not seen; and now head straight home ! Double-time ! Only once did my undisciplined left eye twitch back across the huge billboard . . . . . ?

: And stood there stock-still again, a broken man ! : Up top, where the giantess had just been lolling, a rock garden was now in bloom. The dull green succulents, flowered stars of acerbic yellow, a flagstone path pointed sternly off toward : that chaise longue ! Solitude : the bird in the birdbath was frozen stiff.

Darkness swept a hand across it – and suddenly a new picture : Miss Giantess in a sheet of water. The strong liquid stretched tight like a blue loincloth; her face had opened up, the coarse blonde hair sat totally askew, all to one side. (And now, once again, gone : a pity !)

So they were showing slides up there ? ! Had hung the screen in front of the window, and not given it a thought ? : And so I cozily chose the more favorable angle from which to watch, and crossed my arms over my chest for the duration.

Cities jerked past (almost like Hamburg, huh ?); a vegetable market (and the red tomatoes glistened *so* decoratively !). Cars on long avenues. The tent on the dunes : her lopped-off face photographed though a lattice of lyme grass. So there I stood for a long while in the clear night. Sometimes a couple would pass by, giggling as they joined me to look up, but then had more important things to do, and wandered ardently on. At one point the lamp beside the front entrance went bright : an inebriate balanced his way out, shouldering 2 long gladioli, and made a beeline away from me, on very self-reliant legs.

You could go inside, press the button on the house intercom, and say ever so simply : "Are you the lady in blue in the pictures up there ? : Then I'm in love with you !". In turn, she would open the window and look down in amusement . . . (More likely, however, within seconds two sturdy men would come leaping down, with manymany blows in their muscular hands !). And then maybe she was a woman from some distant land whom you would never see; at most her address.

Maybe the people up there had only found this magazine with the slides in it. Or the developers had mixed up addresses, and they were now watching her strange kismet out of curiosity – on days like this, indeed everything was possible !

Or a dead friend and they were dolefully refreshing memories of her – and so, by way of precaution, I stepped back a few paces; for such complications I'm no longer young and callous enough !

Instead, I chose to dismiss it with both hands; went up to my place full of cowardly determination; midnight had passed thankgod – and, let's hope, everything will be back to normal tomorrow.

ROLLING NIGHT

Even the smallest train station gallowed us with arc lamps; jagged bundles of swords ran at us full tilt; bronze saws glided through every face; so that was how a new German soldier looked without a head.

Because there was one asleep in the corner. First he had had a long look at a magazine : dreadful goings-on in that two-page picture spread ! Some Vesuvius or other stood in the middle of the paper and havocked terribly in all directions. It wasn't tossing up just lapilli, but whole mountains, and the river of fire from its peak was like the Ganges. The town being pompeii-cized at its base had domes like the Kremlin of Darmstadt. From the window of every dwelling, a pair of arms stared out, stretching at the sky; but I couldn't decipher the caption, since it stood so topsy-turvy. Presumably, some journalistic draftsman at his wit's end, but true to the party line, had known no other way to knock off the Soviet Union; once I almost thought I could read ‹Klyuchevskoy›. (‹Dollar› is really tame in comparison; it comes from ‹taler›. But ‹ruble› ? : the first one was hacked off a round ingot of silver with an ax; because ‹rubit'› means to hack : Who can go up against God and Novgorod ?).

It whizzed incessantly. Once again, it made striped torsos of us. Brazen rods bustled by insectesque. The man opposite in the leather jacket demonstratively waved his arm in its sling, and explained it :

He had already supplied 164 churches with golden crosses. Six times now, he had fallen from the roof; once he had tried to grab hold ‹underway› with hands and teeth, and in the process lost 3 incisors that got stuck in the lead of the gutter. This last time he had broken his right forearm; nonetheless he had already gilded 4 more crosses in the meantime with his left, and had orders for 10 more : nowadays you can't avoid hearing the auto-biograms of most of your fellow travelers during these endless express-train nights. (And it's a burden too; especially if you have an excess of imagination, and are forced for days afterwards to come to grips with all those destinies !).

How late is it ? This question from the old woman (who, however, was wearing frivolous-violet headgear for which I knew no name) resulted in a half-hearted discussion of the value of two clocks, one of which was a quarter hour fast, the other equally slow : if they were always together, there would be no problem, that little tad of arithmetical mean.

And the lady was from the East; had owned a little house on the Oder (like most refugees; very rarely do you hear Anyone say he lived in rented quarters); and spoke at greater length about Silesia and its ancient-German soil than was her due by the unwritten laws of an express-train night. I therefore interrupted her as she was about to describe the ‹Breslauer Ring› for the second time, with a question concerning the provenance of that word. "Why, ring, ring" she said huffily, and drew one with her finger against the silky gray stretched across her bosom : "The public square, of course; round the town hall." "As far as I know, that comes from the Polish ‹rynek›" I politely demurred : "which, you see, means ‹market›".

She set her teeth together and exhaled heavily; it sounded like "You cabirus !". "Even if – which I doubt – that *were* the case" she said scathingly : "given the current political situation it would be totally inappropriate to know it." "Quite right !" came the prompt retort of a bass so appalling that I nudged open the compartment door just to be on the safe side. And decided to hold my peace for the rest of the trip; lonely as a pussycat in an empty washtub, with the lid on. But she rescued me herself when her gaze chanced to stray outside the window : "Why it's like a fairy palace !". The factory was, you see, already lit up, from top to bottom, though it was only five-thirty, and stared from its stern facade with a hundred eyes into the winter night, and I thought – thought : I really had to be careful ! – what it might look like inside a head that could let the words ‹fairy palace› slip out at the sight of a textile factory : and her sort is allowed to vote !

"Altenbeken !". Every single express train had a ten-minute layover here; for it was one of those rare gigantic train stations with no town, where diverse main lines cross. Like Kohlfurt near Görlitz at one time : as I child I had always expected to see some technoid miracle at such strange places, a flying man, or a petrified one, or the like. I decided to walk along the platform; stretch my legs a bit, and allow the hostility in the compartment to abate.

The low stone pier outside was covered with gray, coarse filaments of frost. (Wonder if you might get a cognac in that dully lit structurette down that way ? Probably not. And then it'd turn out to be nothing more than the dispatcher's room.)

"Uh-hmm, pardon me –" this was the slight gentleman who had sat next to me the whole time, frail and decrepit : "Are you a Slavicist ? – Uh-Doctor Zeller's my name, assistant headmaster : English, French." Just so that I might have an ally inside later on, I promoted myself in cowardly fashion, graduated and ennobled : "Doctor von Ende." He gave a weary and contented nod; and for some time we regarded the gaunt moon together as it set itself freezing in the white knitted cloudwork. "Could you check sometime in Walter Scott, in the original," the notion struck me to bribe him further : "In ‹Heart of Midlothian› there occurs the phenomenon of ‹the full moon rising grandly in the northwest›." He had languidly held his worn-out profile to me, and now asked in elegant exhaustion : "Why ? Doesn't that occur ?" (In the end, each of us is truly all alone !). "No," I said caustically; and just to be on the safe side we both scaled the running-board step, although we would have had a few more minutes.

Toward morning, our journey raced ahead faster. Fir cripples emerged from white moors; puddles ran past on serpentine paths; many blank birches floated back there through the heath. At a crossroads, a stranger held his stiff bike with both gloves. Rimy board fences galloped along with us for a bit. Then above us the forests cried amok once again.

WHAT SHALL I DO ?

Reading is a terrible thing !

When it's said of a hero who is preparing to do some thinking : ". . . he furrowed his brow and sternly pressed his lips together . . . ." – I can already feel how my face, up front, is distorting itself for the same pensive grimace ! Or : ". . . . a haughty smile played about the right corner of his mouth . . . ." – my God, I must look foolish like that; for I can't even manage an ineffably haughty smile, let alone one with only the right corner of my mouth; it's yet another talent fate has denied me.

It must happen to a lot of people ! On the streetcar in the morning, you can clearly spot the devastation that writers wreak among us; how they force upon us the train of their own thoughts, the most heinous gestures. Yesterday, the young fellow across from me raised – he's a student at the Technical Academy, and was reading someone I'd never heard of named ‹Tennessee Williams› (at best that's the kind of name they called the exotic criminal types in my youth, ‹Alaska Jim› and ‹Palisades Emil› !) – anyway, he raised his head, and stared at me with such undisguised homicidal intent that with trembling hand I pulled my hat lower over my brow; and got out one stop sooner (I almost arrived at work too late. Probably he had slowly cut my body in slices, starting from the bottom; or tied me in a sack and let frenzied madmen in leaden shoes dance me to death !).

Oh, the newspaper novel, the newspaper novel ! Just recently, right in the middle of its prose stood the contemptible phrase : ". . . . he turned his head, slowly, as lions are wont to do . . . ." – the next morning half my fellow passengers gave the impression they had stiff necks; they blinked and made contemptuously protracted snorts. There was no living with the young ladies that day either; they all appeared to have forgotten their handkerchiefs and stared us men down most impudently. Only later did I learn that in the competing paper it had read : ". . . . . she sniffed snottily . . . .".

I've suffered from this since childhood ! While serving my apprenticeship with Henschel & Cie., I once read how a young man had so impressed his boss with his great candor that he was later appointed junior partner – : the next day I was almost sacked !

I lost my second girlfriend – no one has a figure like that nowadays ! – the same way. At the most crucial period, she was reading – quite right ! –

Heinse's sultry ‹Ardinghello›; while Satan had slipped the ‹Middle Collection of the Speeches of Gautama Buddha› into these fool's hands : with the result that I was making a try at lowering my rations to the single grain of rice per day prescribed there (or rather, our more customary national magnum bonum), in hopes that by following such a diet I would within a short time achieve the conquest of space and time free of charge. Also had a head full of phrases à la ". . . wander solitary as does the rhinoceros . . . ." and was attempting to regard her blouse with exanimate will – I can't even respect myself now when I think of those days !

And here I am laboring under the same problems even today. Inexorably, surreptitiously, I am forced to keep tabs on what my wife reads, just to know what she is thinking. I've done this regularly ever since the time she acted so cold and hateful for eight days that even I entertained thoughts of divorce – until I discovered that in her serial novel, the hero had just cheated on the heroine, giving rise to all sorts hate and rage. I have even tried (by clandestine means, to be sure !) to steer her : by providing her with voluptuous substitute reading; there are authors, after all, who know how to describe a hautana in a way that will drive even graybeard accountants mad. (But you have to be careful, too, not to overdose; I'm not as young as I used to be !). (Sometime I'll have to slip a tale of noble creditors into my landlord's mailbox).

When all is said and done, these fellows – these literary types – do with you what they will; whether it's by hoodwinking you with the blessed consequences of regular consumption of Blue Bonnet; whether it's by rendering you incapable of stuttering anything but their formulas, phrases, idioms. I once put off a summer trip simply because before taking it I read the brilliant-ghastly description of a train wreck. On the other hand, I once took a trip to the Emsmoore – my God, what country ! : you can communicate with the inhabitants only by sign language; your feet are never dry; and the rain, it raineth every day – and all because an author had set his love scenes there; love scenes ! : ostensibly the local air was perforce as hot as liquid glass; and the lasses voluntarily assumed positions known otherwise only from the Thousand and One Nights – – : *I don't want to read anymore ! !*

I should give rein to my own thoughts ? God preserve me from that ! : for the most part, I have none at all; and when I really do, they're not first quality. I have tried everything; I've trod the paths of reason and science; I put together a collection of works on Mars, by absolute authorities, from Schröter to Schiaparelli to Antoniadi and Graff : and when I then wandered in spirit across the rust-red desert floor of Thyle I or II and turned down into lichen-encrusted labyrinths of rock – who should come sauntering around the next corner but Frau Hiller, lonely and sly ? (Or, even worse, the depraved daughter of the druggist on the corner !). Historical works ? : I conscientiously immersed myself in the age of Cromwell; and promptly amazed my colleagues with my headstrong and intractable behavior; swore strange curses : "By God and the covenant !"; suggested that our buyer baptize his son ‹Obadiah-bind-their-kings-with-chains-and-their-nobles-with-fetters-of-iron›.

There ought to be books for sleeping : in the most viscous style, with barely chewable words, long as fingers, words that twirl into incomprehensible silver curlicues at the end; consonantal knickknackeries (or at most an occasional dark vowel in ‹u›) : books to *fight* thoughts.

What shall I ever do ? !

Rivals

1. This much I do remember : I was gathering potato blossoms in my dream, and contentedly pressed the pallid blue armful to me; in mucky fields. The circumhorizon was linen-gray; like a puff of smoke, the figure of a detested school chum of yore appeared against it : I promptly hailed blows down upon him, off with him, up in a tree, scat ! (He chewed away for a long time on the python bite; but digested it; and stood there semi-solid again). (Then go to the john, the dream burdened with the usual squeamish-bourgeois obstacles; until I awoke, and quickly did it).

2. Back in bed (empty one beside mine) : voodnbaaba : voodnbaaba went a distant church bell : *that* could be a very great danger of course ! I had been watching her since the day before yesterday : how she took almost the exact same paths I did. Once even with easelette and watercolor box : that's something I've always been rather poor at (although for a writer it's of invaluable help to fix color values ! How often I've brooded over a manuscript, immersed to exhaustion : in this one very specific lighting for a thunderstorm . . . . . ? !). The plumbing in the wall, country-inn wall, began to gurgle, like a drowning man, gulping and spouting, belched and upchucked – presumably Long Michael Grinsnout, the landlord, was up (not his real name of course; I know very well what it is, too; but I prefer not to). If she was a young authoress, then I was done for : those beasts do it all on raw talent ! (I.e., I used to be like that at one time, too. But I'm 45 now and work more slowly, use chronicles and archives; if I greedily hoard all the good turns of phrase that occur to me over the space of 3 years, it ends up a quite passable book; so I'm not quite your little confection on a stick just yet either !). And there are sundry means by which you can knock out the competition; tried and untried : avanti !

3. In the inn's common room; for breakfast (7 marks 50 per day, for 1 room with 2 beds, board and room, wasn't too expensive. Especially since the landlady, puffy cheeked allround, really exerted herself for the meals : "Can I have a look at the register, Frau Schnabel ?"). Ah : here ! (And would you look at that handwriting : I mean if *that*'s not hypertalented !). ‹Petra›, yes, that you could just make out. But now the last name : was that ‹Vandling› or ‹van der Longen› ? (And loitering around in the ‹profession› column was such a corkscrew that all I could manage was a long, spiteful stare !).

4. Now she appeared, in some dress or other. Sat down in the corner by the door, in artificial twilight; the camera strap between her breasts – no : took it off and sucked on her soft-boiled matutinal egg. (A small coalblack cat stalked in on long legs : to her, to her. Received his bit of sausage casing too; her hand coaxed absentmindedly in blackness – wasn't she making some notes or something there ? !). So I went upstairs, and imbibed (against doctor's orders) some Asbach; (diluted with whisky).

5. Château courtyard : wasn't that her sitting at the south front again ? ! I stubbornly took the requisite pictures; always with her, always with her (maybe you could introduce *that* as an episode in the novel, too ?). The wind made crow's-feet on the château pond. And she stood up.

6. Steal over to her easel : ? : well, nothing special. Just a watercolor. Very old-fashioned (probably studied with her father ? You could still see the regulation cross-striping of the first wash; stone remained stone for her, or more precisely, rubble. And clouds like cabbage heads). / To be sure; you could hang it on your wall. All the same. / I went over to the castellan. I tendered him the shallow box of brazils. The five-mark piece. And, whispered directly into the half-profile : "Just in case later on you might give the young lady some wrong dates ? – To err is human. – And plus or minus 10 years doesn't make any real difference : ? – : !". He took it; and outside I watched the pastel blue girl's back hunched over the sheet of handmade paper : my review is going to give you quite a surprise some day !

7. Midday meal : it wasn't quite ready. So she laid down the camera (on the bench beside her); and walked out behind the building with the landlady, to feed the heath-sheep, ‹Why does the lamb love Mary so ?›. A country inn full of the ticking of hall clocks, yellow midday lights, and mine evil thoughts. I carefully stood up : to the window : ? Distance 200 yards ? : So I picked up her camera, opened the back in a flash (and every one of her shots was kaputissimo !); and slyly reset it to 11 : primum vivere.

8. The hollow cudgel of his hand : Long Michael Grinsnout flopped my dinner onto the table (in my thoughts I clove his skull, so that one half lay on each shoulder : ? – But it didn't do anything for him; so I fit his head together again. Just glad it's the plump landlady who ran things). / She received the same cauliflower. Gaped at the wood of the counter. Solar polygons lay everywhere. She gazed at me, an innocent yellow potato on her fork, surrounded by black frame of mouth. (I looked into the stringy-sullen female face – and apparently was nothing more than a stick of furniture to the young thing. Despite my yellow-red plaid shirt of fashion : bah !).

9. The sun disappeared. Wind leapt about. At one point, the shuttle car grumbled past toward Celle. I was tired, true, but had to gather material for my damn book : lighting, objects, idiomatic phrases, Lord set us free.

10. So up and out : Wasn't that the creature sitting out in the open air again ? ! Sitting. Dawdled sullenly up ahead of me. Blocked path and fable. Ripped off a leaf of wild grape and chewed on it; tossed it away and fumbled at her shoelace (tall she was, granted, but skinny). / When she paced off an artful-pointless diagonal across the château courtyard, I could take it no longer ! :

11. "Tell me : are you perhaps an authoress, too, ? (‹ess› : as if I were one !). Confused : "No : a painter." At once I gazed more benevolently upon her : ?

12. Her confession : "I've just got my first commission. From the Natural Science Society in Bremen : 20 watercolors of the château-courthouse-and-environs." After a drafty pause; in round-dance of light and shadow : "50 marks for each picture; 1000 in all." The potato-blossom-blue blouse fluttered; she clapped a hand to her young brow : "How am I ever going to get 20 different motifs ? : ‹The château viewed from the north.› From the west : from the northwest ? : ?". Through the lattice of ashblonde strands (as the wind blew it hither and yon); in desperation : "It's my first commission after all !" (and her father was chief surveyor in Rotenburg). / I took the fluttering lady by her upper arm; I indulgently told her about the château. Gave her 30 motifs for historical paintings ad lib. She quivered and in her delight forgot one theme after the other : Jansen and Massenbach; Schröter and Hardling; Nanne and Blumenhagen. (After all, why had I sat in archives for months on end ?).

13. Oh my dear supperness : she sat feverish beside me; eager not to lose a word. And with dignity I ate of the potato salad (ordered another 2 pairs of franks per head); my mouth went like a mitrailleuse. Rescued, she gulped at her beer, nodded and kept trying to take notes – each time I would take firm hold of her virginal-bony hand : first work through the *whole* complex; *then* select the motifs ! (21 years old she was).

14. "Madam Schnabel ? –" : she was a zesty woman, plump and wise in the ways of the world; but frustrated too and often thwarted. She listened from behind strapping cheeks; her eyes moved back and forth between Petra and me. The cuckoo clock high above us flailed; she shoved out her doughty mouth and nodded : every woman has to learn sometime. (And why not with a hard-working man who's payed 4 weeks in advance ? – Once again a curt gesture of the head : bon.)

15. Petra in my room : we wrote and nodded to one another. Asbach brandy and cigarettes. She breathed easily into a future, and leaned back

gratefully. Let my arm around her, too. And my hand commit demeanors. "Hmm."

16. Her empty dress on the arm : wasn't that exactly the color of the potato-blossom dream ? ! (She was all pink now, and laughed blissdrowsily when I told her about it). The man forever drowning in the plumbing gave one more boozy belch.

AT THE TELESCOPE

Once you're past 50, you can no longer think in the early afternoon hours, (work, yes; that you can do; that's something else); but then again around 5 – or, as is now the fashion, 1700 hours : though that was officially instituted 30 years ago; how ponderous we human beings really are, or, to put it more elegantly; ‹conservative› : make a man weep ! – around 5 then, refreshed by your having been running on automatic, you are tolerably normal again. (17, 18, 19 : *those* are the years !). (But then not really either : promptly off to the military; never any money; your ladylove is sure to marry a ‹rich old man›, as your grumbling curse has it – which in reality means, a prosperous young fellow of 28. What good does it do that you write poetry like Rilke and Hoffmannsthal put together – and that's to be taken literally; because it's really only a kind of transcription – : nah : rather not after all !).

But on summer days, the sun is still shining at 5 as well; roadside trees stand dignified in dust-gray wigs (and if there's a soft breeze, they nudge one another as soon as you've passed : "Look at that fat guy there"). Or, indeed, fiery red kids on roller skates, rowing along the asphalt rivers. I love to hear the pattering of typewriters then too (and in my mind project the appropriate mythological figure : a hyperslim stenotypist; let's forget the spidery scurrying fingers, and replace them with delicate hooves; a zipper pulled endlessly through the silence frees her from the bureaucratic sheath; and she patters away, through wide wild dusty woods, cunning and demure her gaze back at me over the subtle shoulder – on second thought ! : to be 17 again ! – That is to say : now you have to take care of that in your fantasies; which works too; perhaps even better. And yet maybe a concluding question mark all the same; like this : ?).

In the entry hall, then, it was stock-still and tepid; up one flight; and ring Eduard's bell. Waiting quietly. Then twice more : he wasn't that fast at untangling his feet from the weeds of dreams. –

: "Well now ? !" (me; astonished).

Because there are people who, as they open the door, are capable of a look so distracted and dismayed and blank that the visitor immediately feels he's of a lower order; halfway between peddler and tramp; you'd love to cover your face with your hands and storm off, down the stairs; you feel you're shiftless, a hobo, an interloper, sarcoptes minor – oh, out of here ! !

With Eduard, however, that was the ‹normal› expression on his face; I really didn't know it any other way. We had gone to school together : that's

how he'd looked even back then. Incapable of an oral answer to questions
(for written answers, however, the man is yet to be born who could equal
him in profundity and knowledge); fortunately the 2 teachers who called
the shots recognized his sort, and gave him due protection-respect; with the
result that we passed our exams, he with difficulty; I with difficulty : oh to
be 18 again.

Library unchanged; he kept strict order there (which in the end, however, is a sign of weakness; about the same obsessive order kept by some
brain-damaged person defending himself calligraphically against every in-
vasion of the outside world. Comparable to Edgar Poe setting the most
gruesome stories to paper with a hand worthy of a copper-plate engraver :
bulwark against 'orricane and orcus !). The desk fenced in with his favorite
books : again, the same sense of "enclave".

"Ah –" : there on the windowsill, next to his chair, on a graceful tripod,
a telescope : "So you finally managed it ?"

"Yes;" he muttered contentedly : "Once again my great aunt has . . ."
(That was his standing reply to nosy questions or insinuations about major
receipts of moneys. Including purchases of books – I still remember quite
well when he finally obtained the 32-volume, India-paper edition of the
‹Encyclopaedia Britannica› of 1926, for which he had yearned so long (and
there it stood beside him on his desk for 2 months; I fear he did nothing else
the whole time except sit before it, hands folded, and look up his favorite
individual articles : on the Book of Mormon, the island of Tristan da
Cunha; Horrox from Hoole – who accidentally observed a transit of Venus
across the disk of the sun in 1639, and he could get in a real *tizzy* when
speaking of that subject) : in short, he was as lovable as any of the ‹heroes›
of Adalbert Stifter, ETA Hoffmann, or whatever may be the names of all
those vanished potboilers; I'm a textile buyer, and *can't* bother with all
that).

"40 times 60" he described the black-shagreened tube (I knew that much
too : 40 was the magnification, 60 the diameter of the lens in millimeters);
the equally black stand stared atop little pointy aluminum whitefeet; (in
Rubber-Red Slippers).

"Take a look, there !" : I peered through it : an empty cement balcony in
the searing August sun; fenced in by boards; counting from the bottom : 2
white, one red, one white. In the corner a market-stall umbrella, bright
green with yellow polkadots; an empty chaise longue; over the railing hung
a newspaper. – "No; you've got to adjust the focus !" – So I adjusted the
focus; and again; (he was severely astigmatic, and that was of no use to
me) : "Ah !" : now in fact you could almost decipher each of the editorial
headlines.

"It can detect the moons of Jupiter of course. How prettily Mars stood in opposition. The moon : magnificent ! : You know that I'm working on Schröter".

No doubt of it, a lovely item; the image was brighter than the original. He checked in a carefully prepared table, and swung the instrument deftly; pursed his wide lips : there !

A girl. I first measured the ‹true› distance with my eyes : approximately – well – 600 feet (so, in our telescope only about 15). And it was indeed striking : there the skinny gaudy creature sat, her brown thighwork layered at angles; one of her fingers poked into pages of her book (and used it for picking her nose sometimes too; à la nil humani); the profile of an Indian maid, the bosom scanty : ? (And Eduard nodded with shining eye; so it was love at 200 yards).

Definitely; and one after the other he showed me these : a cat on the pickets of the cemetery caretaker's place, brindled white and gray; once it looked down with pity-suspicion at a dachshund howling on the sandy path below, its tail stinging harassment. On ‹Night Field›, a young man who was starting a model airplane freehand; only you couldn't hear the buzzing that ‹normally› accompanies this procedure : most remarkable . . . A dark-green Isetta, being washed by an industrious couple – now they shared, from a crouch, a long kiss . . . . still at it . . . and all the while ‹He› was spilling, oblivious, the premium-pricey window-cleaner from a sulfurous blue bottle (: 18 !). But for the finale, Eduard swung back again, after a brief glance at his tables, to the skinny schoolgirl.

(Apparently, he had got around to the good old French Revolution of 1789 : there lay the Lamartine; Carlyle, Thiers; but Mercier, too, that unreliable, hard-working journalist; and Krapotkin flanked by Louis Blanc and Aulard. On a notecard stood these 2 words : ‹Dieskau› and ‹Suresne› : no shallow mind that).

"I mean take a look at *that* !" – So I took a look at ‹that› : to the right of the chocolate maid, a ‹mother› had just appeared; an argument – inaudible to us – just the arms went; and there was movement in the masked mouths.

"Parents" he said pensively to me. And we both nodded : that's definitely a topic !

"Parents" : "Among the Koryaks of north Kamchatka, useless parents are slain forthwith." / Eskimos ? : "Stab their ailing-weak ancestors to death; and make hasty tracks across the eternal snows". / He likewise brought up the latest African explorer scuttlebutt : "Among the Lobis, no adolescent is considered mature unless he has murdered either father or mother ! And that is supposed to occur as early on as possible; as soon as the young man takes some careless reprimand as an unfounded attack on his manhood. Only then is he highly regarded by relatives and acquaintances; including his finacée, who has been waiting expectantly to become his bride at last. His friends bring him gifts of congratulation; the appropriate dances are danced and songs sung" : "so these parent types had better be careful !"

"To judge by the evidence from primitive tribes then, this idealized children-parent relationship should be regarded considerably more matter-of-factly ?"

For a good while now, the leathern mask of his face – bristly it was; unshaven-hawthorny – had gone tense again. His right eyelid hung low as if paralyzed; he peered and puckered surveyor-fashion across to his wiry statue; his right hand demanded I halt, as surely as any traffic cop.

"Hoffmann, ‹My Cousin's Corner Window›" he whispered : "from which Hauff stole his ‹Idle Hours at the Window›." – Pause. –

"No," he whispered : "At night it's the constellations' turn. During the day . . ." (he fell silent and readjusted for focus – : !). I gazed enviously at the heedless-gray back; he had time for this sort of thing : Voyage autour de ma chambre, and far beyond. With fortyfold magnification.

Then I walked alone down his tawny corridor; stumbled against a sewing machine (now why did the fellow have *that,* do you suppose ? !); and stalked back out, into the sunlight : Baconberkeleylockeandhume : why *do* we live like this ?

TALES FROM THE ISLE OF MAN

Night : and the concrete mixer in front of our new building is finally quiet; the painters in the vestibule have stopped whistling (*and* sneezing; those guys must have cast-iron bronchia !). There are fewer cars now on Heinrich Strasse. And you needn't bother to shave again, either, not for a walk in the dark.

Today there was a special reason besides; my neighbor, an old woman of chaste Valkyrian figure who lived by herself, had told me her troubles from window to window : her granddaughter, a student in her first semester, was arriving by train, at two-thirty in the morning. Total stranger here; and on Saturday night of all times (when, as is well known, all vices have been loosed. Her eyes cast the stony-shocked gaze of a Victorian maiden across to where nothing-but-leg came stalking, scalp lock behind her head, all naked arms akimbo). No, her granddaughter was *such* a respectable girl; in modern languages; and would be here for 2 weeks. She couldn't go herself, on account of her foot. Taking general exception, she motioned with her athletic white hairdo, and gave another, darker bass groan.

Which is why I was making longer loops than usual around the East Station : I had good-naturedly resolved to do the old woman a favor – without having been asked, to be sure – and to guide this woman-child safely home. At my age, you stumble into temptation only with difficulty, and then as a rule take care of the problem in your fantasies – besides which there wasn't the least probability here, given *that* ancestry. But she would have some baggage, and be glad if only for that reason.

2:40 A.M. : back-below, the June night was already brightening again. I positioned myself near the barrier (and took a notebook to hand as well, as if I were writing down selected trains : that *has* to make me look unsuspicious-undrunk !). Ah : it was grumbling in ! An ancient conductor crept numb and larva-like into his wooden shell; only the flashing points of tongs stuck out from where he lurked – – : There ! it tried to bite the hand of a victim, but nabbed only the cardboard bait, and lopped a final, disappointed steel bite.

And then here was the polite little voice right beside me : "Ohexcuseme; could you perhaps . . . . ?" I gave my interrogator a quick look : buttoned-up, proper, to be sure; but with blonde hair and even a flip besides. And, lo, the long family nose ! But whereas there it made a dignified hook, here it pointed down to that nice facade, more like a road sign as it were : here; and here. (Most beguiling !).

"I'm going by way of ‹Island Street› myself," I declared with chilly sobriety, "if that's alright with you ?". It was alright with her (and her small suitcase pleasantly light; and so little detours were not out of the question; at her blessed age you're never the least bit tired at this hour !).

In no time at all, I slipped in an English expression : she responded proudly, full of modest scholarship, laughed briskly at wee-respectable jokes, and tasted the strong alien morning air. "Since you're also studying Celtic, it will interest you to know that I've spent considerable time on the Isle of Man." She blazed up with excitement, and inquired with such intensity, that at once I had to take off down a new sidestreet. And tell about :

"The inhabitants still maintain their unswerving belief in the ‹little people›, fairies and elves. They regard as careless and untrustworthy any man who would retire with his family for the night without having first placed a tub of clear water at the back door where ‹the guests› can bathe. – My landlord in Killabraggan" (enraptured, she repeated the name in a murmur !) "confided to me in all seriousness how he had been walking over the moor one rainy and windy afternoon. It was all suffused with a murky odor, only now and then a stone or bush visible : when he heard a melody as if played by several minstrels. He could not resist the sweet and monotone strains, especially that of a horn, and followed them for several miles across heath and wild brake; as far as a large sheep pasture, where a great many very little people with ashen, yet merry faces were sitting at long tables. They ate and drank and invited my landlord to join them. For some time now he had the feeling he recognized several of the faces; but to play it safe had ignored the fact. Until, just as he was about to set his lips to the silver cup they had proffered, one of them tugged stealthily at his sleeve and whispered : to drink nothing; otherwise he would become like him, the informant, and never again return to his family ! The poor man, terrified beyond measure, decided to follow this advice; he managed with good grace to pour the contents out undrunk – whereupon the music ceased, and everything vanished. Except for the goblet; which he, weary and baffled, carried home and showed to his priest the next day : who of course advised him to present the object to the church, since she alone knew how to deal with such things. And that same goblet is the one still in use to this day for communion in Kirkmerlugh ! I've seen it with my own eyes." – She nodded eagerly, and was apparently receptive for still more.

Beneath the gas lantern next to the athletic field, a car from the savings & loan was parked, with models of houses placed in the windows all around; it made such a nice little exhibition, that we each had to take our pick. (She the smallest, simplest; and her long nose pointed in delight : there. And especially there !). As we walked along :

"Some families appear to be particularly susceptible to such things : a woman from Orrisdale – who brought me my butter every week; a mile north of Ballasalli" (I added offhandedly : that sort of thing makes any anecdote incontrovertible !) "would lament at how her children had had to suffer such things. I was present myself one noon when her five-year-old daughter came home sobbing. She had been sent to the village to fetch a packet of tobacco for her father; and atop a bushy rise had suddenly found herself surrounded by little men, one of whom promptly called out : that she must go with them ! Another seemed to take pity on her – and here the girl whispered in her mother's ear for a long while – and intervened; and so finally managed to bring the others round; all the same, they were so enraged at the innocent cause of their dissension, that they pulled up the little girl's skirt and gave her a sound thrashing. The weeping child held her rear end out to us as proof; it was passing strange : you could clearly see the prints of tiny rough hands upon it !"

She didn't flinch one bit (was she really so childish, or of a free, impudent spirit ? The old woman wouldn't have spoken to me again for 4 weeks !). But she had been paying good attention, and asked expectantly : "Did you learn what the girl whispered in her mother's ear ?"

I nodded slowly and impressively. "Yes; I learned later on. In roundabout fashion. – : The one who had helped her was the spitting image of her eldest brother – the brother who had disappeared while tending sheep two years before !"

And that brought her to a halt (and she shuddered a little). Across the street, two tall youths in black bikini trunks crept from the lonely municipal bath; looked back at us, bawling with laughter, and ran, skinny and soundless, into the distance. We shook our heads indignantly, and turned the last corner : yes, this was Island Street !

"And here we are at number 38 – so I'd guess one of those next buildings." I set her suitcase down at her large maiden feet. We thanked one another. And I wistfully watched her high-heeling off across the cement rocks : and when she spots me at the window tomorrow morning – will that be piquant; or merely foolish ?

FIELD TRIP

Step to the window. (Not pressing my brow to the pane; that occurs, at most, in broad-gestured penny dreadfuls; in fact, the radiator or the long-narrow tiled table prevent it entirely; and the aforesaid bodily part just gets a red and dirty imprint).

Sparrow shouts made delicate cracks in the circumracket of traffic. Wind scraped a dust-dude together from sundry garbage, and made him wallow (until the next car pulled him along and dragged him to his death; together with his one scrap of paper). At my height, then, red chestnut blossoms; on a hundred balconies allround, chaises longues full of creatures hoping to get a ‹tan›; older, wiser folk set up giant, market-vendor-sized shades against the searing May sun, and of such gaudy hues it made your eyes ring : weren't any wiser after all; just older.

Older : and my leg was hurting me again ! Can it be that in your mid-forties the arch of the foot simply gives way ? That all of a sudden, one lovely evening, you find yourself the happy owner of a pair of crude flat-feet ? ‹Life begins at forty›; and nod bitterly.

To be sure, if I had the money . . . . . I'd know how to put it to good use : a tiny cabin on the heath (eight thousand at most; not the way savings & loans do it, tossing around the twenty thousands as if simply letting syllables fall); in its little stall, an Isetta; one thousand vintage books : for once the peace and quiet to work my way through ‹Felsenburg Island›, Stifter's ‹Indian Summer›; or Lessing from A to Z; a real bed to put myself to bed in (no more of this skinny Indian-red rack of a studio couch !); no more need to write for my daily bread, no more ‹experimental prose›, no more refined ‹essays›, no ‹evening radio programs›; only the soundless sorts of clocks would be tolerated, the ones with sand and sun, or at most an old grandfather clock in the hall, which every eternity or so, after I'd spent much and manifold thought, would say ‹hmyes› to itself. Watch the moon set, above meadow solitudes, once it has turned all red, the silver being, as it subsides into ribbon of haze and border of fir . . . . .

A motorcyclist exploded past – they're the worst of the lot ! – : the paper had blown off, and in anger-submission he pointed with the clean-shaven salami in the new direction. And American trucks drove lots of atomic munitions past me, too, and the stench was inimitably that of gas, of sweat of the street, of Nivea cream, what do I know.

4:30 P.M. ? Fräulein Mülhäuser, my only ‹student›, should have been here by now. (I had once placed an ad : ‹Want to be famous ? Become a writer ? Instruction in all phases of the writing profession / given by Otto Lautenschläger›.)

And what rotten luck I had had with my aspirants ! Most of them were totally addled, and wrote in a style like Frenssen's ‹Sand Duchess› – ergo high-grade kitsch; among them had been a reporter, who had come simply to publish an (admittedly, well-intentioned) article about my domestic arrangements; another fellow had taken me to court, believing he recognized ‹his ideas› in my next book – though truly no one would have been more ecstatic than I to greet some real new talent. That much at least I had learned in the course of my literary career : to recognize the good as such (even when you perhaps couldn't acknowledge it publicly : the market was so overcrowded; the competition so great; the instinct for self-preservation prohibited your praising people born after 1870 !).

Ah, there she was coming across the street ! Tall and bony, her strides like a man's, her arms towering out of the pockets of her dark-green leather coat (that was something quite unfathomable too : once, in a very intimate hour, ah, it may well be twenty years ago now, a woman confided to me that a leather coat like that – where we men would of course be enthusiastic : durable, smooth, windproof, expensive & rugged – was pure punishment for a woman ! ‹Doomed to a leather coat› as the plucky woman had phrased it; precisely because the thing was practically immortal, ‹and your years are one score and ten›, 'twas abomination and anathema for every woman who kept pace with fashion's sundry annual changes !). And Ilse here wore one. Hmm.

Doorbell – "Yes, please !". – And there she stood in my hallway, redhaired and lightly freckled; as tall as I; yellow-rimmed glasses rode atop the Iroquois profile; since her father was the director of three local textile factories, I helped her out of the heavy thing.

After a year of instruction (at 3 marks an hour) she knew her way into the drawing room. (My apartment consisted of just that – with impressive bookcases along the walls; a rolltop cabinet full of Leitz binders; living room ensemble – plus a forbidden midget kitchen, in which the much-mentioned studio couch also stood, all of it shabby enough, what's a man to do ?). I called after her – with intentional nonchalance; while putting-her-coat-on-the-hanger – "Take a look at the latest issue of ‹Calabash› !" (The editor, a friend of mine, had finally printed two of her poems, you see; which I had then had favorably reviewed by another editor friend at a second magazine – what's a man to do ? : Three hours a day at 3 marks an hour, that comes to about two hundred fifty marks a month : let him who finds it in his heart cast the first stone !). Therefore remained discreetly outside for a while; while she eagerly rustled around with the magazines inside. "Take those copies along with you, goes without saying," I offered magnanimously.

"Although !" and looked sternly into the blissful-freckled disk of her face : "At least one of the phrases, ‹Lautlos, wie die Araber, / ihr Zelt falten zur Nacht›, might have been expropriated from Longfellow : ‹. . . shall fold their tents like the Arabs, / and as silently shall steal away . . .› !" She blushed almost to tears, and admitted it. "But the translation is *so* good," I continued, consoling her, "that we'll let it go this time. – There are other instances however : do you have any idea what all Adalbert Stifter stole ? His ‹Mountain Forest› is derived down to the details from Cooper's ‹Deerslayer›. Have you read the ‹Old Seal› that I assigned to you ?". She had, obedient and diligent as ever. "Then take out that thick blue one there – yes, that's the one ! – and compare the beginning of Fouqué's ‹Magic Ring› with it : even the names ‹Hugh› and ‹Hugo› are the same : it's downright scandalous !"

And we went through it together, how that sort of thing is done – plagiarism that is; oh, she was learning a few things from me ! We worked our way through useful books, like Wieland's ‹Aristippus›, from which she could study the technique of the epistolary novel. She read the galleys of my books with me. We went to libraries together, where I introduced her to the standard reference works, the ‹General German Biography›, the ‹Encyclopaedia Britannica›, ‹Schlichtegroll's Necrology›; and how to use ‹interlibrary loan›. I took her along to the broadcasting studio whenever I did readings of stories, which was seldom enough, so that she could experience that from the bottom up, too. She typed clean copies of my translations for me (although, of course, for that I could be accused of exploiting her – and for taking care of my correspondence – as a paying secretary; hmm).

Doorbell again. – "Well now ? Can that be my other student already ? . . . . ." And went to the door (I thought it a good idea to maintain this fiction of ‹other students› around her. And *what* tricks I had already employed in order to hide from her that I didn't own a radio ! I had put forward the most refined arguments : how a productive author ought never to hear his old work again; otherwise he'd create nothing new. And that sort of foolishness. But she faithfully listened to every radio broadcast; and reported on it the next morning). This time, however, it was only the mailman; special delivery : the translation had to be in the mail within 14 days at the latest, because they were turning the trash into a film ! Resigned to fate, I laid the scrap of paper aside, and she studied it anxiously : "Yes, but whether we can have it ready ? . . . ."

A quick scan of her homework yet : "Really, Fräulein Mülhäuser, what do you mean by ‹the vocabulary of a man clasped in the maw of a shark› ? : at best he just goes ‹Aack !› – that's mellifluous nonsense !" – (All of it of psychological interest of course; her story titled ‹Dream On› about the woman who can't stop dreaming, sort of the brack water between Ilse's night & day; and other ideas of preeminent uselessness, that is, those she couldn't possibly cope with yet at age 24). Today was Saturday – and so quickly assign Monday's homework : "Write an essay – at least the outline of one – about ‹The Universe of Large Buildings›; that will be our theme for the next weeks and months." And is in fact, in a formal sense, an as yet unappreciated phenomenon of our modern civilization : two things have become typical for humankind, the single-family house and the large build-ing devoted to the products of technology and their management, which is to say factory, department store, bank, post office; in contradistinction to the drilling fields developed from primitive tribal accommodations, à la school, barracks, broadcasting studio, parliament where the elders pow-wow; carnival grounds . . . .

(‹Speech for the Roof-Raising of a Nuclear Reactor› occurred to me : "By your leave . . . . ." – would I ever have something to say to *them* ! !).

What had been that last one ? : carnival. I patted my palm on the desk; I said : "Fräulein Mülhäuser, it's growing dark : come join me at the fair-grounds; as the poet says, ‹Reach in and grab the whole of human life›; and I can do the translation after midnight – bring a notebook along, we'll make sketches, we'll hunt down scenes : field trip !". She blushed; she stammered : "Actually, we've got company at home; my brother, the theo-logian . . .". "Ah, of course. – Well, let's forget it," I said, brought back to earth (I haven't any money really; reckless of me to invite her in any case; as cavalier I'd have to pay; me : for the industrialist's daughter !). But she was blushing so sweetly again and working those large hands : "Oh no, I'd love to come along; I'll just make a quick call home . . ."

Twilight through the streets. The full moon anchored aslant in the cur-rent of clouds : "Besides which, there's a total eclipse of the moon tonight, take a good look; there won't be another one for four years." And accompa-nied her to the nearest telephone booth.

(Strange, standing outside like this : the yellow iron skeleton, filled in with glass plates; the tall girl gesticulating inside, the black apparatus at her ear; turns my way, as if talking about me; falls silent for ten seconds; maybe a villa at the other end, twenty rooms, a distingué mother raises her brows, in the background a fat short father grunts : "Well ? !" And she beamed cruelly at me : "All arranged !".

The racket was growing louder now, the building walls flicker-gaudier. Up above, a little fat zeppelin was flying, down below, the man at the searchlight had plenty to do keeping his beam on it. And contortionists, champagne labels, dancing girls made hoops with their arms and rotated blissfully beneath them; bratwursts sprayed greasy sparks; ‹Pause that refreshes› in the forest of lights; three thousand girlpersons made trimlong legs; red porous faces; lads looped the looped in boat-swings; arms were jostling, ribbons bubbling, belts were cheap as adders; fat sharpshooters snarling inside cheekpads, teddies cowering motley helots.

"Ah, there he is; my brother !" She almost choked on the last tip of her wurst, and pointed her eyes at the tall student now approaching us, who looked as if he were built of black pipes; with high stiff collar and an episcopal look to his face. "My brother Gerhardt . . . . ." she introduced him with slight uneasiness; and I recognized in eyes meant to be ‹stony›, but really resembling boiled oysters, not only the habitual wearer of glasses, but also the proper academician determined to discover by autopsy who this ‹teacher› of his sister actually is. "I know some of your books," he added impenetrably (let's hope not the very early ones, my ‹Sataspes› or the ‹House on Holetschka Lane› !). "And you're working on your dissertation ? Might I ask ?" He nodded formally down all seven feet : I might ask. "The Book of Enoch" was his curt, snubbing declaration, à la : nobody but me knows about that.

"Enoch" I said wistfully : "I always liked reading that." (And vigorous nods at the memories). He turned the sort of furrowed face to me used when you whiff a competitor; to my other side, Ilse's countenance began to beam – she knew me and my remarkable reading habits; she was prepared for anything. "Of course I know it only in Kautzsch's translation," I said icily; "whereas I'm sure you read Coptic –" (he confirmed this with a jerk of the hips) "– but the Dantesque descriptions – or one should of course say more precisely : Dante's Enochesque descriptions – have always interested me; especially after one has got hold of the key, of the cosmological perspective, there's nothing more beguiling really." "The Babylonian ziggurat" he confirmed haughtily, "although of course that still leaves many things unexplained; who can ever hope to understand an apocalypse down to the last detail !". "What sort of ‹unexplained› passages do you mean exactly ?" I asked, "Babylon, to be sure; we know far too little about that; but of course there's an entirely different worldview involved that explains everything." "Well," he said patiently, "for example the beings that Enoch meets on his journey through the heavens; and which he perceives now as human, now as flames of fire." "Hm, well that's really the simplest part," (I maliciously put it just that way !) : "those are the stars and/or their guides around the Mountain of the North." "Mountain of the North ?" he repeated in dismay; and I first had to explain to him the worldview of Cosmas the Indicopleustes – "You know of course that the Book of Enoch was ‹accepted› in the Greek church for a long, long time; and Cosmas *was* in Ethiopia, one need only compare his Monumentum Adulitanum." And so I hastily sketched it for him on the wall of the booth : "The entire Middle Ages lived off of it; Dante; Joinville; even down to Columbus, who claimed he had discovered Paradise in the Orinoco delta, and a mountain towering to the sphere of the moon and shaped like the nipple of a female breast –" (he flinched noticeably, and looked in confusion to Ilse; she blushed in sweet haste; but it really was *too* interesting) "By the by : on the jacket of the oldest edition of Karl May's ‹And Peace on Earth›, without even knowing it, Sascha Schneider depicted an angel as a star-guide – you can have a look at it tomorrow at my place."

He drew up ecstatically tall; he asked : "Is this Cosmas in the Migne ? My father gave me the set for Christmas." "Yes, there too." "Oh, then I'll have to . . . . golookituprightaway" he muttered in distracted excitement; and : "Can you come with me to the car for a moment, Ilse ?" (She made the request with hand and mouth : please do.)

Waiting. Men in narrow black protective uniforms were crouching about in all directions, already laying the fuses for the concluding fire-works. (You have to try and imagine that : the ‹Migne›, comprising the whole 400-volume set of the church fathers, is guaranteed to go for 10,000 these days : and that's what they give out as Christmas presents at the Mülhäuser's ! Wonder if I shouldn't raise the hourly fee by 50 pfen-nigs ? ?). But here she came stalking rapidly back through the plebeian throng : "My brother is quite a fan of yours *too*" she admitted breathlessly. (‹too› ?).

The announcer boomed the news right next to us : "Last ride on the Ferris wheel for this year ! Whoever wants to go ! Who . . ." In no time I had purchased the 2 tickets; in no time had taken Ilse by her freckled hand; in no time there we sat side by side in the gondola, as to the tune of a suitable samba it began the climb to the top.

High; higher still. Alone up top. And dive low into the racket and bright-ness (how does Sir Thomas Browne put it in ‹Religio Medici› ? : ‹And even that tavern-music, which makes one man merry, another mad, in me strikes a deep fit of devotion.› And so on). Newly we rose. Sank again to the bot-tom of the pond of light; into the coral-bright scaffolds; lads rode sea horses; long-legged damselflies tortured bratwurst with tapered fingers, with teeth . . . . .

But Ilse's face : ? : ? ? She was getting sick ! ! I flipped the man at the dynamo a D-mark, and he let us climb speedily off (i.e. I tugged my giant companioness as quickly as possible out of the gondola). "Come on : some bitters, quick !".

And in front of the same booth once again : the black and seasoned waitress poured for us (at a sly wink of my eye, a double for Ilse each time). And gradually her (freckled ?) stomach settled. She took on color again, and moaned in relief a few times. – And whirled around in alarm as the lights were doused all of a sudden. I laid a soothing arm around her shoulder; we stepped somewhat to the periphery (where the tax office is; first I threatened the sandstone building with a furtive fist : ! !).

And now the flailing light was battering our brows beyond recognition; bright sabers were scarving us; a fire-giant let his flowery brain truffle over; and we had diachromatic faces : the right side green, the left a cloudy brown. A rope of light looped in berserk curves across the sky; to the right bonbon red again, to the left a deep frenzy of violet. A cannon blast made for us gowns of flame-colored taffeta (and many faces of fierce roses), until the black thunder pulled the earth out from under us like a rescue net. We moved closer together for safety's sake, and watched the keelhauling of hissing shadows in the phlegethon (but that was nothing compared to the orders troated in bass from vats of light and to the gnashings of fence-high flaming teeth).

"Better come with me" I took the bitters-laden face under my arm; and back through town, down illumined streets, and squares, at whose edges bright dens of commerce loitered : cataracts of hats; black women curtsied with coarse silver hair, many had feathered heads like birdmen. If only you could afford to buy a leather jacket like that.

She hung more heavily in my arm, muttered a laugh, and groaned snugly (had 4 doses of bitters been too many perhaps ? !). She stopped still and pensive before a display window – a pair of black seven-eighths slacks strode grandiosely over blouse bosoms; yellow gaunt gloves groped lasciviously at ladies' lingerie – she was visibly tipsy. "Do you drink at all usually ?" : "Ohnonever !" she hummed blissfully, and laughed and pointed. And grew serious again; and clasped my arm tighter : "I had a look – although it's forbidden – at your ‹other room› : Ohhh !" And placed herself in front of me (the dark passage beside the White Tower was convenient). "I watched carefully, too : there aren't any ‹other students› who visit ! – And your ‹Holetschka Lane› is really so *wonderful* ! ! I just kept stroking your spindly studio-couch, over and over !". She laid both mighty hands around my upper arm; but, well-bred, removed them again, and we walked on through suburban streets that grew darker and darker.

Trees in tawny wigs began to rustle; the distance between the villas was getting larger, posher. On a bench, in the eddy of shadows, a couple were intertendriled. "And that would be so helpful for my brother, your ‹Cosmas› – he wants to be a bishop someday you see !"

And so we took a turn around the cemetery wall; and then straight down the footpath across Night Field; it's cheaper than a visit to a café.

"Aaahh !" and there it hung, a copper gong, very low in the ether : the eclipsed moon. Past scrawny fir widows. A pair of soccer goals stood about, total autism, in the terrain. She looked at me, and learnedly spoke the appropriate word : "Oppolzer !". "Oppolzer," I repeated, and pressed her humerus tighter : considering all the moon metaphors I've concocted, it would only be meet and right to name a lunar crater after me !

And so stand there. On the surrounding meadowlands, the dew was building gently. Sharp-limbed constellations crouched trembling on all horizons. It might be high time to look about for a safer harbor. Her father, director of three textile factories. And I dreamt of card catalogues; of respectable, regular-foursquare work; and you could have children, 3 of 'em, tall and redheaded, not just the everlasting ‹students› ! –

In front of her villa; 14 rooms; up on the top floor, lights were still on. "And now I'll listen to your radio program; with my brother in his room – ah" she confessed. How touching and unfathomably profound that "ah !" was; better not think about it. Or perhaps I should ? – ?

I took her heavy armbones; and laid them around my neck. Mine around her rib cage. For a long time. And we hooked our bespectacled faces, one atop the other. For a long time.

Lunareclipscarnivalfireworksenoch ! –

"And now I'll listen to your radio program . . . . : *Otto* !"

She painfully disassembled herself from me. And kept coming back.

"And tomorrow we'll both visit you : Gerhardt and I." – She laid her large hand to my heart. Caught my face with her own. No doubt of it, life can go on.

SONG OF THE METER

Generally I most prefer to be alone; a character trait that my few acquaintances will confirm without hesitation; that's always the loveliest part, really, this "Ni Dieu, ni maître". As a result, it also seldom happens – I came close to falling victim to the epidemic and typing "relatively seldom"; you really can't be *too* careful ! – that I betake myself to larger collections of humanity, and if so, only to those of a very special sort.

At one time it was the waiting rooms of small train stations (with the emphasis on the "small"; large ones are much too lacking in character : you're never certain that you're not sitting in a hotel or in the dining room of the ‹Queen Mary›; what's missing is the steady, obvious undercurrent of that very distinct notion called ‹railroad› !); and the train platforms of an evening, too, where people with their yellow suitcases stand around like show-window dummies; yellow clock moons guillotine time in jerks; farewells among low iron trees with black rivet-headed bark.

That's been denied me, however, ever since my rheumatism has grown worse. As a substitute, I now take up a position in department stores, next to the escalator (and stay there until the salesgirls lift tails of suspicious eyes to one another); and then there's the spume of streaming faces and voices; you watch as the husband sneaks off when his wife discovers the sweaters on sale : married men, it seems, must buy their freedom with a constant flow of ten-mark bills (and end up reprimanded all the same).

And so evening had come – it has to be evening; that's when everything is tawnier and laxer (the morning's irksome energies have been used up); whoever goes strolling down the streets now, plumage smoothed sleek, even gives an approving nod to the old-fashioned gaslamps (if you bend an ear and wrinkle your brow just a bit, you can hear the monotone hiss of four little flames and tell yourself : that hissing goes on forever, even when you're asleep : most remarkable !); and whoever proceeds to take a peek up top, inside the black iron cap, will see, to his amazement perhaps, that these gaslamps all have numbers, ‹911›, and the next one then, providing food for thought, is ‹1515a› : and there you are, all co-worker at our democracy, starting to brood : what system might possibly lie behind such enumeration ?

As I was about to turn into ‹my› entrance upon returning home from a walk of that sort, I noticed to my surprise that on this winter evening, around 5 o'clock, four furniture vans had come to simultaneous rest before the next building. Right ! : Construction had just been completed, the workmen were still bustling about in all the corridors, little buckets with merry colors made paintbox eyes, pipe-fitters dangled from connections. There was mighty honking behind, beside me, and a new tractor-trailer, its Braunschweig company on the slant, burrowed its ursine head between the crisscross of its waiting predecessors.

"Ain't it grand . . ."; "How the packers are yo-heave-hoing . . .", noncommittal sentence fragments of that sort promptly appeared within my garret parlor, so that I was seized with a desire to pitch in among all those flurried trouser legs and girlish shocks of hair. And so I fetched my old blue overalls from the wardrobe; plus my spiffy-beige beret – wait !; folding-rule in hand; and a remnant of pipe – and cheerfully blended into the hubbub.

There I was yanked along into a loud and frenzied world : here came a cupboard giant tipping my way; hunnish paperhangers laid into me with balata lances; electricians tumbled up ladders with potted lamps in hand, and yet I had such a crack-official look – my most recent meter reading from the power company sticking adeptly, legibly, up out of my breast pocket – that not only did no one so much as dare stop me : but on the contrary : I was a guest in all quarters, an honored guest; the lord of 20 rates; whose goodwill must be secured ! And thus at my leisure I inspected by turns the legs of the furniture and of the women – (both blundering frequently and at length into the wrong apartments); and eavesdropped on what is politely termed ‹conversation›; meaning that mixture of supervisory shouts, husbandly curses (going by the dialect, all of them refugees), children pressing their toy tanks to knitted breasts; female lips keeping silent count. One of them pleased me greatly; a thin, childlike face, ironical and melancholy, very white, beneath her jauntily set fire-red cap.

So get closer ! I purposefully thrust my way into the corresponding apartment : a concerned mother wavered among crates (whose contents apparently were unknown); a small robust father in breeches (the child-brother vanished under the upended wastebasket, quantité négligeable).

I at once took the meter in the corridor in hand (and was regarded with much respect, as I measured and muttered, the tip of my expert's tongue sticking out !). "Ah, you're from Pomerania ?"; and the man-of-the-house eagerly affirmed this; the only good thing about these times is that it's easy to strike up a conversation : "You were expelled, too ? ! How did Ivan behave with you ?".

Oh my; and all waved hands of disapproval. (In return, I helped them shove the furniture into place; had indicated that as a Silesian I was a sharer in their fate.) That is to say, apart from those "tolerably" milder years (and I wished each of our politicians such "milder" years : would their eyes ever grow big at that !); when they marched in, it turned nasty. (And now things got difficult for me : I had to do three things at once : listen to the song of the meter (I don't know whether you've ever tried it : when some night, and all the others have to be sleeping, your own brain has run dry with studying about Schröter or Lamartine's ‹History of the Girondists›, you position yourself in front of the electric meter : there's singing inside, distant voices, the way it is sometimes when you tune in on shortwave and Radio Surabaya whispers in your earwork); so that I had to listen to that. Plus the rollings of baggage outside : retreat of the human army before life the enemy. And finally (and most importantly) the tale of the Dittmanns.

As Ivan arrived, they fled into the woods. It was impossible for the women to hold onto the house, what with all the raping. ("When the drunks arrived and demanded girls, I always went up with them," the dumpy mother confided in a clayey voice.) And I lifted my folding-rule to the lines again, in greater rage.

Then hiding in the woods. (By day they had to work what had once been their property !) They were sleeping forty to the lumberjack cabin when typhoid broke out. (Mixed with dysentery – and one bucket for everyone : yielding scenes that illustrate that vilest of all phrases : "And behold : everything was good !")

"39 of the 40 caught typhoid – and of all people, my own boy, who slept between us two, didn't : that's truly strange !". "And our hair all fell out : completely. We didn't know what to do !"

And here came the little girl (what's with the ‹little› : she might be 18 or so ! At one point I had heard her tell one of her acquaintances : "Say, we've got an electrician up there : he's nice !") puffing up the stairs with a cardboard box. We gave each other a laugh; à la I would that it were night. Slyly-casually, she called something back to a girlfriend. And went down one floor, to this new girl of raven locks.

"Excuse me . . ." (and whatever else it is you say). Then while measuring and estimating for them : "Tell me, what's the name of the young lady upstairs ? . . . Dittmann, sure, but what's the rest ?"

She made a doubtful, puffy-cheeked face (and it matched her silvery eye-kernels very nicely); rocked her head most doubtfully as well : "Then you don't know ? . . ." Of course I didn't know; and she explained it to me : "Can't you imagine why Lisa always wears that cap ? : She hasn't a single hair left on her head ! Bald as a kneecap. She'll never find a man now !"

To be sure, I succeeded in giving just a restrained "aha"; but within me the clouds kept piling up; if you had a girl like that with you – in advanced frame of mind – and then all of a sudden that egg-skull, bald as an atheist ? ! At which I thrust out a pensive lower lip !

(Yes, sure; in Dauthendy, ‹Eight Scenes on Lake Biwa›, there was a similar theme. But that was Japan after all, far away, and more humorous than anything else. Whereas this . . .)

I tore myself away from the raven-locked turmoil; quickly promised new, more kindly rates; and took refuge in my bachelor quarters.

First, page a little in the histories of the French Revolution; Carlyle, Thiers, Aulard and Kropotkin : there were some mad happenings in those days too ! (As I turned in, staring at the white pillow : noo. A woman with a head like an ostrich egg ? . . . : Noo ! !)

The light switch was near the meter, right : it was singing again; all non-Euclidian, outer-spacey and "Hooeyhooeyhoo". Shaking my head yet again : noo. That's most unsettling : I mean with no hair at all ? . . .

MOONDOG AND PINK EYES
(No. 24 in the Author's Faust Series)

1

The night was still; the waning moon brightened the road; away we went on our bicycles. (‹Tarmac›, now that's a more useful invention than.) / (Once again the she-demon had to have a crimson one, of all things, with frame-tubes flamed yellow & looking as if it were wrapped in smoky crepe – and that despite my futile reprimands; her excuse : wasn't another one to be had in the entry hall. Ahwell, I had sold myself to her after all.)

When suddenly, around 3 $^1/_2$ o'clock, in the west, a blackly gray cloud showed up; before we even noticed, and accompanied by violent gusts, it sped like an arrow toward our zenith (‹my› zenith – making me a zenith-owner then ? ‹Who'll buy my azimuth ?› : "Nadirs cheap !").

We watched how just one strong bolt flashed, but heard no thunder, be-tween Görlitz and Lauban; (if the GDR didn't exist : would it have to be invented ?). / The black snaggled woods highwayed slowly along beside us; Doré brambles obligingly opened fans of claws, (if you broke 1 off, they just might possibly heave a sigh, these woods beside the road; and go on suffering their October catalepsy.) / ((In the entry a-while-ago, where we had drunk milk – ‹milk›; you have to picture that ! But then, we did it out of pure wickedness. (And the *way* my she-devil proffered her breast was enough to make a man abandon his senses right there.) – the rooster had stared long into the bicycle lamp, the Snake & the Serpent; and then begun to crow : The Sun does arise, & makes happy the skies. It was also worth noting, that a young cat, which normally produced little electricity (or so that clodhopper said) had, during the recent cold snap from the 23rd to 27th of October, sprayed heavy sparks at the slightest pat; especially long ones, crackling loudly, had come from the tips of its ears. My she-demon – or am I ‹hers› ? – just kept drinking, as noted, milk the whole time; from fiery red palms; with visible gusto.)) / At any rate, we could expect one of the great winter cycles.

It turned so dark we were no longer able to see the road ! (Or wait; get rid of that exclamation mark : the process did not occur with quite that stenographic speed; as it is, people say that I travel about with a handbag full of exclamation and question marks, meaning, full of outcry : it's not true ! !). / A few seconds later it began to hail, and did the stones fall, some of them thick as a walnut. A dreadful wind was blowing; so that the bikes, unable to resist it, were driven sideways instead. Several hailstones that ‹it› thrust against the bells and into the (empty) handlebar grips sparkled; (and at the same moment I saw the tips of her ears glimmering too ! But otherwise, nothing else; no finger-tippy part anywhere on us, nor on the surrounding woodworks, nothing.)

Even my demonessa was getting the creeps. (Perhaps, however, she was only pretending : Show me the man who's included in the Kürschner who knows what's what with demons ? Anybody who claims to, most certainly not. And ‹readers› – ohgoodgod. ‹Readers›, those are the ones who say ‹umbrella› their whole lives long, while a writer comes up with ‹a cane in petticoats› !). / She discreetly reminded me of 1 ‹extended mind game› that long ago, as a young man, I had localized here in the Nun's Bush : ? – I furrowed my most behailéd brow (because now even the upper rim of my (pilfered) rearview mirror had begun to fosforesce). We came to quick agreement; using eyelashed scruples, word shards, lipped perispomena, slights of hand. And, ergo, turned off to the left; (she cunningly let me ‹lead› – and so ‹awaken memories›; they really are *too* shifty.); down the steep clay path, mygodwhatslipandslide : can you call that plank-across-a-brook a ‹bridge› ? . . .

The hail was getting downright life-threatening ! (I & many horses of those regions had bumps and bruises the next day.) / We beheaded ourselves into the under=fir. Crouched beneath the barby weir (= bony wire-hair) of what had perished below. And simply waited. – .

. –. / – –. / : *Pause. The hail* massaged the ever-tolerant branches right-above us. The she-demon counted her paper money beneath (and with) her hooked nose. Figured; and at one point held a brief & indignant debate with her Montessori-fingers. / The hailstones rattled, as if we were living inside wrapping paper; (a cellulose world; we defend ourselves with arms, half-suffocated. Death comes snow-white : that's a possibility *too*. – The nerves of most-of-us would presumably bear up a lot worse under ‹white & soundless› than in Dantesque-rowdy hells.) / She smiled in content, for it just wouldn't end. Begged my leave & gotit. Pulled a scroll from her (fiery fluffed) bosom . . . .

. . . *I salvaged what I could of my ears,* in ski-band & needle dregs; commanded her to speak softly indeed; and the person (?) went right ahead and read, too. Freshly gathered material from West Germany. (But wait : wonder if they, down at Satan's, officially recognize the division ? – : then our sort would do well to ‹adjust› to it, too, right ?) –

2

THE SHE-DEVIL'S TALE

I spent my vacation in the vicinity of, let's call it, Kirchhellen; as an artist, male. Was sitting there 1 day and sketching, in the vicinity of my inn. – / – : 1 car, a convertible, drives by; in it 1 man & 1 young woman (at the wheel). / Lovely weather; high pressure of 30.3 inches, (just right for devils !); and was drawing the next day, too. (A group of alders by the way, near the brook; plus, for a figure, 1 bathing fifteen-year-old, with most big-eyed breasts : cunning !). / The car drives by again. Stops. Drives on. – (I was dead certain now. And proceeded lustily-steadfastly to draw.)

The third time, the respectable-older gentleman got out, and introduced himself : – (some mining baron or other; patron of the arts, owner of yon large villa) : "You have perhaps noticed it ?". (Also large estates in Hanoverian purlieus, where, for personal reasons, he chose not to live at the moment.) : "Would consider it both an honor & a pleasure if you could dine at my home tomorrow – ?"

((And of course my diabolessa had accepted : Now the polestar's red & burning, and the witches' spindles turning. – I began, with pretended indifference, to empty out my trouser cuff – not infrequently you find the most thought-provoking items in there : sand, sure; pebbles; hairs, (from plants as well); little keys. While she went on telling about this mad group.))

: So I went; and met his party. / He : learned academic; totally debauched, and disgracefully rich; brilliant insights into literatures & their histories. The First Lady, a mistress, 25, pretty as a picture : half Burne-Jones half Reubens, and thus ravishingly exciting !, besotted gullet & gut. An ancient-energetic housekeeper, but 1 who kept her rage bottled up inside; (she had been fired once already; the squire was cold as ice in that regard; and only after years of pleading had she been rehired : she knew better now !) : she lived in 1 of the johns, slept in the bathtub, and, fanatically frugal, ate nothing but cold potatoes; she was of noble birth. – In addition, 2 other guests : the 1 an atheist; who, with a bright-red silk stocking in his breast pocket – his money was inside it; and a toothbrush – sat in the large library, and, smiling maliciously, read CANDIDE : a copy autographed by Voltaire himself !

The other – : a schoolchum of the squire. Now a total bust, and so thirsty that every night at 3 he got up, scaled his way down to the dining room; and drank every drop of the dregs. / I stayed there 6 months altogether. (‹By his leave› of course.) : During that time, I saw no drinking water ! There was only beer, champagne, Asbach brandy. In the morning a ‹farmer's breakfast›, so called for purposes of irony I take it : nothing but macaroni, potatoes, corned beef, eggs, sour pickles, and-such, all fried up together; (– I'd like to meet the farmer who eats a breakfast like *that* ! : They'd rather starve; with a loaf of bread under their arm); to drink : beer, champagne, Asbach. At noon, leg of lamb (or the like); to drink : Asbach, champagne, beer. Of an evening coldcut plates, big as toilet seats; to drink : champagne, beer, Asbach. / 6 months; as noted.

1 day the daughter appeared; 13 years old; whom her mother – hoping to vex the divorced husband – had educated in every conceivable vice. Platinum blonde with pink eyes, she drank like Bacchus personified; (or Joyce; or Reuter. "He's a greedyguts" : Jean Paul on Goethe.) I saw her for the first time as girl-in-a-swing & her shadow. She discovered me as I sat a desk – which wasn't a desk at all; it was a wooden lake !. She simply took me up to her room – I mean, you've never seen a room like that !

: 8 windows, ringed by soughing trees : on the pillars, between the windows, gigantic mirrors, in which those poplars were multiplied – ripplings & rustlings to make a saint a nervous wreck ! / (*How many* rooms the villa contained, and *who* resided in them, no one knew any more, by the way; not even our factota, the housekeeper.)

But 1 gifted child all the same ! : "The surfaces of things are more important that their ‹essence›" she claimed; turned ‹Nefertiti› into ‹n' offre tête›; threw herself on her little back, and we twitched for a long while, (and the sparrows joined in the delirium. And afterwards the tiger's eye, red & eyelashless, of the water heater.) From the bathroom window I saw the squire besoming his courtyard : wearing a cap with white-red band, (like municipal garbage collectors); his mistress sprawled nearby, in sheer charlock, orache and oat-grass; 'zounds the Wrytch & Furie; she consisted of naught but midday napping, brunching & boozing.

– even I have seldom lived such a life ! 4 cars, from the most dieseled Mercedes, to a JANUS – the whole house was ‹Janus› allround. / Out of meanness and to peeve his ‹heirs› presumptive, he would make innocent presents of his priceless ‹collected works›, but as individual volumes : "Erna gets 7 & 8; Heinz 3 to 5. We'll toss a couple away." / (And always there were these fantastic notions ! : The 13-year-old was supposed to write an essay on Romanticism for school, and promptly labeled Hoffmann's ‹Leech-Prince› in MASTER FLEA a ‹phallick symball›). / The mistress, schooled in America, had done her dissertation on women's underarm-shields in literature – you weren't permitted to tell her to "Shut your mouth !"; "Shut your doddering mouth !" yes; which she would then repeat mentaliter, blench, ‹much wampum for little word› : thus expressing her thanks, with heart-and-hands-and-voices. God give her 1 hellish night.

The grand seigneur had a gift for the most ingenious analysis of the relationship between Stifter and Leopold Schefer; – ("Tant meiux" the atheist said, who couldn't stand Stifter.) / The ‹schoolchum› claimed boastfully : "I leave bruises behind wherever I kiss !" – though no longer up to it at all; (but did abuse shooting stars for erotic wishes.) / ((1 of the wildest conversations – but that's a story all its own – was a candid discussion around the dinner table, in the presence and with the most heated participation of the ladies, concerning : ‹*Where* would a woman, presuming she had the choice, prefer to have her pimples, warts & wrinkles ?›))

(And there was the ‹excursion into nature's green› – or more precisely ‹into her blue› ! – where, constantly and by turns, the mistress and the daughter fell out of the car, the former to the right, the latter to the left; for that occasion they had chosen the NASH=convertible.)

For a finale, the mistress lay down upon a sofa and began to die. Threw invisible knives into the air, and homicidally caught them again; (wanted, as well, ‹to cut Someone's heart out› – WHOSE was never revealed.) / Finally she died. Was buried. / And after the funeral rites our company went its separate ways.

3

For somewhere around 15 minutes this reading went on. (I never did see the ‹point›, by the way. Unless it was as a ‹tale of manners› perhaps ? – She nodded in confirmation. Economic miraculously.) / The sky now cleared as quickly as it had been turned murky and dark before. We took to our bicycles; (after she had spent added praise at the dignity with which I had borne the tale of Another : not every man can !). / We pushed the frames along before us. First the usual, sticky xylotextiled flooring of light-fishbone & shade, 'zounds Elsner & Tiepolt. Then across the brook, which attempted a loamy surge (and succeeded : up-the-slope !).

On past the ‹Sharpshooters' Lodge› : did the Poles still train around-here ? – As a very young lad I had often harum-scarumed by the place, my bike-basket full of dreams. –

Backontheroad : we were very surprised to see the moon *doubled* ! / We shouted to each other both at once : it was in about its last quarter, some 50 degrees above the horizon in the west southwest. And had, toward the west, at about a 45 degree angle to the horizon, 1 *ghost-image* of equal size, though not quite so bright ! The edges of both disks touched. The sky was now fully covered with thin cloud flora; and I thought I could clearly make out that whenever heavier cloudwork passed, the moondog lost a smaller percentage of light than the moon itself did. (Which seemed to me to indicate that the image had its origin in the lowest layers of clouds : ?). / Nothin' amazed my she-devil any more. Just muttered something à la ‹WHATCHASPOSEHESUPTONOW ?› – I reminded her, impatiently, to be amazed ! – She was amazed.) –

So we let the bikes coast again. / (Conversations about AFANAZYEV : ‹The zoomorphic divinities of the Slavs›. Also, as the barned rim of Lauban approached, about the DOMOVOY, their bodies entirely covered with hair.)

A factory ? : "*In there* lie the ‹Polish attaché› uniforms we'll be wearing next week as ‹observers› during maneuvers." (We grinned, both of us, as we pictured it : FAUST inspecting Bonn's new German Army. Quite possibly those ‹born in 22›. But then had to beat a solid retreat. – : further still. –). –

Was that a light glimmering in the first house ? / – (was only three-thirty after all ! : ?) – / –

: A lunchboxer, with tin thermos stepped out from skwalling garden gate : warm coffee : in the left hand !. / (He hummed – : "What ?". – And Daemona, to my right, obligingly translated)

: ‹Gdye dommov muy ?› : Where stands my parental home ? . . .

PRONE-TOLD TALE

Through the window you could see Rain Street below, made of asphalt patches and black-glass puddles; above, the sky's polygon, nice'n'small. To one side, the death-light of the moon; beneath it the morgue of stiff clouds in fatal sheets. We pursed our mouths in disapproval and went straight back to the stove corner. Frau Doctor watched me, not without favor; set my lounge chair in a more punctiliously comfortable position, so that I lay almost prone, constantly attacked by foppish flames – me; leaning back properly and smoking – her.

Frau Doctor was forty, unmarried, secondary-school teacher; and so clever that I, with my bit of inferior, mossy-frowzy knowledge, fancied myself thoroughly suspect. Besides which, she had her red dress on today, the one with the black polka-dots; and it was my day to tell a story, so that despite the intimate little party we made – we were, as usual, alone – I once again felt terribly abashed.

Which left me with only Norway; and I began with the three geologists whom I had once met there in the Dovrefjell : the finest company in the world; especially for geologists ! It's their nature to halt at every pile of bricks, to make conjectures at every stratum. They smash all stones to pieces, ostensibly to see how the world was made. You show them a majestic pyramid of rocks, and at best it's a laccolith; you mention glacier ice and they begin a deep debate about whether lake-dweller piles might be frozen in it, along with their peat-picks (pretty name that; yes).

Halfway between Dombas and Jerkin, a miserable boulder, upon which I sat, set them into raptures; I literally had to stand up and leave them the spoil of my seat; while they pounded it to pieces, I for my part silently crept away.

And thus, even though I, too, dodge geologists, I do love their science, especially in late autumn. (Frau Doctor listened from behind an Orion nebula of cigarette smoke; you wouldn't have been able to see her eyes in any case, since of course she wore glasses.)

Nothing is cozier than to sit by a strapping fire and debate the formation of the mountainous heaps you visited last summer, to hear chatter about volcanoes, smashed planets, petrefications. And if it gets as far as paleontology, then the mammoths and the gigantosaurs take up the dance for me :

you need only picture such a behemoth, strolling along in the carboniferous forest and feeding its brood with elephants, the way our present-day lizards do with blowflies : long live the picturesque !

My perplexed gaze meandered about the room. Frau Doctor got up (she was as tall as I, 5 feet 11), pulled the cognac bottle from its cardboard prism and shoved the green jack-in-the-box tumbler my way : had she not liked my introduction, and wanted me to hit the gas ?

Dutifully drink; the wind whistled its twelve-tone harmony; and I told my contraband story from 1944 : fourteen smugglers, each laden with a sack of finest Swedish gunpowder, had come down the path. The fellow bringing up the rear noticed that his burden was growing lighter and lighter. Now that pleased him to be sure; yet he soon began to suspect he might be enjoying such benefits at the cost of his gunpowder burden, might he not ? Sad to say, yes : the sack had a hole, and the track lay unmistakably drawn across the borderland snow. He shouted a terrified "Halt !"; at which each of those preceding him first cast aside his burden and sat down upon his sack to indulge himself with some schnapps.

Meanwhile, the last man had had an ingenious notion : He walked back as far as the streak of powder reached, touched the end with his cigarette, his clever intention being to eradicate the telltale line. Three seconds later he heard a strange full thunder whose manifold echoes from the mountain walls and rolling reverberations from the mournfully beautiful valleys caused him no little alarm : all that noise had been made, you see, by the fourteen sacks, which, once the fuse had reached them, blew sky-high.

Pause. The wind shrieked a weak spiritistic cry of horror that no musical notation could capture. And 'tis true : including the fourteen who had intended to enjoy a well-deserved rest upon their sacks. C'est la guerre. Pause.

The cigarette pack was behind me. She arose with lithe catlike step. Bent down over me (that is, for the pack of cigarettes of course !) : vast, gigantic her dress; red desert, with black rock stumps. And her face hovered endlessly too; the glasses hung like two rigid, frozen lakes above me (in whose depths I, fantastic monster, did not move). And planetoid, this moon, oh thou my satellite, did bump against me.

STÜRENBURG
STORIES

An Advance on Life

Of course we occupied only one corner of the terrace. And Dettmer the pharmacist sat, anxious and blissful, at the forward edge of his wicker arm-chair, huffing into his dreadfully thick brazil; the moon had just climbed out of the bushes by the thread of his smoke, and I was free to compare the two round benevolent faces. The retired captain – where had I come across the name "von Dieskau" in history books before ? – swiftly poured two slivovitzes into his lean skeptical face. By way of precaution, Frau Dr. Waring called to her niece : "Emmeline, go fetch me a mouchoir or two." (because you really never knew with Stürenburg's stories ! And the little girl did make herself scarce; but several times I spotted the shock of hair behind a nearby curious lilac bush.)

Indulgently waiting for all these familiar maneuvers of his soirée to come to an end, Stürenburg, surveyor in retirement, whisked the ashes from his cigar with a deft snaky-human motion of his little finger, con-ducted another inspection of the horizon (apparently to check if all the t.p.'s were still in their prescribed positions), and sighed his cozy, intro-ductory "Hmyes". The captain had a most mistrustful look; Dettmer gave an enthusiastic blast on his Brazilian trumpet; and he began :

"You see, I was a still a very young man at the time – uh – my state exam barely behind me – when we were summoned to the Wingst for a surveying course." (You had to know your Hanoverian geography, or you were lost at this point !). "Among other tasks, we twice measured the Braaker base with a Bessel apparatus. And were having a great time of it." (My nod to move his story along came so quick that he inquired loftily; but by chance I knew the venerable names of Schumacher and Andreae, and he gave a satisfied-disappointed growl).

"There was one fellow among us, not a charming man, still less, elegant. Actually, not my sort; but esteemed by all for his steadfast indolence : it would surely never have occurred to any of us to fault him for his poetical vein. What made him remarkable was that twice now he had escaped with his life from some odd peril : first a grave fever. And several days before, he would have sunk to his death in the Ostemoors had not two other mem-bers of the class rescued him." (Here the captain growled disdainfully and let out a bleat full of soldierly arrogance).

"But the peculiar thing was that most evenings he would break away from our amusements – we played a lot of chess; or made a game of calculating the curvature radii on the surface of Mars –, always with unstoppable haste and protestations that he had ‹letters to write› : although we knew full well that he hardly ever received any ! And so we laughed, and let him follow his whim; besides, he seemed to take it much too seriously for anyone to try to make a joke of it."

A gust of wind blew in from the broad surface of the lake, puffing a valet with it, who stammered his report that the surface stood at $^{37}/_3$. "$^{37}/_3$?" Stürenburg repeated caustically : "I mean, those fellows can't keep the same level for 8 days running ! Uh-'t's fine, Hagemann."

"So then one evening we were shooting dice – not for money, Captain : oh no ! – simply to verify in practice the theorems of probability. And here he came, and became quite indignant as we kept on throwing the dice and chatting : good god, you couldn't get one intelligent word in edgewise for the racket, he declared, and departed hence, more than half annoyed. I felt – for some reason or other – strangely moved; followed him, and found him still in the stairwell. I extended him my hand with a downward motion, and asked ‹Surely, Broesicke, we part with no animosity ?›. He pressed my hand briefly and said – he was the elder of us two – in a kindly voice : ‹No, no, my good geodesist, we're both fond of one another : till tomorrow !›

"The next day we were given the task of dispersing ourselves through the area to measure parish lines. He was sent farthest out, way beyond Lamstedt, and was clubbed to death by a farmer who had apparently been playing with the boundary stones." (The pharmacist set a touched expression on his circle of a face, and piously folded his fat hands : ah !).

"There he lay before us, his temple smashed in. We all went through his papers together; and there we found what he been recording in his enigmatic correspondence : letters to his two best friends in our class. But dated many many years ahead, to a time he would never see. Both the friends and he had long since retired; and were living on country estates, happily married and with grown children flourishing about them. They invited one another for jovial visits, remembering their days in the course together as a difficult time, but one that now shone bright and clear – happy the man who could have experienced all that in reality ! – Hmyes. Poesy is surely – just as geodesy – a most ubiquitous phenomenon !"

"Yes, but what became of the farmer ? !" the captain snarled in dissatisfaction. "The farmer –" Stürenburg muttered. Pause. From Lake Dümmer a frail wind sighed. The cigars glowed enticingly. Soon it would be summer.

"The farmer ? : No, not to death. In those days, judges still had to attend executions in person, and so were truly loath to demand that. He was given life in prison. – As far as I know –" he spread his hands in apology, "he's still there today. – Hmyes."

Emmeline arrived, just as the story reach its conclusion; and for today we took our leave from one another.

THE HOWLING HOUSE

The wind whistled more loudly; at times rain would flash in cross-hatchings across the large glass doors of the corner room to which we had fled today; and we all watched, not without pleasure, how the back of the fireplace glowed as Hagemann fanned it brighter with a bellows.

"That's the ticket, Herr Stürenburg," Frau Dr. Waring said contentedly; and then with a sigh : "and this is supposed to be May ! – I think the earth must have turned." Stürenburg, master of the house and surveyor in retirement, raised a somewhat disconcerted hand : "Yes, but my dear lady : the earth is constantly turning !" "Ah, you know full well what I mean" the gaunt widow sulked across the top of her teacup; and Dettmer the pharmacist was quick to come to her aid : "You mean fluctuations of the poles, madam, do you not ?". She just nodded, her mouth at the moment overfull with the sweet brew; Captain von Dieskau stared ahead, highly dubious; but Stürenburg also rejected this attempt to explain the bad weather : "Granted, the earth's poles are constantly oscillating – Küstner, my old teacher, was the first to prove that long ago; and they do so in a kind of circle or ellipse around the ideal center. But such very slow oscillations never measure more than about 30 feet in any direction. Besides which, the motions are constantly being monitored from fixed stations placed on both sides of the pole : one must, of course, be able to state at any time the changes in a given geographic latitude. Thirty feet ? After all, that's a third of the average second of an arc, and therefore cannot be ignored." "Make a note of that, Emmeline" the Frau Doctor said sharply to her niece, who, for her taste, was all too lost in blazing-wood reveries.

The wind's glassy monsters stormed the house still more nocturnally. "The poor sailors" the widow chimed in; "The poor soldiers" the captain grumbled; the pharmacist opened his mouth, but then closed it again in embarrassment : nothing came to mind for underscoring his own profession, "the poor herb collectors" would hardly have aroused sympathy ! Stürenburg watched this competition with ironic eye; then he declared : "The poor surveyors ! On the road, year in year out, in weather like this; of an evening in wretched quarters more than likely –" he waved a hand in weighty disapproval, laid his left hand in his right armpit, took a more contemplative hold on his cigar, and began :

"During the time, long before the First World War, when I was doing my practical training as a topographer, we received the enormous sum of 5 marks per day for expenses if we were working in the field. Nowadays the gents get 30, –, and each has a car. We had bicycles, and were required – though not a man of us was well-to-do – to procure so many books and our own instruments that we came up with the craziest ideas about how to put the aforementioned 5 marks aside. I had been assigned to Rotenburg; being an utterly ‹young fellow›, I of course was given the most remote area, down below Visselhövede – and went on the sad assumption that I would most likely have to spend my money at an inn, when the colleague I was replacing took me aside. We rode our bikes for a good half hour, along back roads that grew darker and darker, finally stopping just outside Stellichte beside a lonely, half-tumbledown house. He then waved me clear round the side into dense woods, so that we could approach the building even more inconspicuously from the rear. We hid our bikes in a fir thicket; locked them; unbuckled our theodolites from the baskets, and entered."

He took a deeper breath of the sweet smoke, and looked archly about our circle : "We're all people with strong nerves are we not ? –" he proposed. The captain merely let his iron cross, first class, sparkle in disdain; Dettmer nodded, somewhat too eagerly, while the ladies confirmed their courage with fear and many words.

"Even I took a step back at first" Stürenburg muttered, "for on the planks of the flooring in the suspiciously empty vestibule lay – a human skull !" Since no one protested, he at once went on : "My colleague simply remarked ‹Aha› or something similarly noncommittal and : ‹Someone's already here›. The way led up stairs, half of them missing and the rest with a disagreeable sag, to the attic. He knocked discreetly at a door; a long knock – I didn't know Morse at the time – and so didn't understand. At which someone softly called out ‹Enter›. And there in the lightproof curtained garret sat two men on dainty stools : a surveyor, from the competition in Fallingbostel; and a gentleman in lincoln green, a forester-in-training as it turned out on introduction. They had a chessboard between them and a bottle of cheap wine; two bedrolls had been unfurled along the walls. I, too, was briefly sworn never to reveal our haunted house; and I then set about to conquer the two chess players, one after the other." He contentedly puffed out his cheeks : "And so there I spent many an inexpensive night. Often in the company of foresters, surveyors, and the rural gendarmery. The first to arrive had always to ‹lay out› the various bones and skulls – another, for example, dangled above the stairs, and would have delivered a ghastly kiss to unknowing intruders."

The rain's Morse was brisker; the wind's yowl unwearied; the good widow feigned a yawn, although she was obviously still digesting that ‹bony kiss›. The pharmacist drew a more manly self up : "What do you mean, ‹haunted house› : do such things still exist nowadays ?". Stürenburg gazed out over his glasses at him as he slowly answered :

"The ‹Howling House› was so notorious in those parts that farmers would spur their horses past it, and at dusk or especially at night, No One would near it. Old people in the nearby village used to say that even the neighboring trees would sometimes take on terrible voices; and one 95-year-old swore by all that's holy : as a child he had heard the wailing screams for several days running. At one point, an enlightened local magistrate had wanted to have it demolished : the very beams had emitted such angry moans that the horrified carpenters had left their axes behind. Hmyes." He patiently smoked while we proclaimed our indignation at such superstitions; when at last we were feeling adequately civilized, he meticulously knocked the long tip of ash into the agate bowl :

"By chance I happened to be in the neighborhood when the forester in charge – himself another initiate – ordered some timber there felled. I felt particularly bad about one splendid oak; but he proved beyond dispute that the tree was rotten to the core and had long since been ripe for felling. And when it finally lay on the ground and the workers were splitting it, suddenly he shouted me over : in the middle of the mighty trunk was stuck a human skeleton, head down !" He brushed aside our protesting and scandalized hands. "They found tatters of cloth from an ancient French uniform as well, and, half hidden in the rotted wood, a few smallish coins." Grimly : "Perhaps a freebooter who had fled up into the tree when pursued by irate farmers, and had then tumbled into it. He must have got so tightly wedged in the fall that his arms were pressed against his body and there was no chance of escape : no wonder that the tree howled and screamed for days on end, and that No One wanted to live in the ‹Howling House› anymore."

It proved necessary for someone to accompany the Frau Doctor home that evening.

SUMMER METEOR

Even from a distance I could hear the piano's nervous lacings beneath Emmeline's dainty paws; viscous bubbles rose; in the bass some porridge burblings (and once again I felt as if I were a boy standing before my aquarium : that was how the geysers of air had always wriggled to the top. Wind promptly wagged its hot filmy tail, all bushes fanned themselves replete with algae-green gestures. Now I spotted Hagemann, with umbraged face, serving the bright glasses – ‹lacour blanc› it appeared, the white bordeaux : all the better !).

By way of greeting, Stürenburg, surveyor in retirement, held his mighty double-bowled pocket watch (in miner's case) up to my countenance : ? ! I tried to excuse myself with all sorts of visitations : by my publisher, my muse, ("sheriff's deputy !" Captain von Dieskau cut in with a scornful snarl); I managed to take my seat, but so despondently and guiltily that apologies seemed unavoidable. Dettmer the pharmacist – the goatee on his soft-round face looked more than ever like nylon – even pronounced me ‹overworked› and ‹hollow-cheeked›, and risked a reference to a nostrum of his own invention, ‹Virgisan› : ? But the snarls on all sides were so scornful that he at once folded his hands imploringly, and withdrew into the strawy clam of the beguilingly uncomfortable apparatus on which he sat.

Emmeline first moled her way through the middle of the Benedetto Marcello; I tiptoed circumspectly inside (ostensibly to turn the pages for her; in fact, to kill some time : I am utterly unmusical, I already said that at best it reminded me of fish, or whatever).

At the bookcase. I pulled out one whose color made a passable impression; dark green leather spine with pale green label : ‹J.A.E. Schmidt, School Dictionary of the French Language. 1855›. I cracked it open at random, page 33 : ‹auget = channel in which the spark-wurst is laid› – I pinched my thigh to verify my own existence : spark-wurst ? ? ! ! (and my life long I shall never forget this ‹auget›; a cast-iron memory is pure punishment !). –

Outside again (and silence; no more tramplings of the piano). Well-coiffed summer clouds wafted above us and away. Above the distant lake evening sparkled; it was still summer, summer (and I took chill again at the thought of the trees along the road doing their danses macabres : in our

November, in our November). The cake had been donated this time by the
widowed Frau Dr. Waring; homemade; at most of geological interest (I
whispered this to Captain von Dieskau, and he blustered militarily : very
good !).

"Ah : There ! !" Emmeline pointed with her wedge of cake to a meteor
leaving, as it sank, a lovely trace in the dark blue : ! I allowed myself to
mutter "Perseids"; and Stürenburg offered sympathetic support. "To be
sure," he said, "from mid-July until mid-August; maximum on the 11th. –
Other dependable swarms are the Orionids (October 20th) and the
Geminids (December 10th). Hmyes."

Pause. Then no one wanted to be left behind; Dieskau had of course seen
whole processions of meteors in Canada on 13 February 1913; I myself had
observed a bolide between Görlitz and Lauban in '32 or thereabouts (was
riding along on my bike at the time, a very young fellow; around 20 or so).
But Stürenburg brought us all to a halt – by nods, by prestidigitations : you
couldn't touch the man ! (Is *that* an advantage of old age perhaps, life begins at 70, knowing everything better for certain ?).

"Dextrocardia" he said slowly; and by way of explanation : "There are
people with their heart in the right place : literally !" He puffed into his
cigar sending sparks flying, like a meteor; and continued : "I was studying
in Göttingen at the time; and a friend had persuaded me on philosophical
grounds – I joined him in attending anatomy lectures for a semester. At the
time a poor studiosus medicus was living in squalid rented rooms on
Weender Strasse, along with his sixty-year-old mother and a sister. He was
unflagging as a private tutor; his sister tatted lace for their daily bread; and
when the mother died they stood before the choice either of having everything sold out from under them to pay for the funeral . . ." (here Dieskau
knowingly pricked up ears and hands : "Or ?"). "Hmyes, or" Stürenburg
replied : "The mother, you see, had, as I've already hinted, her ‹heart in the
right place›. And was thus a medical miracle to set any anatomist to licking
all ten fingers. In desperation, our young man goes to his professor, and
offers him this matchless rarity for dissection – the latter enthusiastically
accedes : for 500 marks."

Here, Frau Dr. Waring, who had been listening with growing anxiety,
called out "Emmeline ! My child : go fetch me my parasol from the beach,
please !" The little girl sulkily obeyed (and I hesitated for a moment if I
ought not to accompany her ? – But no : the new anecdote had first to be
nailed down for once and all !)

"On the last night of the wake then, which he is holding all alone beside
the coffin where his mother lies, he takes the corpse out, wraps it in an old
blanket, and hides it up in the attic, behind the chimney. In its place, he fills

the coffin with straw and stones, and nails it tight as a drum : it is interred the next morning with all honors. – As soon as it gets dark, he sticks the maternal body in an old sack and sets out with it to the professor's house. On the way he is met by a fellow student who asks him what he's toting there on his back ?" Stürenburg gave a mephistophilian wink; and also added the attributive adjuncts : "An August evening. Wind crept the streets. Everywhere in the dusk, Perseids began to swarm : just like tonight ! – In utter confusion, the poor wretch shakes me – ah : the fellow ! – off, with the answer : ‹Let me be, good friend; it's nothing more than an old bass fiddle›."

Pause. Dieskau, the old skeptic, rattled his satisfaction; Dettmer waited, mouth agape; and Hagemann sat perched immobile like some weather-beaten idol on the terrace wall – he surely knew the punchline already !

"The next morning, then, the female corpse was dissected; the reversed circulatory system was duly marveled at; when they began to work on the partes genitalies, the professor tossed off a joke : this was indeed the first classroom of the learned and unlearned alike. Which made me think me of antiquity and of how the emperor Nero had had his own mother dissected and had eagerly watched it all – whereupon said student suddenly fainted. – At the time none of us knew why; but gradually the rumor got about and became the talk of the town. Hmm."

"And ? : What became of the young man ?" Dieskau inquired with a clank (but with no feeling : soldiers are terrible people !).

"He completed his studies at another university" Stürenburg declared, his eyebrows drawn up haughtily : "As far as I know, he's still practicing as a respected doctor in Bremervörde. – Hmyes."

The widow merely groaned; Dettmer the pharmacist was touched, un-pleasantly, and kept his peace; and I too felt anything but comfortable : is it really an advantage to have experienced so much in life ? !

Above Lake Dümmer, a model of a cumulus had formed, textbook perfect. Emmeline returned from the beach, short of breath and strangely flushed. A lean meteor drew a silver brow above the moon.

GUERRILLA WAR

We were all not a little amazed as Hagemann the factotum, by all indications quite distraught, fumbled into the room, closed the door, trotted over to Stürenburg, surveyor in retirement, and bent down to the latter's ear; to be sure, we could not understand his gruff whispers in the local dialect, but we all noted how his face, too, turned pale. "Well, let him in" Stürenburg declared finally.

Whereupon a young gangling policeman in snazzy uniform appeared, laid a smart hand to his shako, let his gaze sweep our semicircle, and then turned to Dettmer the pharmacist : "Herr Stürenburg, correct ?". "No – uhm here, if you please" said the surveyor weakly; accepted the unpleasantly official-blue missive; and the policeman – followed by the sympathetic eyes of Captain von Dieskau and Frau Dr. Waring, as well as the admiring ones of her niece Emmeline – marched nonchalantly out again. A dismayed and disgusted Stürenburg shoved the suspicious envelope away; in reply to a question from Hagemann, who as an old servant allowed himself full license, he merely groaned : "Yesyes, from Police Captain Oberg". "Again ?" Hagemann shouted in bewilderment : "Is there to be no end to it this month, sir ? ! Well, we'll just have to drive over to see our friends in Hanover again I suppose;" he swung the poker like a weapon, and withdrew amid angry mutterings.

Silence, broken only by Stürenburg's heavy breathing; finally he began :

"Just so you don't think me capable of unjustified animosity, I shall describe the whole affair for you quite impartially. Oberg, a former police captain – he's well past 75 now, too, like myself, and retired long ago – has indeed been the cause of most of the annoyances in my life. We went to the same high school together; studied in Göttingen – what am I saying, he studied : dabbled a little in law and economics is all ! –; and a few years later we met again in Rotenburg, I as a surveyor, he with the police. We had always loathed one another : one teacher, who had liked him, laid into me without fail – but, well, our mathematics professor, who was over 6 feet, often provided me my revenge. The postman had a passion for mixing up our mail. We were agreed on just one thing : we were both convinced of the beauty of one and the same girl." He bleated so diabolically that the widow looked up in indignation; Stürenburg apologized, and explained : "And I used the fact to play a practical joke on him : we both wooed this one beauty, brought our gifts at the same tempo; and one day I had my best friend inform him in confidence that I was engaged to her. He hotfooted it over there, just to annoy me, and made his own offer : which to his boundless confusion was at once accepted with a sweet smile ! He then had to marry her; because her father was a government councillor and, since he was right at the start of his career, could have caused him not inconsiderable difficulties : hahaha !"

The captain grimaced his satisfaction at such strategic subtleties; the pharmacist solemnly declared he had never taken part in such flagrant toying with tender female affections; for which he received a kindly nod from Frau Doctor Waring, just as niece Emmeline was given the sweet & sour warning : "Beware, my child, of these monsters. As you can see . . . ." Stürenburg made an obligatory bow, and went on :

"As I said, we were almost always busy in the same region; there are cases where fate seems to take downright pleasure in pairing divergent natures. As each of us in our sphere then came into his own ‹power›, the feud produced the quaintest blossoms. Whenever I would have micro-measurements taken anywhere close to a road, I could be certain that not forty-five minutes later, the heaviest trucks would be rolling by without pause, so that we could go right ahead and pack up our sensitive instruments again : he had had all the traffic in the area rerouted over that very road !"

"None of my surveyors could risk the open air without a whole arsenal of identification papers. He would have each of them called to his car, checking and harassing to keep him from his work; if he could find no errors in the papers, he would at least conclude by saying : ‹There's far too much riffraff runnin' round the countryside !› Once he had had a man, who on my orders was carrying out oscillation measurements to prove an extremely interesting gravitational anomaly, arrested right out in the field and carted off as a dowsing swindler ! He officially petitioned that as ‹honest civil servants› we should all wear uniforms; that we were constantly upsetting the rural population with ‹provocative measurements›, disturbing the cattle, etc. etc. The subordinate staff on both sides naturally took passionate part in the altercation; and we knew how to take our revenge ! When the district built its new highway, our study proved that it would have to run right through his beloved garden. In a trade journal for the mining industry we suggested it was likely that an extensive salt deposit lay beneath his villa; daily, for one whole year, he was overrun with realtors, seriously interested parties, swindlers of every sort, almost driving him mad."

He sighed in contentment. "He had one daughter; the apple of his eye; and in fact a pretty enough thing for a chieftain of the gendarmery. One day the customary young man, with a doctor's degree in engineering, appeared right on schedule; courted her; was given her hand : and did her daddy ever boil over when he learned after the wedding that his son-in-law was a surveying engineer. And a nephew of old Stürenburg to boot !" He rubbed his broad soft hands intensively : "I had promised the young man a not inconsiderable sum of cash if he could pull it off – although, just as I feared, he proved weak enough, and felt a real attraction for the pitiable creature."

We had listened in amusement, and our eyes were automatically directed toward the aqua-blue envelope in the middle of the little round table. His large face clouded over, and he reached peevishly for it; but even as he read it his countenance cleared : "An invitation to the baptism" he announced; and said triumphantly : "A boy. He's named Friedrich : after me ! – I'll have a savings account opened in his name before the day's out. – And the old man has the news served on me by a policeman; just to frighten me !"

We obligingly shared in his outrage; all the more so when he later informed us that to his grief : the other name of the little lad was Karl, after his second grandfather : he had made his toast to Friedrich; Oberg had drunk to Karl's health; the parents had spoken in reconciliation of Friedrichkarl : "The poor tot had looked downright at odds with himself staring up from his pillow" he asserted.

THE WATER LILY

Because we had arrived today somewhat earlier, we found Stürenburg, surveyor in retirement, still busy with his theodolite; the precious instrument had been set up, as he explained while holding us at bay some distance off, on an isolated stone shaft sunk 15 feet into the earth, but at no point touching the cement ring on which the observer moved about. Mouth set critically, he sighted once more in the gauge-microscope, muttered : "10 minutes. 24 point 3 seconds" ("24 point 3" Dettmer the pharmacist repeated reverently). With elaborate groans Hagemann, the factotum, lifted the diverse protective caps over the apparatus; and we followed Stürenburg to our small-talk corner on the terrace, where Captain von Dieskau had just come into view between the two ladies, "A rose between two thorns" as Dettmer remarked with bashful wit.

"Once one knows the exact height of one's instrument –" and the captain was already interjecting 5 querulous fingers of his right hand : what do you mean by height ? The base it stands on ?; and Stürenburg indulgently explained, seeing as he was dealing with an infantryman, that obviously one had to use the hinge pin of the telescope. He gave a listless bleat, and let loose a dusty puffed cone of smoke; "Abajo vuelta" the pharmacist whispered meekly, who had once learned Spanish in his youth and could never forget it; but Stürenburg was already making a testy start :

"Yes, well; we're all to ourselves here, so, there – –. Now you see, this was about twenty years ago – I had been retired early, because I had had a falling out with the Nazi bosses at the time : I'll have to tell you about that someday ! – so there I am standing just like this one evening, with my instrument, taking a few angles; and suddenly across the way, on the beach at Hude, I see a couple coming along. Now I have particularly good optical equipment and so could see the two of them as if they were about 50 yards away. She appeared to be wearing a garish red sweater, and he was holding a little suitcase in his hand. They walked further and further out the pier; sat down on the piles toward the front – : and all of a sudden what do I see but the man letting the little suitcase slip into the water !" "The suitcase ?" asked Frau Dr. Waring uncomprehendingly, and the pharmacist, too, shook outraged cheeks.

"I at once counted the piles out to where it had occurred – meanwhile they both had struggled to their feet, and had strolled back on land. – Then I climbed with Hagemann into our punt and we poled across. Only as we were tying up at the jetty did I begin to have doubts : what business was this of mine ? ! But there we were in any case; and I directed Hagemann into the water; Lake Dümmer is so shallow, you know, that you can wade across it. He felt for a while with his toes, and found what he was looking for; hooked a foot into the handle, passed it up to his hand, and was immediately all grouses at the ‹weight› of it. Now he generally grouses about everything; and so I paid no further attention; whereupon he laid the thing up on the thwart, still carping : and in fact the boat tipped slightly to one side." Dettmer nodded, as if had hadn't expected anything else; the captain gave a right-sided smile at such civilian antics; I took the liberty of offering Emmeline, the niece, a cigarette (which, however, her aunt rejected with the same outrage as if I had attempted a seduction); Stürenburg observed us with amusement, but grew uncommonly serious again, more swiftly than usual, sighed a bit, and continued with furrowed brow :

"The locks snapped open effortlessly; I lifted the lid – and saw : – – !" he bent forward impressively; : "wrapped in blankets, snow-white, a child's face. With large bluish spots; a water lily on its breathless chest". Only now could the aunt cry out "Emmeline ! You're not to go swimming again !"; and "Go fetch me some more hot water from the kitchen. – She may, may she not ? !" this as she turned to Stürenburg, scathingly friendly, who consented in surprise.

"I slammed the lid shut in horror" (Dieskau nodded grimly : horrified at just *one* corpse; oh these bow-tied civilians !) "Hagemann let it back down again, shuddering with the creeps; and we left the place. Of course my thoughts were racing : what to do ? ! : What would *you* have done ?"

"The police. Reported an act of depravity." Frau Dr. Waring husked in indignation. "Murder" Dettmer whispered, pleasantly thrilled. We others scratched our cheeks thoughtfully.

"That's what I thought at the time, too, unfortunately" Stürenburg said glumly; calmed the aunt, who was about to fly off at his ‹unfortunately›; observed his glowing cigar, and morosely continued his report :

"The next morning I rode my bicycle to Hude : correct; there they were staying with a farmer. I met the nice pair in the village. He : tall, slovenly, red hair and freckles to spare; she : snow-white and so thin she was boneless, with black bangs and eyes. The gaze those young faces fixed on me was firm and wicked. An ‹artist› Hagemann managed to find out." The aunt gave a pharisaical snort through her nose; and also came up with : "Bohemian".

"The chief of the criminal division from Diepholz came right along with us. We confronted them : ‹Have you nothing to tell us ?›. They were obviously disquieted; but kept stubborn silence all the same. As we neared the shore of the lake, his pale face fell; she clutched his arm, and I heard her whisper : ‹Wouldn't it be better to admit it ?› – Once the suitcase was lying on the jetty, he wheezed to confess; but the officer had already opened it : by broad daylight, the contents now looked all the more ghastly !"

Here came Emmeline back with the hot water : "Hotter !" her aunt commanded in desperation, and she had to take another sulky departure. "Please be quick, Herr Stürenburg" the widow gasped wearily.

"Sick at heart, we took hold of the edges of the blanket in which the wretched tot was swaddled : it lay in our hands heavy as stone –" he stubbed out his expensive cigar, he gnashed his teeth angrily : "ah, why beat around the bush ! That's what it was ! The fellow had slapped together a spare ‹Sleeping Child› – he was a sculptor – and had submerged it in the lake so that the stone would take on a greenish-antique hue and ‹bring a better price› ! A colleague had slipped him the trick : a lot of people were doing it !" Still enraged even now, he threw himself back in his armchair; while we had no choice but to picture for ourselves the lake bottom : covered layer upon layer with modern statues that were supposed to take on a high-priced patina. Stürenburg stood up, and with an impatient motion of his hand demanded we come with him.

In the shed behind the house, right next to Hagemann's bicycle, lay a small dusty, foxy-red suitcase atop some crates : there you are. Dieskau, baring courageous teeth, opened it. In a scrap of brown-checked blanket lay a sleeping child with pensive smile. "I bought the thing off him" Stürenburg admitted, full of spite "for a lot of money. To avoid a fuss." Hmyes. Even Dettmer the pharmacist bent down over it; suddenly he raised his round head, illumined with knowledge : "But that's not a water lily at all, Herr Stürenburg," he said knowingly of the oversized flower : "that's your common water flag, iris pseudacorus : I'm quite sure, its root is medicinal." "I'll be giddily goddamned !" Stürenburg swore. Silence. Then Dettmer asked shyly : "Why do people say ‹giddily› really ?" We looked at one another; we didn't know.

HE LOOKED TOO MUCH LIKE HIM

"Oh. The master knows stories : he could lure the birds out of the trees !"
and looked up at me with an old man's glittering eye. "Yesyes, to be sure,
Hagemann" I said diplomatically, "but whether they're all true or not ?" He
at once tossed both arms and their still mighty fists into the air : "Why
shouldn't they be ? !" he snuffled in outrage : "What with all that has happened here over the years ? ! – And then all them instruments of his :
Goodlord, if I didn't keep such a cool head – –" he withdrew, amid dubious
mutterings; and dissatisfied, I found my way back to the terrace, where
they were waiting for me.

Stürenburg, surveyor in retirement, was just explaining to the captain
that one could, as a civilian, quite easily acquire better maps of a region
than the ordnance maps generally held to be the non plus ultra. "For 6.–
DM, any land-registry office will sell you their so-called plat maps with a
scale of 1:5000, which likewise record the complete topography – and you
get every single building marked precisely; the houses differentiated from
the sheds by cross-hatching; street names; everything : Highly recommended !" He gave an expert's nod, and notched the end of his cigar with a
special silver knifelet : "Of course there are even *larger*-scaled maps; prepared for the register of real property; they are constantly being updated by
individual topographers, when there's time –" he rocked his mighty head
and groaned a little.

From the lake a gust of wind dandled listlessly our way; spilled like
lukewarm liquid over our hands; the lake air was in fine fettle today. "Good
for the harvest" Dettmer the pharmacist remarked pompously; Frau Dr.
Waring nodded, all mistress of her estates, (though she didn't understand a
damn thing about it); her niece Emmeline surreptitiously stretched her hot-
to-swim legs, but even as she was still looking slyly my way, Stürenburg
had already commenced :

"You all know that twenty years ago, during the Third Reich, I was
forced into an early retirement – I bring that up because it bears a connection with plat maps. At the time I was in charge of the land-registry
offices west of the Ems, and was on my way to Meppen in my car when I
happen to see a couple of surveyors at work near a villa set in a handsome park; one of them has put up a tripod; two helpers stand picturesquely

leaning on their red & white poles : just like we've all seen it. I have
Hagemann stop, get out, and make myself known to the man at the telescope. He doesn't even look up, says sharply to me : ‹Drive on !› Now
that was too much for me : I was his superior once-removed after all;
besides which my old honest geodesist's heart was offended that the
fellow's telescope was directed somewhere at the middle of the villa. In
reply to my remonstration, he said more menacingly : ‹Be on your way !›;
also raised his head : I had never seen the face before; and here when I
knew all my staff ! Now I was getting suspicious of the whole thing; at
the least, this was a case of ‹illegal presumption of authority›. I therefore
demanded that he get into my car and follow me to the next police station.
His face at once turned brutal. He tucked himself up for attack; whistled
for his accomplices; they grabbed me, and would have stuffed me into
my car, if Hagemann had not entered the fray : with a perfect sense for
strategy, he first tossed the ringleader head-over-heels into the deep roadside ditch – marshy soil, I need say no more. Then he came to my assis-
tance. The two strangers persuaded themselves – luckily for us – that they
ought to attack Hagemann's head with their poles; and from that moment
on, the battle was decided. With blows of his fists, butts and gnashing
teeth, Hagemann's head thrust irresistibly forward; the one fellow had already lost jacket and shirt; while I bloodied the nose of the other. Meanwhile the now disheveled countenance of the leader emerged from the
ditch; he shouted an order to his troops; whereupon they immediately withdrew, threw themselves onto three motorcycles hidden in the bushes, and
beat a stinky retreat."

The captain, having listened with interest to the description of the skir-
mish, now poured himself a larger cognac, and Stürenburg went on :

"The first thing I did was to peer through the mysteriously directed
telescope : it looked straight at the front door ! I rang for the owner. A
tall, skinny man, his face ashen with fear, appeared. After I had informed
him of what had happened, he pulled me imploringly through the door,
bolted it behind him, and briefly told his tale : he was a Jew; and for three
days now his house had been watched by disguised Gestapo agents, who
were simply waiting for one of his long-sought relatives to try to sneak his
way in. Then they would ‹pick him up› too ! Once he learned that his
guards had taken flight, he asked me – his whole body trembling, the poor
fellow : it was literally a matter of life and death ! – if I couldn't drive him
to the Dutch border, which lay close by ? When I consented, he ran up the
stairs, and returned immediately with a small bag he had long held at the
ready."

The captain, though not an out-an-out anti-Semite, had all the same been raised to obey every law on the books, and growled discontentedly; while kindly Dettmer eagerly nodded.

"I drove like hell down the road toward Provinzial Moor. He babbled away incessantly beside me, morbidly nervous; pointed anxiously at every possible scarecrow. I made a U-turn in front of the barrier; his smile as he said good-bye was heartbreakingly brave; and I ruminated as I rolled on back across the flat countryside. While I was still shaking my head and discussing the incident with the director of the land-registry office, suddenly the street was filled with the sound of motors; from four black limousines a good twenty SS men emerged and surrounded the entrances : I had to go with them. – yes, of course; Hagemann too. – We were released a few days later, true, since it was not difficult to prove our innocence in the scuffle; and thankgod no one seemed to suspect that I had abetted that unfortunate man in his flight ! All the same, I was relieved of my duties by ‹decree› – and later forced to retire as well : no effort on the part of my superiors proved of any use." He raised his wide eyebrows and cursed through his nose as he recalled it even now.

"The most depressing part was that during that same period I had to read a newspaper announcement of the death of the Jewish physician in question. Having nothing to do, I bought a wreath and set it down beside the open casket – he had been laid out in his own villa, tall and skinny. So they hadn't let him across the border."

From Dettmer and Aunt Waring came a touched "tut-tut"; the captain drank brazenly; and Emmeline fidgeted, hiking her skirt higher; she would probably most have liked to pull it up over her head and leap into the water. But Stürenburg was still drawing inexorably on his havana :

"The strange thing was that 14 days later I received a certified letter from England : containing the fervent thanks of the same doctor, and – my driver's license ! He had known no other recourse, he confessed, than to expropriate it from its dashboard compartment as we rode along : with it in hand, he had been allowed across the border without challenge ! And it was true; for later then, he was forever writing me notes of thanks; at present he lives in the USA and is planning a visit next year."

"Yes but –" the perplexed pharmacist objected "– I thought you saw him in his coffin that day ? !" and we others nodded in confusion.

Stürenburg just shrugged : "What do I know ? Maybe the SS führer, who, as was the custom in those days, most likely had to answer for the success of the mission ‹with his head›, had had the whole commando fall in;" he shrugged : "– maybe one of them had looked too much like him ?"

He spread his hands and stood up importantly. "Yes but –" the perplexed captain snarled : "Yes but –" said disgruntled Aunt Waring; "Yes but –" the pharmacist and I thought, looking into each other's surprised faces. Only Emmeline seemed quite content with the story's ending. And perhaps that was only because it had finally come to an end.

BLACK HAIR

Captain von Dieskau had just concluded his very congenial tale of the plague at Aleppo : how during those days, for simplicity's sake, they had taken to dumping the dead by the wagonload into open mass graves each evening – and then how with every dawn, there would be a dozen plague corpses, who had not yet been quite dead, scratching at the doors of their relatives to be let back in again. "Ohmygod !" Frau Dr. Waring cried in weary disgust; and Dettmer the pharmacist, just to be on the safe side, pulled the legs of his chair away from the carpet where, by the light of the fireplace, shadow torsos and red-swollen limbs of light were writhing.

Surprised at this unexpected failure, the captain gave it a try with a snarling hymn to the sublime desolation and strangely cramped horizon of the desert, the like of which one never experienced elsewhere. "Except perhaps at sea," the Frau Doctor said bitingly (her husband had been a ship's physician); and since the captain had been routed into silence, the pharmacist, always anxious to further his knowledge, inquired : "How far really can one generally see, Herr Stürenburg ? I mean : assuming we regard the earth as a smooth ball." Although Stürenburg's mouth had taken on pleats of suffering at the word ‹ball›, he replied amiably : "Nothing easier than that, Herr Dettmer : you take the square root of your height in meters, and multiply it by 3.5." Noting the widow's irresolution, he obligingly offered the example : "Let's assume you are at a height of 100 meters; the square root of 100 is 10 : so multiply that by 3.5, and you can see 35 kilometers in all directions – approximately of course; it varies somewhat in individual cases." "Make a note of that, Emmeline," Frau Dr. Waring said sharply to her niece : "You can use that next Easter on your final exams perhaps !" Stürenburg, always the cavalier, spared the young lady any comment, and continued, certain of victory :

"And as far as your much-vaunted desert desolation goes, my good captain, : why roam in faraway lands ? It was not so very long ago – as a child I heard it from the eyewitnesses themselves ! – that our own Lüneburg Heath was a match for any wilderness. Which proved invaluable in many an instance; as when, e.g., in 1831 the great cholera epidemic – to which, by the by, men like Hegel or Gneisenau fell victim – wandered across Europe from west to east, but the pestilence, lacking a means of spreading further, came to a halt at the eastern edge of the heath."

Reassured, the pharmacist stretched his legs out again; Emmeline gave me, sitting behind her, a more coquettish shake of her enticing ponytail; Stürenburg, whose surveyor's eyes missed nothing even these days, took amused note of this too, and then got down to his real topic :

"During the French period, around 1810, the area looked so confusingly monotone, devoid of all landmarks, – attempts at forestation came only much later – that the gouverneur, the famous Marshal Davout, had endless rows of posts driven to show the right routes for his supply transports. Now, as is well known, during this period of the Continental System, smuggling was in full bloom; and the boldest of such fellows occasionally employed the tactic of rearranging these road markers. So as to direct the transports, some of them quite valuable, into out-of-the-way barrens, there to attack and plunder them." The captain, who at the name Davout had emitted a hate-filled growl, smiled his approval; the pharmacist, schooled more in healing wounds than inflicting them, stared ahead uncomfortably; and Stürenburg went on :

"It was in late autumn of the year 1811 – on October 24th to be exact – that just such a foolhardy band of smugglers had pulled the same trick once again. They had detoured the French money shipment from the usual Soltauer highway off to the left into a tangle of moors, meadows and brush; and then, as night broke, had attacked from Schneverdingen to the north-west. This time, however, the French were stronger and better armed than had been assumed; there ensued a fairly hard-bitten exchange of fire, leaving dead and wounded on both sides. This went on until the disillusioned smugglers and the no-less-so French began to withdraw in opposite directions; the former to the west, for their untracked heath hideaways; the latter, laboriously and by compass, in the direction of Hamburg, where the seat of government of the so-called ‹Hanseatic Departements› was located at the time. The inhabitants of the surrounding villages, not a little terrified by the steady fire, had trembled and pulled their covers more tightly over their heads and had not budged, determined not to get on the wrong side of either party. When one resolute young woman declared : it was most certainly their duty as human beings to search out the place of engagement; to give the dead a Christian burial, and to care for the wounded. Though her father long resisted, she at last succeeded in obtaining a span of plow horses; and, accompanied only by a farmhand, she bravely drove to the scene of the calamity. And in fact, she brought 4 of the injured, 2 Germans and 2 Frenchmen, home with her; the dead – I no longer know the exact count; their numbers, however, were few – were left lying for the time being. She bound the unfortunates' wounds with her own hands; cooked

suitable food for them; and when, the next day, Tourtelot, the French lieutenant of the gendarmery in charge of such matters arrived from Nienburg
– 3rd batt. 24th legion –", he added in reply to the captain's questioning
glance; "all the wounded were more or less out of danger, though one or
two of them could not yet be transported. While still in the infirmary, the
lieutenant – a handsome, slender man, with large arched nose and coal-
black hair – expressed his intention to have the Germans taken away and
handed over for severest punishment. At that, the young woman stepped
forward, and said to him in the highest German she could manage :
‹There'll be none of that, lieutenant ! I beg you to remember that I could
have left every one of these poor men lying there; so that all of them, your
Frenchmen too, would now be stiff and cold. Let life be exchanged for
life›. The lieutenant, pleasantly surprised by this tall blonde girl before
him, gallantly replied that it would be irresponsible to remove the wounded
from such good care; he would reserve any decision, taking only the liberty
for now of an occasional visit to see how his countrymen were faring. So
saying, he sprang to his horse, shot several very black looks, and rode off.
Fräulein Schumannn took the hint; and when, the very next day, Lieutenant
Tourtelot arrived to visit the sick, he no longer found the two Germans
there; moreover, a half-hour conversation with the young lady seemed to
provide him fully adequate compensation. I will restrict my comments, as
we are all familiar with conversations of that sort – Fräulein Emmeline
excepted –" he added suavely "and be brief : The wedding took place early
in 1812; in haste, since Lieutenant Tourtelot had to accompany his great
Emperor to Russia – from whence he never returned."

The captain grumbled chauvinistically about ‹mixing of blood›; the
pharmacist's face roundly expressed sympathy; even Frau Dr. Waring de-
plored the incident, but haughtily doubtful, went on to inquire : "Those are
indeed interesting anecdotes, Herr Stürenburg : but how do you know all
these details, black hair and such ? That can only be pure invention !"
Stürenburg promptly stood up, and returned in a few seconds with a min-
iature : a young officer in the uniform of the chausseurs à cheval, large
ducally arched nose, shimmering black hair. As it passed from hand to
hand, Stürenburg casually added : "My grandfather on my father's side; the
child born in January, 1831 was my father, who was later adopted by my
grand-mother's second husband and given the name Stürenburg : no no,
my dear lady ! When I say : the square root of a times 3.5 : then it's so !"

"Square root of a" was the reverential murmur from the pharmacist.
"Black hair" came the dreamy whisper, which only I could hear, from
Emmeline.

TALL GRETE

"Back when I was born," the aged man said, "this was all a realm to itself, you see." He pointed very slowly about him from his seat on the grass, as far as the jagged border of firs on the horizon : "Everything was still very different then – –" I understood with no trouble : better; and gave an emphatic nod to keep him in the mood. "Back then you had other folks than these slickers they turn out by the dozens nowadays –" he painfully stretched his worn-down legs and arranged them carefully on the heather "– and this here, you could say, is part of it too : you see, I'm sitting on a grave, young fellow !" Now I can tolerate nothing with less grace than ‹young fellow›; I have, after all, reached 45 years with indifferent honors, and even if I sometimes do look absurdly young . . . . and so I chewed a while on that scrap, while he proceeded deliberately:

"I was still a lad when Tall Grete showed up here the first time, in the middle of her little herd of sheep, and we children would have sworn that those animals were people bewitched, the way they acted so clever and self-assured. Each answered to its own name; she would talk knowingly with them too; and sometimes at night there would be a long conversation about who would be allowed to sleep closest to her this time : she never entered a house, you see, but always slept in thickets, warmed by her animals. Of a morning, when she wanted to get up, she would call the big old ram – Hermann was his name, I think – who would approach, and bend his mighty noggin low, then she would grab hold of his horns while he pulled her up with a simple lift of his head. No sooner would she leave the animals alone for a just moment, and they would start in bleating ever so woebegone; and when she returned, they would throng to her and rub their heads on her hand.

"Yes, she was feebleminded, I suppose; but kindhearted for the most part; and – unlike others of her sort – not at all given to finery or gaudy outfits : she always wore her old shepherd's hat, the brim rolled down; a durable tunic the color of the moors, a blanket around her shoulders; in her hand a long staff, which she used on marshy ground to leap from hag to hag.

"She would tell her tale to anyone who asked : she claimed that she had been the daughter of a well-to-do farmer, and had fallen in love with the shepherd of the estate. The ambitious, and irascible, father shot him dead during an exchange of words; and he died in Grete's lap; left her all his belongings – that is, his sheep and his garb, which she donned without hesitation, leaving her father's house, never to return again.

"One day, Hermann the bellwether wandered onto a stranger's meadow. The ill-tempered owner at once let his dogs loose, who then harried the poor animal to death : for days Grete sat on the meadow beside the corpse; until they finally coaxed her away by suggesting she arrange a solemn funeral for him, to which she enthusiastically gave her consent. We children were all on hand, and to this day I can still see the coffin, fashioned from a crate and painted black, and the tufts of grass and wildflowers that she had laid upon it. She then built a regular grave-mound with her own hands, pressed the sod firm, and fenced it in with willow rods. Until her death, she would come several times a year and set it to rights. –

"In the winter, she retreated deeper into the forests I suppose; and except perhaps in the worst blizzards, scorned any sort of shelter. When she would come by, many farmers spontaneously gave her hay for her sheep and soup for her bowl. If someone teased her all too much, she could also become very nasty, and would call down such awful things upon their heads that, after several such curses had come true, people preferred to leave her be.

"Once, as she was passing through a town, some schoolboys tormented her so, that at last she was at her wit's end and in desperation picked up some stones. Whereupon with loud hallooings, the rowdies likewise began to throw things, finally grabbing bricks, and literally stoned the poor deranged creature to death." –

"And so this here is Tall Grete's grave ?" I asked after an appropriate pause.

"This here ? : Oh no." he replied soberly : "Hermann the ram lies buried here. – The farmer who had him hounded to death drowned himself in his own well 8 days later, of course." He nodded his approval worthily : Justice must be served !

LITTLE GRAY MOUSE

"Yes. Disgusting !" –

The weather had suddenly turned so bad that, shaking our heads in scorn, we at once took our chairs again beside the fireplace. The chorus of flames danced and sang (a reddish blue prima donna puffed herself up royally beneath tapered hair dyed blue), but then was interrupted by another roar from a wind yokel, his motifs taken from Orff. While outside the rain sobbed, disconsolate female – ‹The rainess› would be much more apt : our language lacks conviction and is poorly constructed throughout ! : She lashed her silver hair long across the panes, oh, the Dead they cannot rise; and promptly came back again, aghast : and you'd better dry your eyes; and you'd best go look for a new love !

Stürenburg, surveyor in retirement, gave a decisive clap of his hands. A sulking Hagemann appeared, and received his whispered instructions. A few minutes later we saw, how, near-yet-far from the window, he thrust a man-sized torch into the garden soil, and after several false starts was able to ignite it : the harried flame glowed red and murky in the dusk (*very* attentive : *that* bloodstain was all we needed !).

Such flesh tones instantly reminded the widowed Frau Dr. Waring of her most recent visit to the zoo : feeding of the beasts of prey, bratwurst restaurant (a ‹guide› was likewise still in her purse : 80 west-federal-German pfennigs it had cost, incredible !).

"And ? – But this is, as I would like expressly to emphasize, an underhanded question – : Which animals did you like the best ?". The women, however, had been accompanied by Dettmer the pharmacist and Captain von Dieskau, and, in view of such numerous accomplices, felt relatively unassailable.

Von Dieskau ? "Hyenas !" he snarled with candid malice; plus : "Vultures : very useful on battlefields, ‹Towers of Silence›, as good as the ambulance corps, ha ha." We lifted our brows in chorus, and directed our paired eyes to the next person : ?

The rotund pharmacist, Dettmer, first took a tentative breath; smiled apologetically around the semicircle, and folded the dainty asparagus of his fingers; once more the tip of his foot asked our apology (and here Dieskau began to grunt) : "The giraffes !" he admitted blushing about the goatee : "so slender and agile –" (his hands formed a tall figure in the direction of the ceiling) : "and so – : so bright brown !"

Fräulein Emmeline ? ("You should get married !" Dieskau managed brutally to toss the pharmacist's way). For her it had been the ‹Graceful Flamingos›; which was followed by general approbation-disapprobation. The indecently biological smear of torch outside wobbled wide like an enlarged heart : unappetizing !

Frau Dr. Waring ? She smiled with tapered mouth; the face beneath her sallow-tinted hairwork first displayed its customary libration : "The elephants ! : What strength they must have !" My right and Dieskau's left eye met briefly : ! (‹Strength› : Woman-in-her-early-sixties). –

Stürenburg had benevolently noted them all, nil humani. In the break in the conversation, Hagemann offered his pic of sandwiches; Dieskau let pepper and salt rain; why did Emmeline eat so much anchovy paste ? (Salinity ?).

"Well, Hagemann ?" – Stürenburg had given a brief explaination – : "What is the strangest animal *you*'ve ever seen ? !". He put down the tray of coldcuts in strangely slow motion (almost daring us ? And I eagerly opened to a blank page in the notebook of my memory).

"A mouse, sir : a little gray mouse." Hagemann's heath-grown eyes sparkled ever so wickedly as he stepped behind our semicircle and told his tale (in Plattdeutsch; as a reliable chronicler – I am no more than that – I shall provide the meticulous translation).

"It was back around 19 hundred aught 4 –" he unfolded his face like an elephant; his large hand on his chin : "– or aught 5 ?" (tines spread, almost *too* believable). "At the time we were remeasuring the ‹Oldenburg Ring›, and were looking for the old marks" ("Uh=the Hanoverian survey that had been carried out by Gauss in his day" Stürenburg interjected by way of ill-at-ease explanation : now that was quite interesting, the difference today between master and servant !).

"We were out in middle of the moor with a good theodolite. The chronometer had just registered noon; and as per regulation sleep soon overcame us. Herr Stürenburg's breast rose and fell" (his hands at once demonstrated the rhythm of slumber) : "– and I of course wished to stand watch." (We nodded our approval; all faithful Eckart he was).

"Suddenly his breathing stopped. Strained face – : and all at once a very little gray mouse hops out of his half-open mouth ! Looks about in the grass with sparkling wee eyes; slips into the clearing of firs; I follow of course, keeping a constant eye on them both, Herr Stürenburg and the beastie.

"Soon it stood still; then it came to a little rill, so small any child could have toddled across : for the mouse, however, it was a mighty river, wider than, ah, than the Weser perhaps. Ran anxiously back and forth, now to the left, now to the right, wondering if it could leap across or no ? So at last I took the surveyor's rod, and out of pity laid it across like this" (He showed us : ‹like this› !) : "The mouse seemed amazed at first, but then very cautiously moved onto the red & white striped path, and went across, where it lost itself in a clumplet of moss : Herr Stürenburg was still lying there as if dead among the hillocks."

"Really, Hagemann ? !" Stürenburg gave a perplexed cry : "I've never heard any of this before !"

"Fine gentlemen haven't heard of many a thing !" he merely replied with a saucy snuffle; and was already continuing : "It almost frightened me; for who would believe my story about the mouse ! – When all of a sudden here the little thing comes leaping out from among the stalks, its eyes glistening more brightly still. Looks briefly around. Checks once more before setting its dainty legs on our lacquered scale, and wanders cautiously across to the nill : I quickly snatch up the rod, and follow after. It was almost indecent the way the beast bustled about my master's face; and I was wondering if I should not perhaps reach out and grab it ? – But before I could come to a decision, it had strolled right back into his mouth again." ("Really, Hagemann ! !" Stürenburg cried in protest; but Hagemann's little mouse eyes were sparkling away ! : onward !)

"Hardly was the mouse inside, and the breast began breathing again; a smile spread over the whole face; and straightaway Herr Stürenburg sits up, looks about him, shakes his head as if he wants to toss the last tufts of a dream from his hair, and says to me : ‹Hagemann›, he says : ‹Sit down beside me; I have something to tell you› !

"‹And in fact the very strangest dream ever to visit a man's brain. – I had no more than fallen asleep here beside Bottomless Lake –›" ("A small lake. Or better, a pond." Stürenburg interjected hastily : serves him right ! And Hagemann nodded from profound depths : yesyes; 't's all true !) : "‹when it seemed to me as if I were walking off into a dense forest. Enormously high grass, which soon closed above my head; and all at once I head a monstrous roaring, like great flooding waters : a broad river, whose far shore I could barely make out. I ran this way and that; for something I cannot describe was urging me on, as if I must reach the other side at all costs. I anxiously scouted for some sort of vehicle; suddenly, however, I spotted a broad, red & white striped bridge – with no railings, no breastwork – glistening and dazzling in the rays of the sun. Cautiously I stepped out onto the smooth path, strode slowly forward, so as not to slip and tumble into the mighty forest torrent. I reached the other side safely. After long wanderings in a high, tangled wood, I suddenly arrived at a shadowy cave – and there I saw – : ?›"

Pause. Open mouths about the hissing chorus of flames. The corners of Stürenburg's mouth were hanging low. (But it served him quite right ! Usually it was he who had all the better experiences !). "Well, what was there to see ? !" Dieskau snarled, raging with curiosity.

"A massive square block of glittering gold !" (Slowly and solemnly) : "‹I decided that my most urgent task› – Herr Stürenburg said – ‹was to impress the landmarks on my mind so that I would be sure to find the place again; and left those mossy vaults. Was afraid I might not find the bridge still in place. Then a return path that grew ever more indistinct as it gradually led back into greenery and illumined vegetation. – And awoke in sadness : that it had all been only a dream !›"

Hagemann looked about him in triumph. Bowing slyly, Hagemann presented the plate of sandwiches once again. Muttering : "I then led my master to the spot – though taking detours. We did some digging around – : *and* found the bronze marker of Herr Carl Friedrich Gauss." With sardonic modesty : "That was the strangest animal that *I* have ever seen."

"Really, Hagemann : we found that point by measuring !" Stürenburg cried in outrage; "that is to say : I do recall the dream again now, too ! – But the part about the mouse – : Hagemann, you're lying ! I've never heard any of this before !"

The wind whistled like a peat pumper. "Fine gentlemen haven't heard of many a thing" Hagemann muttered. Left the room; returned stepping more loudly : "Here is the bronze plate from the old t.p. : the one the mouse found." It was passed without comment from hand to hand.

A fine rain fell later. The torch ruddied in the dusk. We departed in separate directions.

COUNTRY
MATTERS

WINDMILLS

1

"What do you suppose is the relative incidence of towns in the Federal Republic with no Coca-Cola ?" he asked; without rancor, although he had to hit the brakes a second time because the cockamamie truck ahead of us was going slow again : the billboard on its stern was now as big as the wall of a single=family=prefab (not to mention that red !).

"Working from Gauss's calculations, about as common," I answered, "as 5 feenixes, 10 unicorns, or 22 occultations of Jupiter by Mars." "Has that ever been known to happen ?", he inquired. "On 5 January 1591, for example." I replied, expert & cold; and he gave a more suspicious snort.

Oil derricks roundabout – Madam Techno flexing her (aptly) so-called thousand-and-one joints conjointly. And in between, fields still all un-aware; (but also a funeral wreath of rusty barbwire around 1 fencepost – and here came our dusty wake to add the widow's veil.)

FRIMMERSEN 1½ miles ? And I spread an inquiring palm Richard's way, because he was turning off. "Deliv'ring a letter to the lifeguard," he declared; "promised the sheriff I would." –

Okay, Frimmersen. / It first distinguished itself, how soothing, by an absolute lack of notable sights; (nor, all unprepared, could I recall anyone of note who might have been born here); but here it came : the cryptic Janus=features of this Lower Saxon village, where someone had ‹struck it rich› in an evil hour. "You mean, in a ‹happy›" he corrected. Conversely, yes. / But it did look very curious : on the left a peaceful old half-timbered house; on the right, the New Well, where a stony prospector was tipping out his oil drum : the jet of water spurted from the bunghole across the pouting concrete lips of Mother Earth – and was gone.

And more evil dreams of concrete & glass, and nickel & black bakelite. ("You mean ‹happy›" he admonished. Conversely, yes.) / The town hall. (Wonder if those flowers out front are called ‹camarillas› ?). / A very New Church. / The crowning touch, by my modest lights, was the Savings & Loan : either these architects were so far ahead of us all ? (And before I could utter the ‹or› my mouth snapped shut all by itself; for I am, like every upstanding person, often weary of my own opinions.)

"Oyster=stew & brawn & shrimp & sliced meatloaf ?" "Go right on in, y' can get it all here," he assured me; "There's even a theater ! Your eyes'll pop like buttons." (Was it possible that in fact my ponderable glance had given rise to his vulgar simile ? He's so terribly uncouth.)

And so a stiff-legged exit, in the direction of the butcher=gutter= meatman. First let the ‹boomer› by, (or the "knallert," that's what the Danes call 'em; the term would be ‹impossible› for us, inasmuch as we possess neither invention nor humor. Among other things.) / And then make room for those two – hmmyes, might one, given the way ‹things stood› apply the term ‹village=lasses› ? : faces of circummopped brown; bodices of poplin; a lampshade swishing round the hips; legs of crimped nylon; flipflopping on very flat plastic soles.

Then into the shop; (even the *ceiling* in these parts gets tiled !); and stammering of requests. Watching the long, mondaine=trim arms of the salesgirl. (The ‹diploma› on the wall; ‹born 16 June 1900›). – "All I have is a 50=mark bill . . . ?" : "Oh, that's no problem." (Of course not; how stupid of me; we were in Frimmersen after all.) / And back out again, to Richard, the packages in the crook of my elbow; into the ‹suicide seat›. –

And he had no more than stepped on the gas, and here the diving tower came into view. We turned in, down a charming elderly grass lane. And then, naturally, it seems to be our kismet, the car heap of a parking lot; (but all the same, just behind the hedge, the pied & simultaneous scurry of demi-figures and -figurines, hilarity and halooing.)

Behind me Richard's masterfull hand flung the car door into its frame. Behind the attendant chainlink fence, the fidgetings of something like a white spitz. (Behind it, then, mallows, of which I am very fond : slim & tall & frilly trimmed.)

"Two tickets; just admission, no swimming, please." Without lifting her eyes from her book, parted black crown aglow, the woman at the window shoved the snippets my way; (ought one want to be the author ? I disturbed her intentionally a second time, by buying that postcard=there, an aerial view of the swimming pool; and now she was forced to lift her head high – and she looked, yes, how shall I put it, quite ‹timeless›; I was at once re-minded of the Savings & Loan in town.)

Richard had been right on my heels all along, reveling in the gaping amazement of the poor savage; and right he was, too : much to see for little wampum.

Lawn shorn to brush-bristles. With flower=collars. / Pop hits from loud-speaker=lanterns. / 3 pools : kiddywading; nonswimmers; and higher up, occupying the grassy ‹slope›, the one for masters of the art. (And just before it, the ‹cordon sanitaire›; for preliminary rinsing of the feet; very good !). / The white, suggestively=gaunt giant tower bowed all ten arms lovingly. / And the well-known bustle'n'shove on all sides : a bright yellow cap with a blue swimsuit; none at all with a deep red. Here the elastic step of the successful courtesan; there a thick pigtail held in perplexed hand; all of them, however, had too tiny eyes in the sun. We held tight along the narrow ledge around the cordon sanitaire, to the lifeguard's cabin.

He was already leaning out over his domain, in a cloud of smoke : shoulders the color of baking chocolate, a belly of old copperplate, feet like those of dear departed Queen Louise – famous for the size of hers. (A little shorter than I ? Maybe by about the thickness of a tram ticket.) The right eyebrow tucked in a martial twirl; a high-set Kaiser=Wilhelm=beard – was this guy a fan of the Hohenzollerns do you suppose ? But his hair hung in simple=unprincely fashion, and his mouth grumbled & mumbled a pleasant plebian.

"Glad to meet y' –"; (was his name Fritz Bartels? The last name had been difficult to catch.) The guy tucked in a robe of vertical yellow and black stripes, sitting in a chair beside him, was dubbed ‹Eugen Soandso› : wasn't the back of it coal-black silk; and with a dragon on it, the jaws about butt=height, the tip of the tail down to his ankles ? He released a large elegant ring of smoke from within him, and examined me critically through it. Until I turned around.

2

Hey : from up here, of course, all you could murmur was ‹Ozean, Du Ungeheuer› ! –

: The water metallic=toxic blue, (as a child I had loved to see ornaments that color on christmas trees; later I learned that the bottom had been intentionally enameled that hue). / The pool itself, into which fiery red ladders led, was the normal rectangle, 150 by 60; at the top of 1 long side, however, was set a broad wedge : and on this new-won short fifth side, the diving=tower hecatoncheir; that way people could turn somersaults, and, right alongside, flail their way down 8 racing lanes : the lines separating them, wide as your hand and the color of dried blood, gazing up from the giddy blue bottom; they wobbled. (So not ‹the norm› after all.)

Each starting block had its crouching Undine, arms like narrow ribbons wound around ultrathin legs; or, around powerfull back flesh, too, not easily spanned; the straps, when any were present, had got small as fingers (compared to those of my youth.) And all, all of them held their smooth, fakir hides up to the blare of light, whether white or yellow or red or brown, until they blistered.

: "They say the interiors of stars are ‹ruled› by temperatures in the millions of degrees." I said in a gallant attempt to bridge our embarrassment. "Must be quite unpleasant," the striped fellow murmured languidly; (and the other two giggled; served me right. – or then again maybe not : someone has to raise up the sacrifice of intellect in such situations.) In any case I had broken the spell, or the ice. "How's your wife doing ?" Richard turned to the lifeguard. "Simply adores me," He replied gloomily : "the moment she catches sight of me, she cries ‹Oh my GOd, my GOd !›". Once we had grinned each other down again, the striped fellow remarked, in an amiable, unpleasantly soft voice : "Make a little bag out of an old nylon; put some E=605 powder in it – hang it in your teacup, and you'll soon be rid of all your troubles." He flung the sides of his wasp robe apart, and one lithe leg over the other . . . . . : weren't those *brocade* trunks the guy was wearing ? ! (But Richard, noticing my bewilderment, at once rolled his eyes *ever so* high; and telegraphed with his whole face, so that I caught on with relative speed, I can take a hint.)

They had noticed none of this; instead, and quite rightly so, they were watching a small-fry (in every sense of the word) teenette lass as she made ready to assault the steps, despite the lifeguard's swishing his big index finger like a majestic scythe; she spread her wee arms up toward us, bellowing her demands. I did not understand her. He, however, begged our pardon with a wave of his hand; took 3 steps back into his cabin; fussed about in there – and at once music rose up o'er the land, ta=ta & boom= boom (Bhoomibhol & Sirikit); and then a jovial bass throbbed : "Red Rider o' Texas 'll bring law to the land." But as loud as it was now & then, you could nevertheless understand the words of the fellow in stripes :

"That gesture of yours just now, Fritz, reminded me of Italy; they've made a real art of gestures there; get more and more expressive, in fact, the farther south you go – very interesting. In Padua=f'rinstance people simply shake their heads no. In Bologna they fan an index finger, much like you just did. The same in Florence; but there they add a, staccato, ‹via !›. But from Naples on south, people do *this* –", to our surprise he sat up and leaned forward; made a broad, massive blade of his hand; laid it, palm down, under his chin, (thumb to the throat); first flashed wicked eyes at us, puffing himself up like a toad – then abruptly thrust his hand forward, toward us, with a dramatic splay of fingers : !. Sank wearily back again, and simply remarked : "Perhaps you can use it on some appropriate occasion, if you like. – It's at your disposal at any rate."

"You were in Italy again ?" the lifeguard asked with distrust. And the

one in stripes nodded: "Me & Gert=Wilhelm. And Sebastian, and Sonny=
Paul; and Ernst=August –". "What ? The ‹queen=mother› too ?" the lifeguard asked, interested; and the other guy gave a measured nod.

"We rented a secluded hunting cabin above Udine, on a quaint little
lake," – (at which Richard, with no other alteration of his face, winked the
eye closest to me; and I gave him an equally inconspicuous tuck, pollice
verso, of one corner of my mouth) – "It was really quite, quite marvelous,"
the fellow in stripes said, laying a hand to his rear as if taking an oath :
"Fresh fish every day – and I do so love the *eyes* – and what adventures we
had . . . . ."; he rocked his long head back & forth, once; gave his smiling
lower lip a bite (something I wouldn't have wanted to do), and mused.

"One day we're walking along a path in the woods, linked arm in arm –
and we hear someone shouting : a man comes wandering up; blinking and
groping. We took hold of his hands – the fingers were a deep yellow, brown
really; but not from smoking, but from mushrooming, there's a kind that
grows there, sort of leathery colored. Well, to be brief, he was pursuing his
botanic interests in a thicket and a branch had knocked off his glasses, and
he hadn't been able to find them again. – Well, we took good care of him; a
nobleman, by the way, a very cultivated gentleman, wrote articles for historical journals. Now, what did he say his most recent one was about ? – :
proof that one of the popes, Alexander the Seventh, I believe, was related
to the contemporaneous Turkish sultan, Mohammed the Somethingeth."
This learned note was greeted with divided opinion; I made the, silent, decision to check it out; Richard gave a dubious shrug; only the lifeguard
nodded bitterly, and remarked that he had no doubt of it. (All the same,
isn't there even nowadays a company, in Frankfurt methinks, by the name
of TURK & POPE ? And I immediately began to think of anchovy paste, and
shrimp in aspic, and all sortsa gooey specimens like that.) The striped fellow set his eyes again; he continued :

"Another time – it had been a beautiful night, full moon – we decided to
get some ‹morning exercise›. We all still had our striped pajamas on, and
off we go romping through the woods. We come out onto an open field – :
and there's a farmer at his plow, the moment he catches sight of us, he
flings his tool aside, and runs as hard as he can in the direction of the village ! – The gendarme who questioned us later – our *nobile* knew him, and
had no difficulty mollifying him – explained it all to us : the man had fled
from a storming troop of striped ‹convicts›." His face a gracefully=vacant
mask, he accepted the applause & laughter; his eyes had long since meandered out over the domain again; at one point he lifted expensive binox to
his pair of eyes.

Now ever since I was a lad, I've been interested in optical instruments.

He obligingly held them out to me; and I took an ample look around, to the hard=right, across to the smaller pools.

: gaudy=gaudy=gaudy; stripes & checks & posies & polka dots. Orion-straddling poses : whoopee ! And on the gentle slope of lawn more constellations of mounded fabric & human flesh. Crouchers sweating in silence. (And a pious constabulary of gray-haired hypocrits slinking about everywhere; and taking, sub specie professoritatis, color snapshots with their Kodaxes.)

A valkyrie ? : Where ? ! – (Yes indeed; that was the feeblest word for that figure !). We all watched for a longish time as she strode our way, in her wide & broad antique bathing suit; you could already hear her bosom seething with exertion. The lifeguard at once went to make a quick check of the maximum berobement permitted by Frimmersen Pool; (laid an index finger to the appropriate line in his regulations posted on the wall inside and compared, several times); and came back, shrugging : "Maybe She wants to earn her lifesaver's badge ?". She strode royally to one of the fire ladders. With each step her weight waned. (And shortly thereafter, her head – no : her dome ! – augmented the number of water-sporters.)

Inasmuch as Richard was beginning to tell an anecdote I already knew – about the two children who had been left alone at home : for the fun of it the older sister had allegedly stuck her merry=babbling little brother into the laundry centrifuge, and then, just like mommy, flipped the switch – I raised the binox anew. / –. –. – / : Across the way, at the restaurant=minitable, a deft highschoolette vanquished a defenseless older gentleman by commencing to do diligent homework right across from him; (doubtless she groaned discreetly the while; and looked at him from great, sweet= abstracted eyes . . . . . : ?) : Aha; he was ‹helping› her now. They were putting their heads together now. She moved around to his side now, for the sake of more fruitfull cooperation. : And 2 ice cream sundaes now appeared ! (And things took the course such dry=ski exercises are wont to take. ". . . by the time daddy came home, blood was running out." I heard Richard conclude gloomily; and now the soft=undulating motions of his hands to illustrate its flow.)

"Luther once ordered, by the by, that a two-year-old child be thrown into the Zwickauer Mulde; because he considered it a ‹child of the devil›." the lifeguard said pensively; (had busied himself, then, reading up on the theoretical side of his occupation as well, doubtless during the winter months, when pool & tower are ‹hung with snow›.) "Hmyes; swimming is not really all that old," the fellow in stripes confirmed, taking his binox back again, nodding thanks; (let them air a bit, exercising a certain self-control that looked good on him, before putting them to use again).

Clouds pert and big among poplar leaves ? The lifeguard peered suspiciously in their direction, through the thicket of brows, out of pond eyes.
Then his gaze wandered back, across the water slide, restaurant, changing
cabins, swimmers pool, and diving tower, ‹all's well 'board ship›. (Actually, I could draw an arrow for north on my aerial view, too.) Then at last
he tore open the letter that Richard had brought for him.

3

And began at once to curse in a high, clear voice : "Damn, they want me
back in Buggersdorf on the first ! To substitute for the local lifeguard for 4
weeks : all I needed !". And stared more angrily at the spiderweb of handwriting. Shook his athlete's head, help= and power=less. (And another
"pfff !"; and more curses in strictest confidence.)

"But why are you so anti-Buggersdorf, Fritz ?" the striped fellow inquired reproachfully : "Cannot solitude be lovely as well ?". And we
decided to wait for the answer – we really had nothing else to do.

"Nono; never." the lifeguard said savagely, casting a shining glance
round his paradise of frolickers here; then, in pain, to us : "Y' know the
place ? – No ?".

"Well, picture a large pond –" ("A small lake," the striped fellow gently
admonished) – "Reeds, duckweed, boggy bottom; thickets of willow and
alder along the banks. The lifeguard has to ‹tend the grounds› : in plain
German, ‹keep it mowed›. And the *frogs* at night ! no reasonable person
shows up there all season."

"2 years ago a whole sanatorium leased it out; ‹with an interesting case-
load› as the decrepit supervising physician assured me every morning : you
saw *things* there that would've converted any Casanova; I very seriously
considered becoming a Buddhist. If only there hadn't been that one nurse :
tall, platinum blond; a pastor's daughter, of most stern countenance; a virgin no less too." I automatically looked at the man-size thermometer beside
me : 88° in the shade ? ! The striped fellow was fingering the stick-pin on
the lapel of his robe, TEAR DOWN THIS WALL ! Richard gave a long & sturdy
nod, and pictured it.

"They put me up in a garret of course : very dark; just 1 dusty, most
slanted dormer window. Giant spiders everywhere, the kind y' find in bath-
tubs; an earwig in your cup every morning. One day I wake up at dawn; feel
something in my mouth, chew on it drowsily – a bug 'd fallen in !"

The striped fellow bent forward : "What do bugs taste like ?" he asked
with genuine interest. – "Ohgod sorta – stinky, reechy," the lifeguard said

flustered; "ghastly at any rate !". But the other fellow dismissed this with a mobile face, à la you just don't understand.

"And the lunatic innkeeper of the ‹Forest Tavern› ! When he had nothing else to do he'd sit under his elderberry bower; the path out to it was lined with beer bottles : *but they still had to have labels; he wouldn't use anything but* ! – The first time I saw him he had a hardboiled egg for a left eye : held down with a Band-Aid; from his forehead to the corner of his mouth." "That's an old home remedy," Richard said placidly : "The fellow had a stye, that's all." But the lifeguard vigorously dismissed this : "Nono. Totally plastered."

"Last year, I walk into the taproom, suitcase in hand – there are 10 men in black suits sitting at the tables, silent as spooks. I checked the clock : in the quarter hour it took me to negotiate with the landlord, not a 1 breathed a single word; not a sound, nothing; I thought I was already dead !" "Playing chess ?", the fellow in stripes asked languidly.

"Up I go to my buggy chamber; change, put on my swimtrunks; and back down again fast as I can, out into the fresh air, to the tavern garden. As expected, nothing but your ancient=awful folding chairs circa 1900, iron frame & skinny slat seats; but I sit myself down all the same, so I can keep 1 eye trained on the little dock, dutiful as always – you can't be worrying about your body in my job, y'know."

"And so there I sit. Naturally, not a soul in the water. The landlord comes shuffling out from the haunted house, average height, beefy, greasy, all noblesse oblige; walks right past without a word, and sits down in his bower. And silence restored. And I stare at my Seven-Up so long I start to get dizzy. The alders rustle disagreeably. At some point something stirs under the duckweed – causing a strange rise in it, as if someone is trying to stick his head up through; for a moment I truly vacillated whether to dive in or not ? And I just kept feeling giddier & giddier, very odd, I've *never* felt like that before !"

"You sure it was just pure Seven-Up ?," Richard, dubious. But the lifeguard angrily dismissed this : "I am a tea=totaler for the most part. During summer." he said hastily, while his hand groped for his whistle : just under our balcony, right at the edge of the pool, stood a hesitating twelve-year-old, still just halfpint ‹offense› but kicking=around. Beside him his mistress of like age, popsicle in one corner of her mouth; her thin long arm, tapered to a menacing point and directed far out into the blue water; the shrill voice announced brazenly : "If y'love me, y'love my ball : go get it." And we thrust lower lips forward, and nodded appreciatively to one another : She's gonna be a good one ! (When we're hobbling on our canes; ‹the vintage cup to come›.) The lad took the death-defying plunge; (‹On the

Freedom of a Christian Man›; ahyes); and crawled along with considerable
aplomb so that the lifeguard took his fingers from his whistle, and continued somberly :

"So 2 hours without any clients whatever. – And all of a sudden it hits
me : *THE WINDMILLS* !".

"At first I thought I was dreaming; it's really very queer how long it
takes sometimes before you're aware of something like that. This time it
was model windmills. The landlord had done 6 of 'em so far; all exactly=
alike : five-feet high; painted green; the cupolas tile-roof red; the sails
snow-white. Everywhere you looked, suddenly there was a windmill on its
man-sized post. It turned; focused on you; and made a slow=gray disk of its
sails. Of course I immediately fixed my eyes on my own tabletop; it at least
was rectangular and steady – although the paint was generally worn off
here too, and the whole thing damned=uh – ‹abstract›, y'know ?". "Can
one be anything but abstract ?" the striped fellow asked in polite=
amazement.

"But do what I might, – count; whittle; think of Jutta –", ("Isn't your
wife's name ‹Hilda› ?" Richard interposed taken aback. But no one paid
him any attention.) – "I found myself staring, again and again, and at ever
briefer intervals, at those windmills. And –", (here he turned to us, index
finger held impressively to his chin), – "keep in mind that garret, too. And
the bugs. And the earwigs. – When twilight fell, I went to bed right away;
after all, my contract reads only ‹by day›." He broke off; because the now=
refreshed valkyrie, the one from before, was passing by : old hands, and
buttoned up tight; but it stuck out from the fabric=facade, like 2 walnuts.
Our disciplined breath followed her; and he went on :

"The next morning I awoke from brutal dreams – you know, ‹war› and
such : crowds circumgyrating in train stations; a merry-go-round of dive=
bombers overhead, firing at me, setting stones aspraying; a doctor who
once came here to swim told me I have a ‹labyrinth=complex›." ("Who
doesn't ?" the striped fellow asked in surprise.) "In any case the whole
circus started up all over again : from inside on my rite, every half hour an
intense=soft ‹au roi !›; rustling alders behind me; the duckweed nicknod-
ding on my left; and dead ahead, those windmills – : ‹surrounded›, right ?
‹hemmed in›."

"Afternoon, around 1500 hours, –" (finally somebody who didn't say
‹3 o'clock›; how very hard it is for an ‹older generation› to die out) – "a
canoe, with 2 young people. And there was some life in the place. They
landed; cracked jokes : nothing was ‹sacred›; neither landlord nor
Botwinnik; neither pope nor Sing=man=ree. They had a bottle of CHANTRÉ
sent out first thing. Joined me at my table; told jokes; we blossomed –

remind me later, Eugen : I have to tell you the one about the chauffeur who tries to curry his boss's favor." (And the fellow in stripes gave a formal nod.)

"So we're quite merry to begin with; I felt rescued. But around 16 hundred 30 hours I notice they're getting quiet. Their voices gawkier; an odd limp droop to their faces; fingers start plucking the tabletop; eyes rove, become mirrors. First one gaze turns rigid, then another – I follow the direction . . . . . ?". "The windmills." the striped fellow said circumspectly to the concrete balcony floor at his feet.

"I jump up – things simply can't go on like this, if only for the sake of ‹business› – and move in on the landlord; till I can see the eggwhite of his eyes, the black under his fingernails : ‹Get rid of those windmills !›." ("Give thought its freedom, sire." muttered the striped fellow, self-enraptured, waspy=slim.) "He doesn't budge. So I go back to our folding table; we wait for hours, gathering our wrath. The others go to their rest; we drink more courage. The full moon, large & pale-gold, starts up out of the elders –" (and both complete the sentence simultaneously; the fellow in stripes : ". . . how long a time lies in one little word."; the lifeguard) : "and shortly before midnight we pull down the windmills and throw them in the pond !". (Both finishing at the same moment.)

"But then later that same night – ?" the lifeguard groaned; (meaning that even 45 inches around the chest can't protect you from the bites of conscience). – "I wake up around 400 hours. I go downstairs – as if drawn, no will of my own. There I find the two penitent paddlers wandering about the lawn; helpless : the windmills are floating across the pond ! Face up." (Meaning the ‹sails› : very int'resting, how he saw them as ‹faces›. Wonder if one could justify calling such a ‹hulk› ‹sensitive› ? Hmm.)

"So fetch the binox : won, too, three; fore, fyve, sicks. The others almost paralyzed; but me, man-of-action, into the puddle; and pull them out : won, too, three. Fore, fyve, sicks." An enviably deep breath expanded his cocoa ribs. But the sun was really heating up, so that the shoulderblades of even the most fireproof cuties, down below, gave a shudder.

"What if someone had been watching this, on the diagonal from uptop : the three of us in bathing suits; scrubbing the things clean again !" "With what ? !" the striped fellow asked eagerly; "With joy," the lifeguard replied gloomily. "Then we nailed them back on their posts. – The landlord definitely noticed; but said not a word." (All the more eerie; granted; the water made ruffs around the severed heads below, too – or more precisely, of course, ‹severed bodies›; except that the upright heads were floating along across the toxic, water=like liquid.)

4

"And I'm supposed to go back there again ?" the lifeguard asked the horizon in a wee=plaintive, quite=inappropriate voice.

"We'll stop and visit you sometime." Richard promised him; (but at the
same time gave the signal for pulling out.) "Ah, that'd be exquisite –" came
his hope=filled reply; and even the fellow in stripes gave a single, majestic
nod of farewell. –

On our right, the patterned tiles of the wading pool : salad of arms & legs
in an azure basin; si jeunesse savait. (Above, the sky's bowl with more and
more cloud dumplings.) They sprayed one another from red=red rubber
hoses, just ripples & nipples. / On past the valkyrie : she had even more
clothes on now; was sitting at the table with that older gentleman, (Aha,
whaddya know); also eating ice cream, spooning and gazing=about. /
Through the turnstile, on past the ticket window; (she was still reading).
The poster in the cement entryway: Closed next week, the such'n'suchth,
for the semifinal play-offs of the German water-polo championship ? And
we nodded to one another in respect=filled amazement : quite some operation, this Frimmersen here !). –

Outside : the snow-white spitz raced behind the chainlink, and barked
much. (But I incited it in equal measure, too; by declaiming in a stage=
whisper, audible at 60 yards, "Master Péter : Ma=sterpé=ter !" – at once it
threw back its head in ecstasy, its tail=feather swishing; it was still cursing
as we climbed in.)

‹Vroomm : Vroomm !›; (almost right under my butt; embarrassing.)
Gliding slowly away. (And we didn't look back either; the letter had been
delivered.) / (But why was my head bobbing so queerly ? Ah : Richard was
footworking again, on the accelerator, ‹And adieu now, dearest native
land›.)

Sunward . . .

1

It was, of course, already much later ‹by the clock›, and although still broad
daylight, we would, within 10 and a few minutes, be treated to a moonrise
– we arched excited brows and smiled appropriately : we had not seen one
in town for a long time now ! The clouds here were not nearly so dolled up
as at home, either. Plump geese (with attendant plump twelve-year-old girl
behind them). A boy using the end of a rope to flog the Coca=Cola sign on
the village grocery's plank fence : in the yard behind it, as if it had accidentally come to a halt there, the flower-potted wheelbarrow (sic ! and the
monkey in me was grandly amused – an autumnal stay in the country, just
what I needed.) "Quick ! – Beat it out !" Friedrich ô Feral roared; and
obedient, I ran after the little glowing corpse of tricky paper and clubbed it
down with the wide end of my pitchfork : !

The ladies still in the bath ? At their artless=bucolic toilettes, (to bring
total confusion to our poor senses, right ? : ‹a beautee oute of mesure›.) We
sighted across the screwcaps of our pocket=flasks, doorward . . . ? Apparently they would be at it for some time; good; in fact very good. Peter was
coming toward us bearing the box of gooseberry thorns; a quivering jerk –
out of pure poet's curiosity, he had simply had to see what might be in
there, and promptly pricked a finger, (moanings & mooings : let me say it
again, a stay in the country ! Cows, with chains around black faces loom up
from elderberry bushes and catch you by surprise. Ledum palustre moves
off, luring and seducing the virtuous wanderer into bottoms – who would
not be susceptible to so much ‹u› ?). All the same Peter, as he came, proposed across his well-sucked finger : "Not ‹cows› : WOMEN ! – Women with
chains, golden chains, around white faces; just picture that now – huh ?".
We briefly pictured it.

Fritz Voss – (why we had come up with ‹ô Feral› for him even I no
longer knew; but he still always got properly irked by that refined ‹o=with=
lid›; probably from some Goethe=Annual or other. Meaning that it could
not have come from Peter at any rate; the true poet, he read nothing but
detective stories.) – Fritz, then, was the first to reject it; he had after all also
been the first of us to pass 50, and presumably treasured his reddish-eyed

Barbara only on a theoretical basis : small & gaunt, skinny white braids
beside saucy eyes, (the other portions of her face rather simple) – and wrap
golden chains around that ? ! "Let not a word thereof be spoken." he also
warned, worried, as it were. Then again, field marshaling, as indeed befits
an insurance actuary, ‹Thou doest smile serenely across the doom of thousands› : "Now put on 2 big forkfulls of hay !" –

– : first a delicate crackle & snap. Then many pointed tonguelets beneath
the Nessus=net of straws. A thick yellowhite blanket of smoke billowed
up; flickered indecisively a handsbreadth above the mound of fire . . . . . :
and then flung itself directly over Peter; (and he was gone; all you heard
now were his coughs, and his stomps of protest. When a mini-veil also
drifted our way, Fritz grabbed the atheroma on his pate with polite disgust,
and used it to pull his head to one side.)

*　　*
*

: "There !". –

Yes indeed. Quite pale, almost transparent, the great vacant face gazed
over the bordering pines. (And the red glassy sun, now harmless as a bonbon, offered its regards from the opposite side.)

"It's said Hagedorn drank like that too –"; because Peter had once again
set his flask to lips much too thick for a lyric poet. "So=what ? ! –" he
replied defiantly; but then he thought of his Gretchen, I suppose, and inquired, with considerably better manners : "We could have another –
couldn't we ?". Fritz let the corners of his mouth droop, and considered
(the poor guy was wearing a tie that looked like the border on an airmail
letter ! but he couldn't help it; his wife picked them out for him; he no
longer paid any attention) : "Well –" he began hesitantly, (and at once was
all ‹system› again) : "– that depends on a) how long our beauties take to
adorn their bodies. And b) whether Dr. Feger and spouse are coming this
evening." "Ohgod; a vet." Peter said disdainfully : "I can't read poems
properly unless I'm just very softly=uh – illuminated : As you know, I
drink with strategy . . ." The word stuck in his throat; for he saw how Fritz
was squeezing his stogie in his fingers so hard that it sent smoke pouring
out from at least 5 places – impending danger ?

But began breathing more easily again; because it was only the brassy
voice of his Lady Barbara : "Well, my chickadee ? How far along are you
all ?". And at once another of her inevitable, pointlessly pointed glances
allround, (with blue jeans flapping round her spindle=legs – ahwell, if she
hadn't always been so frugal they still wouldn't own their own house. All

the same.) "Had I but Amor's wings," Fritz began in polite reply, (and the joke is that if you pronounce it in dialect it sounds like ‹bottom arse› : if only the wind would come from the right direction; just a very gentle breeze . . . . . and I could hear it now rustling up in the Oak Bosket, behind us; now in the young pear trees, ‹Celler thick stems›; and Peter's face beamed, under control). She raised up from the giant rhubarb leaf that she had bent down to spread more decoratively; her eyes still fastened on us, disgusted, as if forced to gaze out over a whole inland sea of alcohol – and I promptly poked my fork into woolly flames and underbrush, so playfully, (and fanning it, too !) – – : there ! She had vanished. From the fumes came the chirp of a withdrawing organ : "Take all the time you like. Gretchen is in the tub. And then Gerda still has her turn."

And how lovely the restored silence. The moon had raised itself up higher still; well let it.

"I spotted the number 2,000 a while ago," Peter said, woolgathering : "set in white bricks. – We really should walk more, y' know." "You, definitely," Fritz confirmed gruffly; but then, getting into the spirit of his idea : "You mean, you *see* a lot more than when you're riding in a car." That was so ‹true› (and at the same time so simpleminded : truth is in fact damn pedestrian, isn't it ?), that we abstained from ventilating the topic further. Peter had his bottle in hand again now. "What've you got in there today ?" a very nervous Fritz wanted to know. But he paid no attention; asked instead : "Are we going to be drinking Canary coolers all evening again ?" (Lady Barbara knew how to mix a bumpkin brew from white elderberry blossoms, lemons and sugar. Though I must say : it actually didn't taste all that bad; quite tangy in fact with seltzer; if you were in the right mood. But were we this evening ? – And since even Fritz's jutting lower lipworks seemed to doubt it, I mutely pulled out my flask as well. And ‹here's lookin' at y' !›. (Shin-gazers; in honey=moon garb and the company of trees. Fool moans for all aethernity.)

The languid charms of twilight. The gaudy big aster pompoms looked flatter, more clothy. Dainty cosmos foliage. Even the dahlias had not all frozen to death yet; (although the black limp leaves ‹afterward› aren't half bad !). The most interesting item this time was the acanthus beside the house : the thumbthick black stalks; (a letter had described for us the pale blue trumpet blossoms; and the column capitals were accurate, too, it said); at present spiny seed capsules sat like little cacti in every branch fork. "More like chestnut hulls. If you ask me." Peter had objected : "And did it really grow there purely by accident ? – Never would've thought it could thrive in our climate : levantine –" he added in a whisper (he just couldn't resist the jawtwisters; ah well, it was his profession after all; people want it that way, too.) "By pure accident," Fritz confirmed, "we had guests from Spain; their car was parked right on that spot for a coupla days – and must 've been brought on its chassis somehow, the aforesaid seeds." (One guy ‹aforesaid›, the other ‹levantine› – meaning truth lay somewhere in between.)

"We ought to take a moonlit walk now." "With the ladies ?". "No, no," Peter said hastily, "I stress the ‹now› – meaning just we three. Imagine it : the soft luminescence always up ahead . . .". But I just shook my head : "In the dark friend ? And over terreign as good as unknown ? – I'd much prefer daylight : ‹Sunward›." "First feed the fire," Master o' the Hall Fritz ordered testily : "Use the stuff from the top layer of the compost heap. And, Peter, you put your hand to the next stack of hay. – One really doesn't know what to do with this constant accumulation of grass," he confided to me with a shake of his head : "Sometimes country life just gets to be too much; the everlasting mowing, and raking, and ‹turning› and . . . And please don't say anything against the vet, Peter," he thought to say as the plump fellow came gasping up neptune-fashion : "My wife swears by him, ever since he vaccinated her cats against distemper. – And it really was quite sweet : the neighbor's little girl, who'd heard something about an ‹epidemic› and seen all the worried faces, brought her teddybear over, and would not calm down until the doctor gave him a ‹shot›, too, and kept a serious face." "‹Sweet› perhaps; though a mite expensive, too, huh ?" I objected; but Fritz pursed his thin lips : "Ohwellyes," he said quickly : "but I have my logarithm tables, and Barb . . . . : to everyone his hobby, right ?".

Peter gave a sovereign jiggle of his tined scepter above the flames, which obediently pullulated high and hissing; stuck the prongs into the earth; draped his crossed arms more tightly around the shaft, and asked profoundly : "Where would you end up in fact ? If you were to walk steadily ‹sunward› ?"

*   *
*

"Starting out in the morning ? – Well, you'd be right back where you started come evening." I declared, overhasty as always; (or, perhaps more accurately ‹fed up› – what another no-account ‹problem› this was ! People like us have to run around scrambling to get an army-uniform contract, and this guy=here . . .) : "Far as the moon goes, you'd probably be best off asking a lamplighter." (Thieves, policemen, the moonstruck were suggested, one after the other; ‹poets›, too; but Peter was no longer responsive : the result of too many bad reviews.)

110 ■ A R N O S C H M I D T

Monsignore ô Feral (– or had we got it from ‹Venetian Legation Reports› ? You really do read the craziest things in the course of a life –) was already shaking his head with great vigor : "No. – Nono," he said : "Out of the question that you'd be back at the starting point by evening. Indeed it's . . . a rather complicated matter . . . . . Go look in the shed; there are 3 or 4 cardboard boxes of old trash; Barb always imagines I can build a fire in winter out of old herring wrappers and sausage skins – we'll pile them right on top." And so I strode, straight across the lawn, on past the ‹stand of rowan›, (set in quotes because all 3 twigs were no more than hip-high and only in Lady Barbara's imagination did they exist as a copse of charming, red=berried large shrubs gracefully gesticulating in the wind : and she wasn't any larger herself, any=where; I had seen her, in years past, in her bathing suit – Fritz must have got some truly bad advice at the time : wonder if he never knew his mother-in-law ?). (But it really was damned obscure here in the shed ! It looked like strange ‹nothing›. Tinny noises hanging from every wall; a breeze heavy with cat shit rose from below; scratchy tentaculata – a rope it would seem. – Aha=here : clammy cardboard cubes. Now, out of this coach of gloom !).

"Huh=uh; depends not just on the date," I could already hear Fritz lecturing; his voice grown most vivacious, as always when dealing with un-remunerative=numerical gags : "but also on the latitude phi of the starting point – and even to some extent on lambda, the longitude. The decisive factor would be the *speed of march*." I pushed the first rather greasy carton into the blaze, (over which Peter had just rapidly strewn some hay, with unnecessary priestly gestures; then some more on top of that). Fritz meanwhile called a greeting over the nearest fence, and we gawked, as always, into Mr. Neighbor's kindly old face – we couldn't help it ! – in point of fact : the fellow looked exactly like Karl May ! The same wicked bonhomie as the frontispiece to volume 34 ! "He could have used Him as a double flat-out." Peter, enraptured; and, enthusiasm running wild : "Something everyone should have."

"What would you want with a ‹double› ?" I inquired in amazement. But then a few business possibilities came to mind; though not nearly as many (nor as cunning) as the ones Peter outlined on the spot – ah well, he was a poet after all, and was required to have more fantasy than we others.

: "You could give readings ‹from your own works› at 2 different places at once; just imagine : double income ! / In the battle with publishers, downing drinks trying to get a good contract : you could trade off; and maybe carry the day that way after all. / You could pull the wildest antics : and always have the ‹alibi› that you were sitting peacefully at home; and neighbor May could swear to it if need be. / In case you're hauled in for

some ‹lèse majesté› or other, you could have the ‹other guy› do time . . .
right ?"

But Fritz shook his head and poked the fire : "The curve wouldn't be *all*
that simple." he declared grimly : "Even factoring in various simplifica-
tions – first you walk east. Then swing southward." "Dead south at noon,"
I risked interjecting; but he just crinkled his high=brow, he was already
way ahead of me : "Then, as afternoon progresses, south=west . . ." ("The
German=Southwest : Lettow=Vorbeck" Peter slipped his wisecrack in, obviously wounded in his double=dream) . . . "and finally to the west :
always sunward."

The gray sky=canvas; the yellow mask pasted on it askew. "Just like at
Joyce's, right, Peter ?" I tried getting him back into a good mood; but he
just haughtily shook his Lord=Brandy head (you could smell it now) : "I
believe in salvation through poetry : I do *not* believe in sole salvation
through 1 single writer !". (Whereas he believed it every 14 days; though,
to be sure, a different one each time; of late, one STANLEY ELLIN – I'd never
heard the name in all my life ! Well, it was not my bailiwick after all.) "At
the equator, around noon, you'd have more or less to jog in place. And at
the pole, you'd end up wandering southwards in a ever=expanding sum-
mery spiral, right ?"

"We are not at the equator here !" an indignant Fritz objected : "No : at
sunset you should – by my preliminary calculations – end up *south* of the
starting point . . .". "How far south ?" I imprudently asked; (after all, it
didn't matter a tinker's dam how we chitchatted away our stoker=shift
here. Or did it ?). Fritz shrugged : "That'd depend on the time of year. –
The simplest thing'd be to have a *practical* go at an experiment of such
abiding interest. : Somebody fetch that bankrupt mattress. But first add
some more hay !"

*   *
*

"With a hay : and a hoe !" resounding sweet and vigorous behind us;
just the way, in fact, a 6-foot, 200-pounder can utter it. In other words :
Gretchen. Ergo, the danger was not excessive; for she had a robust=
sympathetic way of dealing with men; (whether she actually was is a horse
of a different color – ah well, we'd know very shortly now what our ladies
think of us : we had pooled money for a tape=recorder, and Fritz had put
the apparatus in the ladies' wardrobe, placing the mike inconspicuously
in a giant vase of asparagassy foliage, close to the mirror; so we would
see; ‹We›, manifestly dwindlepotent and subject to all sorts of inferiority

complexes, mind-gamers, ‹The name is all, the passion but jangle & smoke› – maybe that was even closer to the truth.) At any rate the fumes separated respectfully before Gretchen, and bright skittering lights surged about her legs. Clear up to there. (Do your butchering in the months with an ‹r›; fall in love in the one with an ‹i›; but the loveliest, to my way of feeling, are those with an ‹o›.)

"Well, what is it ?", Gretchen said, prettily, though not unpleasantly, perplexed; (because we had gawked at her like that). – : "Tsk. – I mean you make me feel downright embarrassed !"; she giggled excitedly; bent down (in shame ?), and spread wide the yellow chair-bottom-sized rhubarb leaf. And strode off again, all ‹haunches›, houseward; (meaning that ‹mine› was now making ready to climb into the tub.)

But : "Did you guys see that ? !". And even Fritz nodded his whole concave face : "How did a penny get in there ? – Peter !". For it was indeed equally puzzling and remarkable : just above Gretchen's knee, there where the thigh began to swell mightily, (until it became a thighway), a copper penny was stuck between flesh and Perlon=hide – : "Peter ? !". But he, too, though indeed a poet and therefore a potential dessous=specialist, knew no explanation; all he came up with was Lessing : ‹Did you ever see / Mistress Betty's knee ?›.

: "A hole in her purse, maybe ?". (Bull : women don't have pants pockets !). "Or just a trick ? To make the men jealous; à la ‹Somebody's been here !› ?". (‹What you Betty's thimble call / that is very good for all !›, But that was really absurd : Who would go to the trouble of finishing off by slipping a penny in there ? Crazy. And our hypotheses were so quickly spent we decided it was better to turn back to the moment's more pressing problem – presumably each one secretly resolving to ask his wife.)

"The simplest thing, as I said : would be to have a practical go at it." dogged Fritz repeated : "Someone takes a compass. Someone else the surveyor's map, and enters, point by point, the line of march. – Even a 1:100,000 might do –" he muttered in conclusion, "or better yet : a military ordnance map." ‹Military› did the trick for Peter; and out of superstition, I agreed as well; (maybe I'd get that uniform contract after all : wishing to be free of the constraints of reason, and thereby slipping into the constraints of unreason; yesyes ! The airy figure of the moon on the surface of darkness.)

But on the ‹longest day› ? That was typical Fritz the Theoretician : "Listen, the farmers 'd have some words for you if we were to stride, in a threesome, through their waving crops ! We'd have to cut straight & ruthlessly across fields." And Peter had the more decisive argument against an experiment at solsticetide : "How long is your sun above the horizon that day ?" "Around 16 hours" Fritz replied distractedly, and was surprised to hear Peter's wicked laughter : "And all the while doing the average 3.5 miles an hour, right ? ! Have you ever seen someone who's traipsed 56 miles in one day, and crosscountry at that ? – Pfff !"

Well then; that meant at the earliest, in the days of stubble. "And if possible without a pause, without refreshment ?" Peter thought to add now : "Pfff !". "Right, there'd be no drinking underway on this trip of course," Fritz declared sternly : "so every wet-eared doubter could add some remark about how we'd imbibed too deeply of the map every time we recorded a curve ? Nono. – Once we're done=then, naturally." But I – someone had to keep a clear head around these two fanatics here; (we are all possessed in the end; and *I'm* taking the scope : staring through it always lends one such an elegant pose !) – mediated the issue : "At least 1 of us has to stay sober. – : Cheers !". "Cheers –" they replied; Peter very pensively; Fritz more mechanically. We tipped pretty much in sync.

*   *
*

"You can send your double, you know," the malicious thought struck me. But just then, Peter, who was about to provide an oral response, had his forkfull rejected : "No; not the nettles ! Put those by the hole in the fence over near the shed –"; (and we approved of this : one certainly does become inventive out in the country : that made it absolutely thief=proof !).

"My double ? He'd have something better to do" Peter explained to me with disdain : "Cash=as=cash=can, my good man. – Granted, you'd have double expenses : always have two have two suits made. And/or buy 'em from the rack" he conceded when he saw us about to break into scornfull laughter : "He'd have to practice your signature. / You'd have to pack his pockets with bon mots; when he's representing you at some soiree. He'd have to answer all the letters from readers, the horror of horrors." "Or when female admirers come to call, right ?", I sneered : "You can forget the ‹child s'pport› : it was always ‹the other guy›, provable by blood-type and rhesus factor, right ?" (And we beasts nodded with oldsters' depravity : too weak for downright sinning; but heads still full of thick maggots !). "Well let's not let our s'port die out on accounta your ‹support payments›," Fritz said enviously : "if I wanted to erect a monument to every good idea I have, the neighborhood 'd look like a bowling green. – Hold out for another fifteen minutes at least, guys : course we'd have to listen to the weather report beforehand; and set out only if there's a ‹high›. Because what if later, halfway into things, clouds came up . . . ?". "Or fog," Peter said, musing : "Why look : here in this box; you've thrown out a whole loaf of semimoldy army bread ! And then you wonder why you never get ahead – now if it were cheese, they'd call it ‹Roquefort›. – I think we can manage 1 more, huh ? Considering we won't be able to touch a drop on our experimental march ?"

We did hesitate though; (true : there wasn't much left; hm.) We already had faces with milky pale shadows. "Comes from the moonlight." but even Fritz declined : "Later when we're conversing with the ladies, they're sure to smell it. – Hey, listen to that . . ." (for distant, wild song came from a tiled=cell; to the accompaniment of splashing that we could hear clear out here. Accusatory palms were spread my way : "Your Gerda !".) "We could talk with our lips pursed nice and tight," it occurred to me : "no vowels, avoiding the ‹u›s : no one permitted to utter words like ‹truth›."

"Hey now," Peter said, mulling this over, "wouldn't be all that dumb : to write a book in a pure ‹consonant alphabet›; like ‹unpointed bibles›. You could vent the freest opinions . . ."; he now scribbled on a scrap of paper, (like all these constructors of word=worlds, he was always equipped with superfluous writing materials); and held the results out to us : ‹dnr s n p› : ? ?. – ?. –

: "The second word is ‹is›, right ?". (And the ‹n› ‹an› ?). But the rest was too difficult. Fortunately, before we could get wrapped up in endless combinations, a shot was fired far to the north. – "Hunters –". And immediately from the south, as if in compensation, came a still more distant tolling. : "What you hear are the bells of Saint Jürgen : ‹on the rope›, Peter Landorf, famous journalist." And at first Peter nodded, at the double= meaning and its flattering prestige; he liked to think of himself as a ‹troublesome author›; (whereas he was eat-from-your-hand tame, as is only fit in our free-speeched West. But furrowed his fat brow now, too, pictur- ing himself hanged ‹on the rope› : ‹auto=matically› ringing those bells ! : The Holy Alliance and its unholy deeds. – Wonder if I might have a better chance of getting that uniform contract if my bishop 'd certify . . .) : "Ah, looka that – !" I interrupted myself; because across the road another neighbor's front door had begun to open; a little=lass came out. A candle inside an old flour sack; and the whole bouncing star=bright tied to a short stick : very droll ! Promptly lifted her voice, her clear voice, for ‹Heah comes Graybeahd with his light / playin' tricks by dahk o' night.›; and faded from view along the privet-hedge – and then it came to me again : the lamplighter ! :

*   *
*

"Cut the ‹moonward› stuff for a moment, Fritz. – You gave me some real food for thought that day – and until now I've been quite unable to come up with a rebuttal – *assuming* that a possible rebuttal exists . . ." (this in reference to so-called ‹trash novels›; about which we had frequently got into each other's bald heads – you really couldn't say ‹hair› anymore; except for Peter : the guy didn't have a single gray 1 yet ! Ahwell, these guys, these ‹poets› know neither shame nor stress. ‹To age with good grace› occurred to me, too, along with similar desperate adages; but the consolation was really too feeble it seemed – nono : better, poor grace; but young !).

"I, for my part, have no objections on principle –" Peter was about to hold forth, as always. And : "But I do !" Fritz protested, implacable, as always. (But his views counted for nothing : if he read at all, it was FRENSSEN at best, whom he considered the last word in modernity !). "I really like to read the stuff," Peter admitted, "You know, 100-part serials, with the craziest titles." And we enumerated them, taking turns, your ‹Heinrich Anton Leichtweis, Dashing Robber and Poacher of the Rhineland, or 13 Years of Love and Fidelity in the Grotto Grave› : ‹Artur Melchior Vogelsang, ‹Fog-Rider›, or the Den of Thieves on Monte Viso› : ‹The Woodland Rose, or Mad Pursuit Around the World, Revealing the Secrets of Human Society; by Captain Ramon Diaz de la Escosura›. "That last one, by the way, is by Karl May," Peter said wistfully : "Moreover, your ‹Fox Hill› here, the one we drove past yesterday, appears in volume 4 of WINNETOU as ‹Tavuntsit=Payah› or ‹Nugget=Tsil›. – but what was it you wanted to prove with your ‹lamplighter› ?".

Oh, right. "Yes; it was before & during World War I," I said : "I was still a boy, and our neighbors, a master shoemaker and his wife, decided to make a little extra money at night by taking over the business of lighting the gas street lanterns." "And/or extinguish them, with one of those long poles, right ?" an inspired Peter demonstrated. I nodded; and gave Fritz time, too, to recall; and then continued : "And sometimes, out of chastest curiosity, I went along with him." (And had no choice but to insert a very brief pause : the memories ! –).

That oil slick, just beyond the high-tension wires – just an ol' yeller spot; as if floor paint had been splattered on cement, (dropplets, bouncing off grainy portland, create ‹constellations›, too; oh shit ! / And ‹bouncing› : on the drive here to Giffendorf, in the brief seconds of a curve, I saw them playing ‹dodge ball› : the 75-inch girl, skinny as a rail (but a pretty pageboy !), endless long snow-white leg-props, (implying a corresponding picket-fence of a ribcage above them). The little lad, on his mini-bike, making a pest of himself by driving in & out : the tall girl cocks an arm diana-like – and hits him square on the head, sending him tumbling from

his microcycle : ! General laughter. And now I knew where the Diana=
myth came from. And drove on=by, on=by. / And Peter's expectant eyes –
all the fellow wanted was some ‹material› !)

: "Bon. I shall skip all the piquant details . . ." (and Peter's hand was
really fidgeting for ‹stuff› now; so act reluctant) : ". . . how one time we
discovered ‹thieves› filching laundry by demi-moonlight. Or stashing
inflation=butter in roadside ditches – we thought the hoofbeats was the
gendarme. Meeting people with no heads – the ‹flashman› took a fever
afterward. And Ewald, the policeman, was always much too slow at ‹making an arrest›, in my modest opinion ! – And then the two of them would sit
there, from 11 at night till 2 in the morning. He would cobble listlessly for
a while; she would fumble around with her empty pots, or her knit stockings – They called it ‹nannykins=nannykins› whenever they slaughtered a
kid. – Hmyes : and so they just sat away the night. Staring into the gaslight.
Boring each other stiff by now. And then she would pick up the ‹serialized
novel› : ‹The Prince of Misery / German Hearts, German Heroes / The
Uhlan's Beloved / The Path to Happiness.› – And after the reading, with
breasts brimfull of situations such as the count's marrying the poor-but-
chaste seamstress, they would have to return to their – hmm ‹rounds› is
much too simple a term for the crazyquilt of curves that had to be described
through the narrow streets."

Pause. Fritz forked in dung and straws. We stood in grass & clover;
(Lady Barbara allowed neither frenchweed nor charlock to sprout.)
"Peter=Pleeze, put a hand to that last pile." Which he did, (departing with
legs as bowed as if already returning under the heaviest burden; also
promptly invited my active fire=fanning cooperation.) "Storytelling does
not exempt you. – And what you were trying to say is that there *had* to be
endless 5,000=page trash like that. If only for lamplighters".

"And/or all occupations," I corrected, (slowly, snared in memories) :
"where, after the humdumb=drudgery of the day, people must keep half a
brain awake through all the black & yellow hours of night. : There *has* to be
something for them to read, totally banal and absurdly thrilling, an ersatz,
so to speak, for shallowest dreams . . . You do follow my gist, don't you ?".
A star blew its nose. And :

"No," Fritz objected : "instead, what keeps running through my brain
is : what do we do in case the border to the Zone gets in our way ?". "The
so-called GDR," Peter said, musing; threw his latest burden on the bonfire,
and propped himself more broadly over the end of his fork : "I understand
you. You mean : even *these* curious rungs in the ladder of literature dare
not be pulled out. So that the public, clear at the bottom, can climb up too ?.
– By the way : we could have 1 more, could we not ? !"

*   *
*

"Ha !" he blurted dramatically, as the flames (paltry; a result of his un-strategic dung=toss) fumed every which way : "The world is mine for yet 1 evening more : / and to such uses will I put this night / that even after generations none / may harvest from the ashes of its fire ! –"; he pressed his hand to his heart and gulped for air. (And the roofs of the houses round-about all jutted like black axes in the sky !). "You shouldn't give way to your passion like that all the time," Fritz admonished dreamily : "Passion & meteorism – if only you didn't have those . . . : once we decide to carry out our experiment, you'll be wheezing again."

Peter was indeed still gasping somewhat beneath the ringed moon. Ap-ropos ‹ring›, it struck me : "Turquoise ones deteriorate in the sun : in case we *should* happen to spend a whole day walking ‹sunward›, we should be mindful of that." "Oh ?" Peter asked with interest : "May I make a note of that fact. – Very nice. – And so you wanted to show that for=uh, shall we say, nurses, nocturnal travelers in waiting rooms – whose train doesn't leave for another 4 hours –, insomniacs, druggists on night duty – or, if you like, lamplighters=in=general – for them there *have* to be these less=respectable large canvases, these masterpieces of muddle. Even if to the more educated mind, or merely to one that's had a good night's sleep, they may seem idiotic parodies ?". I nodded mutely; (I am a pessimist when it comes to the ‹people› – although I would dearly have loved to get that contract for 20,000 uniforms !). But Fritz blurted : "No ! They are *not* needed ! They should be *forbidden.* People must be educated, so that they learn to concern themselves with serious matters."

"Like, for example, walking sunward," Peter remarked : "I have only one thing to add : if while underway, even if we're in mid-hike, I should happen to spot a hen-of-the-woods on a stump : it shall be harvested !". "Can't you remember ‹Polyporus frondosus›, Peter ?" Fritz rebuked gen-tly : "Any interruption is, of course, quite out of the question. And I don't care if a whole harem comes skipping seductively across our path !".

"Then it'd be better you took my double along," Peter said firmly : "One should in any case choose someone who is considerably younger than one-self : just imagine – the copyright for best-sellers could be extended by several decades; assuming that you could come to an agreement, within the family concerned, to make inconspicuous use of sons, grandsons, etc. down through several generations." "Yes," Fritz objected shrewdly : "but what if only the original ‹old man› had known, let's say, Russian ?". – "Then the ‹new man› coolly replies : ‹Never on Mondays›. – Which would in fact be accepted=quoted as a riposte of truly sparkling=wit."

"Or what if He is already 92; and his replacement's ardor gets the better of him; so that he decides to uh=join in when maidens are practicing the broad=jump in a woodland meadow ?". – "The reporters slinking along behind would call him : ‹indestructibly vital : a poet does not grow old : rejuvenation through poetry !›. – And at 130 you'd be sure to win the Nobel Prize, if only for the curiosity value. There's no figuring the criteria those guys there in Stockholm use in any case." (Peter, who had ‹not yet been awarded it, always pointed scornfully at Churchill on the one=hand, and James Joyce on the=other : anyone with any self-regard would refuse it on principle. – The money, to be sure, was not to be despised.) –

And silence. We were slowly getting weary; (should have had something to sit on – Fritz was already perched on the stump of the erstwhile cherry tree) : "What we lack are erratics !" Peter declared, summarizing our feelings. I was still forking away; and inciting flames with the touching faithfulness of a thermostat. / Peter's first urge was to protest – he associated other, older, hackneyed, symbols with the word ‹faithful›; à la Winkelried=Hindenburg, a pelican ripping open its own breast, tin panties with lock appended, (I once knew a Miss Pelican, who did more or less the opposite – if only I had that contract in my pocket ! Then I could be a much freer=thinker.) But then he grasped it, though reluctantly, when I called his attention to the hot=water he washed with every morning : "The boiler faithfully retains – ‹ai› : ‹ai›; the vowel settles it ! – its ravishing warmth through the night, the which you snore away most shamefully ! Well ? !". And he gave it a try – just as I expected; because he belonged to those refined types who employ technology with equal passion and loathing ! – : "The lashless, tiger=eyed thermostat means faithfulness ?" "The grounded=plug provides enlightenment . . ." was Fritz's bright idea. "The hundred-mark bill is dried & pressed freedom !" I concluded in a voice both pregnant & hollow.

"Apropos ‹erratics› –" Fritz began, his embarrassed face turned moon-lightward : "– uh=Barbara has expressed a wish. – We were recently out on 1 of our long hikes . . ." (we immediately got the picture : the two of them, in their ‹macks›, soon became proverbial wherever they lived. She was apparently reminded of the ‹Odenwald Club› of her childhood days in Darmstadt; he secretly counted paces, and recorded them at home on special maps : ‹Lovely lonely trees› / ‹Stand of junipers near Blickwedel !› / ‹An ingrown *chain* in an oak trunk at 35 89 801 right; 58 41 960 up ! : Investigate : why !›).

"Yes=right : Why ? !" an intrigued Peter wanted to know. But Lady Barbara's erratic wish sounded far more suspicious to me, (‹When women wish, men must work› !). And ô Feral : "Hmyes; on the road to Weyhausen, we saw a – truly magnificent ! – stone. And Barbara would love to have it here on our property. – We really do need something like that – as a place for you to sit, Peter; for example."

The weight ? : 40 by 40 by 40; divided by about 9. Times 2 point 5." Fritz, faltering. "Makes ?" Peter inquired; (while I was already pursing my face; 40 cubed is 64,000 right there !). "Well I'd guess about=uh $^3/_4$ to 1 ton," Fritz admitted nervously : "I've already talked with a farmer=here. He suggested : only in winter; on a stabile sledge. Pulled by a sturdy trac-tor. – Bring it in from around back, there. Not across the ‹septic›; the con-crete roof would never hold."

The moon gazed with more spitefull glint through the cirrus=lattice. We pictured ‹snow›; 15 degrees, (or even 25; that would be quite sufficient for discomfort); the woods, a cake with icing : We=Three, wrapped in our camouflage=bedsheets, using crowbars to trundle a giant irregularly= hollowed erratic onto ‹its› sledge – backed up by farmers reeking of hooch and obeying our orders. – Not all that bad; in a leatherstocking sort of way. (And we would finally be able to take a seat around our next campfire= here. From time to time, someone stands up, and stirs the Wild=West red with his pronged fork – getting older every year, right ?). "Yes : but wouldn't that cost an arm & a leg ?" Peter asked suspiciously. And Fritz, miser=ably : "20, 30 marks at most. – and 1, 2 bottles, ‹White Mule›." "So about 50" Peter summarized. (Nevertheless : to have a sort of Cheruscian super-boulder, à la ‹Hermann lies buried here !› ? – Ponder & poke.)

*   *

*

What was causing that square of light in the north ? Ah : the door to the house had opened. 3 Graces strode forth. Their aging limbs freshly laved; (we had once sacrificed our youth to them; and were doing so even now, perhaps. 3 suns rising as it were : ‹Sunward› !).

"Welll ? ! (caustic=courteous) : "Did you=all work hard ?".

Came nearer in triumph. Gerda, (‹my Gerda› ? Who can be sure.) lifting the exact=same rhubarb leaf to reveal a gray microphone=blossom : ! : "And now you may all come in ! And listen along to what you were saying about us." (And those 3 victorious wry=faces above those 6 collar=bones ! : 2 hundredweight; one and a half hundredweight; 1 hundredweight. And the boorish moon.)

(Women=wiles women=wiles ! : so that was the reason for the non= washline strung from fruit= to fruit= to fruity=tree ! The reason for the thrice=broad crouchings : checking the mike ! The reason for the reassuring sanctimonious inquiries !)

What a fine thing that we had something to ‹barter› ! We both pressed the flesh of Friedrich ô Feral's clever hand. We hung up our pitchforks on the rack, under the porch roof. We strode inside behind them (still triumphant, and all=unsuspecting).

Was that a honk there in the near distance ? Vet & evening call ? – (Well, come what may : ‹Ripeness is all› !).

AUTHOR'S AFTERWORD

Desoccupado lector – : read; and having sneered duly, consider. –

The preceding story does in fact cloak a serious semi-astronomical, semi-geographic, -geodetic problem; which – assuming you are still confident you command the requisite mathematical knowledge – you may set your fine teeth into.

An ‹elegant solution›, suitable for teaching my heroes a thing or two, might consist of a 1:100,000 map on which are described the curves for seven lines of march, one for the 23rd of each month from December through June, each originating in my hometown (BARGFELD, district of Celle) and each assuming a strolling speed of 5 kilometers per hour; (the particularly punctilious may wish to include – properly dotted – lines for 6 kph as well.) / (At this point I hear savants whisper ‹CARROLL› – not quite, friends. In his sly modesty, that great man usually contented himself with tantalizing=diophantine equations. But not I : Not=I !).

I therefore warn against any preconceived hypotheses, such as assuming that an adequate solution can be achieved in the hour between sleep & waking ! As regards astronomy, the exact moments of sun=rise and =set, and their corresponding angles to due east and west, are matters of ample consequence; not to mention azimuth, height, Central European Time, equation of time and that mysterious penny in Gretchen's silk stocking. In matters of geo=graphy and =deosy, it is quite permissible to discount any local aberrations in curvature; but since it is said, and with good reason, that the earth is an egg, a simple spherical calotte, with the corresponding radii of curvature for ‹my› latitude, should suffice; all obstructions may likewise be regarded as nonexistent. Nevertheless, difficulties – the more exact the method, the greater – will arise in the drawing of correct lines of march for our 3 heroes. (And in Manitoba, or Lumumba=Land, the matter would look quite different.) –

Correct solutions are to be submitted no later than 1 October 1961, and are to be addressed ‹SUNWARD›, *to the East German Academy of Sciences, Berlin W 8, Otto Nuschke Strasse 22-23.*

TAILS

Granted, it was a little cramped : if one wanted to get into the wardrobe one first had to shove the studio couch aside, (and then one couldn't get the window open; ah well, it made for just those little tensions one requires as an artist; after all, we weren't detergent=moguls who can exist only amid electrical ottomans and running dictaphones.) And the prefab cottage did look devilishly respectable from the outside; set in its .639 acre – that had been the coup, and quite remarkably clever of Caspar, who had talked the rich farmer's dim-witted heir into a large family mausoleum; and what's more, executed it himself : our lot here had been his honorarium. (Said heir's furious relatives had then promptly had him declared legally incompetent; but in our particular case there was ‹nothing to be done›; inasmuch as it had been an ‹act of childlike piety and consideration for bloodlines, which happily still characterize our rural population›, or so the opinion of the typically out-of-touch judge – nor had Caspar been chary with victory runes and cruces grammatae !) At any rate, there were times when one could stand here & look about (if one were not thinking of the mortgage), and suddenly find oneself in a damned polycratic mood.

‹Refuge› ? Hm, sure; we were all heading hard on sixty; and I had begun to notice some time ago myself that there were literally things ‹eye hath not seen nor ear heard›, (I guarantee it was the same with the other two ! But they didn't admit it; they weren't honest enough.) / ‹Meals› ? Why, at the neighboring farmer's of course. It didn't matter to him if his wife cooked for 15 or 18; each of us paid our 100 marks a month, (and they stood in respectful awe of how we came by ‹so much money›; ah, sweet innocence.) / The cleaning lady came twice a month; (simultaneously taking care of the rubric ‹love›; of which she provided us three a superabundance; it's only a kind of pornographic fun-house in old age anyway. The worst – in this regard, and as always – was Caspar; a crude sensual fellow, with urges equally strong and unrefined. Ahyes.)

At the gate, then, the hulking sign:

CASPAR SCHMEDES, Sculptor
JAKOB MOHR, Composer
J. B. LINDEMANN

The last being myself; I didn't need it. I mean, after all, Jay Bee Lindemann meant something in the editorial rooms of provincial papers; they were happy to publish one of my menagerie=articles once a month : about writers averse to bathing; writers on the farm; writers hypersensitive to noise; ‹Writers Falsify History›; ‹Manuscripts Lost in Fire›. (Admittedly, 7 marks 50 per article is not overwhelming; but when the same piece is reprinted 20 times over the years, that comes to 150. Minus 4 marks postage; the cost of paper; and not counting one's time spent retyping. – One can't get near the major dailies, their mission being, apparently, to finance ‹experimental› writers.)

All the same, *I* had the great advantage of having to make no ‹investment› whatever; everything came & went via the post, God bless her. Whereas Jakob, poor fellow, whose only income by this time consisted of giving piano lessons, ditto violin, was forever brushing up his black suits – bicycling about on dusty country roads and farm lanes was gradually taking more than its toll on him. The only thing that sustained him, his only recompense as it were, was that he could claim he was keeping in touch with the neighborhood, and so, too, our good reputation therein. And when he returned with payment in cans of homemade liverwurst, crocks of ‹brawn› and pounds of ‹jerky›, it was indeed an appreciable contribution to our frugal evening meals. (We had known no breakfasts for over 20 years; not only because it was cheaper and easier that way; but because rich breakfasting makes the mind flabby at its work, and on one happy occasion I chanced to recall the absolutely irresistible catchphrase, that venerable commonplace, ‹the learned man's morning fast› : ergo.)

Far the most money was earned in fact by Caspar – he had made a pile in the last 2 years ! New commissions like the large set of cookie-forms for Greinert Confectionary – which would have set him licking his fingers at one time, in the bad days – he now treated quite en bagatelle; and did we ever have to nag him simply to consider it : it is after all a branch of ornamentation ! (What finally tipped the scales was my quote from Giambattista VICO : ‹Heraldry, the language of the Heroic Age !›. We certainly are compassed about by advertising with crests and mottos, ‹Philip Morris›, ‹Hershey›, ‹Second to none›, ‹Pause that refreshes !›. And he did take it on, though with a grumble – such fellows are indeed defenseless against real, solid arguments – but first I had to show it to him in print; Caspar at 6 foot 6 is all for ‹heroes›.)

On the whole, then, we still managed, in comparison to so many others, to wriggle cozily across the gelatinous shoals of our time. Whenever Caspar would motorcycle into the county seat, he faithfully brought back the items we had requested of him : mustard & sole inserts; gypsum for himself; a new pocket comb for Jakob; a brown typewriter ribbon for me, (and from the public library, some old forgotten book – ordered through ‹interlibrary loan› – which could now be stolen with impunity.)

We sit on the porch of an evening. He describes the frantic bustle in town : the buildings of pale-gray concrete and black glass; the teenettes at that bewitching age when the tongue is still their only lipstick; (and here comes a gust of wind to flip every leaf on our old willow). Jakob contributes anecdotes from the families in the vicinity, mostly about rich farmers; (in the woodshed, snorts & skittles from our pair of hedgehogs, for whom we set out our garbage in a flowerpot-saucer.) And then I may well expound on WITTGENSTEIN : "What's most repulsive about the PHILOSOPHICAL INVESTIGATIONS is the smart-aleck way he keeps addressing the reader as ‹you›."; and we all three nod : no one may do that to us ! Farmer Lüders drives by with a Augean wagonload of manure, and calls a friendly greeting : "Nice fresh air today.", (and although one can barely catch a breath for the stench, it is said without irony; noses are fully superfluous for the Messers Granger. Perhaps even incommodious.)

And the bottle, 6.50 or at most 7.75 a fifth, makes its rounds. –

*　　*
*

Until, after 3, 4, and of late even 6 months, these certain days arrive.

(I've not yet been able to recognize a ‹law› in this. Wonder if it's some sort of ‹bio=rhythm›, (though we no longer have much to do with those; as noted); or perhaps it's somehow connected with the weather? Maybe the moon's at fault; one of those 14=day highs, when the sky is always clear, and one can keep a steady eye on that fusiform inconstancy, now a dagger=star now an ashen orb; one sits on the chair with the fractured leg, the typewriter tarantellas at chest-level; one can't help taking notes on the ‹voices of the door› : it can whisper and squawk, growl and fulminate, hiss (the front door, especially when someone first opens it and it pushes against the drifted snow of winter=outside), and rattle, too; and, if Caspar is in a bad mood, thunder, he really must learn to control himself !)

And one notices the same thing with the others, too : their looks grow gloomier; their gestures more abrupt and savage (Caspar is capable of bowing off the lowest branch of our young yellow-plum tree when greeting the woman next door !). Utterances turn more menacing : "We=artists, to a man, can easily do without the so-called fatherland; but the fatherland cannot do without Us : look how quickly it tries to appropriate Us once we have become great, *despite it* !". One can hear Jakob standing in the middle of his room and muttering his name, over and over; and if he does come out, he passes us by, askance and angry; and if he uses the ladder, normally reserved for the chimney sweep, to climb to the attic, to that steep triangle of a room where one practically has to crawl – then we know for certain. (10 minutes later he is sitting behind our largest gooseberry bush, with an enormous dusty odd-shaped volume; and I know – I in particular know ! – what is on the cover, without ever looking :

THE WOODLAND ROSE, or Mad Pursuit around the World. /
Opera seria in 5 Acts.

And although it has been some 30 years now since I wrote the libretto for him, I can tell from the same number of yards away whether it is open to Doctor Sternau's grand scalping=aria; or to the trio sung while dangling above the alligator=ponds – the fog follow you all !).

And when one walks past the shed, with its roof of glass shingles, the ‹atelier›, there the fat Gargantua stands at his joiner's bench, his palms propped on it, a shock of drawings & sketches spread before him – all for his RIO JUAREZ, the symbol of Mexico, where he once sojourned for 8 months in his youth; and, quite right, inspired by his first ebullient total= recollection, he drew up his plan utterly to outdo the NILE=grouping of antiquity by attempting the creation of ‹the symbol› for those exotic regions : BENITO JUAREZ, ("Portrait; the greatest Indian brought forth by the race" came the inevitable comment at this point), stretched out naked; the head propped at an angle against a swelling mountain shaped something like a female breast, on it the hint of something like a face; the taut hair liquid= smooth; in his indolent right hand a macquahuitl, the ancient Aztec serrated sword; atop the opened fingers of the left hand centauric Indians perform equestrian feats; beside him a teocalli, (a stepped pyramid; but then every child knows that since CERAM); in his pubic hair reapers hard at their mowing; and round=about women dance fertility ringarosies; his right heel nonchalantly crushes a machine=armed White man, while another works to polish his big=toenail for him. (All to be done in variegated sandstone; Caspar worked, if at all possible, in natural stone; he had the muscles for it – and we had the noise, for which Jakob's piano would have sufficed. Well, perhaps the day will come, and, it would seem, a not too distant one, when I shall rejoice in every sound I can still hear.)

But – : *What is the point of it all ? !*

I mean, one is not that much of a dupe ! One has in one's day stood beside ponds and let it rip :

"Fooples cruggle / cloaders drallop, flappies sillit / swiddle clinner guller flanger / tazzles toofer mockits dooser / wipples ellow plinter leesher . . . . . ."

so No One needs to boast to *me* about the ‹avant-garde›, no matter *how* long the hair ! Or when I think of my comic epopees, ‹THE CRACK IN THE DYKE, or the Pastor's Daughter of Weidau›, (ahyes, for all I care, SWEET= SUZIE plus PRÄTZEL, I admit it all; and all the same I wouldn't want to have missed it for a whole woods full of squirrels ! – By the by, ‹Otto Krabgrass› my erstwhile pseudonym. Ahwell. Nowadays I provided snide glosses on writers of historical novels who have the moon shining on nights when it stood neither in the calendar nor the sky.)

Then, after our vile midday feed – some innardiana or other – there we sit, of course, in rather precarious companionship on the veranda. (Ah, what's with ‹precarious›; one ought to be much more matter-of-fact !). Bright overcast. Hot. Teeth abaring and skinny little trees (we'll not see thick ones; Old Harry may very well drag one of us off any moment.)

Disgusting, this sitting=here ! White-locked clouds in bellowing blue. Diverse walls of foliage, patched of many greens. (Leatherness cross-hatchery taperedness someyellownow ? If one were to suggest a game of papacy to a young lady, she would most likely be terribly upset; whereas ‹Pope Joan› is quite civil.)

At any rate, on such days one should be rather careful around us bald= mouthers. Jakob can be downright ‹rough-bass›, (which doesn't suit him at all; indeed is not his strong=suit; HÄNDEL, of course, could hold a soprano out the window with his outstretched arm.) I dream of a ‹Royal Electric›, which costs about 16 hundred : one could write ever so nimbly, ‹and swift is their dance as they move through the wood›, and maybe even dash off my SATASPES (Herodotus, iv, 43) again – I can sit there dozing over the typewriter=brochure, for hours on end . . . . .

It is definitely advisable not to speak to us on such days. (And even less so on the day after !).

*   *
*

It was on just such a ‹day after› that Jakob returned home at a discordant hour. I heard the bony tinkling; rejoiced in its audibility; and then cursed the untimely bicyclist, (it could only be something unpleasant; at our age ‹special occurrences› is another term for the tricks of fate); and went to open up, straight through the mad noonday sun. Past the ‹atelier› – : he was chiseling away in there like a lunatic ! In this heat; the fellow was indecently healthy, no doubt of it; (and lowered my head deeper still : it was, in fact, a ‹day after›; 'tis best we not disturb him.)

And Jakob as well was swinging his textiled arms like the lunatic he temporarily was : "Faster faster !". "Get back from the barbwire" I replied gruffly; (and we conversed on this basis for another minute, until I got the dangling padlock off.) : "What's going on ?"

: "She's coming ! She's coming ! She'll be here any moment !"

And he slowly got it off his whistling codger's chest (He was in fact much further ‹gone› than I; on the one hand regrettable, on the other, perhaps one ought not be quite so resigned just yet ?) : that Fräulein von Kriegk, the wealthiest heiress in the village – what's this ‹heiress› ? She had owned the place for 2 years now, an unparented orphan. What's this ‹orphan› : a 24=year=old female, ‹independent›, ‹educated›, ‹PhD.›, ‹germanist›; (and consequently, local reporter for our county paper at present) – Fräulein Brigitta von Kriegk, then, had announced some time ago (via Jakob, who was giving her ‹composition theory› lessons) that sooner or later she would interview us three, and intended to write it up afterward as a suitably=thoughtful report, to the melody of ‹Bloomsbury›. (Refusal impossible; she was the only person who paid in both cash & hams.)

The interior of our home flashed across my mind. Then that of our souls. – "She was gonna follow you in her car in 15 minutes, you say ?" – and now we hastened in on spindle=legs; ("Leave the gate open, dammit ! How's it gonna look if we don't !"); past the shed, apparently the armory for all this year's thunderstorms – ?. "Ah, let 'm be. Don't disturb him. You know how he is on days like this." (hypocritical. On the one hand unfair; on the other we could put on the crucial makeup.)

Decorating : dirty dishes into the cupboard. Ditto laundry into the bench=chests; (should have informed Caspar after all; we'll never make it all on our own !) We very quickly gave up; and each decided to disappear into his own room.

Put on my modern sandals ? (Though the stiff wooden soles were torture for the older human foot; though of course they did lend a modern touch; ‹open-minded›; we absolutely dared not have lost the connection . . . . . laudator temporis acti . . . . .) / Another quick touch-up shave; (electric; Caspar had had to deliver a ‹coat-of-arms› for the entrance to the industrialist's villa : a bolt of lightning and a juicer crossed; I had provided the motto CAVENDO TUTUS, ‹Secure in caution›. Like most of his pack, the fellow paid exclusively ‹in truck›; ahwell, he might very well have gone bankrupt in the meantime.) / Fingerwork flying, check through my note=box under ‹APHORISMS› – 3 of 'em, learned by temporary heart and then impressively ‹rattled off›, that'd probably suffice. But which ? (Germanist, 24, lady of

influence & wealth . . . . . this one here might do. Or was it too ‹frank› ? I
knew her solely from Jakob's vague non=reports; the fellow was simply
incapable of objectively describing the smallest matters of fact; his testi-
mony was totally irrelevant !). / In case she should inquire about ‹publications in book form› – and she was certain to do so; she *had* to – things could
get unpleasant. A haughty smile would not do the trick; my one English
detective tome would have to be trotted out, translated in days of yore;
and James Morier's HAJJI BABA; the only linen-bound volume I could produce. (Should I perhaps drape my manuscript of CRACK IN THE DYKE across
my lap ? There it still lay, from yesterday, from ‹the day›. As if I had just
now had it ‹under my pen› ?). / One could make mysterious mention of
‹radio broadcasts›; impossible to disprove that. And now I gently raised my
heart=hand, and in solemn=flippancy declared to the wall : "Its (= a
report's) purpose is always to reveal the creative process, to educate concerning our literat=all existence . . . . ." (get nastier) : "amid this neighton
of ‹poets› & ‹thinkers› !" –

: ? . . . . . : "Honk. – Honk=Honk=Honk !"

(And I was feeling pretty queasy : Jakob was sure to have put on the
same spectacle. But he was he also sure to have performed for his shaving
mirror; basic opera hero. – And how I envied Caspar !)

"Hooonk !" – very like a threat, wasn't it ?

*   *
*

And sit on the porch. And silence. (She was therefore, thankgod, a little
embarrassed as well.) / The blaaazing heat ! The bird in the elderberry bush
now let out another scream, like an older make of bicycle bell; what sort
of bird I don't know. Under a haywagon 4 gaunt wheels drudged along
through frizzled dust.

(And what a kid, this=woman here ! Almost $6\frac{1}{2}$ feet tall. Lean; but
lovely=lean. Charming. The giant shoes soled higher still with wood &
cork. Very smooth sandy bob; the wind lifted each individual hair. (Eye
yolks & nostril hairs). / She pulled her pad & pencil from her leather purse
first thing, and laid them before her. Her watch to one side : but what a
watch ! glass fore & aft, (one could see it bustling and ‹turmoiling› inside;
owning a gizmo like that would make me nervous); the whole thing set
in a kind of mini=car=tire, but raised a little so that it was drop=proof;
ahwell, They've got the means. But the erection of such a ‹bulwark› was
also a wee sign of insecurity; which was enough for an old psychologist
like me.)

"Yes. Unfortunately still a ‹Monte Testaccio›." (The CRACK IN THE DYKE; she had noticed it at once, and, reverence in her little voice, asked about it – giving me the courage to offer, number 1, said ‹mound of shards›.) / The tender chasms of her toes. Just a breathy whiff of smudge on them : kissable ! / And sultry, sultry. And when she declared : "Oh, I love thunderstorms." it came to me – triumph : sometimes things do come to me ! – "Then you must be a renter ? – What with our inventory of works of art in the house, we have no choice but to feel a certain unease whenever there's an excess of sheet lightning." (Smile : general relaxation; she happily made a note of it.)

Jakob she knew well enough; she didn't grapple much with him. (Though, granted, she did call him ‹maestro› once; but that was ample evidence that she regarded him as a gramps. He was the man, after all, who whittled marks in our clothespins; periodically recounted them; and could get vexed all over again if 1 was missing, from all this mighty sum. Though it's unavoidable.) / Her long dress pearl-gray & clove-brown. And pale green with heliotrope would definitely have looked good on her, too. (Ah, one should have been able to storm downstairs, in athletic bounds; a mighty volume of the BRITANNICA spread like a falcon on one's palm; the carpenter's pencil athwart one's mouth, like a machete forged red-hot . . . . . : what did she want to know ?)

"What did I have under the pen at the moment ?" – (with nary a blush, and using precisely the term I had foreseen. Somewhat disenchanting.) "THE ‹REGICIDES›" I informed her with dignity; "some time back" – (to wit 1930; oh, set the finger to the mouth !) – "I wrote an extensive radio script about those who sat in judgment over Angleland's Charles the First. How they were later executed; emigrated, fled – curious fates. And frequently dealt with in serious literature : SCOTT; COOPER; PAULDING. And so forth." And she made interested germanist=eyes; (unfortunately at that very moment 2 Coca=Cola delivery men clad in dark green and propping up a drunk passed our cottage; so that my nonchalant, "It is also my honor to deliver the worst=seller year-in & year-out" fizzled to no effect – I knew nothing more to add.) And more boring now, too; verbal abortions, born ceaselessly from moist=red mouths, through thick and thin lips; (one ought to claw one's face till it is unrecognizable in the mirror. She was still a pretty little bug; but all the same, judging by the bony frame, she would live long enough to turn out considerably less attractive.) Anyone with ‹connections›, she explained, could have his telephone number put on his license plate. (So she had connections; got more inane from minute to minute !)

"You have a sculptor here as well ? – We represent all the arts, right ?" she, delighted. And we diligently accompanied her to the ‹shed›; (serves

Caspar right ! She stopped once underway, for graceful discourse with a young rowan tree – of my planting. Her throat smoother than oil.)

For safety's sake, to prepare her – we didn't know ourselves what all we might get to see; it was indeed the ‹day after› ! – "At least you may conclude from the state of things that our life here is characterized by a high degree of innocence & simplicity."

*   *
*

(And thunder and lightning. The closer we came.)

And open the door – : there the giant stood ! His large (spongy !) muscles twitched and addered; he had set his chisel dead center in a horse's fanny, and drove it up=in, as if it were clay and not Königshain granite : ! : ! ! : ! ! !. – And was that a sight to see, when he turned around and the thin=blue arabesque of vapors, in a kind of art-nouveau line, puffed up to his menacing face : his cigar in his navel ! (Her eyes, at first boiled=fixed, began to glisten, like rotten wood. What a beast !).

"That's quite some thunder you make ! As one gets closer." This, then, Fräulein von Kriegk. And Caspar in reply, after Neanderthallic scrutiny : "If I were lightning, my bolt would strike only you !" (With bloated mouth and swollen eyes; she wasn't even trying to avoid the shadow of his fist now.)

"Might I ask what it is at present that you=uh . . . . . ?" (‹have under the chisel !›, she didn't dare it this time; but had done it to me with no further ado.) And Caspar took his standard impudent bellows=drag on the stogie; stuffed it back into the middle of his gut; and bawled auThor=itatively :

"TAILS !" –

She shuddered; plum-eyed; held out. And sanctioned, lips slightly open no less, Caspar's explanations : ‹before the war› every German city had gloried in at least 1 equestrian monument. All steeds rearing; atop each, the man in question, clad in metal tux and plumed hat; a pointer in the right hand stretched toward the observer as if to say : "You too, sir, prove yourself less and less qualified from day to day !›. Now the horses' tails, all grand princely=curled, were usually mounted at one, or at most, two small points, predestined, that is, to give way at the whistle of a bomb. With the result : after '45 almost every statue stood there sans tail !

And Caspar was not only a specialist for animal sculpture; but he also knew the appropriate government undersecretary from their schooldays together; with the result, disons le mot, that for 2 mortal years now he had made *nothing but tails* ! Horse tails, bison tails, dragon tails, peacock tails, anything=having=a=tail – he betailed it anew. (And with what subtle consequences – since on principle he fotografed all mammalian=rears, (had to, had he not?), he was pursued by officers of the vice squad : § 176; ‹Bestiality› ! At the zoo they had been hot on the heels of the poor wretch, who was constantly peering up the wild beasts' asses; ‹sodomy› is no trivial matter. In the end he had taken to carrying several official attestations to the effect that he was the Person=Who repaired damaged monuments, and had general authorization for activities of this sort.)

They looked at each another : the skinny goat in her summer dress; the Polyphemus with ironwork in each fist; their mouths were at almost the same height. His broke into a smart-aleck wrench : "Would you like to see the designs for my RIO JUAREZ ? !" he commandeered; (it was of course still lying inside ‹from yesterday›.) : "Naked. In the right hand a macquahuitl. The head propped on a mountain : shaped like a female breast !"; and so brutal was the bellow, the bastard, that we looked about in real terror – ! –

He held the door for her. With chiselated fist. More (disgusting) bulgifications in the muscle flesh. "Mejia –" her threadlike mouth suddenly recited her school lessons : "Miramon; Bazaine; Kaiser Maximilian : MIRAMAR !" And at once, promising much, he grumbled : "Miramar."

She vanished through the maw of the door as it opened wider. She simply knew too much : made defenseless by over-education. (The bastard threw us a gloating & majestic wink. And the cotopaxi of his paunch fumed away. Conjunglutions of obscurridada.)

*   *
*

And sitting on the veranda again.

Me, immobile, before the CRACK IN THE DYKE. Jakob was hugging his favorite cat; (went inside once, too, to ‹put things in order›; I heard him, as per his ghastly habit, counting each manipulation – stuffing away 1 shirt took about 25; damn=a=lummox !)

30 minutes. The sun began to bleed; oozing out red below; no gray cloud napkin would help. A lad, the truncated=oval ‹4711›=sign at his scrawny chest, galloped, with a roar and a birch=lance, at the neighbor boy – maybe an article : ‹How Modern Writers Are Inspired by Brochures & Billboards› ? Jakob reappeared, and reported, in a curiously=aged voice, about the civil servant and his wife, who lived in the county seat and whose offspring he instructed in guitar : He had recently pulled out the little

water-clear bottle from behind the scanty reserves of his bookcase; inside, the embryo; proud :"My son !". "Then She's sure to come up with her gall-stones soon." Poor Jaycub.

(Didn't I hear tantrumming & fooleration coming from yon ‹tavern= house› ? But he – who lived from ‹his ear› after all – simply gave a negating motion of his high=gray head: "Just the hedgehogs." / So take myself in my arms again. For lack of anything better. / And keep silence; crone's bliss.)

After 90 minutes then a "Bridgy –"; (Caspar's unmistakable voice; but, then, who else could it have been ? Idiotic.) "I'll walk you to the gate." (Follow with peeping eyes : wrinkled skirt; at least 2 buttons missing from her blouse; her hair significantly misheveled. And Jakob's hand automatically beat time to the ‹Wedding March› from his WOODLAND ROSE; when the Grand Duke of Hessia=Darmstadt comes striding into the festal hall. Beside him the Duke of Olsunna.)

*   *
*

Pointless to remark, the marriage took place 8 weeks later. (We, as was only natural, stayed on in our cottage; I have no desire to disturb ‹young happiness›.) / (Rather sit on the veranda; with my CRACK IN THE DYKE : the Grim Reaper's sure to show up one of these days.)

Have a lot more room now, too. And less racket. (Meals are delivered, though; from the oversized servants'=kitchen. Right after every meal I ‹turn out› a song – GAUDY, or some other total unknown – Jakob promptly sets it to music; and ‹Bridgy› boldly ‹sight-reads› it. I'm all for paying for what one gets.)

(‹A charity case›, right ? – : not yet, not by a long shot, for Jay Bee Lindemann !).

*   *
*

Chr. M. Stadion :
J. B. LINDEMANN, PLAGIARIST

I believe that in raising the sharpest protest to the preceding production, I speak for all upstanding citizens and readers !

And not only because of the incredible ‹intellectual posture›, which does not shy from the most repulsive obscenities for any cheap effect – said posture being duly censured elsewhere in my (unfortunately still unpublished) manuscript, ‹History of the Decline of German Literature since 1945›,   Part 4, ‹The Decline of the Short Story›, II, pp. 743 ff. – but above all because of the so-called ‹expressionist poem›, of which Mr. Lindemann once again has the seeming insolence to boast. For some years now I have observed the activities of this, I make bold to say, CHARLATAN ! I have also contrived to obtain, among other items, a notarized copy of said ‹poem›. Here it is, then, in life-size; (the marginalia – and I note, after the fact, my veritable irresponsibility in summoning such good will – come from my own pen) :

COUNTRY WALK

i.)
Cloaders drallop
flappies sillit
fazies sliper slinkle sulpy   on the bank of the pond
swiddle clinner guller flanger
seevers plumple rulsits swicker
(nixies mummle ?)   Nonsense ! Nixies don't exist.
tazzles toofer
cowlits slutter hootoo flather
swerdels glither mockits dooser
wipples ellow plinter leesher   water=surface, embossed by fish ?
sedges reedick taishes taggle
(oken ?)
fooples cruggle.   i.e., frog croakings

ii.)
Sprainicks wurtle oasids laxit
flatties spouner bishes broostle   apparently a wood's=edge begins with
kintcher prushit rengies dendle   mosses and heathering

iii.)
Muckits molder fistles buffix   Aha ! : ‹mushrooming›. – The author
kunzies truffle bollix killit   is famous for this motif.
morels cereb rimple brainer
rushids nolly blighties muckle
purlurds nipple spongies stubber

iv.)

Dingles marger roddigs lingle
hilping flurrits nemnicks illig
roalets rasple rickle groanter
brickles scashop grample spurrit
fratticks=flassers=scrubies=diggits
tarckies tackit sordies splagle
sprickers outchit rishit ramrood
bramburrs speardle treaple mully
thittles rincher
sungies oakle
aspens hessles lindens millick
loungle jeckle patty yuggle.

‹margin›
Stand of fern? Hard to say.

So, indubitably thorn=thicket & under=
brush – but why must he walk through
it ? !

‹Brambles› ! – We've picked up his
scent now !

Ergo, hard=woods; in other words,
another wood's edge. – Since without an ‹r› :query : plagarized from
Brockes ? ! I wouldn't put it past
him !

v.)

Ryeroes swather scythle coxcome
sickles deschamp reeshes sedgit
sockles thistle straidle stickers
sadders ivy wutters jocker
maltchies gaddit klepper kossit
heavits swirmer millets josser
cloudly strappish clillows buckit

Fields; apparently overgrown with
weeds

yes; well, are cumuli piling up, or not ? !

vi.)

Fobies leanick ottens limmer
navies puttle glannel pluster
whealies figger lilax gumple
spanglers rummitch ? Rhombix tringle.
loxes lorry teeter alber
poppies noddle glumers neelit
markies gracen elpers gindle
framids gurtle tardles velver
lorshes grishit brauner questen
cruppies coonit
rishes beetle
winders myrtle in the wake.

He doesn't care – a whit !
‹bluster› ?
probably the flapping back & forth of
umbellate flowers

First ‹stone=garden›; then softer again

‹question› ?

Beetles ? Pests ?

vii.)

Pumpkits nabble toppit bulber	almost *too* easy ! – The adjacent fruit=
doublix nodle	garden of an acquaintance, of course!
clammies tordle	
scrubbles twittle	
newels peakle	
surges prumer gories whispit	From ‹plum› or ‹prune› ? – More
vowsers drooter rullies hulkit	precise, please, in the future !
hollies humper neelies sumper	‹ump=ump› poet's slump !
heppits wolcker burries wurgle	
cabbicks buttle crackits carrit	
fillips mimper wilkies spargle	
milders cressle nittles snopple	
cumbers droople ? Bulbers urchin ?	
what – : the very sparcuts rampit ? !	Asparagus ? – That can hardly be !

*   *

*

Risum teneatis, amici! It is not merely this; rather, let the horror be uttered : *every single ‹word› in question can be found in OKEN'S ‹Natural History›*, where each is forced to function (in pointlessly teutonized fashion) as a designation for the genus of plants or godknowswhatall ! Oken may be forgiven; but in thunderous voice the people cry : Quousque tandem, Lindemann ? !

*   *

*

J. B. Lindemann :
A NECESSARY WORD OF EXPLANATION

Now that the feigned professional indignation at ‹plagiarism› and ‹stale expressionism› has abated much more swiftly than the self-appointed malcontent had hoped when he published my creditable experiment of a ‹COUNTRY WALK›, with neither my knowledge nor consent – i.e., illegally : we have still to settle the matter, Mr. Stadion ! – the following must be said, and may I emphasize that it is ‹a matter of genuine concern›, to use correct Federal German. For in the very near future humanity will be confronted by entire empyrean worlds, MOON=VENUS=MARS – stones of every design, curious landscapes, lifeforms hardly comme=il=faut, not to mention the experiences of space travel (‹love by zero gravity› : it is not only our good Mr. Schmedes who affirms the senses, in moderation, but we=ourselves, Mr. Stadion !).

In recognition of this fact – though it takes little to ‹recognize› it, plain common sense will do – a young author, in his recent book ‹$\frac{B}{M}$OONDOCKS›, has indulged in a thought=provoking jest (presumably an unconscious realization of my=own insight – my inky hand being not so quick to allege ‹plagiarism›). He has them cart a ‹namer› along with them to the moon, a ‹genuine poet› of course, who, being therefore equally lethargic and anti=technoid, proves a total failure. And although I cannot sanction the frivolous manner in which said author treats his material, the problem= itself remains for that very reason an earnest and urgent one. (Though our German, to my melancholy regret, will hardly be of service here; presumably Russian & English will be more appropriate as eventual languages for our solar system.)

* *
*

What is needed is total linguistic flexibility, so that, be it on the basis of orthography, phonology, or root=words and =morphemes, a speaker would be capable, à la New=Adam, of providing a quick and vividly=persuasive inventory of, e.g., the circumsplashing lifeforms on a liquid surface; indeed, brutally capable of ‹appropriating› them.

For which reason – and let me stress : I am convinced, more so presumably than most of my contemporaries, that the situation is earnest – I indulged in the aforesaid non=jest with my good=uninformed readers :

there once was, in fact, here in good old Germany's midst a ‹school› that might well have commanded the requisite mastery of language; I shall call it, after the name of one its leaders with whom I am most familiar, the ‹School of OKEN›.

Lorenz OKEN (actually ‹Ockenfuss›) was born in Bohlsbach, Swabia, on 1. 8. 1779. He studied medicine in Würzburg; pursued his studies further in Göttingen; and was very soon a privat-dozent. In 1807, at Goethe's prompting, he accepted a chair in Jena – though resigning this=same professorship, again at Goethe's prompting (for what reasons I will return momentarily), in 1819. Working as a private=scholar, he stayed on in Jena, where in 1822 he convened the famous ‹Meetings of Naturalists›. In 1827 he moved to Munich. Under pressure there from certain ‹circles›, which it is not opportune to name these days, he soon left and accepted a call at the University of Zürich, where, unflagging & frugal to the end, he died on 11. 8. 1851 – having just turned 72.

This Lorenz Oken was anything but a shallow mind !

Quite apart from his, rather famous, dispute with Goethe concerning priority of discovery of the ‹intermaxillary=bone› – in which dispute, by the by, ‹the generally well-informed› ENCYCLOPAEDIA BRITANNICA (a descriptive phrase to which, as I well know, only the RHEINISCHER MERKUR is actually entitled) clearly takes Oken's side ! – he published a large number of very provocative works; and terms like the ‹Rotating God› or the ‹Universe as the Continuation of the Sense Organs› ought to sound quite sweet in the delicate ears of our fashionable=modern mystics.

His absolutely most important achievement, however, was his periodical ‹ISIS›; appearing from 1817 through and including 1848, it not only dealt with the ‹Feeding Apparatus of Insects› (as malicious reviewers, and/or the authors of rejected articles, liked to put it), but also played a leading role in several areas. I shall mention only literature here – for instance the famous dispute with FOUQUÉ; the first translation of the KALEVALA; or those most charming innovators of language like K. Fr. Wildenhayn. Nor were politics neglected – in which respect, I grant, we are dealing with a thoroughly ‹unGerman› publication. Politics, by the way, served as the lever for the hyperaforesaid Goethe to interfere in a loathsome=energetic fashion; presumably still annoyed about said ‹intermaxillary›, he found a roundabout way, via the grand-ducal=Weimar cabinet, to force Oken into a ‹choice›: did he wish to suspend his ‹ISIS› or resign his professorship ?

Except that Lorenz Oken – presumably for the rarity of the thing; only the ‹Göttingen Seven› were comparable ‹men› – unexpectedly ‹chose›= otherwise : he resigned his lousy Jena=professorship, preferring instead to continue editing his grandly=notorious ISIS in Rudolstadt ! (Here might be found enough stuff for several dozen doctoral dissertations; for the material contained in 30 years of publication is truly inexhaustible : re=printers, give heed !)

But, mercifully, Oken was not only a ‹natural philosopher›, but also from 1802 on, he published important and increasingly=bulky reference works on biology. The last dated is the

‹GENERAL NATURAL HISTORY FOR ALL CLASSES;

Stuttgart 1839-42; 14 volumes›;

(and it is recommended that anyone having a particular interest in the matter compare the original with what the so justly named ‹GREAT BREHM› cribbed from it – I guarantee it's over the hurdle of the 5%=clause !).

As he had also done in earlier publications, Oken here provided a comprehensive new ‹German Terminology› for the plant & animal kingdoms – one so superior that it has never found a home among us, although the names, and by far the greatest number of them, are absolutely delightful in their vivid plasticity ! (Based on the work of predecessors like NEMNICH / ILLIGEN / WOLCKE; which I therefore promptly worked into my ‹poem›.)

Since such an experiment acts as a stimulus, i.e., is indispensable & exciting for every thinking person – and not just ‹readers›, but presumptive ‹specialists› as well – I took rogue's liberty with all the ‹orders and classes› in volume 3 b, pages iii-viii (Roman), and trotted them out on the bridle of a ‹Country Walk›. (And I wish it particularly to be noted that I have done no violence to the Okenian nomenclature, but rather have kept aquatic plants in the pond, fungi among the mushrooms.) –

‹Fooples cruggle› – : do you know a lovelier ‹croaking in the rushes›, (to use the phrase from Voss's Louise) ? Can anything be derived with more charming simultaneity à la Joyce from both ‹fool› and ‹tadpole› (i.e., the ‹foolishness of Messers Frog› !), or from ‹croak› and ‹gurgle› ? –

: What We lack are not career =officers, =diplomats, =theologians, =jurists : we need ‹NAMERS› ! ! ! –

Such, perhaps, Mr. Chr. M. Stadion, would have been the tenor of remarks that a thinking and honest man might make about my ‹COUNTRY WALK› – with both of which attributes, of course, the author of a ‹Decline› and the translator of a ‹Republica Intelligentsia› may well find he can dispense.

Cows in Half Mourning

1

At one time, as a young man, I suppose I, too, imagined that the language of looks & gestures had been invented by lovers – you know, ‹neighbor children›, held hostage at precautionary arm's length by ‹strict parents›; (though I had dark presentiments that bit by bit problematical matters might have been telegraphed, waved, signaled back & forth; be=guiling be=guiling.) Later then, I thought it might have been clever thieves, by night, in inadequately lit jewelry shops; or even circumbugged politicians, in the Seven Mountains, reposing on a leasward, ready to coalition. Today I know it must have been two elderly men on a circular saw; after about 40 minutes.

2

: "C'mon; may our morning be white !". Otje invited with affected vigor to a breakfast of milk; and though it was only our second such breakfast, we regarded the glasses of maternal-pearly liquid ever so tentatively . . . . . (Plus ‹in the open› : a sparse woods behind us (within it, however, bold twipperings); odd scrawny bushes ahead; then ditch=direct to distant green.) / A long limousine submarined through a faraway sea of grain. – "This early ?" : "A hunter maybe," Otje listlessly proposed. I promptly reached for the telescope, whose long-arm always had to lie beside us, (urbanites, you see; who regard every crow as a spectacle of nature); and peered sternly through it : – – cloud igloos everywhere, (presumably more ‹thunder=showers› awaited us). The refined ‹birch=bench› was hurting my rear end . . . . : "Ah=Ha !". For the distant bright=smooth tin wall now split asunder to bear a whole litter of colorful reaperettes. "What ? : Reaperettes ? !"; he demanded his telescope. – "The yellow one –" I heard him mutter after a while; (I, too, had noticed the plump one right off; ‹neighbor children›; with 300 yards between.)

For whoever cannot buy a house – and Who can manage that; unless he be bold as Caesar at going into debt; besides which, once the deed is done, you are punished by taxes, for ‹capital gains› : nono; diligence & thrift are quite out of place in Our=Land ! – rents a little hut in the heath. "For 99 years; like Kiao=Chow of yore." Otje was quick to wave this aside; he knew only too well where I had first seen the light of andsoforth; (ah well, as chance would have it, my father was a sergeant there, and at age 2, I made the proper move for a respectable citizen back to Germania. That is, was moved. All the same, I suppose I did have an organic relationship with the Middle Kingdom; and the right – or was it the duty ? – to page through DU HALDE. And nice success with the ladies at one time; whenever I could weave into the conversation how I was actually Chinese.

Given this fact, we had therefore taken a long-term lease on $1^1/_4$ Hanoverian acres for Ourselves & our Wives (marriages fortunately= childless; but that meant in turn higher taxes : I repeat, the man who takes responsible precautions is always the loser in Our=Land !). For a song, by the way, since it was considered ‹wasteland› – farmers don't understand 1 thing about nature & its beauty. I had thrown in an extra 50 marks a year on condition that the ‹scenery› dare not be changed; (are they going to be surprised someday, the Messers Granger, at what it was they, the town fathers, had put their signature to ! Upon reading said paragraphs, the lawyer had puckered a smile, too, and slowly rubbed spidery fingers.) / And so add our little hut, 12 by 18; (‹second=hand›; had had to be deloused first, too; but you didn't notice a thing anymore). / And now the job was to ‹make it livable›; a task incumbent primarily upon us men, it seemed; the ladies had merely ‹insisted› on a birch=bench, and collected a couple of pinecones – our intention was, in fact, to spend a few winter weeks before a blazing snapple=crackle popping fire : except that the requisite ‹chimney› had cost us a small fortune (even though the village mason had done the job ‹under the table› : the 40=hour=week is not for the thinking-person; and for the non=thinking it must be downright unbearable !). / But I wonder if the enclosure was worth the price ? – Otje had bought 200 old military=cot frames cheap; and we had used them to ‹win› the requisite number of fenceposts, simple but tasteless. (And got ‹military›= and ‹cot-frame›= memories for free : any one of which would have sufficed to keep us semi=codgers busy the rest of our lives !).

And we, therefore, all ‹operation underway›, were now here to ‹produce› the requisite wood. (The ladies still in Hanover; to be on the safe side, they weren't coming for 3 days, in a taxi full of pillows & blankets : "They don't ‹sacrifice› their maiden names; no sir : they take ours from= us !". Otje, angry; but he's right.) / Noon meals for the 3 days provided by the innkeeper; mostly ‹Tender Liver› on tomato-dyed rice. 9=50 a day for us both; (on the one hand, expensive, given a region with no tourist=sights.

But if it had more charms, it'd 've been overrun years ago, and no longer an ‹oasis›, healthy as aces, so they say. And so remarkably clever of the local innkeeper, his 9=50.) / Equilibrium, ready to topple after the meal, is laid out on the cot – we had set up 4 of the aforementioned, 2 each, one atop the other. Amazing, how suddenly just after 1400 hours and in sheer synchronicity, each informed the other : the doctor had prescribed a minimum of 1=hour's daily napping. (Now & then blink the other's way; checking if his eyes, too, are stoutly closed and every mother's son is wrapped in invigorating, healing sleep : ? Fine fine; we are wrapped. My fantasy is still sufficiently intact, knockonwood, for me to close my eyes for 60 minutes at a stretch and set up a mind=game. Some people are always quick to scream : "Imprisoned ? ! Oh that must be awful; I couldn't take it for even 3 days !"; meaning they can't be great intellects, (presuming they really think that way; which you never know); you'd really get far as a POW with fatuous maxims like that !). / And then, shortly after 1500 hours, ‹awaken›. And, eyes shining & refreshed, roll your shoulders.

Quickly send off a couple of postcards; and brief letters (nowadays even the village grocer=here carried cheap ‹Stücklen's Vexation› : the new, very thin=sturdy stationery, it takes 14 of those $8\frac{1}{2}$ x 11=pages to make a half=ounce letter : how else can you keep up with the periodic rise in postal rates ? Nono; quite okay. Though the postcards appeared to be from the twenties – it didn't look like that anywhere around here these days !). And address them to envious co-workers at the plant : ‹Best.›; and ‹Best !›. Here, give Bachmeyer an extra prick . . . . . hmmm=uh : ‹Some spots on earth are just *too beautiful* !› : "Sign your name, too, Otje."

3

We had the trunks delivered of course. Likewise the railroad ties, (some ‹substructure› or other in the vicinity was being redone; and we, ever attentive, as is only proper for good merchants, had swiftly interposed : *solid oak !*). To be sure, the ladies had fancied that we would somehow ‹gather› the requisite rolling hills of logs from somewhere – fell=roll=saw by hand; then stand atop the chopping-block, all Siegfriedian, with legs astraddle and the 2=hander tossed way back over the shoulder, ‹Notung's wrack he'll not hector from me !›. (And finish off by ‹dressing› our numberless proceeds and erecting them in delightful country ‹ricks›, to put one in a most squirrely and woodwormy mood. And ‹while=we=were=at=it›, collect several hatfulls of chestnuts & acorns – THEY intended to set up ‹feeding stations›, ‹HELP THE POOR NUTS HATCH IN WINTER›.)

The negotiations with the farmers in the matter of transport had not been all that simple – suddenly they were all busy ‹with the harvest›; (though we had inquired about the exact when & where of the gathering-in : 'twas all a swindle, to jack up prices !). Once they grasped the fact that good cold cash was about to flow to the next village, they rather quickly displayed something akin to reason. / And so trunks climbed socially high and black, ties higher & blacker=still. And stores of ‹root=wood›, too, round the property, clawlike, never to be cloven by human hand – and since Otje, totally taken by the bestial shapes, had been babbling about ‹the grafick element in winter›, I refrained from words appropriate to the occasion, so certain was I of being voted down : there are better things to do with *that* nervous energy. A ‹demolished› barn still littered the ground; boards, lathes, posts; all of it (how would HOMER have expressed it so aptly ?) ‹richly nailed› : "Just don't say anything to the owner of the saw !"

Because the procurement of the circular saw had once again shown rural humanity at its worst ! / First, with vacant gaze, striding across endless beet fields; potatoes (‹SASKIA› brand : sic !) lupines graminoids; everything a man doesn't know 1 damn thing about (disgusting, really. Ignorance, I mean.) With furious=flat palms broadslap the horseflies : arms, belly, chest, "Oh=shit ‹clean shirt› !", (you end up with pancakes for balls because of the lousy beasts ! Well who cares; didn't amount to much anymore anyway.) / The one solace : step aside now & then behind the lane's companion hedge. Where, however, instead of the lily, the flask of KIRSCH gets shaken : ∼ . ∼ . . . : ! : at once everything grew brighter; at once the most splendid besprinkled stones lay there in great waves, all colors grand patterns; these farmers truly did not know what they had. (Subject for colorfoto=amateurs : ‹FLINTS OF 61 AND SEVERAL OF THEIR CONTEMPORARIES›. One ought indeed to acquire a hobby like that : a good reflex camera; with lens attachment; granted, that'd mean the add-on of a projector, too; so around a thousand, hm hm. That presupposed, however, a region teeming with flintstones. : But here we were; right ?).

And above all, take no note of the name of this nearby village; not yet; at 55 you have to reserve your memory for what is most necessary. / Colorless & gray, the mechanical. Unpleasant long face, (what they call ‹practical›; that is : like Gay=Lussac & Fischer=Tropsch together – they learn it while still in ag=school. But so do we: every inch an inch.) But with the appearance of the fan of 6 hundred-mark bills in Otje's wallet, against black-velvety doeskin, Tropsch could resist no longer : with an unnecessary handshake he promised the saw and 900 feet of power-cable for the day after tomorrow, Friday. / And back again over very sandy paths. Inhaling the thick=fat country air. Cows in half mourning; among ‹moorwort› and

COWS IN HALF MOURNING ■ 143

withered bog=birches. (Toward evening, that blanket of fog again at 1 particular spot, not all that far away, out of which a coal-black bull=poll came
soundlessly charging : !. (And afterwards real ‹sounds›, too, like at
THOREAU's; brrr !).).

: "Shall we make a brief stop at the inn ?".

4

: The life of man is short; anyone hoping to get drunk has no time to lose !
/ And evenings at ‹ZIEBIG's Inn› were not that unlively. (We at the bench=
corner for elegant folk; the only one with something like a cloth on it. And
beer & serious stogies.)

Yokels fetch ‹cig=ritts›. Buxom village lasses plod in cheekily for
bottled beer. (Harried wives for ditto, sloven=aproned, with low-slung
metacenter, rude dugs under cover of loud duds.) / The view of some
‹Hamburg harbor› or other on television; endless; (we'll see who holds
out longer : flash it 1 wicked smile every few minutes . . . . .). But now it
starts to oblige, the gray-blue flickerwork; stretches a thousand limbs
at once; and the machine discharges the familiar ‹half truths› : Whoever
calls a black-bound book ‹black› is an utterly honest fellow in the FREE
WEST. (And if he claims it's ‹red›, he's a liar, sure.) But what sort of fellow would constantly try to convince us : it's ‹not=green› ? ! / So, then,
Bonn smiled & flourished. It appeared no official idiom was as yet established for ‹Burr=Geeba & Bee=zerta›. (Not all that easy, either : whoever is for ‹freedom› in this particular case, rubs ‹Day=Gall› the wrong
way; and vice versa.) ‹Gug=garin› treated briefly & snidely; (meaning, all
the more copious news about the latest American ‹Ex=Ploarer›, promptly
50% unsuccessful once again.) At home, laity assembled for Protestant=
halcyon Days; if you pushed the inappropriate button, kolkhozes blossomed and sweet was the fragrance of komsomols : ‹hmm, bare ass meant
averages›.

And the steady murmuration of the Messers Granger. / Some of it not so
dumb maybe; (though they kept peering over to check how we were con-
suming our beer : they understood the ‹Green Deal› about as well as
EINSTEIN did the atom bomb; i.e., on the one hand quite well, on the other,
not at all !). / Local data, divulged by accident, some of it right interesting
: how that odd small=round redoubt back in the swamp owed its genesis to
the only (and presumably inadvertent) air-mine drop of the war. Plus details : how the grass & bushwork had been ‹shaved clear=round›. Claimed
that deer with ‹lungs ripped out› lay decoratively about; (using hands to

draw the suitable broad=cannibal gestures : I saw plenty of that during the war, with *human beings,* amigo ! You can't have seen much of the world yet !). One fellow even claimed he had seen=heard the thing whiz past his attic window, about 1 in the morning – but since at this point the local cop, who happened to be on hand, cast a broad (and unnecessarily familiar) glance our way, yes winked, we knew that the statements of the gentle-man=in=question were to be received with caution both now & in the future. (And so it was : 2 glasses later and he was already claiming he had ‹been to sea with Karl MAY's brother›. – "Did he have any siblings ?" Otje didn't know.) / "These hula=hoops –" an eminently squat fellow lectured his crony (whose face gloried in a quite critical lower lip – most unseemly for his station) : "– do they ever induce pelvic motions . . . ! : The Thiesses' little girl nextdoor . . . . . ? – : Cheers !". "Cheers –" his crony replied, word for word (and their eyes twinkered like cathouse panes in the twilight).

Some remarks to the imminent ‹20th of July› : *one* ‹statesman› had held a noncommittal speech; (à la ‹not=green›, see above). And an*other,* shrewder, had silently ‹laid a wreath›. The *one* praised the ‹soldier who thinks for himself›; (but then the next orator was quick to spell it out : in case of ‹immoral authorities› ! Even a general, with certain reservations, was said to be in favor of thinking for oneself – wouldn't that have opened BEN AKIBA's eyes wide.) / And bless the jukebox, all you need is 10 pfennigs to push in at one side, and out of the slit comes ‹HEIDECKSBURG=HURRAH›; (or one also has the choice, 'tis said, of ‹ONWARD, CHRISTIAN SOLDIERS !› – at present the difference is audible only to the well-armed ear.) / Now & then, over at another, even gaudier apparatus, some brave soul would give a rou-lette whirl to 3 buttons : here, too, you could win something, theoretically, if you had ‹luck›, oh lady luck. (A nation strangely miscarried : hardly anyone among us wants to do hard & peaceable work; all they all want is to ‹win› somehow, bingo lotto wheel & war, at which one can only be a notorious loser – the science is called ‹probability calculus›.) / More inter-esting, faith !, was the scoop on the capacities of the village whore. (Query : whether the hot affections of one's own spouse might be recaptured by laying a rose in the bathtub each morning ? She might respond perhaps with a small ASBACH brandy. Or even serve it up naked . . . ? : "Otje !". And he, too, gave a heavy slow nod; and pictured it – loveable senile dreamers we, the=2 of us. But : "Screeches by day bring impotence by night." Yes; sure. Definitely.) / And meanwhile the plastic box was leveling heavy curses at ‹the East›. *More* wreaths were laid. (And no one called ‹barracks› ‹soldier=stalls› – granted; we knew only those of the Hitler years; the=ones nowadays were quite, quite different of course, I had read it again only recently in the SPD press, simply no comparison. All the same the ‹Reich› had cost me 70 months, equals 2000 best days, of my life – in compensation I had lost all my goods & chattels, except for 1 busted aluminum spoon : not that I'm in anyway proud of it, au contraire; but just in case those ‹of another opinion› should be all too quick with their ‹bellyacher› !) / "Cheers, Otje." : "Cheerz=Carlos !".

The mood of the paraquadrupeds was turning more frisky. / The Farmer Senior (with silvergray head and goldenred mustache, with woollyclad chest and leathery footwork – *and ‹Senior›* : what titles they could invent for one another !) stuck a knife=handle in his, still passably firm, mouth; set a glass of schnapps on the blade : – ! : – and balanced it clear across the taproom – : "Braaavoo !". (And he, too, promptly ‹won› another prize for it : what a folk !). / The hired hand, in baggy drab buckram overalls, got 1 last glass of hootch for the road; and demonstrated the ‹Prussian Parade March of 1910› : ‹Bum=Búffa Búffa Búffa Búff !› – At the sight of which we decided to wave the innkeeper over; paid abstrusely; and departed. (For a good while we could still hear a psalm new and fine : ‹Higha Bovethy Hillsthe Winddoth Pipe. Socolld.›)

5

And today around 9, I've already mentioned it I guess, said=rented saw was to appear. / To be on the safe side, we had arisen at 6. Had had our ‹white› breakfast, (in order to have all our athletically fit energies at the ready). And now we were waiting : Tropsch gave us a fine lesson on the meaning of ‹eternity› ! / So we reached for the peep=pipe now & then, and peered under the skirts of the distant reaperettes. Each selected 1 for himself; led Her off into a suitable ‹fir bower›; and did this & that to her, mostly that. (Naturally only in our fantasies; we had a load of sawing to do after all – the mere sight of those gray, nailiferous planks . . . . .). / Why was Otje constantly taking off behind the ‹HOUSE› – as we had agreed to call the thing – meanwhile muttering something about ‹check if he's coming› ? There were just woods back there : Tropsch definitely wouldn't appear out of them. Came back. And smelled as if he'd ‹struck it rich›; (and now a pointed sniff : hff=hff. – Granted; the morning *was* raw. Hm.) / Conversation about ‹female menopause› : "But shouldn't you be able to expect the exact opposite ?"; (that is, for them to be more apt to ‹let› you : be securer freer less prude ? A shame about all those cruel hips, plus fittings; each almost good as new.) / "Only eight thirty."

Another topic : "Do you think there may be trouble ? Sawing like this today, so close to the 20th of July ?". And I, with no hesitation : "Aw go on ! First, here we are in the middle of the woods. And besides : when would we have the time otherwise, huh ? Nono; just let someone try !". (But 'tis a curious corner of the world : this morning, out back, in the center of the glade – where there'd been nothing yesterday evening ! – a ball a foot in diameter. Yellow; spongy=scaly; when Otje hit it with his stick, it gave a muskety pop, and then emitted a shallow, dull=toxic=green circumdusting=cloud : "A bovista ! – Young ones 're s'posed to be edible." But Otje, with massive=disdain : "After all, you're ‹edible› your=self, too. – Case you don't taste all too goaty."

6

: "There !" –

Gay=Lussac appeared with his wheeled apparatus. / : "Well finally !" (Because the fellow dared to mutter ! Inspecting his horse-kisser I somehow felt rising deep=inside a desire for ‹sauerbraten› & potato dumplings ‹À la thuringien› – it's a fact, a person's thoughts are fully irrelevant : "Give 'm a stogie, Carlos." : "Don't keep callin' me ‹Carlos› !").

This=here, then, the switch. / The button in case the trunk is too thick; the saw gets stuck, and the fuse pops up; bon. / This the tilting=shoe. / : "And don't go sawin' through any nails ! – Or –" (and with what disparagement the houynym dared regard our charming root=wood !) : "– stones, for that matter. Like you often find in stumps like that." (Beat it, friend !). –

Alone with our monster – : shouldn't there be *three* men to saw, just in general & on principle ? ! We looked at one another. We weren't insured. Not against this sort of thing. / The morning air grew heavier; gaudier, too. I savagely thrust my jaw forward; strode around to the handle; and gave it a forceful jerk – (full jerk; full=jerks thwack) – : ?. / – – : ? ? – / : !

: zzz=zzz=ZZZTTT – and the hmyes ‹sound› sent such a wicked whistle through the sultry silence, the tool vibrated so violently, that we first had to re=collect all our courage. / : "Thinnest pieces first, okay ? –" –

: – –. / : – – ! / : – – – : – : ! ! ! –

My, it worked like a charm ! / Now, groaning softly, I heaved a weightier round log up onto my (rusty) forearm – : "Careful !" – (and add my high=thigh underneath; and gasp and hang on, holding the thick=lower end. Meanwhile, the bastard, upfront, effortlessly sliced up the ‹crown› (and smiled superciliously at his ‹own strength›, huh ? !) : Well just you wait; we'll be switching places, too ! / Zzt, Zzt, Zzt : those were measly=thin boards, no match for us ! / It spat & screeched & whistled, in the drive=belted draft. – : "Damn; it's *oak* besides ! !" (Be-

cause the railroad ties made regular sparklers ! "Wonder if Tropsch=
Loossack will mind ?" : "Screw Gay=Fischer !"). Okay. Although our
shouts could surely be heard clear across the riverlet – several nymffs were
now looking this way it seemed; (and *what* they were actually doing there,
we couldn't figure out either – could it be they were scrubbing the edge of
the grainfield=there ?).

A racket like in war ? You bet ! / : "Tell me, Otje – did you do any
notable ‹thinking for yourself› during your days as an artillerist ?". (The
‹20th of July› had popped into my mind again. Besides, here came a whole
heap of thin=short pieces; we were therefore standing close together, and
could shout=chat.) "Hmmwell," he replied indecisively; adding a couple of
dilatory ‹zzt=zzt's› : "– but we once had a battery commander who was
always thinking. He once told me, later on in a Belgian POW camp, the
following story" : Zzt=Zzt ! : "In early April '45, in the Oldenburg retreat
area – I think the town's name was VECHTA – he hears on his walkie=talkie
that the town has been declared a ‹hospital station›, and friend and foe alike
are transporting their wounded there. 1 hour later, however, some ‹colonel›
or other – in command of that section of the front – suddenly radios him :
‹This is an order ! : Blanket Vechta with 200 rounds !›. To his inquiry, plus
most submissive demurrer, if wounded haven't just been . . . ? the answer is
as simple as it is brutal : ‹Shut up ! In 15 minutes I except a report of
mission accomplished ! – : Out !›. – Now tell me, Carlos, what would you
have done ?". And turned toward me, as if in fact he was the man the anecdote had happened to. : "Keep your eye on the nails. – Or better yet : let me
take over !". –

And give the broad santos=brown beam an expert once-over – for iron
inclusions; for ingrown gravel – and the machine let out a roar, ursine=
irate; and devoured its way, in a shriek of dust, through the substance :
clear through ! (It was a captious question, of course; because ‹an order
was an order in those days›. And refusal, refusal. / And I had been a coward
now for ages & ages. And although years are said to make one generally
‹more infallible›, o rocks; surely not any braver=too. And so I made my
decision, after the third beam) : "Hmyes. I'm sure I would've ‹got sick›."
And, since a blind man could have read the disdain on Otje's face, quickly
and vigorously added :"Don't tell me you would have leapt up; and hero-
ically shouted : ‹Never, you immoral major=ity !›. – Or, rather, that your
‹thinking commander› did : best bring those last couple of beams; then
we'll take a little break."

: ? – : "A break ! !" I screamed; because the fellow was holding, no
stretching, such an uncomprehending ear my way – short=white hairies
growing in the fleshy sack; all I needed ! – and wrenched such a disgust-

ingly quizzical mouth, you could only feel sorry for the poor woman who'd
have to open her eyes every morning to that Flemish countenance on the
pillow beside her.

– Break. – / Only when I caught myself staring intently at his lips (he
seemed to speak strangely low today !), did I realize my ears were ringing,
too, or more precisely whimpering, (if not bawling). And hurt, literally : I
had the irrefutable feeling that the left, having been turned toward the saw
longer, was slightly swollen, and the pain wasn't at all vague : could that
be ? ! – / : "Noo; he did as follows : wrestled with himself for 1 minute. A
la ‹heroic refusal› ? : he'd be shot. ‹Get sick› ? : then the nearest subaltern
would do it. No no : not a solution ! / So he bent down over the map –
‹winning time›, sure – took coordinates; then gave the orders for ‹range
& elevation› to the gun-captains outside. And, once the ‹200 rounds as
ordered› had been fired, reported ‹mission accomplished›." – Pointless; I
shrugged disparaging, broad=drooping shoulders. But Otje filled me in :
"But of course, he had, as he confided to me *after the capitulation, outside
Brussels,* ‹measured wrong›. Mistakenly placed the field=plotter on an
empty fork in the road 500 yards this side of town. Can happen to the best
of us, right ?". Not bad. "Eichmann would've said : ‹No wonder we lost the
war›. – Look at that, over there !"

For 1 monster=machine was tottering through the fields. And turned
with a snarl. Moved voraciously in our direction again – – : "A combine !";
Otje, the expert, with the peeper to his infallible eye. (Then I was allowed
to look, too : up on the captain's bridge all sorts of pied folk. Strapping
rye=mamas; trolls that looked puffed from blue linen; sacks large=lovely=
plump=dry=many). – "Pretty." –

– : "C'mon, to work : the ladies'll arrive in an hour or so !". / The long
hyperheavy trunk; but it (the saw) devoured it (the trunk) all the same. We
held our heads, nervously, to one side now, listening to the ululation. Neither of us was going to fight for the joy of sawing now. (Rayed by the sun,
a power=pylon. : What are these profound roarings of yours in my pretty
ear ?)

Otje : "And what about the *next* war ! I have a sister in Görlitz : when I
picture me getting an ‹order› to ‹blanket› her with 200 rounds ? ! – : Good
thing we don't have to play soldier anymore ! You'd have sundry such
ticklish questions every day. – : Look !" (for the fat=yellow female was just
passing by voluntarily : we promptly heaved those trunks with less effort.
Smiled (though it probably looked like illustrations for Part I of DANTE);
and gawked in her wake, with sweaty Passion masks. I made some remark.
Otje replied. : ? – We showed each other empty palms : we couldn't hear a
word now. / : *"WHAT : IS : IT ? ! !"*. / Until he finally used gestures to assist.

Hooked the tips of his little fingers in the corners of his mouth, and pulled
it wide, rapidly=repeatedly : ! (And supplemented by pointing after the
ocher=lady vanishing : !). – Ah, that. Yes; guaranteed. But – and I raised
my left fist, the pinkie sticking out limply; and gave it several gloomy
snaps with my right indexfinger : . . . . . And then, an overemphatic=
resigned shake of my head: "Not us anymore, Otje." – And he, too, understood; and lowered a broad melancholic brow over the saw-blade. (Which
seemed to hurdygurdy much=much more softly than at the start : maybe
‹being deaf› wasn't so great a misfortune ?). / But jumped all the same,
at the death=rattle, when he started to chop up the barracks=window-
frames; and in his perplexity showed me the split ‹stool=brace› : ! Sheepish
face above. : "It'll cost us 3 marks more now, friend : mission accomplished !". (He didn't understand me of course. But on the whole, things
were moving very happily to their end – I just gave my own temple a tap,
to signify a belly=full; made the gesture of counting money; (while raising 3 fingers : I I I ? ! – He flinched his shoulders; and still didn't get it :
"That's okay."). / And properly look forward to the moment of general
collapse !).

7

: "THE END ! ! !" – / (And, leaving everything hanging, stand there; sort of
stumped.) –

8

: A hand on my shoulder ? ! –
    And Otje made a ditto startled whirl . . . . . : Each stood face=to=face
with His Own ! / We hadn't heard a thing, not=1=thing. : "Well, have you
gone deaf ?"; and were deliciously amused by our dirty, anxious=listening
faces. And idiotically petted us; and nodded to one another, at us poor
wretches.
    (Appeared to be in a good mood & remained so; because underway they
had met up with some queer bird or other – judging by their flatter=and
screech=mimic, "Dix=Huit : Dix=Huit !", could it have been lapwings ? –
/ Else capsized her doeskin hat to demonstrate : dived for it (and her rear
end went broad as a washtub : lovely !) and caught it again – definitely
lapwings. / In the telescope we showed them our Ark of Noah soundlessly
plying seas of rye. (And both at once, objecting : "Well now, ‹soundless› ?

– It's making quite a proper racket." – We heard nothing, neither 1. But meanwhile laid out the groundplan for the 2 wood-ricks they had ordered up – : it would soon look sort of like this=then. : "Lovely."). / Sniffing – : "Say ? – : Have you 2 been drinking ? !" – (And promptly made those familiar disgusted faces : that's the thanks you get.)

Great Cain

1

Ella was still enthusing about ‹Berlepsch Castle›, making puppet eyes to match puppet's mouth, describing its garden terraces at greater length, when suddenly she gave a dreamy shake of her puppet head : "It's ir=rash= ional." (Her watchband polyringed like a flatworm. I at once looked over to Ernst – ?; and he affirmed, for only me to see, that this was the latest phrase. Ahwell, now & then we need to call in company, so we can realize how good we usually have it; besides, they'll be on their way again tomorrow.)

And lazily let eye & ear stray=up and/or =about . . . . . : / That most pilose line with towels, and crucified shirts; (and a great many empty clothespins : touching, really, these homely minigadgets, faithful for years; ‹mute› occurred to me too, ‹real=wood› –, – : well, anything especially refined want to surface ? – nope, nix surfacin'.) / Geese agaggle ? – aha; Brauer's little girl on a drive. (that is, she's not *so* little anymore.) / On every house-wall, caterpillars struggling upwards, trying to pupate; and me, promptly turning to Ernst : "Who in fact first realized a caterpillar & a butterfly might be 1 and the same ? Buffon ?". "Dunno –" he hastily replied, from over his Eisenmenger, ‹JEWRY EXPOSED›, the second edi- tion of 1711; "– that is : not *at the moment.* You can look it up . . . . . anytime . . . . ."; (this last word very muttered; footnote=filcher was only half-here again.) / So more slurps of the gas=pantomime, heralds of the approaching low : long white cloud shrubs, dilldolic and hemlock=budded, lashes fibers worsteds, in takeoff over behind Steinhorst; grayish rags eager to scurry in from the west; (‹sticky afternoon› had been issued as the password. Say no more.) / Out of cussedness, ought to ask Ella : just who was this Berlepsch of hers; that would set her red slit gaping nice & wide. (How had Pythagoras put it ? : ‹Sire no children by a woman wearing gold !›; and she had several teeth of it. (Of course, it seems He propounded nothing but stuff like that : ‹Piss not at the sun !›; ‹Above all avoid every black tail !›; ‹When it thunders touch the earth !›; andsoforth : junk not worth the mention, the whole of antiquity !).)

As a table-base the spare tire ! Verily, there was something ‹in› these VW=CAMPERS. / Ahwell; Ernst has been making good money for a few

years; and the ‹filler=upper› for a big paper doesn't have it easy, either – I
now raised (in homage as it were : ‹To the spiritus, rector !›) my pale
murky tumbler to him (yckh : ‹grape=fruit juice›, oh rocks !). But then he
laid another soft gray slice of bread so handily against the glassy brown
rim, pressed the butter so firmly into its pores, as if part of it; spread the
brown strong-scented jam, thicker & thicker –, – (and my gaze did indeed
relax now : Will you be surprised, friend, at how cathartic it is. And dia-
phoretic : spread away.). / Cookies allround, ‹GOLD MARIE› & ‹PITCH MARIE›,
(the latter with chocolate, that's why.) Cigarettes & tobacco; (‹tabarettes &
cigacco›). The chestnut in Ella's hand (above it, Ella's wild'n'woolly armpit). : "Like a smoldering coal."; (I meant the chestnut; Paula, however,
promptly jealous : "You=two still have the mowing to do today.").

And further breakfastatic exchange of news from the three months
since we had last seen one another. / Ours about the hedgehog couple in the
shed. – : "He still alive ?"; Ernst, in English & softly, (as if afraid the
hedgehog could hear him; or understand German.) / Then about the ‹bird in
the chimney›. First, very queer loud peepings; for hours. Then the hard job
of localizing : ? – : clearly audible only in the kitchen; around the house
outside not at all; (Paula was excellent at it, flutterheart & sootphobia.) He
finally ventured out through the opened damper : hop=hop – and ‹brrr !›
out the kitchen window (prophylactically opened, of course), into the mix
of leaves & country air that was his by rights. (But moving on now to
Weighty=Generalities, the conversations cultivated with the chimney
sweep : how they frequently find dead birds there, especially owlets,
strange to say. Ernst made a note of it; Ella's lips formed the requisite
pucker of empathy.)

And retaliated with the exciting account of that Irish Night o' New
Moon; when through the kissing window, left open in the sultry heat, a
felonious hand had come groping : – : first twice on his nose. Then on
Ella's practically bared left. And she, resolute wench, not uttering 1 word,
fumbled in the toolbox for the pincers – listened – right : snuggle number
four. She latched onto 1 finger of the party in question with the aforesaid
tool : !. – All quiet; nobody said nothing. – Except outside, something like
more rigorous breathing. Trampling. And a penitentiarial wheeze now
& then. (And she kept squeezing ! Charming. But you probably need a
puppet's conscience for such deeds. – Nevertheless, I now examined the
ingenious mobile home with admittedly greater interest : at 7 feet 1, how
had it ever made it through our entry=gate ! ?).

2

: "Hey look at that !" –

– ? – ! : 'sindeed; a small advertising=zeppelin drifted ever so merry and silverfishy above the farthest vapor=woods' edge. "‹DUJARDIN or TRUMP›, aut=aut !" (But you couldn't make it out, even with binox. Individual trees, yes, as if puffed from smoke : with hat-shaped heads, and some like champagne goblets, troops of paintbrushes; they stood, presumably, on the floor of their ocean of air, swaying back & forth in sync. And that ‹transitional low› wasn't going to be all that bad : otherwise they would never ever have gone up in the thing.) / The tall television tower, a scrawny=red stripe, was clearly visible, too. At first Ernst mistook it for no more than an innocent smoke=stack : ? : "The tallest edifice in Central= & Western=Europe, dammit !"; me, outraged. And he, impressed : "Where exactly ?". I showed them all the spot on my 1:100,000=map : "East of federal highway 4; near Bokel." / ? / And, being agile autopedes, elaborate the plan for a drive= over. / ? / Until the ladies approved it; and hastened the clearing of the table. (A tire as a base; what all won't them collij=kids come up with next !)

Meanwhile Ernst & I by ourselves; smoking. / He definitely does *not* have it easy! As ‹filler=upper› for one of the largest papers ? He must regularly provide

   a) the column ‹FIFTY YEARS AGO› (the ‹Panther› pounces on Agadir. / ‹TWENTY YEARS AGO› on Stalingrad. / ‹TEN YEARS AGO› ? : Ah=ah=ah already stepping on toes). (But preparing now for new pouncing; not to worry.)

   b) the ‹Letterbox›; 90% bogus, 10% real=idiotic inquiries from ‹readers›, (always the same ‹strata› by the way : cantankerous retirees, bar buddies, high-school seniors despairing of ever seeing themselves in print otherwise) : "Why is TANTALUM called tantalum ?" / : ‹Are salted herring hung in cherry trees effective against thieving magpies ?" / : "Where does the brand name MONDAMIN come from?› (And the stoic= inane answer : "E. Kr. in D. – From the Indian; ‹Grain of the Great Spirit›, that is, maize. Your friend has won his bet.").

   c) Or, sometimes, a half dozen times a day on average, a call from the editor-in-chief : "Quick, a filler with 6 lines : PDQ !" (Whence edifying Tartar=canards, à la ‹Camel Bites Child›; ‹HOLOFERNES, Inventor of the Mosquito Net›, cf. Jdt. 13:9; ‹Willi Brandt Nominated for the Nobel Peace=Prize ?›).

As a result of which, Ernst was condemned to peruse the motliest reading; forced on principle to read pencil-in-hand, affix every tomfoolery to a scrap of paper, and slip it into the appropriate stockpile=folder. (They carried queer labels : ‹LEARNED WIND; a) schmaltzy, b) ancient, c) slightly risqué – CAVE !› / ‹ADJECTIVES CONTRA GENTILES› – it was after all an ‹independent› rag, i.e. Christian Democrat; (and *what* a Socialist he had been, around 1930, when we were in school together ! Ahwell; back then there still was an SPD.) / And as noted, ‹5=LINERS; 6=LINERS; 7=LINERS› – I was once allowed to visit his ‹Cave of Winds› : *Never again !*). All his closer acquaintances were likewise trained to collect pertinent items and present them to him, for he labored under a permanent shortage of material; so his next question was predictable. : "Y' got 'nything ?" (I now pulled out my list of findlings.)

: "‹MASAK›, Reversal of Circumcision." – "Can that be done ?" the letch asked in initial delight; but then began rocking his head dubiously : "‹LEARNED WIND, slightly risqué›" I heard him mutter considering; "Hm. – Well, hand it over." / "2 kinds of alien spirits could, in the opinion of rabbis, invade the bodies of the living; either those of the Babylonian tower-builders, or the wicked who perished in the Flood." – "Well okay." / But at last I had touched his stony heart; and it was a fine item, ‹THE AUTOMOBILE'S FATAL PROGRESS IN 1908› : "During the past year, within the entire German Reich, 141 persons were killed by automobiles; of these 12 were drivers, 22 persons riding in the vehicles, and 107 third parties. It is obvious, therefore, that it is less dangerous to drive an automobile than to cross a street populated with them." (41,727 cars & trucks registered at the time. And with a smiling second of silence we honored the good-ol'-days, when grandpa ran down grandma : 141, tut=tut !).

"Is A-1 SAUCE allowed on Fridays ?" – "You crazy ? !" he asked in dismay. I just fell sublimely silent; and then he too grew serious, he had recognized the Gordian nature of this seemingly harmless question. And shifted his shoulders with growing uneasiness : "Oh=oh. – Pfffff : listen, don't mess with *that* !" He formed an orator's claw, gazed into it, and shaped his pronouncement – : "If a coward wants to prove his courage nowadays, he protests against the atom=bomb=in=general. That's so chic & safe you can ask in the most nonchalant causeur=tone : "Ah, so you're against the bomb, *too* ?›. But it's best to say nothing nohow about ‹religion› – about Christianity, that is" he added more precisely. And, fully out of sorts now : "Besides, on independent papers we have special chaplains for such things : Nono." Arose ponderously, (had the elderberry jam started to work ? Hardly this soon.); gave an unsightly stretch of elbows, and pointed with a chin topped by a yawn, to the corner of the house, around which now . . . . .

"Girls, you can't go like *that* –", Ernst & I, in anxious chorus. "At least take a sweater, it's turning overcast." (Quite apart from the fact that they really were exposing a great deal : if Paula took cold afterward, I'd be

making tea again.) They gave a concerned look upward. Then at themselves. And had seen through us. Paula simply reposted : "You're still
going to have to mow." –

3

Was Ernst ever driving fast again ! – I had the feeling of being telegraphed.
"60"; him, imperturbed. / A droll feeling, really, sitting in this thing : we
two up front; the ladies nonchalant & mondaine (‹GRAIN OF THE GREAT
SPIRIT›, ought to have a bottle with us) in the tin parlor behind us; (on the
return trip I definitely 'll have to snoop around in there, too).
  "Left or right here ? Highway ahead." True, I saw nothing of said highway; but these drivers have their own penetralia when approaching inter-
sections, or other witching places : "Turn left at the GREAT CAIN." "Odd
name" he said disparagingly, (and to my joy had to slow down considerably). "Well, not every one can be named ‹Ernst›." "No they can't," he
admitted; and brightened up, and made the same remark I'd often heard
at this turn : "Judging by which, not far from paradise, right ? The scene
of the celebrated incident." And I, with gravity & wit (likewise well-prac-
ticed : one cannot plagiarize oneself) : "Quite right. Where even today
chauffeur Cain, having spotted his pedestrian brother Abel=uh . . ." (and, a
few quick allegorical ‹final strokes› of the hand). "Cain was far and away
the more interesting sort." he declared testily, (using, consciously one
would hope, one of those Federal Germanisms : ‹far and away›; ‹to confess
oneself to be›; ‹a genuine concern›; yesyes). We were scampering (not
‹campering›) down the hi-way again at such a tempo that the leaves at the
road's edge did wobble and bob ! : "Anything else ? !" he inquired, not
without trenchancy; and : "You ought to ride with our local reporter sometime; that'd set you searching your soul." And after a while, fully disdainful now : "Lord, are you ever backward here in the country !" And at ever
fuller tilt, ever onward we went, Nobodaddy's children, with esprit and
fiery=step, ‹THE AUTOMOBILE'S FATAL PROGRESS IN 1961› ! – ? : All I needed !
Music had struck up behind us : Pretty=Ella explained how the new portable worked. (All we lacked was for them to play ‹Nearer, My God, to
Thee›. To put you in a real titanic frame of mind.)
  "And now a right." he said, just to make sure, on the far side of
Sprackensehl : "By the way, that's by Robert Kraft, the ‹ADVENTURES OF
DETECTIVE NOBODY›, right ?". While the last village flowed by on both sides,
sensibly slow. The last house : gray wooden swords set around it, points
up. ‹HEATH ICE› ! / "I'll beat your barge into a pram !" I screeched into his

Judas ear, as he was about to ‹step on› the gas (or whatever) and head down
the narrow, empty asphalt ribbon – quite obviously newly paved : "We
have to keep an eye-out for the side-road to the right !". He muttered obedi-
ence; (or contrariwise, obediently muttered : it must be just *too* difficult,
with 34 horse=power at your feet.) / : "Stop ! There !". (And keep to the
right of the balk, my son; 'tis good advice I give.) / Climb out. / "Please be
good enough to roll up the windows, okay ? – You folks'll never learn."
(And pompously ‹checked it himself›. And locked up.)

4

Up the path : you couldn't possibly pull your head as far back as would've
been necessary here ! (And since I had no choice but to inspect the sky's
frizzy grayblue canopy, added : "Well ? Wouldn't those sweaters feel good
now ? !". But they just emitted, 'tis the wont of women perhaps, a
uni=scornful "Pffff –"; and then let their wind=groom link arms ‹straight
off !›.)

The cement blocks, to which cables had been anchored, were huge, like
sheds sunk into the earth. Each surrounded by its half acre of sandflat and a
7=foot=high fence. "Well, yours can't be all *that* much smaller." (Ernst; it
had the unequivocal ring of remonstration.) / Technical flat-roofed huts of
clinker-hued clinkers; here & there on the clean sand=strewn ground, taste-
fully sparse, lean twin=pairs of young birches, very nice and austere – but
from those large tin lunch-boxes hanging on several walls, you knew that
something was not quite right. Protective link-fence here too, of course;
(and I mean the most expensive=thick gauge; I knew all about it; after all,
as Ernst had alluded just now, I had only recently had to repair mine.)

But the grand slammer was & ever would be him, HIM : THE GREAT
TOWER ! ! ! –

Way at the bottom, the skimpy round cement base : "Barely 1 hand
above ground ? !". "Listen, it goes deep enough," Ernst cautioned out of
the fullness of his gazetteer's erudition : "Given the weight it supports,
there's a good 60 feet of it ! And cone-shaped, too, I'd say : widens as it
goes downward." (‹And sometimes tends to move lieward›; but that the
tower=itself should taper to a point at the base, like a carpenter's pencil,
for once he had no explanation, either.) / Pointless to ask the 3 visible
Babylonian tower-builders : once they noticed we were taking pictures,
they started acting like megalomaniacs with their long white metal canis-
ter. (One even had the gall to approach the grating and ‹warn› us : no pho-
tos whatever at present; a matter of top-secret components ! Several warts,

boon companions, on his cheek. And the two harelipped spooky bastards
yonder promptly carted away their crap, and with what flank-sergeant gestures, as if they were invested priests of TELEVISIUS. – "The fraud –" Ernst
grumbled agreeably; and clicked & shot away lustily; he enjoyed anyone
who took his job seriously. Not me : I only have to hear the word ‹SECRET !›
and I feel like I did under the late Hitler : the bankrupter the gov'ment, the
more ‹secrets› it has to have !).

   "Well – : 7 feet; 7 feet 4 inches –"; the diameter of the tower, that is.
(And it had to be very hollow : you could see 2 damn dungeony little doors
in it, topped by semicircular arches, heavily riveted, in triple & quadruple
rows. Nor had they spared rivets in general. And the skinny, cocky=
contorted ladders that climbed to those doors ! Into the fiery red tube : let's
go !). / We looked at each other, Ernst & I; (what the women were thinking
we didn't know; of the hmyes ‹counterpart› perhaps ? – Redskinned &
hollow : wonder if it might not be more correct to think of TELEVISIA ? No
doubt the spiral staircase inside, cunningly emaciated, wandering up &
down all 1150 feet, like at Piranesi's : Someone with a key could, were his
heart so inclined, walk right out onto one of the 4 allround pulpits, (way too
high for leaping off), and in muezzin fashion, all ABU LAHAB, all ‹Father of
the Flame›, call out to the federated folk : ‹O come all ye faithful to the
quiz; hie ye to the tube !›). / CHANNEL TWO : "Do you know the triptych by
Eberhard Schlotter ? With text by Dr. Mac Intosh ?". "I don't know names
like that on principle." was his initial retort, official=obtuse; then, however, unofficially softer : "Course I own the portfolio." –

   The craziest part was the still unravaged landscape ! (‹Crazy› in con-
junction with this monster here.) Once you turned your back on it, sandy
paths suddenly ran away from you; so lonely, that should you ‹trod› one,
it's guaranteed you'd still find your own footprints again 3 days later.
Merry=indigent farm woodlets on both sides; (they never gave anything a
chance to grow big, the Messers Granger; more than enough of them in our
village who never paid for an ounce of coal – "course they own a TV !" –
but instead in the most invegetane=barbarian fashion dispatch half a grove
through their sooty stoves over the course of a winter. "The other half,
then, in summer : axe & saw ought to be legal only with a ‹license› !".)
Fields (how do Binding & Co. put it ?) ‹swelling gently into the blue distance›. (And, even bluer, far to the rear, to the east I suppose, some ‹fell› or
other.)

   : What was purring now so impertinently ? ! – Ernst turned reproach-
fully to me again : "Y'see : you *are* allowed to drive your car up to it." But
I, shaking my head : "No, you're not. That's some guy from ‹Behind the
Curtain›. A technician, I bet. – Ah : y'see ? !". For the fellow in question

had the key to one of those pot-galvanized enclosures; he diddled, threw a cursory=intense glance our way; (and took an even longer decorative time locking up : you too, my friend. They were all obviously grateful for the change we provided.) / And nevertheless glances slid down, nefarious & nimble. And played our way in closer – ; –. For behind the authorized fellow, a disembarkation had occurred, a chic curio, (our wives sauntered over inconspicuously as well) : a white=violet burnoose, a ditto shawl, (for up here, on this naked rise at the foot of the tower, it was drafty as a barn now !). "Odalisque" I heard Ernst mutter : her skin pale reddish & chapped; a wide=scenting nose; mother-of-pearl buttons that seemed to grow from her wrists; she set her eyes far & snowy, and submitted herself for inspection. (And more and *more* wrinkles the closer you got ! Even Ernst now cited his disappointment : "‹Ah, but pull the strings and the puppet doth play.›".) And then the little boy climbed out of the car, did a few rounds of go=between, and then crowed : "You'll have to wait, mom; your husband's not ready yet." ("Irrational –" I heard Ella murmur critically.)

And back to the camperette. / Ella, awakening with the unlocking : "How late is it, Ernst ?" : "12; on the dot." (‹Pan sleeps›. And we chit-chat.) / And puffy (seemingly hollow) clouds, beneath which we swiftly drove on.

5

: "In *this sticky heat* ? ! –

But Paula was implacably gentle; Ella quietly amused; (and beneath the sadistic gaze of Both, as with tucked-up shirts, unseemly=little bellies and disgruntled sheepfaces, we took up our position – helpless as once upon a time before the ‹draft board› : ought to bang a fist on the table !). "Oh c'mon, Ernst; there's no point." But they weren't letting us go to it yet, not by a long shot; first the Xanbiddies held those sundry little favorite lectures.

: "A *good* mower gets through $1\frac{1}{2}$ acres a day." (Paula. And since we were dealing here with a mere third and 2 men, the application was self-evident; we held sullen peace, and merely probed our navels.)

: "And please=please don't harm those salmon-colored dahlias ! : They're *so* sweet." (Ella : as if we had intended to. (That is to say, if They pestered any *longer* . . . !). A quick turn of the tables.)

: "And what do *you=two* plan to do meanwhile ? !". But they were irony-proof. "Us ? Stretch out on the chaises longues." (Ella, innocent; so totally matter-of-course.) "We'll cook you guys a pudding." Paula; by an impactful hint – I can speak Federal German, too ! – the more sympathetic.

Alone at last. / : "A pudding ?", Ernst, peckish; but I just shook my head dolefully : "Dregs left over from ricing elderberries, then boiled with sago : one eats, but one does not prize it. – That is to say, tastes do vary." I added hastily, so as not prematurely to smother his lust for work, which didn't appear excessive as it was : "Go fetch the scythe from the shed on the right." (And He actually went ! – I first waited until he was halfway inside; and then, in an inopportune fit of charity, called out to him : "But don't knock down that wasp nest with the handle ! Firstly, Paula sets great store by it. And the secondly I'm sure you realize all on your own." He uttered Cromwell's curse, 'tis true; was, however, just as I had figured, too much a coward to make the decisive turnabout. And happily brought the entity out into the dingy light of day.)

A child of the asfalt, he was, praise god, morbid enough to be greatly fascinated by the tool : the ash handle; the honing block (but I fiddled away at that homicidally long blade *so* enticingly=supply that he promptly beamed like John Paul Jones, WE SICKLEMEN !, and strode forth, legs in atavistic spread.) / The rake (of alderwood !) ? : "Nono, Ernst. We'll leave the hay-raking to the lovely reaperettes, ‹from August weary›."; (and at once swallowy twipperings from the elderberry bushes confirmed it. "D' you know that swallows never nest on Bismarck monuments ?". He didn't know. "You folks below the Main know very little.")

"First cut a border clear=round –"; I demonstrated, (and he walked merrily alongside : Just wait, your little bell will toll shortly !). I entertained him as best I could with bucolica : "D' you know that piglets get sunburned, too ? : On the ears !" : "Don't need to know," he reposted testily; "Why do y' s'pose we have a Farm Column ? Have enough squabbles among editors about ‹jurisdiction› as it is. – What're all these wooden pegs in the yard ?". "Oh. Paula's probably planted something there –"; I tried to keep my voice as expressionless as possible, (all the while executing an egg-dance around the spots in question; with most bitten lips, and seething breast, and an urge to drip from every sweat=pore; at 1 point I struck a ‹Lovely Stone›, and they could hear it 3 versts away : ! (and of course ended up spending 5 minutes whetting the resultant nick.).)

Sooo. / Stand there & pant; (with a hand to your mouth to keep your tongue from hanging out : if I survive this once more, praise be !). Imploring Ernst : "Haven't you got something in the car ? You know : ‹It refreshes the palate, sweetens the breath, and spreads good cheer› – ?". He puckered unbiased lips, and fetched something. / But : "You too, Ernst ?". Yes; him too. / "Let's hope the pictures turn out," he said with some concern; "That tower might – theoretically – emit some kind of ‹rays›, mightn't it ?".

Theoretically, yes. And the beverage had so refreshed my palate that I could swing the scythe around more potentatally : DEATH, THE FRIEND !; (And Ernst delivered an appropriate eulogy over every third=fourth swath.) / And another break after an ambit back & forth. – "How many ‹laps› like this 'll be necessary, did you say ?". 25. He was about to pull a wistful face; but instead had to strike a blow at a rain-fly thirsty for editorial blood (and in the process gave himself such a swat on the testicles that, unrestrained as ever, he let out a roar ! "That's a chunk of life, too, an insect like that" I admonished buddha=assisi=cally; but in vain, the dull pain had evidently been too great.)

"Nono, Ernst : all the more reason for you to mow. A steady back & forth; ‹boustrophedonic›, very simple." / Now *I* walked alongside, now *I* made asinine chitchat. / And laughed like a frog for glee when the old pettifogger – now why had that gooey word occurred to me ? – promptly lopped off half a dahlia bush : "Ernst, *you*'ve got to take the whole blame ! : You're heading out tomorrow; I'll be the one left holding the bag." To which on the one hand he acceded; on the other, however, he was afraid of Paula, and not without cause. With heaving breast after the very first round. (When I noticed how he was covertly eyeing the gaudy headscarves over in the potato patch, I quickly fetched him=us the binox, to keep him=us in a good mood.)

First the rotating rotund rooting=rotor; beside it the petty bumpking : foxyred face with whitish bristles; a hide that would have bent a hornet's stinger; and raised his arms in a most incongruous priestly gesture, (the commando=bark of pipes that doubtless accompanied it could, happily, not be heard this far. Diafragmantic rabble. – "You can tell 'em : ‹Sharpening a new pencil on Wednesday brings misfortune at home› : they're so stupid that 300 years later a folklorist'll be able to come along and, awestruck, collect it as ‹wisdom›." / And back. And forth.).

: "Break !". He screamed uninhibitedly now; directed his backside toward the Orient and let a gas formation advance to the rear; (all that elderberry jam, right ?).

: "Hell, like a POW camp !" (He meant, 'tis true, my pretty new fence; to keep him in the mood, however, I first handed him the bottle. Then the binox; (and right off he focused lecherously on the 6 potato diggers in the furrows, nudipedalia with milkmaid arms). / "‹'Tis no mask she wears – grown ebon rather fro' the sun› ?" He nodded agreement, and continued to level musingly on those color-taut buttoxes. / "Listen, the conversations they carry on sometimes ! I hid behind a bush once and eavesdropped for 5 minutes – : the army's a nunnery in comparison !". (Here, as if she'd understood us, a young tan gazelle arose from out the local fertile plain; revealed herself as a saucy brat of 14 at most, who looked our way – and promptly, with resolve, tucked her skirt higher still, tormented by her own sex. Ernst ogled her all the more; (‹forest-primevally sansculotte, having been seduced by the zeitgeist›; "What d'y' say, Ernst ? : ‹TO THE WOODS, TO THE WOODS› !". Naturally something morbid=letterboxy occurred to him right off : "The French Republic enacted a law on 9 September 1792, whereby every youth of 15, every maid of 13, was qualified to marry." ‹Qualified› sure. Whereas I, wise with age, (and because he was whispering so) : "C'mon, we'd better move back & forth."). / But then I could resist the notion no longer. – "Why not swap for the night, Ernst ? : You two can sleep in the house; us in your minibus ? !" (And he honored it with a nod; and gave the frailties of the ‹flesh› their due. Gave thought as well to varietal raptures; and assented, ulti= & legiti=mate : "Agreed.") –

"C'mon, stick it out : let's have six more back'n'forth !". / For Helios was now showing us his rear wheels. The potato maids, chassis totally dusted, trudged homeward. And naught but dusky=fruits of reading began to run through Ernst's mind : "‹AVALON›: a sun that sets eternal there behind the apple trees abloom. In the midst of a meadow, IDISTAVISO, the ‹Fountain of Forgetfulness›. ‹Heroic shades›, hollow & glassblown, lounging there in English ray-grass." – : "Sure would be lovely –"; me, gasping crick-backed sweat-drenched stoop-shouldered cataract-eyed bedazed semicircular tract-scything autochthonous . . . . .

. . . . . and jerked up ! Such female screechings behind me : "Care=full= now ! The sloe=tree=Carl ! !" – / And whip back the homicidal tool : ! : ! !. / And for starters gape stupidly at where the dark red ran from the toetips of my right foot. : all fivevem properly slashed ! (And only then did there come a fine, most scalping pain. The nylon=sock was shot to – uhm=hell, too.) / An opinion poll yielded the following. – ELLA : "– perdu. – : Irrational ! –". PAULA : Y' see; 1 of the branches is gone ! – I'll put SAGROTAN in some water for you." ERNST : "A beheaded person's torso vomits sometimes." – (My first urge was to reply. But then I pictured the aforesaid bubbling of blood & barf by the beheaded. – And, limping decoratively away, exited; to the bathroom.)

6

(It sure looked snazzy, the bright red bathroom=line, bandaging the end of my 5 toes now. (And would be bandaging them for a good while yet !). And the LYSOL=ersatz stung : well, go ahead'n'sting ! / But it had its good sides, too : Ernst had to finish the mowing. Me, nursed=indulged=pitied. (And the inevitable evening ring=toss and badminton would be spared me for the next 14 days, too – grimly rejoicing, I stuck the BAND=AID on firmer. (Although naturally ‹blood-poisoning› crossed my mind as well, 'zounds amputation & pension ! – Aeh : wouldn't be so bad if you could chuck this job=shit !) – Sure=stick. No=stick. Poor=stick !). –

And lie ‹suffering› in the chaise. (While the other Three, in a trigon, bounced & badmintoned – Ernst with such a charleyhorse non-grace that my eyes wanted to bug with taloned wickedness : serves him right !). / Then – as is probably inevitable with rising high pressure – the great wheel of the stars emerged, (‹MISTER ORRERY›; head of the local planetary system – and I instinctively thought of the TV tower again : might there be some connections there ? / And the folks=yonder hopped & skipped. On a freshly mown meadow, ‹over which now the cool of evening ran›, and dallied with themselves.

Gathered, taking deep breaths, about the couch of the notable=invalid; (and a covert odor arose, panaromatic=blend of female sweat & incipient hay : rocksdrops, up benn, down dell, a craggy road for rambling : lovely.) / And distant rumbling ? – I particularized testily : "Strauss & several of his contemporaries. The artillery ranges at Munsterlager and Unterlüss." (And heard Ernst trying it out : "‹You are mistaken. ‹CANONICUS› has nothing to do with erstwhile corporals in the heavy artillery; there is indeed no such rank in the new Federal German Army.›" – Idiotic; & lucrative : this con= and de=scription of us=All !). –

And offered the three youngsters – I was afterall & sadly=sadly the eldest ! – the binoculars : ! / : "You can see it from here every evening." – : "Not there : on across that horse pasture ! – Adjust the focus a bit, kids." – And then at last they spotted it too : 2 red lights, 1 above the other; far to the east=north=east. / – : ?. – : ! : "The TV tower of course ! From this morning. –. – Prob'ly for airplanes." (And they gazed, 3 memory-stirred youngsters, more mnemonically in the alraunic twilight.) –

Plus the hasty eating of that ‹pudding›. / Ernst & I exchanged several furtive swapping=signals : !. (Each had evidently already informed ‹HIS› in 1 stolen moment – they were oddly defenseless, ‹puddingish› in fact.) / Ergo they entered the house. / And we the wee=double=you=camper : the curtain was quick to move in submissive greeting; (as we opened the door. – Or was it merely a draft ?). / "Say. – Look here. –" Paula greedily felt the unfolded leather sheets; and EVERYTHING in general ! (Were the pincers ready at hand ?). / (You saw nothing but green grass with clover when you got your eyes=closed – : – –).

7

White fogbow stands. The arse embedded. (Damn narrow, this rack here, extolled as especially ‹roomy› ! Was all the same to Paula of course; right afterward, she made a soft mattress of me, and fell asleep.)

The OWLET THAT COMES EV'RY EVE flew about our tin-smithy here, too, with thin ‹hoohoo !›; (and ‹hoho !› and ‹Bassa Manelka !› and ‹Seest thou, good landlord ? !› and ‹Adieu !› and ‹Faretheewell, good landlord !›. And inside the house those two were using john & bath worse than the Prodigal Son; (and now & then 1 wee voice recited sweet & matter-of-factly "It is irrational". – ‹They saw the grandduke's car approaching from afar !›; I had to chuckle a bit; and as my ribs jiggled, Paula murmured in her dreams, (the wife of the railroad man next=door, who always polishes too well, slipped and fell herself yesterday; and cracked two ribs on the end of the marital couch ! : mine jiggled again now; and Paula murmured longer (endlessly distant, the lugubrious dragon=howls of a freight train : red-skinned, long & stiff, the tower=today : cables, tightening down over you, like cages, (a sometime ‹fellow=traveler›, now named ‹Ernst›, was very determined to hide me from ‹pursuers› ! (and signs of danger were indisputably at hand : wasn't that a wart=face pointing something this way ? ! Wasn't something white & totally camowlflaged slinking round=about= me ? (I first hastily wrote my name in the snow alongside : so at least Something of me might remain on earth ! (Then Ernst shoved me ahead into the ticklish=low door, (that promptly got even narrower ! Didn't Someone from the Coalition have hold of my foot now ? ! : ‹I FEEL AS IF SOMETHING HAS WOUNDED THIS FOOT OF MINE ! !› : ROLAND DÄUBLER ! (but Ernst slammed it rattling behind me. He thought nothing of it & followed me ! And I began, laboriously, to climb the spiraly spun=yarn of the hollow stairway, (and the wire snare got ever more tinny & tight – no air – : ‹JUGURTHA : JUGURTHA ! !" . . . . .)))))))). –

8

(First thing next morning I had to produce printed proof for Paula that it had *nothing* to do with a *woman's name*. / Ernst, sneering : "Old-fashioned nervous=nelly ! – You'll never make a real automobilist." Ella, teasing : "Bye=byyye !". / At first I wanted to remonstrate : ME ? : old-fashioned ? ! – But then decided to spare my nerves the energy; after all, anything is possible !).

TOOLS BY KUNDE

i

I like to get up early, (and not just in strange houses). And I mean really ‹early› – not because I am determined to set the brim of my hat against fashion; but it is so wonderfully quiet then for work, in the winter around 2 and 3 : as a BACHELOR, (which is definitely not the same as a ‹single›), you disturb no one, and the dictionaries are used to it. Especially here ‹in the country›, at 4 on a summer morn, I would have had to be a fool not to thumb my nose at my travel alarm's face (just as it was about to flash at me there in the sine of my angle of incidence). For it was indeed alluring roundabout, sitting here in the easy-chairlet on the little porch THE HOUSE & THE DISTANCE :

Quiet takes back her folded fields. Tranquille thanks, + U ! (I have to translate that ? ‹+ U = add you = a dew = adieu› : Say long, Madame Night ! As Lord Sun ope's his eyes. So many, marvelously submissive letters of the alphabet.) And wheaten bells bide breathless. Tiny tattling. Starlings whistle like horse-traders. (At one, younger, time, I would on such occasions normally peep round the corner : do they mean me ? Long-legged days back then. Nowadays I am no longer quite so megalomaniacal.)

: "Well, Conte Fosco ?". (Martin's powerful, white-gray tom.) But he was not about to flatter me : the cat is the symbol of our possible (i.e. to the extent compatible with civilization) freedom. That's why. (And it is in fact 1 of those rare cases where the singular is more than the plural : at best, ‹freedoms› are granted to peoples; FREEDOM nevermore. But it is probably quite right so; the older I grow, the further I deviate from ‹the people›. ‹40=hour=week›, pff ! For me the minimum is at least 70, and often it's over 100.) / : "Leave those titmice alone !" – but they had already noticed. / –.–. / : ? – Very distant tolling of bells. East southeast; and permissible at such distances. When the ‹dix=huit› of pewits is louder than Ben Pandera. (All the same, 1 shake of the head to send it packing.) Go on dozing.

ii

And perk up my ears ! Who could be stirring in the house here at half past 4 ? / Definitely not Martin; He's far too comfy, time out of mind. And since Karl=with=a=K is sleeping with his Ida in the car, logic demanded it was ‹She›. (Unpleasant.) / And indeed came creaking down the stairs ? ! (Still 1 chance : She may be going to the john.) But no; scratching & nestling at the front door now. Chaste chink of the chain-lock. (Whereupon, as a gentleman, I cleared my throat, preferring to make myself audible – no way of knowing just how She might emerge, mornings at half past 4.)

Mutual scrutiny then & there, cold & curious. / Crude naked feet. Then, clear up to the neck, tightest-fitting gray stockinet (had been black yesterday evening; and of course it's not stockinet, I know that, but tantamount to it); small acute V=neckline. And then that face ! : broad & red-marbled, (as Her whole body may well have been; there are such); the mouth a brutal gaping slit of exactly the same color (being fully unlipsticked); the hair short as a brush. Not the least inkling of a bosom. (Hmyes, was that any better than the hand-painted floozies running about in general ? Neither= nor, I'd say. Happily, I succeeded in non=shrugging; She would've noticed right off. / And suppress the grin of memory, too : how upon arrival yesterday evening, Ida had taken to task the ‹Young Fellow› sitting there on the fence and playing with the Conte. It had been quite a surprise.)

She placed an (equally gray) bag, plastic & shining, on the table, between us, and sat down. "I have to do my morning toilette," she said : "Would that bother you ?". Now I had long since noted that in this case plain, forceful honesty would be the wisest (granted, yet another way to cloak oneself; but she obviously made far more mental notes about Karl's & Ida's bourgeois phoniness). So then, earnest & honest : "If I might watch . . . ?". Then, (somewhat wily & self-ironic) : "I'm seldom so lucky anymore." And now a quotation (intimated by a slight lift of the hand, as well as somewhat louder & drier diction) : "‹The gray=ness hither creeps, Thy pride is worn and spent.›" (And the series of masks, along with appropriate quips, met with a certain amount of success – I'll gladly walk over my dead body.)

She nodded approval. "Me, too," she confirmed. Sat there. In her own mighty underbrush of bones, her left foot to the right region of her groin, almost flush with the belly; and with large scissors cut the callus from the (inner) edge of her heels; she carefully laid the orts in a little pile on the table. Between us. (Pieces like woodchips were among them; they slowly curled in the course of our conversation.) "Who is that by?" she inquired, studied=bemused; meaning the quote just now; and I replied simply :

"Opitz. – Or so says Adelung." (That is to say, it wasn't exactly ‹simple›; if you dismantled it. And She was the type to do it if need be : psychoanalyst, and in the middle of her dissertation. One really couldn't help but hear Martin's call for aide; his letter (and an almost identical 1 to Karl) spoke of "fiendish analyses" that would "slaye him yet," and how he feared he might well end up a "bye-word" in medical circles – which Karl & Ida had taken seriously; I took much greater umbrage at all those obvious gummy diffthongs : He had never before spelled aid=with=an=e ! (In any case, we had all Four, including Madam Ida, gone to school together for 9 years, until graduation, and had never lost sight of 1 another; on the contrary.) But Karl, apparently less and less taken by subtleties of that sort, had shaken his surly head and bellowed coarsely – they had brought me along in their car; and the world-whirlwind whistled at our hats & windows – : "Nono : She wants to inherit the farm !". Which Madam Ida, nimbly over her shoulder to the wheel and all Yolk=mouth & Silk=tongue, had translated thusly : "Marry.")

And meanwhile, it was the right foot's turn; she snip-snapped. (Good thing that I am accustomed, moi même, though I arise at 4, to adonize myself after a fashion. For we eyed 1 another now & again.) / Ida's "marry" was of course absolutely asinine; the epitome of chic hebetude, at which she and 80% of the adults of her generation as a whole – hmyess, but then I suppose I cannot use the term ‹excelled›. That Martin, rich Martin, in dealing with this orphan child – (and then, I really could not help myself, I had to gaze at Her : the word ‹orphan› was hardly commensurate with *that figure*; more with the iron-gray outfit; and perhaps most, and most eerily, of all with the ‹intellect›, half Sheffield half Solingen, which appeared to dwell therein) – so then, that Martin, who had provided Her (the child of some more distant erstwhile cousin) full funding for Her education, and had granted Her 1, 2 years of asylum at no charge so that She might pen Her dissertation – that Martin might well have dallied with the notion of seeking some bit of compensation at some point was quite conceivable, given his old fellow's sentimentality, indeed it was perhaps quite ‹natural›. But for marriage, he was, if not too wise, most assuredly too comfy. (And since I had now seen *this up-to-date miss* here, I was thoroughly convinced of Ida's misdiagnosis : She had best be careful not to expose herself all too much to this orphan maid !).

iii

End of pedicure. She laid the long scissors so heinously on the table that the points were directed at me, the narrow mouth gaping with whitefish lechery. She gloated for a moment at my resultant uneasiness. Considered for a moment. (But here the flutterbird from before came to my aide, just above mead & fences – lookathat : I added an ‹e› myself ! Is that how things stand ?). : " 't's that ?" the very=learned=lady asked, a little nettled. And I allowed myself the antiquated joke, and called to It sharply through my hand megaphone : "What'sssss your name ? !" – at once it lifted pugnacious wings my way, black wings, with broad=white bands : "Peeee : Wittt !". And I gave her a ceremonious nod, as if introducing them to 1 another : "Miss Seidel." (And with something of an apologetic smile at my own gaudypied bag of tricks : We are in the country. She was, however, quite aware of the slip-up; and being refreshingly obsessed with omni-science, she was also most surely embarrassed by my failure to exploit my ‹victory›.)

"I have to specialize first," she said nervously, "then I can take on Generalities." Set her mouth more rigid, (for a curselet had wanted to take flight : aimed at herself, sans doute, because of her quasi=excuse); and now turned suitably brutal, ('tis only seemly for an orphan child, humbled for decades, to be brutal for the next several score of years).

"You're a translator –" she began; "Uncle Martin has all your books. I glanced at them again yesterday evening myself : a great deal of middling stuff; but a couple of the Great Men of Literature are included all the same." And let her gaze rest upon me, in a manner to which she was in no way entitled as yet; (although 'twas my due as a minor artisan in the great wide word workshops : there was only 1 means by which to hinder her from unmitigated stupidities – if only to save her from later post-embarass-ments; Ida, of course, out of pure meanness, would have let her go rattling on – to wit: gentle warning, distraction. 'Twas indeed a merry little duel.)

"Yes –. Yesterday evening –" I replied, gazing absentmindedly past her : "OWL-RUN is what the farmers here call the last dusk; when a tag end of the moon is romping in the oaks. –". (I deliberately drawled it out somewhat : if She is truly clever, she'll do a few cosmetics, and leave. If thirsty for revenge, gymnastics. / ‹Yesterday evening› she had served us a beer soup. And Martin cautioned; as if to say ‹Eat carefully : She's perfectly capable of dosing it with something to make you tell All !›. Ridiculous. After that, Karl & Ida barely sipped at theirs – it tasted good to me. / And again, when she had gone to get me seconds, Martin hissed to us : "The ideas they're coming up with nowadays for making rural folk happy ! Reading= Writing='Rithmetic ? : None of that ! And to replace it, ANAL EROTICS as they call it – must indeed be quite some fancy stuff." he added, pondering. Madam Ida had at once spread her hands in denunciation. And I had shaken it off : erratur.)

But she was in fact neither wise nor thirsty for revenge; instead, she
simply got down to business. "My dissertation is on the SUBCONSCIOUS DE-
PICTION OF PHYSICAL STIMULI IN LITERATURE," she explained : "You're more
widely read than I, surely – if you perhaps might know a few more examples that I could include ? I would, it goes without saying, mention your
name at appropriate points." she nonchalantly added. (I hope I was able to
keep the grin off my face this time, too : she must still be really very young
not to consider a reference of said sort to be a rather melancholy=curious
goal in life. But she noticed nothing; She was too deeply involved in the
matter). "SCHERNER –" she said reassuringly, to steer the calcified trickle
of my thoughts down the right gully; "But perhaps you don't know him
either ?". (The ‹either› could hardly refer to my erudition, (the possibility
of which she had just now at least been polite enough to assume), but
rather, unmistakably, to poor Martin's. – But her topic was really important
& interesting. Piquant as well. (Pee=cunt). Nowadays Wise Virgins apparently have a little oil on hand as a matter of principle.)

"Naturally I cannot produce utterest profundity off the top of my
head," I began; "I shall give it some thought, however. – And if I might,
‹think aloud› as it were – ?". "That would be lovely" she rejoined, as hungry for material as her voice was hard; (though it did resonate with certain
scruples. Quite correct.) Me, countering : "Not always." Pause. Then : "If
you hadn't placed the accent on ‹subconscious›, I could recommend the
diverse ‹asses› in JOYCE. But as it is, you must by now have come up against
the peculiar dilemma : that, on the 1 hand, you would love to have examples from *high-brow* literati –" (she nodded) – "but in as much as they
work on a muchmuch more conscious – ergo more encoded, ergo more
opaque – level than the reader ever dreams, it is the famous pennydreadfuls
that can provide you with much richer material –" (her mien grew still
more astringent) – "for their authors are accustomed to scribbling in a sort
of ‹imperfect trance›, which not only permits of no corrections, but is indeed also inimical to them, yielding therefore, of necessity, materials of
particular transparency." She had meanwhile crossed her athletic wrists,
being a habitual listener. "Examples." she now demanded automatically.
"*German* examples ?". (And I seemed to have struck a weak point; for she
made 1 motion of those mighty gray shoulders. Noticed that I had noticed.
(Charming. Sharp mindette.) Yet had solid foundation enough to admit it
with dignity) : "If possible, yes." Alright then : "Potential candidates :
Retcliffe=Goedsche; Samarow; Robert Kraft. – : KARL MAY ! Him above
all !". And then, as Her lips (unlipsticked : few there are who can endure
such kisses !) let out an automatic buzz TONELESS ROULADES – : "1 million
copies a year even now ! And ‹subconscious› is what you need. Besides,

there is reason to presume that on occasion the man may have been an invert –" (her crudish countenance began to shine) – "and since indeed we are dealing with THE TOTEM OF THE GERMANS, you could in this case substitute quantity for quality. – For example – –"

But as suggestive as her glances may have been, we did not get round to the examples quite yet; because

    a) Conte Fosco deigned to sit upon the table between us; and it was such an honor that I was immediately called out of my superstitious & for a literatus highly improper fondness for said author, to watch this fellow=here, as He licked his ass : the way 1 fur=leg=stilt sticks up so high in the air ! . . . . . / Also : "For a cat, a house must really be like a HOLLOW MOUNTAIN : with treasures inside; lotus-lands, warmth – and ‹dangers›, too, granted; like all hollow mountains." / She watched me sternly the whole time. (My studied dispassion is presumably no less inhuman than is this assiduity of hers.) – But

    b) further sounds were coming from behind the shed, where the vehicle was parked . . . . . ‹sounds›, I say . . . . . I have, I suppose got up 20,000 times myself; and the guilty party was without doubt Karl, who as gardener . . . . . / We both got up in sync; and stole his way, almost shoulder to shoulder, shirt beside cotte de mailles . . . . .

iv

Down along the shed's overhang – the GRAY SCREW of a rope; the wormy glass body of a nylon=line, clenched in clothespin teeth – 1 young plum treelet (they still looked like olives) – and peep through the jasmine : – –. Now & then we looked at 1 another : – (wouldn't you know, my grayer temple was turned her way : to think that one can still be so sensitive ! As undeniable as it is ridiculous. Well for that matter, she didn't have a bosom, either. – And yonder dialog as stimulating as our eavesdropping was unseemly.) –

Both fumbling around at the rear end of the vehicle : "To think that we say ‹rear-end› for it : SUBCONSCIOUS DEPICTION in language !". (She nodded. An excursus was already planned : "Anthopomorphizing Idioms in ‹Weather Reports› : ‹Warm air is flowing in from behind.›"). / Absurdities of truly astrocomical dimensions : he a nil, she a nilnil. They fiddled; they bickered; fiddled. Came out, stooping – and his eyes stopped veritably dead in their tracks : ! : "Dammit=woman. Don'tcha have any hair left on it ? !". (He was dealing, of course, with flesh-toned BELINDA pantyhose. But it was indeed eye-catching.) Ida laughed, till the tinny cage echoed; Karl's answer was a shrill hiccup. (A gradual squeamishness tried to rise within me; but Her hand made *such* a plea for delay –. And material of such (how had I expressed it just now ? ‹genuineness & transparency› ?) would be hard to come by again any time soon. She pled once more, inaudibly, pouting her escapading maiden lips. And in the battle between old acquaintanceship and scientific integrity I was, of course, worsted THE MALE MEMBER AS SYMBOL OF FICKLENESS. Although with some very anxious pursing of brows.)

Argument about some sort of system for stowing baggage – she spatted him off with a curt, consummatory ‹Dowhatchawant›. Me (it made no difference now) whispering into a red ear=sack : "As a young bride : she once *embroidered* his portrait." – ? – : "Nah, cross-stitch." And she nodded at once à la ‹Physical Stimuli› : "Crossed = Itch !". (Satanic.) / Karl=yonder briefly bared his dental apparatus. (What was that in his hand ? : "Nippers ! ‹TOOLS BY KUNDE›." I explained. – Not familiar with it ? "Before the war the most incomparable garden & workshop tools were produced by the firm ‹Kunde & Son› in Dresden. Karl still swears by them even now; you'll hear about them at some point, I guarantee.") But first he had a question : "What're you moaning about ?". "Aeh; just in gen'ral." (At the packing; really quite legitimate !). – All of a surprising sudden, she pulled her torso out of their ‹Hollow Mountain›; turned around and let loose with a morning kiss that set his head wobbling. ("Sensed a deathwish," came the nornic murmur beside me. "Or a libidic=urge ?" I politely reminded her, in the same artificial language. She began to gnaw at her lower lip; was entertaining obvious doubts about her theory.

"Strange dream last night –" Karl slowly commenced, while gawking with visionary discontent across the lawn, ("BERLIN ZOO MIX" Martin had proudly declared yesterday evening : a great rarity of course. "Needs Thomas meal; that's all !" Karl had grumbled) : "toward morning . . . . ." She hooked her fingers into my arm (and did she have a grip ! Even if it was only the left) : "Something to write on –" she hissed, THE CHANCELASS WITH THE IRON FIST; while I tugged my notebook from my hip, and gave it to her. She propped it with her left hand against her breastless bosom and simulstenographed; with enviable ease – even in his best days, Karl could never= ever have spoken that fast, not even if he had done his uttermost; (she'll make a good literati=wife someday). She even found time at one point to let her gaze wander to the top of the left page, where apparently *my* last entry still stood; (let's hope it's not all too – what was that now ? Check later.)

"I'm standin' at home in Pforzheim on that little traffic island – y'know where Pferdner= and Hinterstädter=Strasse come together. Where the trolley stop is." "And the bus stop," Ida said expectantly; "we've both used 'em often enough." / "Yeees – it was a real cloudy day; but some sun. I wanted to take the Dresden=Eula line; 'nd single cars stopped, but none of 'em had a second car attached, 'nd always the same sign on the brow, number ‹8›. The odd thing was that 'nstead of usin' the real tracks comin' from Treuhofen, they were all comin' down Pferdner Strasse, where there aren't any." Ida first nodded to confirm this, but then shook her head. / "Which, y' see, is on my left in my dream; to the east. A coupla insignificant people next to me, although the lady in gray keeps distractin' me with her comments : 'cause I want to board 'em all; but every time either the car's jamm=full, or I end up missin' it." (Here Ida began to smile in indulgent delight.) / "At one point, 'nstead of a single trolley car, a big open automobile appears, a real old-timer, with the roof folded back – your basic hemorrhoid buggy – but once again, so packed that even a coupla young guys 're standin' on the back bumper – seems like it was 2 scrunched up on the left; then a gap; then, 1 on the right. Between 'em was a little open space : 'nd I tried with no success to climb on the rear with 'em." / Obviously THE END. / We stole back. Behind us, though quickly no longer understandable, Ida's voice, like soup with a raw egg added : "But that's really quite simple, Karlykins . . . . ." – –

And sitting on the porch again. With her. (She had briefly pointed & made a plea of her face : ? . I had nodded. Ergo, she had torn out the page. (Upon receipt, quickly compare the note at the top=left – ‹The face wanes, odors wax›. Something disagreeable after all. Her most likely thought, however, was THE FIRST REASONABLE OLD MAN I'VE MET; but ‹old man› all the same. Ah well; I shrugged (but all ‹on the inside› for safety's sake).).) / Really no need to fear then. She was studying those icongrafic lines like a tiger. Her incredible mouth lengthened, improbably, further still to the right and left WRYTHED & LAUGHED; a hem of teeth came into view; she was nodding now, uncanny sway – / – (and was suddenly a child) : "'fonly I had a typewriter !" – she groaned her wish. (That's how They are : either lacking all feeling; or almost crazy with feeling.) "You can write up a clean copy on mine later," I offered : "to be on the safe side – just in case I might get some work done underway – I brought my li'l ol' portable along." "Ohyes," she said, in genuine relief. Folded it once, for hominid noises were encroaching on all sides now; hid the (abstruse ? ; although for years now I'd been too lazy to give great thought to Karl) junk in the wrist of her sleeve. Stood up; stopped to turn at the front door, the figure of new sheet iron, the face of copper; nodded to me, (but I was not about to let her extort any play of my features); and vanished then inside, presumably to some sort of iron-sided=round-headed deputy-housewife=duties AND SWIFTLY DID THEY CLOSE THE DOOR=BEHIND THEM.

V

And veritably flocked in upon me ! / Karl, broadly striped. "What're you shakin' your head at this time ?" he wanted to know. : "Because you look like BROOKLYN=DODGERS." / Then Ida, in her shimmering robe of gray silk, (and I managed the old chivalresque "Ohhh !" this time with such admiration that it extorted a smile of deluded grandeur from her; she simply loved it when a man pined for her in disciplined=hopelessness for decades on end. But also) : "Gloves, Ida ? At the height of summer ?". "Hangnails," she explained; cross at me for the bewilderment I had allowed to creep into my voice. / And finally Martin, all in beige, like trousers like shirt, both cut to the fashion of the reasonable man. We greeted 1 another in silence; (he was the one I liked best). / (Me nimbly johnwards : the gaskets spring leaks, are willy-nilly sneaks. And the old reticent face of the carved hermafroditic head of the portal opening to the can; and the annulet of the tap was smooth to the hand as always : blessed days of youth, when a man still hears voices in the gurgles of the john ! – I believe I am well known both in heaven and hell. And expect no special reception in either.)

Outside again; still entre nous. (‹Miss=Seidel=inside› was sure to be frying eggs, making tea, slicing cake – Ida was purposely not helping. An impulselet called me to lend a hand to the orphanchild, a minority of one, but I doughtily subdued that as well.) / First the mutual plaint of woes, round the circle; (we had not seen 1 another for – welll ? – almost 9 months now). Swiss Cheese ogled us with such subservience OSTRICH BRAIN & NIGHTINGALE TONGUE rustic glowed the toaster=oven. For was that singing beyond the woods ? ‹Units› were apparently trying to stage a maneuver. "Easy to drive the roads to smithereens, hard to come up with the taxes." (Martin; also) : "Yes : every other knife has broken off of late !" (Another deed of the Invisibles; int'resting. But I might have known.) "She doesn't care a whit for Stifter." (Me neither; that only spoke well for her in my opinion.) "Recently we were discussing something. And I finally said : ‹I'll definitely have to run that through my head›. – And she takes my wristwatch from the table, and checks the time !". (Even=I didn't catch on all that quickly. He continued his tale of woe) : "Shortly thereafter, as I was standing there in the john, it struck me." (I'll be damned ! SUBCONSCIOUS DEPICTION : was She ever sharp !). Unfortunately one discerned all too little of it; because she was deft, too. (Would make a good literati=wife someday.)

Chitchat at the breakfast table. / Martin divided his fear into 2 halves (the fear of Her; and the fear of Her pronouncements : and now he could almost bear it), and put away a quite substantial meal. / Karl gorged himself in any case like (yes, like Who?) in person. "My wife hasn't washed her face with soap & water for 20 years," he informed us in midfodder, being a cosmetic ignoramus. And gruffly rebuked Miss Seidel when she had to shove his beloved garden sheers a little to 1 side : "Hey ! – Those are ‹Tools by Kunde› : high-efficiency instruments !"". And immediately explained it all : brass seams, tempered blades – Martin just managed to wrench it from his hand as he was about to demonstrate by snipping off a thick=dry branchlet. / With a flick of her dainty tongue, Ida kissed the sugary glaze from her fingertips. Whereas the Other=Lady was gnashing into plain=hard=rolls with vandallust; apples, too, unpared & unwashed; (and was visibly delighted by our denture-wearing shudders; and no less by our metafyzical ones).

"Had strangely unpleasant ‹visions› again myself last night !" Martin admitted nervously; and (with skittish=saucy gestures of his head in Misseidel's direction; who for her part had tuned her countenance to ‹stony›) : "Don't tell her anything about your dreams. She'll construe some ‹meaning› into them that will set you on your head !". But Ida just gave a maternal smile. "But that's all easy as child's play," she said THESE YOUNG-STERS, "and particularly since men 're put together with such amazing simplicity – one truly doesn't need a doctorate for that; any really intelligent person knows what's what right off. I have just the prettiest example for you, Miss Seidel : tell about the dream you had this morning, Karl." (Strange how I still react to ‹Karl›; even though I write my name with a ‹C›. But to be called CHARON was even more macabre : that probably has cost me quite a lot ! Even though, godknows, I always write it without an ‹h› ! No wonder if a man makes nothing of his life, when his name reminds everyone (including himself) of the ‹ferryman of the dead›. Maybe it would have been best to move to the Orient, where people would think nothing of it AN INDIAN LASS WEARIN' GLASSES can there indeed be Any among Us who would *not* be taken by that ? I looked up, and my eyes met those of Miss Seidel.) For Karl the Gardynere was beginning : "Yes, well I'm standin' in Fortzheim on a little traffic island –". "Could you perhaps stop chewing while you talk?" Martin said testily. And I seconded this, too, (just to annoy him a bit; since I was somewhat annoyed) : "It would make it so much more exciting, Karl=with=a=Kay." He gave us a nasty=bulldog glance; choked down the sweet dumpling of cake stuff; and continued; (just as WE=BEHIND=JASMINE had already heard to our surfeit. With a few things omitted (forgotten ?), however. That furious meowing in the distance ? 'Twas the widowed peahen at the castle, Martin explained.

And Ida played the gentle, indeed indulgent interpreter. Threw her arms back around her light chair, letting her considerable bosom jut out the

more, (in Mockery & Scorn of all bony sorts ‹whom it might concern›). :
"My aunt – who took the place of a mother for me –" (Karl confirmed this;
by biting clear through a piece of apple tort) – "has her birthday today, the
8th. On the other side in the so-called Soviet Zone, near Dresden. And we
were saying yesterday : How nice it would be if – she will be 85 – we could
have driven over for the day." She smiled. Brought her left (plumper) arm
forward and bespooned the hand attached to it & stirred her cup : "The
‹meaning of the dream›, Miss Seidel, is quite manifestly *that* – ?" "Manifestly." She repeated in a flat voice; and Ida gave an ironic shake of her
head, amused by such great dullness of mind – : "Why, that we would have
loved to drive over ! Pff, mygod." she concluded scornfully.

And turned victorious=magnanimous mondaine=coquette LA DAME AUX
CAMÉLIAS : "And here's a kiss for it, Karl." And we, well-trained, risked our
old gag one more time : "Karl with ‹K› or Karl with ‹C› ?". Whereupon she,
as was only proper, voluptuously : "Both !". (Karl got his square on his
gardener's mouth; I a glancing blow from on high, at the left edge of my
widow's peak. And meanwhile my eyes met those of Miss Seidel.) Ida
decorously took her seat again. / Martin made some allusion to a piece of
property he had recently sold in Hamburg; (the fellow had inherited a lousy
quarter of an acre ‹in the heart› of that city, and every 5 years peddled 1000
square yards of it : and lived off the income ! Did He ever.) Karl's eyes
wandered about in that most gaudy bed of cakes. Miss Seidel sent a series
of fleeting glances his way; mulled it over; poured herself some more coffee as well; (at 1 point she slipped a piece of paper from her sleeve, and
read – and the tip of her tongue crept out along the rim of her lower lip, and
rested a while there, musing – leaned back, took a deeper breath, and the
breadth of those shoulders was downright felonious !). I – oh=alas=I; I
decided to pull a disparaging face, and offered emulsifying comments on
all sides.

Ida, duly fatigued after her Great Victory, let her hard-boiled eye saun-
ter o'er Martin's twae acres : now came a broad stretch of lawn, green=
hirsute. Latched on. And her sleepy=mouth remarked : "That thick cop-
per-beech there – such a splendid solitary tree : the trunk so powerful &
red . . . . .". ("Cuckoo !" it began to count, somewhere in some distance :
"Cuckoo : cuckoo : cuckoo.") Interrupted once by Karl's "Ohshaitan !",
(had he burned his tongue ? Or bitten it ?) : "Cuckoo : Cuckoo" – ten in all
DEAREST SWEETEST, JUST ONE MORE ! (But ‹meantimes / tentimes, sad to say !
the tree had borne its bloom & fruit› – and couldn't keep it up any longer.
Goethe, of course, who else CLASSIC FORM APPROACHING.)

(But it did indeed frequently appear in literature as a PHALLIC SYMBOL, the
‹copper beech›. Although the LOVELY GARDENER'S WIFE was happy not to be

counted among Those who knew such things.) : "Let us cut this short." she simply decreed (what a shame; I hadn't caught what that was about just now). "Oh Hail & Dampnation !" Karl cursed, who once again couldn't cope with something somehow. (Meanwhile I was picturing to myself the various ‹professional journals› in which the two of them would soon appear : the feeling of being analyzed was sure to be new to them. – Well, they would never get hold of any of them anyway.)

"I propose : seeing as how it's already eighty-in-the-shade, that we go for a walk. What do y' think, Martin ?". "Glad to, Carl."

And Misseidel quickly carried everything inside. And Karl grumbled approval : NATURE always suited him just fine. And Ida (already sweating & doubting whether she would be able to master the 15 tight=spots in good style, and so spiteful as well) : "Just send her packing, Martin !". In whom egoism and pity were waging a small, indolent battle –; (but as might be predicted, the ahwell=realization won out : that it's all much of a muchness in the end ?). I cleverly sidestepped him; and merely asked if I might be permitted to carry along his good=expensive (and therefore light) binoculars.

vi

It was all magnifi=cent of course !

First, for a few hundred yards, village openings. / Karl, at the sight of the fields : "Here with us in the West, the potato varieties are usually given girls' names; in the GDR, it's birds'." (I'm always glad to hear these things; it's something to take note of : for translations. Trans=Lay.) I turned at once to Miss Seidel, who, flatteringly enough, was walking beside me for the most part : "Potato-leaf juice – extract, that is : is said to have the same effect as henbane." Something for us poor bastards, right : ? (She looked straight at me. And we believed one another a little, 'twould seem ?).

MURM'RINGS : cows, cooling their feet. (1 stood, not far off, pumping water over itself with its head. "Not all that un=intelligent; are they ?" She made a note of it.) / Karl=preceding=us, wearing some sort of CONTI=soles, kept imprinting ‹names› in what without him was the glorious dust of the path. (Cheap stimulants, gratis if possible; sure, it's a problem). / Giant= brushwood piles along the path's edge ? : "The sort of stupidity that goes by the name of ‹peasant cunning›." / Yes, that does exist : fungi on fungi. "Even on dead caterpillars." (Obscenity). She wagged her head all scientific. She accepted both, animal & plant abuse. / Hare droppings rosaried. She permitted me to inform her about said black strings of beads; considered=stared; and then decided : "Looks nice." / "Do you hear that ?" No; (poor hearing, perhaps ?). And so lead her over closer – : ? – : ? ? – : ! ‹Tick : Tick : Tick› : "Storage cells for an electric fence." The early howling heat had already swelled her not unlovely face an even redder hue. / "I find it very congenial that telephone poles are numbered : INDIVIDUALS y' know ?". Saunter=shamble; (those were badly tattered shoes she had on CLODHOPPERS). "NUTMEGS if ‹misused› are also said to cause numbness & babbling; just sleeping in a grove of such will make you dizzy." "Much too expensive," she grunted.

: "Lookathat ! – How romantic. –" – / We had caught up with the Three= Others. Of Whom, Ida stood ponderously pondering the ‹plain› birchwood cross. Karl meanwhile lopped the sere branches from a firlet, (and there it stood now very proper & loop-skirted !). Martin had unobtrusively stepped behind a firthicket, and was administering a prophylactic dose against snake- bite. Of which Karl took advantage (his master-forester's eyes missed absolutely nothing) to demand his portion of the serum – – : "Damn ! Now that's a beverage of veritable hellfire !"; (Karl, with satisfaction. I passed, though not without inner struggle : when it would soon be 85° in the shade ? !). / "Boyscouts." Misseidel, in a flat=disdainful tone to yonder CROSS THE HISTORY OF AN ILLUSION; and I, too, gave a negative tuck to my bit of lipworks : They do indeed stop thinking all too early on. (And they'd lit themselves a ‹campfire› as well; all dandy skills that would stand them in good stead in the military. / "You can't imagine how I've wrangled with my father=in=his=grave because he wouldn't let me learn Russian back then, too." She nodded approval. / Or : "They make it so easy for us to fulminate against the GDR – they literally give prizes for it ! – that a respectable person avoids taking part in it to the extent that's possible. Indeed, is almost tempted to laud this or that praiseworthiness 'cross the border." She nodded approval : "They learn a lot over=there. In some sub- jects." she confirmed.) –

"Well, Who's going to climb up ? !" (The hunting blind.) She was al- ready striding toward the spraddled wooden skeleton, and, without chang- ing her pace, moved up it, not quickly, but ineluctably DIANA OF THE BEARS turning once she arrived up=top (what We were waiting to see, right ?), and static there, gazed for a long time down at us. – Then the other way around. And Karl's eyes stared blankly at the broad (but flat) butt, the gray plan- etary surface that moved slowly through green foliage cirri. And set. / There : a ‹bee hedge›. – The whole blooming field hummed ex=orbitantly CALLUNACALLUNA 100,000 most diligent puritans in the most raging sun A DAY'S WORK BEFORE BREAKFAST : "That's something !". And her face lowered to a dignified AMEN. / A pile of human dung at the side of the path – : "Fieldhand; uncommonly strong" Karl diagnosed. The lizard, nervously pacing back & forth ‹in our immediate vicinity› (strange habit), but He didn't recognize it either : "Lacerta such'n'suchia." And instead, gave us the biogram of the nearby shrub : "The buds taste like capers. The leaves 're good for diarrhea. Good wood for cabinetmakers. There's a variety with white blossoms, too. Turks plant it in their graveyards." / And wander on. (At least I had started clumsily to lift my feet toward me now.)

She had suddenly come to a halt in our (wandering) midst. Lifted her (once again more reddish) face, and nostriled the air – – "Water –." And Martin nodded endorsement : "Ponds just ahead. A couple hundred yards yet."

vii

Rest. On a ground of slanting=brown needles WORSTED HERRINGBONE and relax & enjoy. (The ‹Woodland Breeze› provided an acoustic rinse, the water=bobble below an optical, most ideal vacuity of brain – plus the gurgle, triton=lusty, from yonder drain into the next=adjoining fish pond.) And head nodnodding in ever more delight, look=about. / "Like a little BRANDENBURG LAKE, isn't it ?" (Martin, proud. Something to that.) "But a *very* little one." (Karl). I could only show my content with head & shoulders : for 'twas indeed downright idyllic. Naught but Voss + Louise. (Particularly since Misseidel was sitting beside me. At a little distance, true; but considerably more ‹beside me› in any case, than beside the other Two.)

Below, hidden from the opposite shore by a splendid model of a fir, a veritable Apolla among young trees, (whereas we had a clear view), Ida disrobed, with equal cunning and chastity; we saw naught but DAPHNE opisthe, not for a moment she did neglect a certain ‹decency›; (though the 2 mighty spinal dimples were never lacking either, of course; the same could be said of the globi aft). "Were the earth a ring, you would be its gemstone. Ida." had been Martin's gummy compliment down to her. (More substantial than most of those one normally saw in our epoch's mondaine swimming pools – sunburned, polyribbed stuff; batting their glued-on horsehairy lashes – that beyond doubt !). And so I seconded it : "Were I a bolt of lightning, I would strike only you : Ida." (Though it hadn't come out all that convincing, to be sure : Misseidel=thusly would've int'rested me far more. – I must have automatically glanced her way; for she had apparently noticed, and moved her right shoe (half solace, half surrogate ?) 4 inches closer.) / "Don't *you* know how to *swim* ?" Karl, the allround=idiot, had asked. "Sure." "Well=then ?" "Not today." "Why not ?" (And with *that* the idiot was made visible : she was having her period of course. And Martin's asinine=endless whispers, before the fellow ‹got it›. – Or had his ‹subliminal› disappointment, having beheld the aforesighted planet high on the hunting-blind, been so great ? And at once I caught myself, if I wanted to be honest about it (and I did want to be, fairly often), sensing the same wish : I, too, would not have been averse to gazing 'pon those large-pored parts myself. Although in quite different. : Damn ! was I really so much ‹like› that nitwit ? Now that would be a disgrace. I looked across to her, in search of aide – ? She took an elderly pinecone in her mitt PHALLEN SCALY FRUIT held it insensate (probably just a scepter); and that brought me back to reason.)

Below us, the slow swimmeress IN CONCENTRIC RINGS. Higher=up the fringe of fir, (in which We=Others just sat around.) Way up=high, skiff-shaped clouds. (Hay=days. : What would Conte Fosco be up to in the meantime ?) / And was suddenly all child again – : "There !". – ? – : a goldfish= couple (although as large as smoked herring) slowly pushed ahead through the water. "There's another." Where fresh=green fern mixed with last year's golden (wanted to be on=hand, too). And here we were of divided minds (?) yet again : Karl started babbling fluently about fish hatcheries; Martin, the artsy 1, about "red accents on blue"; (one *can* put it that way. Unfortunately.) What occurred to me (I told her) was : "3 transformed farmers. – Who once upon a time forbade the weary stranger seeking re-freshment to swim in their pond=here. And as punishment – the stranger was some ZEUS or other; what else – were changed along with their wives into goldfish." She had first looked at Karl. Then at that sheik, yon Martin. Now she turned the mars-red globe of her face to me; a pair of rasped vocal chords demanded : "And their names ?" – (*You* aren't going to best me !) : "Hintze. Meyer II. Aitchsingerräderloh." Obligingly. (She pulled out a ‹mental› slip of paper, and made a note of it. But I at once raised my hand palm to her, and shook gaudy eyes : !). She had come to realize it seemed, that I did not do such things to no purpose. Took, therefore, the proffered binox; and sighted in the direction indicated : . . . . . : . . . . .

(It did look wild, enlarged like that. / I had long ago noticed it, en passant : the semicircular sand=wall. The concrete=table in front. (With an iron hoop around it, as if afraid it might fall apart; 1 pipe for a leg). The tiny lunulae=surfaces. And then that sign, jutting on its post

NO FISHING
H. SINGER / RÄDERLOH

I was quick to put the pistol to her gray breast) : "Does it annoy you that much that I saw it first ?" She vigorously opened her large mouth; and slowly revealed the tongue thinking inside; (she was enjoying ‹meeting› this passably intelligent fellow, a pleasure so long denied : ‹Rencontre with tongues; at 4 to 8 inches›.) / Karl & Martin conversing in the background. : "Never let a woman wash your back." Martin, baccalaurian=hyperdoltish : "Why not ?"; (he probably imagined something more in the piquant line, the ignoramus). : "The mondaine claws they've got : they'll scrape your back raw !". – To which Misseidel casually remarked, through the field= glasses : "Sounds about like : having a man shave the nape of your neck." Which silenced Them. (Though one could see the rage of refutation on Karl's face !) / And got up too, after brief savage silence, brutal. Stomped a few treelets farther away, (unmistakably=obviously not far enough). And actually took a leak, the old swine ! (The other Two at least only had to hear & smell it; whereas my kismet, of course, had seated me so that I *saw* it as well : the Pit and the Pendulum THE PENDULOUS LILAC BY LOCH NES.) And the shot of schnapps had a truly infernal stench ! And that's supposed to be ‹erogenous› ? : could make you sick to your stomach ! (There should be apparatuses for minimizing odors. Or maximizing those of flowers, of course. Or of certain spices. – ‹Can patch porc'lain with it› Karl had boasted of those juices erenow !). / If possible, I wanted to apologize for Us; and made inquiries : – – (and clapped my mouth shut again in shame; in any case, She would have to resign herself to people's permitting themselves just about Everything in her=presence. But our eyes had met.) She appeared to have understood the PLEASE escaping from mine, for her lestrygonian mouth smiled. But her – yes, at most I dared call them ‹organs of sight› – shim-mered so blunt & hard that I first furrowed my brow; then lowered it with might & main. Even Martin may have sensed it this time; for he demi-coughed (as Karl loutishly made his way back), and directed a diversionary inquiry her way (it was, by the by, the 1st time that I had ever heard him speak so directly to her) : "What=uh – what do *you* have to say to Ida's INTERPRETATION OF DREAMS this morning ?". Karl, troating a cry of confident victory : "Y' got 'nother swig there, Martin ?"; then, it sounded downright condescending : "Well, miss; what does that dream o' mine mean ?"

At first nothing of her moved. (The worst sign !). Then, after a little while, the pair of lips (and, therefore, 1 invisible tongue as well) : "Your dream expresses a recurrent desire, nurtured in your subconscious, though never realized, to engage your wife's aunt in coitus a tergo."

!

And the reaction was threefold=phenomenal. / I – wellyousee, it was as if *I* had walked into a bright room : the urchin was right ! It all fell together with nary a hole. / Martin, at first desolately shocked. Then amused; (he had a good sense of humor as long as the joke was on someone else); he was starting to giggle with glee. / Then, of course, Karl presented us with an out-and-out ‹picture› : he had been just about to sit back down in ponderous=relief; but now he froze there, sort of clumsily hovering, eyes wide agape and mouth goofily nutcrackering for a while, before he fell on his butt. (Serves y'right, you puppy : caught RED=TAILED, weren't you ? – He searched & searched for words.) / And meanwhile Ida beached down below, full-bodied & good-humored. (Had she got a part in her hair from swimming ? – bygod, that would've looked good on her, too. And went on wiping & broad-rubbing water from her cooled loins.) Next to me, ever & always, leaning back stony gray, trained by her teachers for every wicked-ness, our JUDICATRIX. –

"A tergo ?" Karl bellowed at last; (he still knew that much Latin). And would have gone into a frenzy if he only could. (We, however, were staring at him from every side, all blighted. "Have a swig of raspberry=schnapps," Martin suggested. And the foolish fellow actually took one : oh to be so primitive ! And/or lacking in character; gauche at the very least – or was it perhaps the right thing to do in his situation ?). Ida, below, wrapped more and more concentric cinctures, belts, sashes about her, (as if afraid she might fall apart). : "Get up here, Ida !" Karl began to shout in a vicious=alien voice; from the bevel of his raspberriest aperture (ape=urger up=itcher a=butcher oh what permutations there are !), and was planning to add a good deal more. But She merely reached up her tightly gray-clinging left sleeve and pulled out just a piece of a little folded slip of paper, her eyes always fixed on him – so that's how a non=murderer gazes at her non=victim ! A breeze felt obliged to add a meddling, mollifying gust, (if not to cool, then to warn). Ida sluggily mounted the slope, ‹checked in›, and made general moan. His only sound, the lamenting clamor of his bowels. As a diversion, I told the anecdote (and Martin came to my aide by moving the troops out as well) how a foreigner had once confided to me at a swimming pool : "My fathurr vas a verrry gud=uhm – –" (and had searched for words; shaking his fists at the crawlers there; pressed his hands to his face in desperation : ? :) : "– a verrry gud SWIGGER !". And I, pensively : "Mine too." (For he could swill to shame a silenus; enviable talent.) And further paltry matters.

viii

Our new path was perhaps even more lonely.

Strewn with whitest sand. (At one point ash-gray & powder-fine, too.)

On both sides the walls of immobile=high hatched green. At most a clearing would open up now & then : wee thing, tended by birch nurses. Or
mile-wide meadows. (On such occasions, the air was like liquid glass ! Or
DANZIGER GOLDWASSER – Methought that now, in faith I did, I'd gladly down
a draught, a most great draught of it –). / Our sequence of march kept in
fairly good order this time : up front Karl & Ida; they debated. Then 30
yards of Lüneburg Heath. Then Martin : he bore a switch in 1 hand, and
slowly lashed his fleshy calves with it; (as if to keep from growing weary;
his brow lowered; as drowsing he was dawdling). Then another 10 yards
of paysages. And finally, me & Miss Seidel, staunch & mute, in her gray
CHAIN MAIL, and she missed nothing (She had an ‹eye› like the sum of 1
forester + 1 old constable + 1 mushroomer !).

Flung a brief "Ho !" into the air, bringing me to a halt : ? She held two
branches to 1 side, and peered through the jagged window into the underbrush; (I had just walked a few paces past it; the others, of course, long
before) : ?. A quick look, and I called them all back : "Hey=martin ! – Hello
Ka=arl ! !"; and here they came : Martin, indolent à la grandseigneur; Ida
gaudy=haunched. Karl, (who did not venture to lift his eyes above our
waistlines) stumbling in embarrassment. Took a tumble, almost sending
hat, glasses & dentures flying, (and releasing 1 nervous little fart behind,
puny & short – " 'xcuse me !" he muttered distraught : He wouldn't be
rudifying any orphan lasses from here on out !); cast a glance at the
pumpkin-sized yellow spheroid, which had got caught, about chest=high
above the ground, in a tangle of branches, and immediately pronounced it
(he had indisputable experience with subordinate sprouts of the earth :
gardener's assistants & hired hands & the ladies who help them weed) :
"An inflated – (and hesitated yet again, cathartically minding his manners.
And uttered the crude word apologetically, softly, only to Me & Martin
actually) – "rubber, for crissake ! These yokel=roughnecks can pull off
tricks y' wouldn't believe : can y' imagine the giggles of his amazed
sweet=heart ? !." Martin first thrust his princely lower lip way out – ? : then
gave a few unbiased nods : he had been living ‹in the country› for 20 years
now and TASTES DO VARY – it seemed plausible to him. But She was already
shaking a gainsaying head (just 1 efficient shake; more as if she were shoo-
ing a fly) : "There's a tag hanging on it. A kinda cargo=label." And pushed
her hulky=elphyne way in (saith Gjellerup), all 4 paces. (We=cowards
waited outside. Curious=prurient, as is the wont of cowards.) –

Came back, the thing in her hand; ("Yuck=yuck –" Ida whispered excitedly, as if some thing might be new to her). And held it out to me=alone,
the translator : ? ! – (and did a favor to them all as per protocol – 'zounds &
'sbloods : that actually rhymes ! – and took a fussy seat, as it were (as is the

wont of learned dervishes); laid a conspicuous spectacle=harness round my head; first gave 1 extra, peevish=perusing look on past them=All : ! ; solemnly cleared my throat – of course All theoretice, ‹in reality› I simply stood there, & took a look at it) . . . . . :

‹BALLONWEDSTRUD.

Het kind, wiens ballon de verste reis gemaakt heeft . . . . .› ("German, speak German," Martin advised languidly. And I off-the-cuffed) :

"‹The child whose balloon has traveled farthest will receive 1st prize, a splendid AUTOPED with pneumatic tires.›" (" 't's that ?"; Karl, who had to make up for his base skepticism somehow. / "Ah –" Ida, arm in arm with her CON=DOMINUS; she listened and considered. / Martin, with a satisfied smile, rocked his plump brow : always somethin' in these parts, ain't there ? ! (And, above all, no need to get upset : just like at the Stifter's, huh ?). / Only 1 Rational=Woman : "Where's it from ?". / I gave her a nod of approval, & continued)

: "‹Whoever finds this card is kindly requested to fill in his own address and mail it back. You will receive a memento if your child wins a prize. / The card must, however, be postmarked by 26 July 1961.›" Today was June 8th.

: "TIME OF DAY ?" (for I didn't carry a watch; & She didn't own 1). From 2 sides, Karl & Martin, came the obedient answer : "Round 3 o'clock." : "2 till." She demanded a second time, (more caustic, ‹to even things out› : "Where's it from ? !". – I looked only at Her : after all, I had been dragomanning the whole time ! And she apologized at once by directing her eyes sandypathwards. (Looked very nice. So that's how Middle High Germans apologized. The mouth that divulges nothing will always attract the thoughtful tongue : now wouldn't that tongue make a fine dessert !).

: "‹Balloon released at Vaassen, on 6. 6. '61; by Johann Koetsier, Vaassen, Mersenseweg 17; boy; age 11 years.› – The ‹MEISJE› has been crossed out. – Now We have to write in the time & place it was found; as well as the address of the person who found it - : THE WOMAN WHO FOUND IT !" I corrected myself, significantly, (and gazed at our meisje; She was indeed the most significant among us. Or at least the most efficient TOOLS BY KUNDE hardened for anything). But : "We'll do it with my typewriter, once we're home." / And pilgrimage continued; sequence as above. –

This time We all stopped at once : ! : where 2 sandy paths crossed, a tilted wooden signpost : (the arms hanging low in sorrow; at one time they had been inscribed IN THE KINGDOM OF HANOVER.) But the idiotic part was the wicker chair placed below it ! When, as Martin informed us, it was at least 3 miles to the nearest village. Spooky. / Stand & shake our heads. / With unruffled=long strides, she made for it. Sat down in it; (‹took› her seat;

seized control). Crossed the beknitted columns of her legs; and granted her countless thoughts & impressions an audience, those We hadn't seen (or rather, hadn't had – her face taking on so hard, indeed so disdainful an expression that the wicker chair creaked ! And turned sublimely red & calm again QUEEN O' THE HEATH a kind of decrepit vizier, so near to the throne, I watched Her Majesty's limbs at play, standing somewhat back to 1 side; (my face now suffused with the impenetrable reverent suave muttonheaded expression) as void of every wish as possible.) / Very distant paradiddle of a tractor. Under a fern, something wee & gaudy ? (Ohyes; ‹maneuver=doodles›, disgusting.) Filicales : "To keep love alive, the farmer's wife once secretly sewed fern=spores in the hem of some piece of *HIS* clothing." She gave a folkloric nod. (Only 1.)

But I was still curious as to particulars. : "Tell me – and it goes without saying you're right; 'bout the dream – but . . . . ." She explained it All as we walked on. Likewise pulled the piece of paper from her sleeve; (commended the brown cross-rulings; I, coolly informative : "That's old as Babbage : logarithm tables." She gazed eagerly at me; and was happy to learn that neither Freud nor the anthroposophists had discovered that. : "What I like most is writing with brown on chamois : that's the least strain on the eyes. White on black has much=too=much irradiation for me." And she nodded eagerly : 'd someday. an ideal. Literati=wife.) But here goes :

"The several fat yellow trolley cars – even the big old-fashioned automobile with the folding top – those are the aunt=herself : the trolley number is her birthday; their signs give the destination as the city where she lives, with a lusty addendum. The ‹single› cars, with nothing ‹attached›, tell us, I would bet, that she was ‹unmarried›." / Curious, I ran ahead to Martin, who had, long ago, acted as 1 of the ‹bride's maids› at Karl's wedding : ?. – "Ohyes," he said after giving it some thought : "Her husband died on her – after hardly more than 2=years of marriage; and since then she's been as good as single. Strapping wench by the way : a rear end like a brewery horse :" (his hands depicted it animalistically enough in the summer air. Then it occurred to him that She could doubtless see it; and in fright returned them to his trouser seams.) And, psychoanalytic page, I hurried back with said intelligence; and she added it to her notes, using the sawed-off sur=face of a fencepost, (an elliptic blend of graygreen & blackgray). / "‹If granny had wheels, she'd be an omnibus› came to me. She pursed her rude lips, (and it was a veritable Bismarckian mouth; though most impressive !), and lowered her head in concurrence : it, the adage, could indeed have contributed to the transformation of wish=to image=matter. "Sure. Decisively in fact." Going on : "That's very important, that the first thing Uncle Martin recalled as well was her buttocks –

therefore, without doing violence to the truth, one may –" (if you closed your eyes, you could literally see her writing on said sheffdoovre) – "assume it is indeed especially impressive. So that the wish to climb on, indeed to mount her ‹from the rear› is clear enough. That's the reason for the back ‹bumper› on the car; and the ‹gap›, the same with the ‹open space›."
THE HEMORRHOID BUGGY. "That for Karl the wish remained subliminal can be inferred from the very fact that it is disguised, a masquerade, right ? And that it was never realized is demonstrated by the constant=refrain of ‹occupied, jamm=full, missed›." At first she shook, then nodded her head. / "Isn't the balloon getting smaller & smaller ? !" Sure was; was visibly shrinking; in her hand HE SHRIVELED IN HER HAND. ·

At the simultaneous edge of wood & path : a young (but very tall for her age) birch; so badly hunchbacked that her crown touched the earth ! An impeccable greening semicircle with a radius of 6 yards. I risked it, and touched the arm of the Lady of Thoughtful Gaze with my indexfinger –; – she awakened a little, and made polite=larger eyes : ? – "Would you perhaps be willing to walk through it ? ARC DE TREEUMPH You've earned it." (It must have come out rather affected; for she mustered me.) Then walked through. No : stopped 'neath it ! Turned back, and looked at me. (And only then proceeded.) A little further down the path she reunited with me. (What turns of phrase these were : Her with her ‹doing violence› a while=ago; and here=I=came à la ‹reunite with me› – were we slowly gettin' ‹subliminal› too, maybe ? ! / She cast her piece of paper another glance.)

"Particularly exquisite, the cunning transformations the dream effected in the secondary details : that the whole thing takes places in ‹Farts=heim›. Where ‹Horse› & ‹Behind=stander› streets come together. Deft, too, how the trolley cars don't arrive as usual on their normal marital lines, that is, from ‹True=hofen› : they appear from the ‹left›, representing perhaps the nebulous ‹sinister› sense of things." Me, accommodatingly : "Don't forget the expression ‹left-handed marriage›." (At once and with a masterly degree of delight, she lifted her right indexfinger, and nodded to me in praise; made a note of it, and then continued) : "And also, that this ‹left› in your friend's dream was likewise ‹east›; where, from his point of view, Dresden lay. – The term ‹traffic island› is a way of cloaking what in many respects is the ‹isolated situation› of the GDR." Me, more villainous : "Speaking purely lexically, might it not also conceal the little words ‹terrific I land› ?" "Precisely !" she replied emphatically. And fully diabolical, I now proposed : "‹Traffic island› ? : invert syllables and you have ‹I'll try fick aunt›." She stopped in her tracks, and turned fully to me BROADSIDE – "That's grand –" her face whispered, its ugliness so pure it was beautiful : "Listen – : this will be a classic case ! And of course within the word ‹traffic› there is . . . . . implicit . . . . ." (now she was kneeling in midwoodland-path before a flat stone, and writing; ‹fixed› ‹concealed› ‹cached›).

The gangway below us had unexpectedly become a narrow asphalt ribbon, (our shoes resounding upon it). In the fragrant wake of a hay wagon; (so, near home sweet home). The wee balloon was dreadfully withered now, drooping below the back of her hand; and I was really pretty flabby myself toward the end (There ! Once again : ‹toward the end› ‹flabby› – was Something up with me now ? Better add a few supplemental subtleties; and/or self-evidencies) : "The one ‹woman in gray›, who kept distracting him with her comments, was therefore –". Her broad hand was already pointing ahead, where the Three, their feet drag-flapping now, too (pff we were all in need of training. And, granted, were no longer the youngest, either) were slogging along side by side; to judge by the disgruntled look of her stern IDA'S WIFELY ROBE. / Casting a longer, severe glance my way, (as if I should prepare myself for something : what else might be coming my way ?), she said : "‹Dresden=*Owl*› ! Which, as far as I know, does not exist. : The owl is a bird that seeks its *meat by night* – !"; pleated her mouth like a physician : "I could show you *a great deal more,* too . . . . .". (And as slightly=embarrassed as I truly was, I had to grin covertly : *naturally* you could ‹show me more›, my subconscious child; considerably more. / And grew more downcast; (for peanutty nubbins on pink plates were trying to juggle before my eyes. And bright bast hair=tussocks –) : STOPPIT ! Nothing for me.) The weaseling Bundeswehr jeep came to my aide (with an ‹e›), the switch of its antenna swinging long behind it. : "I can't stand Them." And she nodded with equal coolness; she, too, knew better things to do in life. (The MACK right behind, with a white spitz next to the driver, pleased us both all the more.) / And accurately done, her analysis ! She'll be eminent in her field someday. (That is, if She works hard & lives long enough. Have another talk with Martin later : to keep up His support of Her !).

‹Speak of the devil› – here he came toward us, gesticulations rich in disappointment, genially outraged : "Why're you guys taking off again so soon ? ! Karl claims he's got to be in Pinneberg by this evening." (Aha. – Well, probably the right thing to do.) He pouted his lips to a thick sackful; and pleaded : "At least *you*'re staying on, aren't you. – ?". (She ‹walked at his side›, ‹hands behind her back›, ‹And spoke nary a word› – whoa!, now wasn't that a nice collection of formulae.) Above the woods to our left a mighty ash-gray face appeared THE FIRST CLOUD the erstwhile balloon in her hand looked exactly like Karl's hypothesis; (‹good aft her moon !›).

ix

: "Well, Conte Fosco ?" –

(Me; in Her room. Alone.) / Afternoon sun in heavy web of clouds. And her captured image stirred, and wanted to free itself. ("May I be so free, Doctor Seidel ? !" – 'twas HIGH TIME to depart.)

Raised the hand beside me (‹mine›), in which the little portable hung, up onto the desktop. Brown ribbon. A thin stack of (cheap !) chamois=paper. Twice as much onionskin. (Very little carbon; I wished it could have been more. – Maybe send her a package ?. ?. No; better not; that would only have confused things. And unnecessarily made it that much=more difficult for Her to accept.) / Which I needed to make easier with a brief note in any case. And so insert 1 sheet of $8^1/_2$ x 11 – that way she'd think ‹He's loaded; drop in the bucket for him›. Fits. – Hmyes, but now what ? / : ‹What from your fathers to you came, now fossilize, to make it yours.› Not bad ('cause it's malicious), but too long. And too melodramatic, in the last analysis. / ‹You've earned it› ? Nice & short, true, but too much ‹critique›; to which I wasn't entitled. / ‹GOOD WORK !› : that was it. (But without the shout=mark.) Type

1, 2, 3, 4. Space bar. 1, 2, 3, 4.

And roll it up a little – okay. (And then put the cover on. I didn't even know her first name ! – I've always pictured the ‹aging Goethe› as a queer duck, like Adenauer.)

Waver=linger=dawdle. / ‹Soirée=sowery› : Martin had availed himself of the elegant term, and regretted that he would be ‹alone again› this evening. The nitwit ! / I shifted gears, in my mind, sneerfully, and by way of precaution, back to my own bachelor quarters. My ‹cell› (as the refined types 'mong Us=humans, and their number was legion, would have expressed it. ‹Ex=pressed›, per anum a tergo : "Puh ! How unwhisperably so !› – And it looked about like FINNEGANS WAKE page 182 ff.)

NOT BAD

I gave myself a proper wicked smile. And betook my=self to where Karl's motor was catarrhing & belching. (‹Staying on› would mean that She'd want to pay for this bit of portable right off, the puritaneuse – Have to send her CARLYLE'S CROMWELL ! Besides, almost still a virgin, like all these freudened misses – huh-uh : best thing was to get out in Hamburg.) –

And, spiteful=drossified, stand to 1 side. / Karl asserted that the point of this trip had been a visit to a colleague in Holstein, to study THE EFFECT OF SUNLIGHT ON THE COLORATION OF APPLES : paste 1 stencil onto 1 unripe fruit; and, who woulda thought it, promptly a FEDERAL EAGLE appears 'pon ripening ! (Only a malicious man could entertain objections to that). : "Nono;

We *must* be on our way !". / Martin, gloomily propped on a window=
screen, like a monument to himself, (a pose to which I immediately dis-
allowed him the right : not=you, you !). From the ‹distant› kitchen came
janglings – as if knives were being broken into little pieces ? iron-gray
break – and He, suddenly timorous : "What am I to do ?". "I consider it
worth my while to have made HER acquaintance," I firmly declared. "Sure,
you," he reposted unconvinced; and, more urgently : "Just stay here then :
that way y' can get to know Her *real* well – how 'bout it ? !" I first threw
"Curséd pander !" into his ham'n'eggs face; (thought then, however, of the
typing clatter awaiting him, which would not be at all unbefitting his syba-
ritic lifestyle, either : ante he had no *idea* !). And so I most cheerfully shook
his fattened right hand : "Tak for sidst, Martin. – And treat Her well." / Ida
was already sitting behind the wheel.

While we slowly nosed away, a last look from the window (to the other
side, for safety's sake) – – : and the sun was making a coppery horse under
an elderberry tree ZECHARIA ONE=EIGHT : had we not, this morning, assumed
a comparable pose in the jasmine ? – We were moving faster now. (A different ‹we›.) –

"‹Now adieu, ye goddesses of the fields; now adieu, thou green delight› !". Me; after some time. And Karl, at once nasty=mocking : "Opitz. :
In Adelung." (A practice to which I could have put a stop merely by allud-
ing to ‹Ida's naunte›. But *because* it would have been so very simple. /
Better just close my eyes. And tune to the zero. As'ponadayunderhittler.)

X

AFTER WORD : 17. 10. '61 / In the mail, 'mong other items, 1 package. – : My
name on it somehow more familiar to me than usual ? Until it jogged me,
and I recognized my old portable : Return address ‹A. SEYDEL›, in sham=mé.
(Now I knew the first letter at least. But I had not been prepared for that ‹y›;
I had always imagined Her, I don't know why, with an ‹i› : ANNA AUGUSTA
ADELHEID, ADELAIDE ANGELINA AMALIE: ‹DOTH LIVE MY 'MALE YET ?›).

(Unpacking – – –) –

: in most transparent clear-glass wrap, 2 Dutch dolls ! All in folk cos-
tume, and with veritable wooden clogs ! HE red jacket, SHE sash & lace=
bonnet JONGE + MEISJE. / Plus the letter of the department=store that had
sponsored the competition THANKS . . . A MEMENTO . . . REGARDS and the little
fellow who had let the balloon go had actually won first prize WONDERFUL !
(His ‹Vaassen› by the by was about 3 miles north of Apeldoorn.) / The
couple looked natty from the rear A TERGO, too : her skirt was an artful

patchwork, red middle panel & white side strips; his high-waisted trousers wide & black & multi=folded. THE RED JERKIN. / Nothing else. No matter how thoroughly I searched the packing paper. (And all the rest, too, of course : NOTHING.)

Might have ‹written› of course : then it All would've taken its uncle= like course. ‹Uncleless›. (& Antyless : ‹Torments of Tantylus› : subliminal Karl certainly suffered from those. Without ever knowing; very curious.) / Even a ‹VISIT› was possible; She was sure to be there still. (Pretext : new paper supplies ?) / But ultimately that did seem quite foolish; (as it doubt- less was, too). Better just to take $^1/_4$ tablet of CYCLOPAL, (pills, boli, troches, dredges and pastilles – I had to go to the trouble of learning all=such anti- quated officialese for my imminent translation of JOURNAL OF THE PLAGUE YEAR.)

: ‹Weigh well our fates; speak, which demandeth hotter tears ?› (Weisse in Adelung : my generation.)

And so We'd best let it be.

Dr. Mac Intosh:

‹Piporakemes !›

(The author is a guest=lecturer at one of our universities; a valued essayist in his home country, known and respected here for his study of Benda's (1775–1832; ‹Goethe year›, an easy mnemonic) translation of SHAKESPEARE *– he makes a point of writing that great name in majuscular form : a fine token of a reverence devoutly to be wished but largely abandoned by our ‹angry men›. An expert in his field & a man of candor, he has put his finger on one of the worst festering wounds in the hustle & bustle of German books – a "grim ‹wolf› in our most Abruzzian dens," as he remarked sarcastically upon delivery of his manuscript – and, after due deliberation, We have decided to publish the article entrusted to Us, unabridged & with all names named. Not because the opinion of our editorial staff is 100% identical with that of the author; but rather, because it is to be hoped that the discussion initiated thereby may ultimately result in consequences that prove highly salutary & beneficial for the general state of letters among us. –)*

1

Presumably – no : indubitably – I should have held my peace longer still and continued to collect materials in ‹all patience›; inasmuch, however, as I am unlikely to discover details any more incriminating, even were I to grow as old as Thomas Amory, I have decided here & now, though far from providing a full treatment, to offer a brief sketch of my topic. I would therefore request that my paper be read merely as a prodromus to a planned exhaustive study. (In providing quotations, I have used the American original of WILLIAM FAULKNER's ‹New Orleans Sketches›, 1958; and the – I will not venture to call it corresponding – German book in question, published by Goverts in 1962. / Further, I shall make every attempt faithfully to reproduce fonetically my interlocutor's outrageously curious mode of expression; although this has cost me no little inner struggle, and will make, I grant, utterly unreasonable demands upon my readers – but ‹truth above all›.)

2

Since on principle one ought to give one's adversary every benefit of the doubt in matters that might lead to his exoneration (if not his exculpation), it is therefore not superfluous to mention that the days preceding had been marked by dry & hot weather – I am myself sensible to atmospheric pressures, and therefore also keep both baro= & thermometer on my desk. The sky, then, consisted of white elliptical squama, across which a sun (now questing for a bronzer hue) very slowly proceeded.

(It goes without saying that in preparation I had sought to inform myself about the tenor of the mind (?) I would be dealing with. I therefore conscientiously consulted the excellent new lexicon of authors published by Herder – what a name !; and made further inquiries of that well-known critic & savant of modernish German letters, the acclaimed author of ‹Mankind Unhoused› . . . . . : I wish likewise to note straightaway that the data gained thereby proved unimpeachable : not 1 word too many; though indeed many to little purpose !).

In any case, after a longish odyssey I succeeded in finding the hamlet where the gentleman in question resides at present. (Remarkable for what it reveals of the vox populi, is the dyspeptic information provided by a strewer of Thomas meal when asked about the house by my female companion & driver : "Yup. : Got wunna them=theah in town now too." / The next person grumbled something about the ‹ath'ist›; while metronoming, expressively, with a thumb over her shoulder. / A third person, moreover, raised high the fringed curtains of his eyes, and whispered : "Reg'lah *big* cheese !". – That in order to utter this formidable phrase he had to hold onto our ambassadorial vehicle, as well as bawling ‹hick› between the various syllables, may indicate what ‹weight› ought be given such a statement.) / Stop. / Climb out. (By way of precaution, I left my assistant in the auto for now.)

3

Behind the 6-foot-high fence – heavy link, with 2 ropes of barbwire on top; (and the overgrown arbor vitae hedge besides : typical : never co= operate !) – stood a man with a thin, ghastly=red plastic garden hose in hand, amid a sparse bungle=mowed lawn, (give me Our HAMPTON COURT any day !), spraying a row of little newly planted thujas. (‹occidentalis› ? I would rather not commit myself.) / I first, quite intentionally, stayed behind a spruce; and He, though he must have heard the noise of the approaching auto, did not look around.

(And wait. I had resolved to be icily patient.) –

–. – –. / – – –. – – –. / . –. – :

: He adjusted the nozzle; (one could tell by the change in the swish of the water). / "Damndest thing since Noah joined the navy –", I heard him mutter; (I had of course been told to be prepared for blasfemies). / Obviously suffering from crepitations; (that is, if it was not a malicious token of contempt, though this is not the place to resolve that issue – the question being so clouded that even=I am irresolute in my verdict every time I consider it anew. He laid his head on his left shoulder, and appeared to hark to the mefitic tones –) "Whole flatland's snorin' –" he ventured laconically. And a pause. And more aqueous whispers. / Then, when 1 distant birdcall broke his silence, – : "Ere song or mumble ever were, the cuckoo was Caruso." (Nice maxims ! But I am acting purely as a reporter here. 'Twas time, I thought, to step forward.) –

– : "Dr. Mac Intosh." –

(He had in fact flinched : had he perhaps *not* assumed our auto pertained to him after all ?). Took my measure, sulky & foxy; (and in his glazzy eye there was something *else* that would soon make itself evident). He pondered. Then he said, equally cumbrous and impertinent – (and that was the mixture that characterized our entire conversation : the way every now & then a look of overwhelming wiliness appeared in his murky eye !) – "Mmyess. – Not everybody can have Schmidt for a moniker." He squirted; while looking blatantly away, as if hoping I would withdraw forthwith. And, amidst downright hunnish importunities, tugged the hose one length farther across his self-made world. (And the sprayed foliage rustled like the pages of bad, experimental novellas !).

"I have come to talk with you about your translation of FAULKNER –"; but at once he, rudely, interrupted me. : "Nah." he said. Made a trapezoid mouth & aimed. (Peered wickedly around 1 corner of his glasses : ?). "Wouldn't y' know, Willyemm Forkner –" I heard him growl; (poor pronunciation : that rounds out the picture decisively).

: "Might I come nearer perhaps ? –" I essayed, to help him along. "Nah." he said, and shook his head. / : "Do you know that you're being impolite ?" – : " 's=it any politer t' come burstin' in here like an assault troop ?". / "Your great GOETHE once . . . . ."; but he interrupted me again. " 'm an author m'self." he said to snub me; (& jehovial grins & slovenly oyeglances – so the megalomania was showing, aha.)

"I have done several studies of German translations of our important Anglo-Saxon authors," I began again with some restraint; "here, for example, my book on Benda's rendering of SHAKESPEARE . . ." – (I held the handsome linen volume out to him, between barbed strands & linkwire; he

gazed at it a longish while, but with his eyes closed the whole time). /
"Benda –" he then said, musing; "old stock –". And said not another word;
and sprayed. / : "I was hoping to write a piece about your FAULKNER=
translation . . . !" He gave an impartial shrug. And sprayed.

: "Are you actually listening ? !" I, more sharply now. / And he, after
some serious consideration – : "I always listen with jist haff an ear." –

: "Might I begin with the title ? – You have omitted the ‹SKETCHES›. :
Why ? !". / He looked at me, comparable with the same astonishment a man
might show when advising a mason about the repairs to his chimney and
the latter were suddenly to use the word ‹levitation›. "Honest Injun ?" he
asked suspiciously; (I did not know, quite rightly, what he meant !). "Have
y' ever met 'n editor, or a publisher – or a ree=viewer – who didn't know
ev'rything better than you=y'self ?". He; I waited circumspectly; (he was
obviously thawing outer). Pulled a flask his from rear=pocket, (2 jills,
'proximately); gave the cork a vulgar rub till it whistled; gave me a mean-
ingful look from across its glassy orifice, and ejaculated

: "LONG LIVE THE RAPACKI=PLAN !"
(I said nothing, naturally : wind-bagging that bagged nothing for anyone ! /
Whether he had too much proof, I cannot venture to say; you never can
figure that out with practiced drinkers; he asked slyly : " 've y' ever written
'nything yourself ?". "An epic poem, with MOSES as the hero." : "Moses ! ?"
he replied with an unseemly whinny, and sprayed in wider arcs. – *How*
had that gone ? : ‹There is no end to the wealth of his abuse : repetitive
plethora›; *every word* of it true !).

"*I* woulda – bein' an old great here'n'nower," he interjected, "suggested
a totally diff'rent title." "And what would that have been ?". – ‹OUT OF
NAZARETH› he quoted with relish; and looked, at an angle of 45°, into the
tepid cloudworks; (as if somehow then one's gaze penetrates farthest !).
I gave him something to think about : "Might it not be possible that
many people – and not the worst ! – would have been offended by such a
profanation of all that's holy ?". – His face wrenched most singularly !
Struggle arose within; he strove with his entire body. "Now listen here –",
he gasped . . . . . : – ! ! ! (and sneezed ? ! ! ! – in all my life, even at Oxfart,
I've never given ear to the like !). "Did y' hear that echo ? From off the
walla the p'tato=shed ?" he asked, proud & ex=hausted. "I would have had
to be deaf." I replied in disgust.

(But be magnanimous, and give him a chance to blaspheme to his heart's
content) : "Wouldn't that have sounded all too questionn=airish, this ‹OUT
OF NAZARETH› of yours ?" I offered for his consideration. He arched approbatory brows, and nodded his interest, several times. : "Just pickcher
it : a questionnaire; filled out in Benn Pandera's very=own=hand ! : Offer it

to CHRISTIE'S – ?...". He absolutely beamed with odious elation : "A man'd never have t' do another licka work ...". His voice slurred over; he aimed for a sprucelet, under its green jagged skirt, and sent it bending backwards in embarrassed surprise; (Motifs like those of Félicien Rops : the foolish Vice=Heathen ! Let's get back to the topic, and quick.) : "So that the title, let it be recorded, does *not* come from you – nor is it to your taste ... ?". He offered no response to this point. (I gave my notes a brief glance –, – ah yes.)

: "It most assuredly filled you with great pride that you were entrusted with translating a book by a Nobel Prize-winner, and I can well imagine – –"; I interrupted myself all on my own; for he was looking about with *such* a face, upon which much was afoot. "Don't lay it on too thick;" he said disparagingly : "I didn't have all that much use f' Forkner b'fore; but after translatin' him, I can't stomick him period." (I truly was not prepared for *this* !) : "Are you trying to tell me ... ?" He nodded. : "Precisely." he said; took up a few yards of hose, moving the same distance toward me, and spotted our ambassadorial vehicle. "Hey, 's that *your* neckmobile ?" he inquired with mistrust; and, more indignant : "There's somebody *else* sittin' in there, too !" / (Seasoned by now, I had almost recovered; just by way of precaution, however, I let my eyes wander a bit, until I regained total control – – : "What y' oglin' my larches for ? !" was his interposed caustic question – – Keep calm; just keep calm.) "If you're not *fond* of Faulkner : why did you accept the job ?". He stared at me open-mouthed for a moment; then began to smile, and shook his head in languid=amuse-ment (And with a hat size well over $7^1/_2$, I would guess; well it could be water, too). " 've you got your head that far up in the clouds ?" he asked, with unfeigned glee : "For the cash, o'course ! *And* the publicity. – D'y' think I did it for love o' the science ?". "So, purely out of ice-cold calcula-tion then ? !"; I, outraged. And he, nodding congenially : "Ice-cold cal=Q= lation."

"Are you not fond of Faulkner in general; or is it only this 1 book in particular ?". "Not 'n gen'rull. And in p'ticular def'nitely not." (I hooked both hands in his linkwire, (‹held onto me›). And an absurd situation, actu-ally unseemly, this disordered conversation absent every basis, ‹behind bars› – I persevered only for the sake of the subject.) "*Why* don't you like the ‹New Orleans Sketches› under discussion here ?" : "Cause the *tone* is so false !" he shouted rudely; "cause almost ev'ry single piece is sentimen-tal & meretricious ! ‹Poor nigger looks for local ferry to Af'ica› : that's where we get our nigh=eve ideas of colored folk as lovable ‹big kids› : We'll all be makin' bugeyes 1 a these days ! – There was 'n Arab here not long ago, he just about went berserk when I made the mistake o' quotin'

him lines from Rückert's ‹Man in Syrian Land› : Damned dirty trick, 'nd
his native land of all places; to hell with Hariri; 'nd then a lotta stuff in
Arabic. So we just whiskt him off to the swimmin' pool, so he could get a
dose of his normal harem fantasies – wrong again : the fella was gay as
Winnetou ! Until fin'ly a teacher arrived with a classroomfulla boys, 'nd
that satisfied him. Kept goin' ‹Mash Allah›, 'nd there was no gettin' him
away from that pool – quite a crazy scene, Him standing there like that :
motionless, arms crosst at his chest, short full beard; his dark cape
billowin' so slowly b'hind him it lookt like Somebody was already doin'
the job – 'nd all we could think of was more Rückert. – But they had some
classy ice cream there; I s'pose I tuckt away haffa dozen servin's easy myself; musta lookt pretty weird t' the waiter –" at which point I interrupted; I
was not of a mind to let him slip through my fingers. "Inasmuch as you
found the ‹tone› of the book, as you chose to put it, so repugnant : did you
not entertain doubts of capturing it faithfully ?". He gave a nonchalant
wave of his free left hand : "For me it's about like ventriloquism. All the
same I was glad t' put the whole inflated & bloated caboodle b'hind me."
"But you don't reject *all* the pieces in the collection ? – You used the word
‹almost› a while ago." – "I dunno why I'm botherin' to respond t' your
questions," he said, disgruntled; "Haven't 'xactly ‹taken a shine› t' you. –
Aeh, two of 'em, maybe." : "Which two ?"

He clamped the hose between his legs, greasy, medium-brown
Manchester goods, (and it looked truly opprobrious, the way it protruded
from him, long & monkey=thin, and let water like mad – good thing Miss
Whytefoot had stayed in the auto; it almost gagged me ! – on the other hand
it was very like a nightmare, filled with eternal foreboding, where one cannot see enough. (And whisper that eternal foreboding now : ‹Take up the
White Man's burden, / send forth the best you breed; / go bind your sons to
exile / to serve your captive's need; / to wait in heavy harness / on fluttered
folk & wild, / your new=caught, sullen peoples, / half devil & half child.›
Yesyes.) *Now I knew* why as a matter of principle, our peers, our Grand Old
Men, spoke among themselves, even yet, of ‹huns› : "A German !".) I must
have involuntarily let it slip sotto voce; for he gave a despondent nod. But
then I understood as well – : He had merely wanted to free his hands ! (Yes,
but then he could just as easily have . . . . . laid it in the grass; or given it to
me to hold ?). At any rate the flask had now reappeared twixt his fingers; he
fumbled. ‹A German› he repeated after me : "A ‹germ› man : Saynt
Appun=Olius !". "Which two ? !" I; and fixed my gaze on him, (‹in patience to abide› –). He already had the tip of the flask well into his mouth,
but he pulled it out again, and inquired in a feeble=sullen voice : " 'f I tell
you – : will y' go away ?". "I shall remain as long as the topic demands."

I replied sternly. He drank. / "A man with emission –" he said scornfully; and : "The next thing I'm gonna do is p'tition the local c'mmissioner : t' let me lay a minefield round my place." He drank. / "Well the 1 piece about the LIAR. 'nd then maybe CHEST. – Not that it's all *that* illustrious, either." He held out the flask at an angle, and suspiciously eyed the wee=slant of the liquid's level, (which, touching to observe, attempted in vain to adjust itself to the horizontal in his trembling potatory hand); shoved it back into his hip, and swung his left leg backward over the hose. And as he did, apparently noted my restrained=outraged face; broke into a grin and nodded to me : "Walter=Scottian char'ckters," he said : "You prob'ly consider y'self the flowera knighthood ? Me too." He gave the local firmament another grimace, but abruptly turned more earnest when he spotted all those cewmewli=buds; scratched his cheek indecisively : "If I knew f' sure that an imminent visitation awaits my impluvium t'day yet . . . . ." and in doubt & disgust shifted his gaze back & forth between the airy messengers of foul weather and his garden hose, (which, with the typical ingenuity of the drunkard, he was still able to aim with tolerable precision. He set his foot more violently upon it; and at once the syringes quavered).

"On page 195 of the American original –" I began anew – his face darkened; he repaired somewhat deeper into the yard : "Alright; now you'll have t' talk louder." he remarked sardonically. – "– it is said of an automobile that ‹she was only doing sixty=six›; which you have chosen to render as ‹Sir Car was disposed to no more than 110› : might I ask –" (and from here on with cutting irony, ‹watch sloth & heathen folly !›) – "why you uhm=chose to replace the simple ‹she› with ‹Sir Car . . . . . ?" "Aeh, that's easy 'nuff," he said ingenuously; and proceeded to lift his eyes in visionary fashion to the wide waving fields of rye, above which pollen rose, a veritable smoking foundry. "Fumes of smelter skelter –" I heard him mutter, to my surprise, (would never & ever have thought that he might perceive such subtle subtleties); also "7 oak=ages long –" came trailing after; (which had nothing whatever to do with our addressing the tasks of our present situation – at least *I* could recognize no nexus.*).

: "We're sittin' there, in the settlin' dusk, with an acquaint'nts – he's got a car : *I* don't even know how t' drive" he interjected with regret : "I go

---

*) I have since determined that these two expressions occur in sudden proximity in ‹Invisible Maid› – said gentleman's latest, notorious work – in the way of a describing an evening sky. (Upon this occasion, I did not, however, hear the words appended thereafter in the text – ‹Nihilnull. All we need now is an angelanglo.›; given the author's certifiable tendency to run amok when free-associating, the genesis of such an addendum would be difficult if not impossible to establish.)

back to pre-electric days, when men shaved with knives – in the ‹Han-
niball›, a café in Weyhausn. The wives 'd come along : mine 'd held a
ladybug on 'er finger for a long time, quite an amazin' sight !". He sprayed
& mused. / "And so it was slowly growing dark –" I gently nudged. But
he gave a staid shake of his head : "Nope," he said; "it was the heighta
summer, when it never gets all that really dark; ‹subfuscous› I'd call it. –
The waiter comes out, cantin' heavily from mindin' all his p's & q's;
adds wrong : eats some 'umble pie for us; recalculates, 'nd comes up with
an even *higher* bill. The John Darm – who lives in the same building –
comes marchin' in 'nd arrests some guy; the sorta drifter y' can find in
all Mary=Dianes : completely crocked – really dreadful, ain't it, when
people booze like that ?" he added slyly. I just fixed my eyes on him,
earnest & stern; and he gave me a depraved wink. But suddenly turned
mistrustful, too : "Y' sure your name's not Hintzemeyer ?" he inquired :
"Y' swear you're Mack Whatsits ? – Y' see, I recently met a fella who was
xactly like you." I looked right back, unblinking. "Ohwell, s'pose it's
possible," he said (and it sounded almost like an apology); "but 'n case y'
just might be Hintzemeyer in disguise . . . . ." "So you were sitting in a
café somewhere and=uh – ?" "– and drinkin'=uh cake." he voluntarily finished my sentence for me. Considered. Then, flatly : "Nah; the tramp'd
already set 'mself down. – All mellow & tells us : how at one time, or so he
claimed, he was on the ‹Emden›, 'nd knew an ad miral ‹Tirrpitz›. And
acourse starts bendin' my friend's ear, allà ‹Gimme two bits !›; 'nd when
He doesn't give him anything, he curses our car : how it'd end up in the
junkyard, an object of wonder & razzberries ! Then the cop collars him;
they practic'ly fall into the flowerboxes at the window. So we get aboard,
too."

(His blather was slowly getting to be too much) : "And so that is your
‹Sir Car› ?". He lifted a hand in protest : "Not yet." he said; conceding :
"was 'n Opull Captain acourse. No matter what, it woulda been a bad &
sandy road, quite an unreasonable hike on foot – which edimal logickly
comes from ‹ratio› – but that was morer less present; 'nd the nine miles o'
woods were rustlin' ever so attractively : ‹The Unmaskin' o' the Woods›."
(‹The unmasking of a poor translator› ! But he was obviously sunk deep in
memories; and I let him have his head now : Who knows, what useful materials might yet result, though all=involuntary on his part : just spray
away.) : "So he takes the wheel; 'nd We climb aboard : an old fox & a big,
heavy car, what's the chance of anything much happ'ning, we thought ? –
'nd so up the sandy road !".

"First came a house : small, plank siding; very isolated; scratchy firs
allround : a sweet young thing sittin' at the door. 'bout thirtteen – just the

age when the beasts turn coquette, right ? – skin yellow as straw; wearin'
not quite a beekeenee; stares stonily our way; 'nd then paints a circle in the
dust on her belly, right round her nav'l. Her head trimmed with sorta long
brownish hair : natur'ly we pulled to a stop. – Round the corner a fire-blue
bakelite bucket. But otherwise, nothin' 'cept that endless plantin' o' firs,
'bout man=high; 'nd threat'nin' intch by intch t' become even *more* endless. / A steady ‹Ping=Ping=Ping› comin' from inside the house; 'nd the
kid notices we're list'nin'; tells her belly : ‹Pappa's a goldsmith.› 'nd starts
drawin' a line cross the circle. Lifts her head, stares right at us, 'nd adds a
vertical : ‹And a Sweed'n=borgian.› – Let me tell y', that bowled us over !
Doll Tearsheet, right b'fore the Phall."

   "In the middla bein' so bowled over, here the old man comes boltin' out,
'nd he looks like Dapsul von Zabelthau, too : holdin' a teeny=weeny droll
hammer in his hand – int'resting : I can stand there lookin' for hours ! –
That is t' say, natur'ly not ‹for hours›," he confessed; (although my indignant stare had more to do with his dissolute manner of reporting than his
exaggerated particulars as to time). : "The way his gray arms rose from his
body once he learned where it was We were headed ! ‹Don't go !› his face
kept shoutin' : ‹Don't go; there's somethin' horrible in the woods=t'day : I
am a Swedenborgian !›. ‹That's no news t' us,› I say; and my friend adds
some spare answer or other – I don't recall what 'xactly, 'scapes me now. –
I woulda loved t' talk with him a little, cause I'm missin' a bona fide
Swedenborgian in my collection; they know the most curious verbal
dingdongs, ‹Xaldnipter› 'nd the like, hm hm hm."

   All of a sudden he cast me a searching look. : " 're you the Guy who
always signs his articles in the Frankfurter with ‹zoroaster›, maybe ? No ?
Y' sure you're not ? – 't's funny." he added, brooding. Shuffled off dragging another length of hose; I followed in dogged pursuit, around the corner of the yard; (and stood there now on a very narrow, totally overgrown
strip, wedged between a softly rustling wall of stiff blue-green stalks, taller
than myself, and that ridiculous fence; the brutal Vandal up ahead : what *a
situation* ! ! – ‹Wigalois› came to mind automatically, aventiure ix : He
stands there much the same way, amid the spiky circle of mace & sword,
and behind him the ironwall of fog ! (The deceptive pale moonshine there
matched the elflocked hokum here : ‹Rural Hours› is their name for it I
suppose !). – "Nix Zoroaster : nix Hintzemeyer –" I heard him recapitulate
under his breath : at noon today I would have thrown down the gauntlet to
Anyone presuming to connect those two names, and associate me with
them besides ! A groan wrenched from my breast, whether I would or no.)
I tendered : "But now you drive off into the woods : please go on !". He at
once gave me a laudatory nod.

"Happy to;" he said. "Granted, the gray fella shouted his warning after us : that the moon was about t' rise – but that was more a bonus for us, wouldn't y' say ?" (I hastily confirmed this with head & hands, merely to urge him on to a more spirited narrative.) "My friend gives another glants at the gass=gaydge – nine miles 'nd nary a house is no mean thing – I even remark about the stayta the tires; but he dismisses it energetickly : ‹Nah› he says : ‹Not for Sweed'nburg : Piporakemes.›. Steps on the gas, as once Odd is Zeus at Bully Fame – and into the mix of gloom & green : in the nama the fetter, the sol and the hollichrost !". "You can leave the inscrutabilities out of your disreputable word=play !" I decreed. He bowed & scraped, tipsy & polite outa spite; turned more serious, and tentatively inquired : "Don't y' think maybe it could be *just* the methud t' get a little closer t' the inscrewtabilities ? No ? Y' sure not ? – Wellthen, not." he said resignedly. " 'tanyrate the wagon=trax 're gettin' more'n'more rutted. The Capt'n weighed in heavier & deeper – like sittin' in sea=swells – behind us, our wives' faces start exchangin' whispers. Alleva sudden my friend pulls to a stop, 'nd brakes into curses. – I'd just turned round t' look at a pretty= strappin' birch," the lecher added, with unnecessary intimacy, " 'nd hadn't the 1st clue ‹why› ? But We All climb out, 'nd stand there at a – hmyes, wasn't a mere ‹crossroads›; was a downrite ‹multupull in'ersexion› ! I don't wanna 'xaggerate, but about 6, 7 roads diverged from the green- sward. T' 1 side there's 1 helluva boulder. We're curious, acourse, 'nd walk over. Shrubs b'side it –" (he gave me a glassy 1ce=over) – "almost as tall as U=ther; specially the nettles. But charlock, too. And on 1 side there's a . . . . ." (he bent forward a bit, pondering. (And came close to wetting my whistle ! "'sxoozme –" he muttered.) Then) : "‹Here lies –" he broke off again, and made a carplike mouth. " 'm not gonna lie," he said with hesitation. Resolute : "Nope, no way : nothin' 'bout ‹with GOd›. – " 'tanyrate ‹Head Forester of & for. In the midst of woodlands he created.› And then came –" (he lifted his besmirched indexfinger pregnantly) : "shot dead by wicked poachers, on the evening of the such'n'suchth› : 'nd it was 'nfact *the very day* We'd stoppt there ! – I look around, so that's how it thumps & gambulls in moribundom. And had to grab my friend's arm : there, rite in the dead center of a glade, a red besotted face, with a black ear flap : lookt like 3 Communists ! – The moon natur'ly," he added to mollify me; "but all the same. And starts in cursin', too, my friend does, ‹'zounds pollards & saplings !›. I don't wanna be left b'hind, and say : ‹Oh LOrd o' Hogsheads !›. 'nd so there we stand; and really haven't any notion whitcha the superabundant non=hi=ways t' follow; our map wasn't all *that* good. – But I don't wanna hear 1 word 'gainst the Shell=Atlass !" he interjected, inanely punctiliousness, at this point.

"Which brings me t' your question," he said amiably. "We betake ourselves back along the 20 yardsa thick greencheckt twilite, 'nd climb in. First the ladies – whose faces 're wax=cake pale from all the 'lumination; with a dark fringe attacht uptop : Each gives His a passifyin' kiss –" (he smacked with savage onomatopoeia, musketshot of air : ‹Pff !›) – "with *me* last. And then, before sittin' m'self down, I say to my friend : ‹Okay›, I say & I point : ‹drive down thataway. But be careful : give Sir Car his head a little.›".

Fell silent. And measured me, puffed up & princely, à la ‹Never woulda thunk it, wouldya !›. / "And on the basis of this – I shall be accommodating : ‹experience› – *you* have taken the liberty when translating mankind's greatest living author – – !". "Justaseck !" he said threateningly, (and his spurt sizzled in the grain right beside me; I neither dodged nor ducked !) : "We're just chewin' the rag 'bout Forkner. – Y' needn't worry –" he calmed me : "I won't hit y' : it'd be much too great a waste o' my water." Made a quick grope up front, for the brass nozzle; and now it sprayed fine & gentle across the elderberries.

"Dontcha wanna hear 'ny more, how it ended ?" he asked, disgruntled : "How we got lost, as was t' be expected; nothin' but bucks & owls ? Alleva sudden we're at a pond ! Very black sloppy water; the trees standin' moon-rotted allround; on the far side the drain's gurglin' –" (all slack=closed eye, he immediately imitated this with his mouth : "Bubbubbubbubbu . . ." – Lunacy ! A netherworld, it was; inverted & heinous !) : "And our wives simply went crazy : ‹We wanna swim !›. Un=dress; slip into the water, in bras & panties; 'nd swim figures of 8 round 1 another. My friend starts in, too, fumblin' at his pants, 'nd steps b'hind a bush. : ‹My bladder's very words›, I respond, polite as always –" (he shot me an uncertain glance; and I nodded to him, grim & uncompliant : !) – "go & do likewise. And when we get back, standin' there, with as good as nary a thought, oglin' our Undines : alleva sudden 6 shots ring out : ! ! : ! ! ! ! – P'r'aps they thought we were ‹wild=dux›, ?, can't say t' this day. 'tanyrate we start in screechin', a/o bleatin'. They come scramblin' out. We stuff 'em into the car, just as they are, soppin' wet & stark naked –" (he slowly wiped the rim of his (definitely hootchodorous) mouth with the tip of his tongue. / ‹Pornografy› ! : I've got your number, you ! / One has but rightly to picture that : shoving=pressing=stuffing 2 dripping defenseless women, only in their brassieres, into a nocturnal automobile ! And a man like=that may very well – I had heard such from the grapevine – translate the Brontës' ‹Angria›, a Brontë=saurus : it *dare* not happen ! Publishers of the world unite ! / He, lost in thought) :

"We trundle along; 'nd brace ourselves mentally for havin' t' spend the night in the car –" (at this point a near=distant call interrupted us. – : "Black & White & Mul & Min !". My godfather – what did *that* mean now ? He, too, hearkened to it, obviously troubled; and spoke more hastily) – : " 'nd then I see a light, a little t' the right uppahead. ‹And though you offer me the foreskins of 100 reviewers,› I say : ‹we're makin' straight for it !›. Reluctantly, he lets the motor rumble a bit, ‹twixt 2 mountains a bear doth grumble› – lemme tell y', the things he can do with that Cap'n ! He can literally make it speak; it's p'fectly clear what he's thinkin' – but steers in that direction. It takes a while; but at last we pull up before somethin' decorous=wroughtirony. : Two guys in uniform come stormin' out !". (He meant, as was immediately & incontestably apparent, in ‹livery›; once more signifying the inadequacies of his vocabulary by having to call upon excessive gesticulese). "With hurricane lamps in their hands. Keep bowin' in fronta me –" (he once again made his meaning patently clear even as he spoke, pulling courtly grimaces) – "'nd said ‹your Serene Highness›; and another ‹serene Highness›. 'nd *even I* was startin' t' feel all princely, as if I'm gonna have t' bite Some=body's head off any minute now. But acoarse as a respectubble proletaryan I get a holda myself : ‹Gentlemen; you're in error.› Give my friend a signal t' fork up a cigarette – I don't smoke – 'nd He swears softly; but holds one up t' the window. I take it, 'nd hand it on. 'nd he lights it rite there on his semi-lantern – the things're open at the top, y' know ? – 'nd while he exhales our smoke, he remarks t' the other guy : ‹Ain't him this time either.› So He comes over our way, too; 'nd, let me tell y', He has a beard like the king of New=Zembla, endin' –" (he held his free left hand halfway up his chest) – "in two spikes, 1 right & 1 left; so that I automatickly bob a little bow 'nd say : ‹GOd preserve Franz our Kaiser.› I can hear my friend shakin' his head in the car –". : "How could you *hear* that ? !" I interrupted in desperation; "And probably couldn't see all that well either : surely it had turned rather dark by then !". "Y' can hear it with him," he replied candidly : "there's a crackin' in his neck whenever he moves his head real hard – but it's nothin' serious, the doctor said. – 'tanyrate, he volunteers up another cig, 'nd I hand it onto Hairy, 'nd He takes it, too; tucks it in somewhere, 'nd then starts takin' aim with his lily o' light : 'nd only then could y' see *how soused* he was ! Focuses, & lurches; 'nd promptly has half his face stuck in the top of it, 'nd it stinks like burnt hair ! : ‹Sonarumbeetch –›› was his affable comment; meanin' he's from East Prussia; 'nd after we – me & the other lackey – recovered from our laughin' fit, we pull him back, 1 on each sida his beard; 'nd he sets fire to his L & M, 'nd puffs happily away. Ahead of us, way uppin the air, there's a sound like chains startin' t' rattle, seems a clock is preparin' t' strike : 'nd the two=guys flap their arms 'nd shout ‹cuckoo› right along with it – real malevolently, y' know ? ; ‹four for the quarters & twelve for the hour› : ‹Cuckoo ! : Cuckoo !› – Worsen 'mong the Nopanders ! Well, outa courtesy I flutter my hands a little, 'nd add my own ‹cuckoo›; 'nd then start in with : ‹We'd 'preciate knowin' which passable road 'd take us t' Haidkrug –". Then I hear, more, even *heavier* footsteps; 'nd here comes a typicull housekeeper headin' our way, 1 a your real viragoes : two'nhalf hundredweight, blackgray brissles under her nose, 300=watt=eyes. And my friend – who's got a real weakness for the type; purely plattonick acoarse, but he's completely unint'rested in women under fifty – does a swan=neck out the window, performin' a regular tongue=show, 'nd's about t' say somethin'. But she's already bellowin' : ‹Get outa here ! I been watchin' you ! These flunkies don't do a lick moren what they have to : you're on the state=assemblyman's prop'ty !›. – Woulda made quite a scene for an impartial observer." Head=shaking & laughing, he bit his lower lip, and set his hydrocephalic skull swaying for a good while. "Are you=uhm – a Communist ?" I asked, as casual=businesslike as possible, about which fact my informants had provided a plethora of hints. He shoved his lower lip out far beyond what I would have thought anatomically possible. : "*Not yet.*" he said calmly; and also added gloomily : "To communists a socialist, to socialists a communist." Strode musing, ‹To Guelfs a Ghibelline›, over to the nearest clover=patch; (and I right behind, in shameful=parallel, along the fence – degrading !).

"I would love to have a look at the reference library you use for your translations. – : Might I come in *now* ? !" I asked testily. "Noo !", he reposted crudely, pulled the flask from his trouser pouch for the last time : "I'm too great a man t' have any other drinkin' companions besides the Pherkadan –" he explained; then, menacing : "Your cup's about t' run over, too." "And *yours* will soon be empty," I countered fearlessly, pointing to his flagonette. "Not bad," he paid me coldblooded tribute; lifted the container to his mouth of depravity, hectically gulped the rest down and burped. Then : "Whaddya mean ‹liebrary› ? : My ol' Muret=Sanders; a trained slater doesn't need 'ny moren that." "*Not* your=own brandnew, *extra* large Langenscheidt ?" I asked scornfully. But he denied it with dignity : "I compared the letters A to K once & counted it up," he said placidly, " 'nd even figurin' magnanimously, the verbal substunts of the old edition 's about 11 to 7 compared t' the new. – Natur'ly I've got the new 1 *as well*."; (but gave the standard work yet another shrug). "And nothing else ?" (I, boring slyly; after all, I needed evidence to hang him) : "No Webster ?". " 've got two=Websters – three 'n fackt : 1 from 1854 – for Cooper, of whom I'm a lot fonder than I am of your Forkner; at least as far's translatin' goes – 'nd the latest from '61, too." disgusted : "But they're all useless ! Nono : praise be t' my ol' Muret=Sanders." / "Do you own any dictionaries of the German language ?". (At this point we were interrupted; the invisible voice called in an even, cuckoo-clock tact : "Blanca : Silverbeard ! – : Blanca : Silverbeard !" –). He shook his head to ease my mind : "She doesn't mean us," he said mysteriously : "not *yet*." Turned his torso on shaky legs, and roared obediently across the lot : "Not hee=ere ! !". Then turned back to me : " 've got an Adelung," he said cantankerously : " 'nything else ? !". – "‹Adelung› –", I repeated mechanically : I had not heard *that* name from the mouths of modern=factfinders in all my life ! (Or could it be a trap ? He was notorious for his – and now I don't want to confuse them : criminal or criminalist ? – forebears. Adelungadelung – I could not, simply could not recall . . . . .)

: "Wait ! Wait !". For, as I stood there thinking, concentrating with my hand over my eyes, he had tried to sneak off. (What was that rule my venerable Oxford=don had given me for interviews ? : ‹Limber the tongue either with alcohol; or, with clever provocation of the interviewee.› And since, in terms of alcohol, this=fellow seemed beyond influence, I had only the alternative) :

: "Why did you deliver such mediocre work, when in fact – as well= informed parties have advised me – you pocketed a fee of *twenty=thousand=marks* ?". – : Hey now ! That hit home ! Here he came again, galloping out of the depths of his garden, (and with the hose snaking fiery-red right behind him – had bit him on the hand, it appeared; served him right). : "What a lying basturd !" he bellowed; his eyes casting drunken bolts (no wait, not really; too dull for that : ‹sheet-lightning› at most) his tongue grubbed & pawed : "Who was he ? !". His spurt missed stroking me by a hair; but since this time it was obviously a matter of genuine excitation, I said nothing; which is to say, merely goaded him on maliciously : "Only too true." "Dammit ! – : not s'muchas *two*=thousand !" he troated indignantly. (Aha : judging from which, about 18 hundred. Int'resting. – Well, more than enough for that bungled job : impudently inventing a ‹Sir Car› just because somebody once drove *him* in an automobile from X to Y !). / At this point my companion displayed a clock=face through the windshield : ‹Time to leave !›. And I nodded briefly & resolutely her way : !; (we were duty bound, after all, to employ our energies for more serious matters. – : "Othello ! : Sufficient Rea=heason !" I heard the female voice call anew : that tipped the scale.)

"I'm coming. –". / Enough. (Yes, more=than !)

4

On this side of the Aller bridge in Celle – while we waited for the JOHN DARM up in his high-stilted glass bird-cage to tender us permission to continue our journey – I spoke again for the first time. : "Do you by=chance happen to know, Miss, what the term ‹XALDNIPTER› might mean in German ? Or ‹PIPORAKEMES› ? – You have after all been in this country=now since '45." "Oh, Dr. Mac Intosh –" she replied, (and smiled devotedly with the entire right half of her face; while the left diligently monitored the tydesque chaos of the traffic) – "if *you* do not know : who then would dare presume !". SIR CAR I gave her a well-measured nod : Good. (Indeed *very* good : knows how to express herself. / Her father, rector in Cranmer, Essex; author of the ‹Wednesday Evening Sermons for All the Year= Round on Justification by Faith›, a clear thinker indeed, no SWEDENBORGIAN he, but rather, best middle=class=family. Perhaps.)

The sun set for good & all. (Which is to say : it would be standing above Great Britain yet; quite different native=soil, that's all.) We drove off into the grandeur of God GOD PRESERVE FRANZ OUR KAISER. And she shone beside me, HIGH=SERENELY, illumined, THE LILY O' LIGHT, her long teeth sparkling like red ivory. (Perhaps one ought : her mother Eliza, née Michelson. A forebear who had not=fallen at Marston Moor; on the right side, naturally, ‹the lane along the front was held by skirmishers› : wellll, it was something one could always check into. Perhaps one really ought INTO THE CAR ONLY IN BRASSIERES the reprobates : could it be that the fellow was trying to pull my leg with inventions like NOPANDER & PHERKADAN ?*) *Was* it possible that the iniquity of an author=afterall=too and therefore also, in some sense, a prisoner of intellect, THE SORTA DRIFTER Y' CAN FIND IN ALL MARY=DIANES, would go *that* far ? !).

I turned vigorously to my charming chauffeuse (‹37› : actually just the right age for a virgin SINCE NOAH JOINED THE NAVY perhaps one really ought sometime DOLL TEARSHEET might it be that, inspired by me & the manner in which I introduced myself, the smart aleck was parodying the Swan of Avon, and with his anniversary year so imminent ‹no respect of place, persons, nor time› yesyes and such a man bears human countenance

---

*) Apparently not. – According to information supplied by an Arabist friend, ST. A. RICHMOND, we are dealing with an allusion to a certain King of H'îra, Gedhîmet Elebresh, who in his pride drank with no one except the Pherkadan, two stars (in Ursa Minor), for whom, whenever he himself drank a bowl, he would pour 2 onto the floor – that I observed nothing corresponding to the latter part of this rite surely needs no special mention by me.

well it certainly looked like it !). : "Would you pull over to the shoulder, please – : I have something to tell you . . .". / She steered, simultaneously confused & confident, under a precocious pear tree, which even now had begun to bear reddest fruit. Compelled the motor to mumble more soft & lovely. And looked at me FOR LOVE OF THE SCIENCE while the last=red snippet of sun dis=sipated behind the line of trees BUT OTHERWISE NOTHIN' 'CEPT THAT ENDLESS PLANTIN' O' FIRS 'BOUT MAN=HIGH (THREAT'NING INTCH BY INTCH T' BECOME EVEN MORE ENDLESS : We were alone. Rendered all animated Great British; and German objects nonviewable to human watchers.)

: "Uh=hmm. – Miss Whytefoot. – Shall We perhaps put to the test ?. – : Whether You could be Mine ?". /. –. –. – –

She gazed at me, in steadfast bliss. Her jaw struck the harp of Her breast. Sweet & ductile, half Austen half Brontë, her flaming face stammered (or was it the scalp of the sun RIGHT BEFORE THE PHALL ?). She raised parenthetic hands – and risked it, and latched them onto my shoulders – : "Oh, Dr. Mac Intosh – !" she said, still quite incredulous at such good fortune.

5

–. – – –. / – – : "?" – "." / – : "? ?" – – ". . ." – / : ! ! ! ! ! ! ! ! ! ! ! ! ! ! ! ! !

6

(Utter darkness now reigned in the NECKMOBILE SUBFUSCOUS in fact. / "You are so very clever –" She, ever & again, TEENY=WEENY DROLL HAMMER IN HAND – –).

*   *
*

7

To the matter at hand. –

My theory states, in brief, the following : that he who translates a book in language x into language y be chosen, if at all feasible,

   a) according to age & sex : he must in fact, *quite* apart from childhood memories, possess approximately the same biological elasticity.

b) according to cross-section load, i.e. the quotient of ‹height divided by weight› : it will not do for a man (woman) 6 feet 6 inches tall, and weighing 240 pounds, to translate the book of another man (woman) 5 feet tall and weighing 240 pounds : the first has no idea what to do with his (her) strength, the latter cannot ‹catch his (her) breath !›.

c) according to sentiments & social background : a child of the working classes, educated in Marxist class-hatred, will unhesitatingly intro-duce an envious, malicious tone to descriptions of refined milieus; the bald-pated atheist will, whether consciously or no, prefer satirical turns of phrase when rendering simple god-fearing sentiments.

d) according to education & vocabulary : in the inky hands of the demi-educated, the delicious delicate overtones of learned allusions – often suggesting to the thoughtful reader totally new, unanticipated and perhaps even revelatory perspectives – must perforce fall ineffica-cious upon even the best of soils, misunderstood and/or made unrec-ognizable by lumpish, truncated dialect.

e) Should it involve a living author, (respectful !) consultation with him is a fundamental prerequisite, mere mention of which (one would think !) is utterly & absurdly superfluous : only in this way can obscu-rities (on the part of the translator !) be redressed; (and let every sub-ordinate sharpen both pencil & ears when the master commences to speak !). / (Might I add here as well : that *I,* should my study of the Benda rendering of SHAKESPEARE 1 day be Germanized, my translator will *not* be left to wriggle his way through that easily ! ?).

f) To achieve this most desirable goal – for indeed, truly cocytic abuses scream in particular to high German heaven !, as has been made abun-dantly clear by my not unimpressive description thereof – I propose the erection of Translation Centers supervised by a public=academic governing body. In the future, the publisher acquiring an Anglo-Saxon work would simply apply to said institute; where, by means of punch cards & sorting machines, the most congenial translator (covered, moreover, by a pension plan) would be automatically ascer-tained according to criteria a to d; point e being a matter for official-dom – said translator then would promptly beply himself frugally & diligently to his task.

Thus my impressions of our threatened situation, thus the antidote.

Would God that my proposal were acted upon on an international level ! – : In my mind's eye I see Translation Centers large as ministries; teaming with civil servants of the word, dynamic=godfearing, scintillating with in-telligence & alert to responsibility, reference works in their indefatigable hands, their sterling character matched only by their bibliogenephilia !

(Forgive me, please, my enthusiasm; but when I think of that epitome of homo=non=sapiens – of that hose-riding, booze-mouthed lazzi-jargonist and his koboldlike dodging of every serious discussion – oh for Oxford= clean air ! – I had best break off this unedifying bramble of a protracted period on my theme.)

(When I informed my Bessie – i.e. my fiancée – of this & analogous trains of thought, she listened not only without once interrupting (inestimable quality !), but also responded with nods of approbation & eyes glistening ever brighter. And when in my own rapture & fervor I concluded my portrait of the ideal translator with the – admittedly indelicate – words : "I will sire him !"; she blushed sweetly; chewed for a while; and then responded – I had to bend low to her to capture her whispers – : "I will bear him. –" / Any further word were a profanation !). –

8

EDITORIAL AFTERWORD. / Though the issues be ever so woefully apparent, in order that we might preserve inviolable the precept of audiatur et altera pars – a principle fundamental to every independent newspaper, and therefore to ours as well – points a through f were sent to the translator portrayed in the preceding article for his comment – as is his wont, he did not reply. Since, however, the imperative of objectivity required that his own views be contraposed to the noteworthy theses submitted by Dr. Mac Intosh out of his high sense of cultural duty, we established contact – at a considerable sacrifice of time & expense; but truth above almost=all ! – with one of his very few more reputable acquaintances (very few, indeed – his lack of social contact is as notorious as it is medically significant); who, in a display of truly phenomenal patience, succeeded in eliciting some resemblance of a reply, though obtained only in passing and at irregular & widely spaced intervals and under the camouflage of desultory small talk, that being his sole method of communication. And although our learned readers will thus have to forego well-formed, definitive responses, the statements obtained in this fashion are themselves so revealing that we dare not withhold them – here they are :

to a) "So 'cording t' him, if 'm gonna translate Cooper, I'd have to be 180 years old, right ?"

to b) "Cross=sexion=load, that's rich ! – Maybe for the Brontës I oughta turn back 'nto a virgin ?."

to c) "If a millyunaire takes up writin' it'd be pretty 'xpensive t' ‹dovetail› things. Or whatabout a gay : 've I told y' about my recent trip

t' Bad Frimmersen by the way ? 'bout the lifeguard ? . . . . ." (At
this point he once again wandered off into one of his endless=con-
fused & =confusing anecdotes – something about ‹Windmills›.)

to d) "Bull. It's all as plain as the nose on your face : fifty p'cent of all
translations 're better than the orij'nulls anyway."

to e) It is said that he grew very animated here and swore that ‹like hell
he would !› : "'m not gonna let some for'ner horn in on my German
text ! I woulda had a few things t' say t' Joyss, what with his
German=gibber : ‹es ist eine Hundesleben›, oh carry me home to
die : 'nd somebody like that's gonna maybe dictate t' *me* how my
translation's s'posed to sound, 's that it ? ! Or when some sev'nty-
year-old d'cides his little timid blass=fummies & love=sceens
from when he was twenny-five 're ‹reprehensible› now; 'nd 'd just
as soon deny he's ever been laid; 'nd now wants t' supply some
‹corrections› usin' the detour o' my translation : No way !" / After
further lounging about on the porch rail, and more grumbling, he
provided a concluding summary of his views in this matter : "No
sir : protect translations – and the seckunt eddytions, far as that
goes – from the awethors ! : ‹What's ritten is ritten›."

to f) "Now wouldn't that be awef'ly nice." –

His more general criticism, however, concerned a problem – in his opinion the most important one – that had not even been touched upon : "The
ona=raryum, acoarse ! Just 1 more thing publishers 'll *never* learn : when
they fork up 3 thousand marks for a translation, they get a 3=thousand=
mark translation; if they shell out 6 thousand, they'll get 1 for 6 : 'cause I
can take twice the time with it !". To the cautious demurral of his acquaintance – who, as can be well understood, prefers to remain unidentified –
that under said circumstances most ‹artists› would then produce the 3-thou-
sand version and simply dawdle away the other 3 : and whether this might
not be *the* obvious danger ?, he offered the coldblooded reply : pretty
damned obvious, in fact.

THE WATERWAY

1

Not that you could say I didn't know my father : half of him, the lower half, I knew that all too painfully well – the odor was almost always too much for me. (Uptop, then, a smoky high baritone; consequently, the kind I don't like to this day); I involuntarily gauged above, with astigmatic eagle eye : – ? –

– a veiled, very choleric afternoon sun; (‹The veiled 1s are the worst›). But the first cloud all the same; who was in such a hurry to cross the sky that she lost a piece; (all the same, ‹thæs yeres thridde quartre›; really ought to hold till evening –). Ergo, a firmer grip on my hiking stick, (it only looks massive; in reality it's juniper wood : very light, but tough o'course, ‹oh t' be young & tough again›) : "Hold the map a little more accommodatingly for the ladies, Felix." He groused, and complied. And the ladies, who, touched & boggled, had till now been admiring the bucolix busy roundabout – the eloquent geese; the grazing equine silhouette, all ‹leg adandle›, of smudged sheet-copper; the little dogcart, steered into meadow=expanses by a female whose biceps were as large as the legs of an urbanette; the whitegray=taciturn cat on the alder stump : "I treasure these beasts – 'deed I do : plants as well – almost immoderately; if only because they are non= kristians every=1." And so the ladies drew closer.

Ruth, fullbosom=bellyfull, (a desert sheik would have offered 2 oases for her), grasped the survey map by an end; (and her no=rust=ring, with its stone from the Berlin Wall, was already glimmering damned ‹tarnished› : on the one hand a man should be glad he's a bachelor !). Hel, too, took a stride (of fully incredible length) forward, with all her teens together; and I looked up all 80 inches once more : 16½, and a skeleton=spook, who gazed gracefully down upon my six feet one ! (But she got it from her father; he was ‹six feet eleven›, too, topped by that little, ridiculously bereted head. / Apparently hadn't ‹grown› in the last year – which would've been fully unnecessary; she'd have it hard enough as it was : if you only could've seen at least an *intimation* of a bosom ! But nothing, nothin' atall, no trace of that appy=cycle; what this=Miss concealed within her drab bikini was, guaranteed, naught but a work of art. Instead, round her neck, threaded on

a medium=thin cord, a zoodiac of hazelnuts : ‹No greasyguts fuming in
his massive armchair shall offend thee›; or also : ‹Divested of frame, my
members discarded, I became but a shade. – yet 1 pinch of dust now, and I
am enkindled, a spark hot ascending !›; title ‹My Godchild›.) Lady Ruth,
however, in high black rubber boots & russet shorts – her plump breeches,
side-by-side, looked like 2 mandolin cases – now impatiently planted her
parasol (hyperslender ballast) in the thin alluvial soil. And I declared,
bachelordly :

" ‹Before there e'er was gold, : the golden age had dawned !› – "
(and, with all my powers of solemnity, pointing roundabout with my free
left : – ! –). "Laydeez 'nd jennts : We are presently located at the mouth
of the Small Water; at 10 degrees, 20 minutes, 50 seconds longitude east;
albeit at 52 degrees, 42 minutes, 30 seconds latitude north." (And the
tiniest of pauses : no one protested my, granted, idiotic ‹albeit› ! Most remarkable. Hence, proceeding more boldly) : "At roughly 203 feet *above*
sea level – in consummate contradistinction to ‹Captain NEMO›, : kwoad
veeda !". Whereupon, only Felix had promptly nodded, the aforementioned
copper jade made a couple of wanton forehand leaps upon the ultra=green :
! : ! ! : ! ! ! : (and farted the while, sheer rending the air : GOd preserve us
from a strong government ! A weak 1, yet versed in the arts, were much my
preference – – but why had that occurred to me now ? – I gnawed away at
my left indexfinger. But did not know for all that.)

: "Its length : in toto is no more & no less than 10 – in words : TEN !
kilometers; from the Greek ‹chilios›, that is ‹thousand›. The ladies will
moment=airily pace off this : ‹waterway›." (The gentlemen walking at
their side; it had been so agreed.) / "The local political status is likewise
not totally uninteresting : this entity, having presumably existed for several tens of thousands of years now, arises near the village of Blickwedel,
in the district of Gifhorn. – Which, by the by, was once an independent
duchy : Felix, do remind me that we should pay a visit to Gifhorn Castle
soon, won't you ? – : Why are you gaping at me like that ? !". For his face,
above, displayed a somewhat ‹ravenous› expression; (was he hungry perhaps ? Although the potatoes-in-jackets had been downright good at lunch;
and the ‹attendant› headcheese ample & tolerably=tasty, juicy in fact.
(‹Hot & mealy› crossed my mind for the spuds, too.) Well, ask about it
later; when we're alone.) : "I repeat : the source at 10°25′ uhm=lambda;
52°40′ Enn=Phi; altitude 295 feet six inches. In other, more impressive
words : a falling gradient of over 92 feet for its full=course, right ?" They
did not appear excessively enthusiastic. (Therefore moving quickly=on;
pile up details; overwhelm with the ‹blisses of enumeration›, with rith=
micks)

: "Wide, if not to put it bluntly ‹endless› woodlands : spruce= & fir= mamsells, jagged-skirted man-high green-haired" – and now something for the ladies – : "Oak scaleywags, gnarled, as hard as they are tall, unembraceable. Trigonometric points hem its irenic course : feeds ponds . . ." "How'd yóu like t' feed whole ponds ?", Ruth inquired, (and promptly gave a shiver, in response : brrr !). "M'dears, please don't distort a man's words when they're still in his Broca's area !". / Tributaries ? : "Oh 'ndeed, Hel ! – On the left, that is from the east in this case, the ‹Räderloh Brook›; an equally not uninteresting – and likewise all too little explored – watercourse, roughly calculated, some $2^1/_2$ miles in length. Several rivulets, to which I may perhaps introduce you shortly as well – ?". They pouted pretty=thick lower=lips, and rocked their heads in amiable neutrality. / –. / : " 's it form islands ?", Hel inquired, giving me a look, from under her black bang=tufts, of ravishing gloom. (If only she weighed fifty pounds more ! And I simply couldn't, really couldn't, get used to being gazed down=upon by a woman. And it was also a matter of dodging her captious=belittling question) : "Islands –", (I knew of none in fact . . .); "shall We not, as an indispensable basis, first complete our survey of the macro=geographix ?" I said sternly. "It flows, then, into the Lutter : here : at precisely this spot : 'sindeed ! –"; and stretched out a long arm; (and added the tapered finger; they obediently turned their heads). "Might We not therefore justly call our standpoint" (and decoratively stomp the foot, thou stompst, further ascending) "‹Co=Blents›; ‹conts›, verily a ‹cunflunts›." / And whither this ‹Lutter› ? : "Into the Lachte." And it ? : "Into the Aller. – The latter into the Weser, near Verden. Which then enters the North Sea. : And so it flows ever onward.", I concluded allargando, (yea, sublimely. Or would ‹further› have been even more poignant ? Felix rubbed his hand over his chin; a gesture that, as I well knew, customarily signified a fecund ferment of impatience plus indecision. It could, however, ‹stands to reason›, have been merely his beard.) I nodded encouragement to him. Put an arm around Hel, to pull her closer; (to the surveyor's map, naturally, Sir Vieux's mop, and it was, in turn, like hugging a broad plank, poorthing); and tapped the various localities=roundabout with 1 of her fingers, (the born pointing stick as it were), as I enumerated them, 1 after the other :

"Bustling ELDINGEN – poor region for rainbows," I was forced to append ne'ertheless; (and to produce the grave face of a charlatan). A perplexed Lady Ruth looked right into it. Gave a curt shake of the head, and asked : "Why *that* ?". Felix, too, had ceased chin-rubbing; he simply held fast to the thing, and gazed at me; (Doubt + Insecurity among Them=All : today's the day I succeed !) The only one who thought it over was, once again, Hel. Fixed on the situs confluens beside us. Then on me; then on the map. And began, slowly, to deduce the why of my wherefore. : "In the south –", she said, growled & protracted : "And whereas the sun spends the m'jority of its time in the south. 'nd rainbows by definition occur *opposite* the sun . . .". And now I interrupted her; patting the white staff of her forearm in praise : "Move up 1 chair, Hel ! – And/or, *should* y' prefer, accept a holy meteorological kiss from your godfather – ?". She spread her mouth wide; and sniffed pertly; and slyly declared : *"That'll* take some deliberation." (Then *yet* more wanton shoulder gestix + grins like at the Beatnick's : " 'd rather have a mark.").

"HEESE – where We saw that heavy hailstorm last year. You remember, we were in the car, like sittin' inside a tin drum !". They remembered. "Actually it's called ‹Spitz=Heese›; t' differentiate it from a ‹Breiten=Hees›, up by Ülzen. We get most of our snow from this 1 here." / The mighty municipality of ENDEHOLZ. / Richly wooded MARWEDE: "A curiously large number of hares between the two ! *And* pheasants," I added, since they didn't seem to be following with sufficient enthusiasm. (And so go on.) / "WEYHAUSEN, an erstwhile hunting castle of elector=princes. Even nowadays, y' can still tell by single, splendid solitary trees." : "Isn't ‹single= solitary› redundant ?" Felix asked indignantly, (all bookdealer & re=print= fan); for which Ruth, however, compensated by rasping : "Say, does that have 'nything t' do with ‹Weyrauch› ? I was reminded of ‹incense› recently by that juniper sawdust –"; without even asking, she seized my hiking stick, and sniffed at its knob with great pining; (held it that way, too. I quickly threw myself into the breach) : "To the north and east, then, the magnificent, secluded" – (now why were both, Ruth and Hel, nodding again so dark & dreamy ? ‹suck lewd ?› : ‹nifty scent & suck=lewd› ?) – "the numerous fish ponds of RÄDERLOH, splendid for swimming. / Then come great moors, and the ZONE is close at hand –" (this last mysterious, all long ‹ooo›. It did, however, deliver us the sun every day; and of an evening the mooon) – "inestimably desolate regions, 'specially in thunderstormy air, all hot & blackgray : grass tall as reeds; cows gawking, plagued by flies, like authors by reviewers : one tree with an in-grown *chain* ! –", here Hel's mouth slowly gaped; (it had really been a mad dog=day : first the very small, deep-green, fire line in the stand of woods, toward STEINHORST there. A sand-ditch=halfmoon-bank, its rim fuming uptop; some sorta ganef must've been campin'. And the path quickly splayed three fingers. And each of them, I had doggedly followed every 1, ended blindly in flats of swamp bog & fen – there's more to report there. But I preferred to jerk my map-pocket in place; that would definitely lead us too far astray at the moment. The ladies gave their napsacks a jerk, (it's catching); and Felix laid a groping hand to his snapsack – ‹schnapps=sack› : I had indeed

noticed him fill it with his kwan=tum a while back !).) –
So then : "Might I ask the ladies to climb aboard ? –" –

2

: "Justasec ! – Not yet." –

Ruth. Licked her flews. (Even showed her fangs.) And all of a sudden started issuing orders in such a barracky voice that, ‹old veterans› that we were, we obeyed automatically at once

: "HANDS UP ! !" –

There we stood, just as once in that epoch of uniform=glory. I would have lowered mine again right away; but Felix, the poltroon, continued to raise his wed=crippled ‹victoire›=signalement, (and so I kept him company, as it were). Smiling grimly, Ruth walked up to him. As regarded me, she merely did an over-the-shoulder twitch of the thumb – : "Hel – –"

And actually frisked us, the TAMPAX=trix ! Indeed, gave us a ‹beating› with sinister dexterity. / – / – : ! Lady Ruth now extracted his flask. Lustily lifted the backside-pocket lid – / And meanwhile Hel fingered me, with nornic brusqueness. Went deeper. (But I had long since figured on that, given Felix's latest hints : we shall see, which wins out: manly courage versus femalice!). But she had already discovered *my* potables. And kept gnawing away !, evoking my soft warning : "Hel –" – and grinned, 'tis true; but proceeded somewhat more businesslike down to where my socks merged into my high shoes. (As weak recompense, at least a peep into the décolleté of Lady Ruth's one-piece bathing suit : left a graspful; right a graspful. Poor Hel.)

Stood back up. Retired; meanwhile secreting our confiscated goods in their napsacks. Then Ruth's silver-anniversaried grin : "So, *now* we can get started. – pretty spot for a house by the way –" she added, with furrowed brow and a practical look around. / But now it was my turn I suppose. Grumbling : "Justasec ! – We at least want to measure the width." Hel was already descending adroitly, 1 end of the tape measure in her right hand (quickly superseded by the left) – (whata picture : those very flat green sandals; teeny pantlets, even skimpier halter !) – danced-macabre to the ‹Far Shore› : ?. And I read it off, thunderstormily – : "Ten. – Two."

Then they lined up, a debonair & devil-may-care sight to behold. And We marched off, All Four, upbrook. (: ‹Cop you late !›) : . . . . .

3

Above all it was his beret that had such an extra flat and flaming yellow quality today ! And he sanded, as was his wont, his earlobe, (which, as it was, already stood out like half a crescent roll); hissed : "Shit ! – couldn't we 've at least called and raised ? – Now we've got nary a drop : you're wastin' away day by day, too !". "Worry 'bout yourself !" I reposted in outrage : "If Ruth were *my* wife . . ." : "You'd long ago 've taken to your cane !" he cantankerously finished my sentence.

And malicious silence. Striding along the semi=road. (While yonder, in meadow verdancies, 1 buxom and 1 polyboned UNDINE slowly, long= groped along. / At times parcially hidden by alder=drapes, windows into Eden, mazes of delight.) But we were still in ‹inhabited regions›; multiple Messers Granger were still fumbling roundabout us. / (Question : do there *have* to be people who chop=down a solitary=birch of exemplary growth simply because the next=burnable 1 is 10 tractor=seconds farther away ? Not to speaka alder=copses; titmice in their green hair, ‹schools› of fishies flitsermousing away=below. F'rall I care, farmer=people can be ‹at log-gerheads› up on the banks : ‹I hold nothing animal foreign to me : HOMO= SUMM !›).

: "‹In blameless joy slips noon on past the husbandman› : ZACHARIAE.", I began soothingly; and pointed to the sand=path, perforated sexfold by a ‹prong=rotor› : ?. / But Felix kept shaking his spurning head. Deep=n= thot : "Hey. – Ruth wanted a swing=bar, i.e. ‹trappeez›, for our silver anni-vers'ry just=passt. : What d'y' say t' that ?". / : "‹D'nammick› p'r'aps ?". But he, curt & gruff, "Y' think so ?". / And grew, it seemed, even *more* enraged; and gazed malignantly at the fields beside us & those farmhands who'll take any oath easy. – : "Lookathat ! –"; for a plowjockey was slink-ing, ostensibly to pluck weeds; deeper through shamrocks & hairfoot clo-ver. But instead laid his paw on the nearest maiden=rump – ! – ! ! –

"The scream of the person pinched is really no standard by which to measure any pain experienced," Felix said sternly; after having had to smirk briefly; : "What's the actual populaytion density round=here ?". 59 to the square mile. "Blessedly few," he said : "Why d'y' drag=around that beast with=you – ? !" – he cast a nasty sidelong glants at my tella=scope, in its thick=brown leather cylinder, which hung (clumsily, I grant) penn= dulous down over my (broad) chest : the hardrubber ocular cupp peeped out, black & fingerwide. / While we, dowghtily, strolled along beside the rowans : the berries still in the early stage, yellow, or very pale brown; (lovelier, really, than their later, almost too energetic fiery hue). / : "And a guy like that's perfectly capable of envy –"; Felix was, in thought, still with the pincher. (And so discuss other thematix that somehow derived ‹logickly› therefrom : ‹Might it be a token of kindness to sire children gratis on the locull country maids ?›. Some remarx on ‹barley›; which, it only struck me now, too, had grown muchmuch rarer since our childhood – around 1920 or so; strange. "Can y' become a member of par=lament with your nose cut=off ?").

: "Vexed by your golden vein ? !" –. / "Nah. : gold=water salvation"; he replied gloomily. / As a salutary diversion, I told him of my most recent mishap : how, in order to get preference on delivery from the Rhenish Paper Factory, I had represented myself as a ‹writer› – me, the poor registrar of the Eastern Heath – but Felix, surmising & peevish, began to grouse : "Well ? So wha'd they say ?" : "‹Pay in advance, please› !". And gloomy grousing. / : "Dallalla=Hú=Hüh !" – came the very distunt & sweet & rawndly yodeled call. Siren rabble. (Ducky jaunty. Aspen=quiverish behind black-green curtains. "Could kick m'self in the butt !", he rankled, in well-drilled self=hatred. We did not respond.) –

Why off to the right ? : "Well, it *is* our first rendezvous=spot." / Through a woodlet; which, however, barely betrodden, grew more open; now the path descended a little. And a long=long=flat troughlet of a valley, filled almost too high with grass. At whose edge we stood. / "I dunno," he admitted, much more indulgent than before : "Whenever I'm s'posed to walk out onto such a great=swampy meadow, I always feel a need for a certain corage." I just coolly wiggled my pucker : normal funomenon among urbanites : "C'mon; y' won't drown. *Your* head 'd peep out of any pond round=here." And forward=into the touselheaded grass. On past voluptuous growths; ("Caused by cow pies"). A lacewing on the thorn of a thistle ? : "To him it's about as ‹pointy› as a kitchen stool 'd be for you." "Maffwá –" he said in amazement.

And uttered his "Ah –" of delight once we stood at brook's edge. (These urbanites really notice nothing : Our sort would immediately have noticed a priori & infallibly, if not from the bare fact of the primal glacial valley, then at least from the attendant bushes, that this had to be the abode of a vigorous little watercourse.) Lovely the alders, oh yes; more lovely the simpleton bridge. Lovely the water o'er sand; more lovely the plants soft wafting therein. And gaze back & forth; and observe the glassy entity. (" 'Zounds wadi & whiski" he murmured pensively.) / But here they came now : 1 hop-pole striped black & white; one robust & round : Undine Melusine Anna Dyomene Anna Livia Russalka. "Oh, I do love them," he said calmly; "but all the same I'd not be averse to a proper snort." Then, seeing the ladies, gleefully battling the knee= and/or calf=hi flood, approaching – "Seest thou : ‹Lady Flooth›", Felix interrupted me, in

approval; gloomier again : "‹battling with the Flooth› : such as is nour-
ished in bottles; ahyes." (‹And forgive us=our puns› : "You're an A=sot."
I swiftly declared. For they were, for diavologues of our sort, too near
now. – ‹Naila› came as well.)

4

Us *on* the footbridge; (2 long round logs; planks nailed tight over them,
2´8˝ x 8˝). The ladies, obliquely below us, in the water. Lady Ruth braced
her hands on it, (and cuddled thighs together); Hel lumbered in, elbows
asplay, (the girl had calves like a condor's). Before I could intervene, Felix
had already begun to babble most wretchedly à la "a swig=pleeze !" – but
They had only cold smiles for the weakling (quite rightly so, by the way);
while I casually lectured : on sand ways, on deer ponds, on whitefish species, on water plants : "‹Vingt Mille Lieues sous les Mers›; I'd be glad to
read you all some chapter or two from it 's evenin'. – But first measure the
width here, okay ?"
  : Seven=three wellokay. (But it varied mightily. Right at this spot. Hel
had to apply multipull tape=endlets up & down the current – the Steinhorst
flank of her ribb=caged was conspicuously brighter than the side opposite;
probably purely a matter of solar position; I noted it in my notebooklet.)
Felix meanwhile gave a poke to several alder twigs, (‹Northpaw, Tacto=
Compulsive›). Ruth patiently waded tredding water. Hel (her labor done,
so wrested she Gudrun), laid on her very own back, bên ze bêna; (‹Saucy
Gelimida› : I know you well, you, sous les mères. She promptly sent a
sulky and lusty smile high & away, somewhat to my=left.) I spake ever-
more as befits a Landlord Wondermild. While she lay on her back and
cooled herself. Swiftly rose up again for no reason what=ever. And stood
there dripping; (‹coerced him that he stood all dripping there› – or ‹stood
all trembling› ? Indeed I didn't know at the moment).
  What this was here ? – : "Marsh rosemary. In more unenlightened eras,
aboriginal humanity prepared a tea from its leaves, ‹Labrador Tea›. – But
seldom drink it; for in that form the stuff has a keen narcotic effect, offici-
nal no less. Therefore clever farmers in turn were wont to add it to their
beer, for more triumphant results." Felix at once wanted to inconspicuously break off a sprig, with the barefaced intention of inserting it into his
wide mouth; but Ruth's parasol scorpioned (core=spined, yea sting=rayed)
up from below, and stung him casually on his (truly unstingworthy) shin : !.
"Do better t' chew a mugwort leaf; y' won't get so tired walkin'. – :
‹Fook=Lor›", I tauntingly remarked; and he glared more nastily again.

Whereupon we All glared at Hel : who, while we were stoutly climbing the Tree of Knowledge, (and/or of m'Alice), had mutely buried her long= righthand in her own bosom. And after ample rummaging, the beast pulled out a *cork*. (Now why that ? Was she a secret boozer ? ! She was right in the middla that biological period, not to say epock; and with No One to come to her aide, with an e; neither theoretically via FREUD, nor practically via the prescription of penis vulgaris. ‹THE UNCLE'S RESPONSE ABILITY› quite true; but I would've had to be ten long years younger.) / Ne'ertheless it turned out, as almost always in life, to be something *quite* different. She rotated the upper rim of said cork – : and twisted it off ? – : and lo, it was hollow ! She upended the hollow part onto 1 of the many bridge=planks : !. (First looking up at Us again – : was I mistaken; or were her eyes indeed resting on regions of my groin ? ‹Groin wine›, in goatbags : as a mattera ‹fact› she was just the right age !). / And so 3 tiny dice. Which came to rest at my feet in an (imagined) periferal circle with a 2 inch diameter. (Rest roost root. Roots of march.) a black 5; a white 5 : a red 6 ! – (: "a farmacist, from Brem'n; a client," Felix whispered, "sent'em as gifts to *his* clients for New Year's : ‹THE BREMEN DIE=CUP›. She snapped it up first thing. Why ?, I dunno." : "I shall marvel, by your leave –"; for it really looked like a per- fectly ordinary cork ! All the same, I kept my head enough for)

   : "I'd like to say that this red SIX=Hel tips the scale. – Have y' ever actually tried – in a series of throws; that is, statistically – to determine which is *more* ‹loaded› : a white 6, or a red ?". She examined anew (& pensive) the 3 screwy dice. (Each 216 cubic millimeters, I'd guess). Then me again. And finally shook her long, black=rimmed skull. (That I didn't deserve, girl !).

   So best continue. / : "Mesdames ! – After about=um 7 eight hundred yards, we'll meet again, near the district border." / They ducked (from the English ‹duck›) under the bridge, another creature whose die had been cast. We=however strode, rudely, off to the right through a small ferny corner : ‹Swilly tubble !› –

5

I performed a stage=evesdrop : ? – "Y' hear it ? The brooklet ?". Also came to his aide (with=e=again !), by laying hands behind his hairy ear=mussels. (His mouth flapped open up front; by means of such contrivances, he then heard it apparently.) Gave a slight nod; superficially ‹engrossed›, (or only just confused, as is the wont of urbanites, who after 100 trees cannot differ- entiate one from the next ? Anything's possible really with these asfalt dudes.) But then finally said : "Pretty. – Sorta swishes, doesn't it."

But also the voices of the ladies now & then & here & there. / He mulled
a while in his nose. Then erupted : "Why do I have so little self-confidence
t'day really ? !". I merely shrugged my handsome shoulders : a man can't
know everything. (Felt, however, a smile on my lips. Let him go ahead a
bit. On past the Great Anthill; (the juniper beside it; looking like the
double=pointed flaired beard of a playing-card king : Ahhhh !).) / Heard
him, as if from faroff, bickering : "What're y' forever peeping at through
that telescope ?"; and also, more sardonic : "For that little bitta Hel . . . ." I
mustered him coldly for that : a man whose one eye was smaller than the
other=pff ! / And pilgrimage continued. Erect in the green. The tough=stiff.
Staff in the knobba my hand. He began to laugh listlessly

: "Say – d'you know this one ? : ‹HIS HAT TRIMMED WITH POSIES ? –". In
response to my headshake, he demanded my hiking stick; and I, in utter
surprise, handed him said staff; amazed. He turned briefly away from me
(Moving off some 4, 5 yards as well.) And here he came toward me again;
and sang as he came, booming & monotone :

"‹HIS HAT TRIMMED WITH POSIES HIS STAFFINHISHÁND› –"
he was swinging it so hard that you *had* to look : (‹wide-gestured› would
have been the forced=poetic expression for his behavior) :

"‹THE LONELY MAN WANDERS FROM LAHÁND=TO=LAND› –"
he gazed, weary of hiking & life, to lateral expanses; his hand, which until
now had so decoratively guided the cudgel, somehow broke ‹free› – :

"‹HIS HAIR IS DU=HUSTY, HIS FACE IS DARK=TANNED› –"
sang Felix. My gaze grew more'n'more fixed : why was the stick positioned like that ? Aslant in fronta his body ! At his fly : butthenthat'dmean !
The fellow wasn't born with a prehensile tail ! ! – :

"‹AND WHO'D BE THE FIR=HIRST TO KNOW THE LAD'S FACE ?›"
(And from somewhere, wayoff on the lefft, soft laughter emerged, from
grassiest wilderness, most muliebral in the brooky c'anal.) And it tugged
my mouth very wide as well – : "A top-drawer buck –", I whispered, in
instinctive=amazement. He 1st bowed his thanks. The hand took over
again; (while the indexfinger stuck through the slit, in the usage of hell,
wriggled & squirmed); Felix shriveled, he faltered (and ‹altered› visibly :

"‹HERE CAME 'N OLD WOMAN AT CANE=WALKIN' PA=HACE› –"
: hunched over my own juniper now, he gave me such a olladylike=scruti-
nizing look, ice-gray stooped cataract=eyed : ? – / Drew himself up, more
collected, to his full 6 feet 11. Gave some measured tips of his beret; (while
the pinkie kraken went back to holding the truncheon aslant) :

"‹GOD BLESS=YE! HE SAYS. BUT STANDS SILENT IN PLA=HACE› –"
and I could hardly have done otherwise : I leaned against the nearest stable

sturdy=stemmed fir; and whinnied district-borderwards : "‹PITTSHAFT the Unflagging !› – Hey, 'fonly your pitch didn't stink so bad of sulf= & foss=fur !". And also, since he was baring such frustrated teeth : "Well c'mere : 'nd take a peep through the field-glass !". And demand silence of the dubiously approaching little=pig : "I am more than adequately familiar with the basseuse of your mauvais goût : you're not worth it, but you're in dire need . . .". / First he inspected the, slightly protruding, ocular cup with disgust. Which I, ditto slightly, raised – higher still ? – : ! Only then he did notice the flask beneath; it literally took his breath away : !. "But o'coarse y' first had to belittle at length the ‹unpractickle tool›, right ? – : Quiet ! –". (For, from far in the distance, came the sound. Like a sweet laughter; a sweet splashing. Phraises like ‹up to the waist› came to mind) : "‹Ydor or the Wanderer from the Watery Realm›. By Josef All=wheeze GLEICH." And : "RAIMUND's father-in-law," he followed up, "but so what. – : Great Franz in heaven !" : ther reyzed he up and dranck. (‹Set the spyglass to thy lips : In the roses. Thou drinkst the Holy Ghost in sips›) : "Dammit, smile some applause or . . . !". But he was already smiling on his own, refresht & addickted; a freelance sot in the great cylindrical wheels of time : the fern=here luxuriated up to even=his high waist. And a comely fragrance had, faith, spread through the e'ergreen nook here : "D'you take it all back ? !" : "I take it *all* back –" he promptly replied.

I had led him deeper into bowered yurts; ‹yet once more, Robert, before we must part›; but he took fright all the same. : "What if Somebody chances in here ?" : "She'll back right out again." I mollified him. "Pretend you're relievin' yourself." But all the same, looked so greedily into the clouds that I had to tear the ocular from his mouth – ! – / Aahhh –. : "What's this stuff cost ?". OLD CHANCERY : "Haffas much as your Asbach." He rocked his high head in approbation : saaaved ! / : "Let's move on, Felix. We at least have to begreet 'em from the High Bank." –

– : "D'y see that ? ! –"

for the two gillyfrillies were already veryvery near. / ": Genus ‹five-toed slapfeet› !" I called to them through my hand-hecklephone; and, softer, to Felix=beside=me : "C'mon. Sursum cauda : give a yella your own." The Old Sir Chantsery=Countslur pondered. (Farted instead, as if wanting to force an alteration in his state of aggregation; fortunately I was standing up=wind : "That won't quite do it, Felix.") "Total lacka desire," he reposted sircumspectly. (Add ‹for a yell›. While the muliebrity, circum-rubbed with sea-sand & almond-meal (or whatever they call the latest smearacles), trudged our way on 4 legs : 2 strapping bowling=pins, topped with a Danaïden tummy : RUTH. And Felix spoke the while, with an oddly puffy tongue) :

: "Our so-called ‹for=bears› were really as stupid as turds, too. : That a man ‹weakens› a female ! –" (and right he was : puttin' the cart before the horse) – : "Just picture it : not long ago I came skipping up all lust & love, a real rarity of late, alla ‹Shall We ? !›" – (‹anxious the pleadings of a love-sick man›, and then those obstinate perverse Adam's riblets; oh, I could picture it easy 'nuff !) – "Put her on my lap. Busily=unbuckle her hooks at the back –" (I just nodded, bitter & sex=starved : ‹auld lang syne, long sin› !) – "start=in strokin' her collecktive err=rutch=inous zones" – (his hands duplicated the deed, ohmy fatutitty; I begged him, by gestures, to proseed more quickly, I, too, was but a sexual fallow. / And had moved in closer meanwhile : 2 longskinny legs, Hel even lifted 1, & gazed at her own sole – : "Greenfoot : Greenfoot !", I shouted into her 50=yard=distunt face. She noticed, most definitely, and earnestly. Felix, the Unflagging, continued for the nonce) – : "wander up the thighways – : ! 'nd, insteada vaulting voluptuous lips for me, She breaks into shivers : !, and allegedly has t' go sit on the potty : said My hands were too cold ! – The=End o'coarse !". (‹Studies for the Right Hand› : ‹She's for Lou=Mumba; whereas He, with a European eye, is for Chomm=Bey›. All the same, once again, it was all up to me) :

: "Go ahead, please, about another five hundred yards –" I shouted, with a polite smile, down toward Ruth's dun-hued belly; (an unpleasant wide-spread navel actually; that literally smirked at you. / And 1ce again a goal that I=alone of Us=Four could see : now, is that to be envied or perhaps a curse ? (The mere fact that it could be formulated as a question was sufficient answer for me.) But go on with my instructional pilot=cry) : "– there's a meadowy x=panse, with a three=quarter rotted bridge : we'll afternoon there ! –". Hel was already making the turn – not simply ‹turned›; there were far too many limbs (and allevem far too long) – along the stony dam=steps; ‹The Virgin's Peturntions›. Felix nodded & shook his head as they departed; then : " 're you aware that you're not the first uncle= type ever to have an itch to go to bat for his niepce ?". And I, promptly= indignant ; "I'm only bidin' my time t' see if I oughta just pinch your blas- phemous tongue, or a quick dose of E 605 –". He waved this off with knowing=nonchalance; and we scrambled, though lending 1 another sup- port, across the border ditch & its barbwire barricade : M'arse of the Bar- bary Pirutts ! –

"By the by, your pantomime of the ‹POSIES› –", (and I let curiosity stretch across my face : ?), – "that's the *one method* for getting ‹broad segments› to listen to that p'tickular sorta kitsch & schmaltz without promptly breakin' into whinnies of laughter." Lifted my endless indexfinger, too; importantly : "Y' can depend on it : it's the *only=way* ! for scoffing such

junk right outa the brain=wrinkles of the workaday mob." Takin' that
slant, I could use that little genre painting . . . so then not just a fool in
foolio ? . . . or wait : "But what would you replace it with, usin' your
method ? !". Whereupon he testily demanded the telescope again, and
peered so deep that the tendons stuck out on his neck – "Careful, Felix :
we're definitely gonna have to justify our halitosis later ! So be sure y'
demand a swallow from your confiscated hip=flask right off, as a cover=up
rinse."

"Did y' ever thinka castratin' yourself when you were young ?", he
asked, (apparently still on some other topic; but all the same volunteered an
"asshole" to the crude log obstructing his path : who had *not* given it a
thought as a young high=minded fellow ?). I dissented, too, only very
curtly & chattily; then : "Felix – couldn't y' maybe jot down a coupla my
book wishes ?". He squared his (skimpy) shoulders; and then moved right
in front of me, challenging, ballpoint fixed : ? / So, then, what int'rests me
at present . . . : "Words that *don't* appear in the BIBLE, Felix." At once he
pursed his specialist face (a walnut=hue) – : "Y' gotta go at that the other
wayround; with the aide of a BIBLE=concordance : that'll give the words
that do appear *in=the=BIBLE*. – CALWER –" I heard him mutter besides; also :
"Y' don't wanna spend much on it." "As always : no !" I said indignantly;
(and saw him underline the ‹Calwer›). / "The old magazine for boys, ‹THE
GOOD COMRADE›, from 1888, the second year of issues; it's got KARL MAY'S
‹The Ghost of the Llano› in it. – But 'f possible, don't stamp the stuff on the
fore-edge this time." And he reacted as always : "Mygod; just 'cause I did
it once by mistake ! Or, rather, habit : y' simply *have* to with books on loan;
otherwise y' won't have 'em in the shop very long ! And even *then* there're
the ice=cold types." While we shoved our way through green & brown
pesterations.

And once again, somehow ‹touched› anew, gazed into the meadow,
some of it curly, but more of it stringy. –

– : "Is'is it ? Our rendezvous ?" –

6

And sit at last, and rest, (even relax; we were permitted 1 teensy swallow;
now each & every aura of our vapors, be it sweat or chancery, was justified :
"You=two, o'course, can keep nicely moist & coolish allover !". They nodded self-righteously and from a brook-cooled bottle drank of that nervous
stuff, ‹soda pop› or whatever it's called.)

: "The table's been laid for you –" / – : well-buttered pumpernickel, and

‹cold smoked loin›. He, a sandwich of drippings, with added FONDOR
fumigants; slave of spices. "Show of hands, Who has never taken a lick of
the A-1=bottle," he parried amiably. And I, (the courage to confess has
never been my forte; but I was always adept at diversion), as if in sudden
enlightenment : "How would it be : if, in celebration of luncheon, we were
to address one another by first & middle names ? Just for these few minutes." They beamed excitedly; even they, bereft of their city, gladly accom-
modated themselves to the peculiar opportunity; (In heavy=pregnant
coquettery, Ruth twitched shoulders & hips. So break the ice)

uhm – : "Helene=Franziska ? – : Could you pass me the salt=shaker ?";
(and reach with a fist for the fistily offered long pot, in penis=format, with
a thick fiery-red head, rather portraitlike, SUPER CHIC : sly fellows, those
manufackturers; "Thank you." : "Don't mention it. Frans=Friedrich." she
replied slowly, and very ungodchildlike.) / "Are you aware, by the way,
that in some brooks of the Lüneburg Heath – for example in the Small
Water here as well – one can find *pearl oysters* ? One can view large-broad
antependia embroidered with them at Isenhagen Cloister. Tawny heath=en
ladies wore whole necklaces of them : MARGARITANA MARGARITIFERA !". (Not
quite large as pigeon eggs; ‹bitchin' aches›). "Uhm – Felix=Oswald," Lady
Ruth commenced : "Hand me 1 of those mommified hard-boiled eggs –";
unwrapped yet another slice of bread from the rhubarb leaf, in which it had
been swathed (my advice !) to keep them country fresh; ancient custom.
But ‹eggs the cleanest food› ? : "I once had 1 with a wriggling=live earwig
inside ! – And if I'm not mistaken, a certain ‹Bremen Society for Scientific
Research› has quite some others matters to report : Nono !". / On the
whole, the air seemed full of slips of the tongue : using an allegedly=En-
glish word, Felix characterized the ripple=tracks, down in the brook sand,
as ‹nipples›, (a claim which, strange not to hear, went unchallenged). Ruth=
Susanna merely gave a dreamy tug of her halter, setting the ambrosia jello-
ing. And Hel elongated a leg to the far bank; held it in the air for a while, (as
if considering : where to put it now ?); and then placed it beside her, at an
acute angle contrary to all police regulations. Sighed, too, for the man ‹who
would her equall be, in berth, in stayte, in propurty›. (Which wouldn't be
all that simple; granted, THEUERDANCK only means the totals of ancestry &
acreage.) / "What doest thou think & fancy, Felix=Oswald ? !" – : ! –

: ‹Enter 2 hares !› / And we froze; their jaw=bowls full of chew=pap – :
the way those=guys sat up ! And did semi=headstands : hoppety pop. And
were real joy=boys in general. Until Ruth hicked, (a malicious soul
would've said ‹belched›) : startling the fellows. Made very clever figures
with their ears : ? : ! And dashed headlong under the nearest fir's petticoats.
/ And we could breathe again; (first swallow; and did both profusely, too).

"The BIBLE declares hares ‹unclean› : 'cause we were speaking of it a while ago"; (Felix). "Totally addlepated," Hel grumbled; (there were some things about her worth redeeming. A ‹task› which in my cowardice I preferred to duck; and instead spoke of hares' & deer's notorious fear of thunderstorms) : "But thunder really does resound unpleasantly in these woods ! – By the way, ‹antler-stump salad› : was an 18th=century dish !". (Whereas we contented ourselves with mortadella; Felix with tinned=fish in fact) : "If herring had names, no one would eat 'em pickled," he said, equally passive and filosofic; chewed, (fair eats fowl & fowl eats fair); and rebutted with his ‹Free Left›. "Like a monkey chewin' putty," his spouse remarked; astoundingly unmerciful, as is the wont of spouses; gave her head a shake as well at the lusty play of his mandibles. And then offered me ‹in compensation›, with the most ravishing mons=veneris=smurk, some of Her scorned Saint John's bread : –. Now granted, I, too, would have preferred a toast . . . but must I, when challenged in this manner, really be ‹better› than he ? . . . and so dutifully pitched in ‹pit chinned›; if possible the smallest of the shucks. Hel was already munching, childlike & unthinking). "Did you know that those famous ‹husks that the swine did eat› is merely another one of Luther's 18,000 errors in translation ? What does the Holy Original simply say ? – : ‹carob pods›."

And lean back. Doze=digest. / Even if you turned a closed eye there would still be wind in the woods. (Int'resting, how I avoided the word ‹blind›; lookathat.) The smacking sounds of the Small Water here. Grass husked remonstrations; (and ceased them. / Barking fit ? – Not all that far away; or was it ? / And, faith (‹concert today, it seems›), the hyperdistant, subsoft internal shaggings of a tractor, he just keeps roal=in' a long, presumably from the WSW, was a better match for Ruth's rustling=grapples as she packed the valise : even as a child I always found it ex=citing and =hilirating (one & the same thing, I suppose ?), when, on the early radio of the years after 1924, half a dozen stations maccaronied their nocturnal jumble; (and if you *really* pulled yourself together, you could indeed ‹separate› 1 from the other : how the first would whisper piratically from ‹Cherna=gorra›, and be promptly & brightly contradickted by his sidekicker : ‹Nono monnte Neggro !›; (and the whole scale of mere two-worders staunchly joined in, substammering teeny-windy with ‹dididd=dádidd : ditt=dáa=dáa=ditt !›). What impoverishment we submit ourselves to these days, letting ‹governments›, with all their FM or TV programs, have their muttonmouthed way, ‹axe=ept› it in fact ! Prior to 1930, if a radio dealer didn't offer the most comprehensive short= & long=waves, it was grounds for a right hook. I submit, that if I can speak English : then I also want to hear Great=Britain's broadcasts. (And all the more so those

of Greater Britain : nothin' but ‹Ottawa› and ‹Melbourne speaking›.) And
whoever truly wants to limit himself to German, should add 1 station from
the GDR for every Federal Broadcaster he listens to; and finish off with 1
Austrian and 1 Swiss : that way he'd know 20% of the ‹truth› at least.
(We're All really dread=fully stupid; and the Nabobs of Bonn are right
to torment their folk à la ‹Channel Two›.) But there are other firms that
do produce lovely export=receivers, with first-rate short= & long=wave
bands, especially for South America, SOUTHERN RADIO CONSOLE TANGO; a
man should have one of those, 'zounds Kalundborg & Motala.) / And the
ongoing rustle of wax paper across the heath.

Why did Hel have blood on her leg ? : "Let me have it, you : 'nd I'll give
you a peddycure that you'll feel till y' come t' the blessed enda your days."
She lay long-stretcht over the dilapidated footbridge : below toes snapping
mockery; above her sloppy tongue looping the last sweet=pulpy traces of
Saint John's bread, (and gone, into the cheekpouch). She languidly un-
jointed herself, and laid the green moist end of her limb, heel ankle, in the
middla my lap; (inciting *my* blessed end to sheer rebellyun. But with firm
hand stuck the Band=Aid around the onset of calf.) : "‹Hares unclean› –"
she said in her sluggish way, and gave a lazy & chiding shake of her head :
"‹Crischun› – : that's somethin' very stoopid, I think, don't you ?". Let her
leg rise like a tollgate, clear up to verticul; examined my plaster=work, laid
her head at an amiable slant, and gave several sequential nods. (The arts
of unbelief, that's all. And the barking really was somehow ‹closer› perhaps ?). "Not a bad spot for a house, actually. This hi-rise," Ruth muttered
critically; and finally sat up. – "*I* propose –", Felix energetically forced
his way in : "t' vanish for a bit." And Ruth propped herself up onto her feet;
in such a fluid motion that she no longer needed a ‹meatoo›; Hel followed
her mother's example. / I first waited politely until all three had grown
invisible in the larch planting – how quickly that could happen in the
woods – and then did the same at the foot of a remarkable fir, (‹the hand of
Douglas is his own› ?; 'sindeed it was). (But these fashionable underpants
again, with a thrice=moral safety=slit ! I stamped and, snout aflare, cursed
the company responsible, be that whoever it might be : searching myself
silly ! – finally . . .) . . . : revolving many mem'ries : wonder if Felix still
preferred to keep his right foot forward in the process ?; he was the only
man I've ever seen do it; (but then he was a queer duck in general. And Hel
was his daughter.) Near=far I heard Ruth pushing her way through the bush=
high larches, alreddy heading back down to the bridge; (women really can
ur=inate lots faster). / But all pretty=healthy treelets, of both sorts, (the 1s
with yellow-green, and the 1s with blue-green needle=leafage – I had automatically taken a few steps forward. And consequently froze at the long

snowwhite=planked back rising up there from moss & greensward ! In
the middle of a bearskin=capped guard of june=nippers : a short copper
rod slowly thrust its way out of Hel. Toppled over=below; (while ripping
off up=top). Then arose a slender but very long tone – like someone whistling whistfully through his teeth – and I hastily re=moved myself. All un-
discovered : 'xcuse me, eavesdropped larch : 'xcuse me, unshushpecting
Hel ! – From the moment I first saw & heard it, I couldn't stand the word
‹BITUMEN› : just retreat !).

But stopped stock=still : *so boorish* was the strange voice asking
"What're *you* doing here ? !". / Lookathat : a mini-puppy; with a half-size
young=forester on the leash behind it. (Carrying his gun, naturally, à la
‹Lord o'er life & death› – well let's just stride a little his way. (Although
Ruth was Lady enough to down 6 pieces of *that* sort, and before lunch.)
He heard me coming, too.) / And stand there; hands (contemptuously !)
behind the back. (Even *I* was a half a head bigger than this Green Horn : are
you ever in for a surprise !). Right away he turned more polite, (but just
‹somewhat›). : "What sorta=uhm cook=out is this ? !". – (Would make a
‹good soldier› someday); I merely bowed, and picked up my hiking-stick.
Watched with satisfaction how directly behind=him, and soundlessly, the
‹bushes parted› . . . – : "What's your name ?", he automatically shouted,
spotting the silent=cold face hanging there in the sky above him. / (You
asshole ! Everything that voluntarily ‹dons a uniform› . . . but ‹be silent, my
heart !›; for I live in a state of justice & rights.) And, oh, behold the splendid, young-boned aide ! . . . / : "I am the Princess Ilse. – And dwell in
Ilsenstein." : Hel voluntarily & sorrowfully forestalled his predictable next
question concerning her ‹permanent address› – young as she was : she al-
ready=presumably knew what ‹officials› are capable of. The ‹Woodprince›
(NEHEMIAH TWO=eight : another one of those LUTHERIAN translation jokes !),
kept looking in confusion for the chair=below (the one this Lovely Child
must doubtless be standing on). When, from the other side, came a dis-
sonant=courteous greeting of "Tally=hó" : ! – : How bout that ? : Was even
taller, wasn't he ? !. (And a slow, dank sound arose behind Felix – *what* it
was, was promptly revealed by the odor.) / But purely as a picture, 'twas
indeed ‹delicious› : this aide=decamp to hunters, a little greasy=type, and
all too big=mouthed for his age, allround loden plus hunter's shirt. Between the two candidates for spookhood, spookhootch=Asbach. / "You can
go on ahead," I said, forbearingly; sympathetically, in fact. / And He actually left ! Let his little terrier (apparently it didn't feel all that well either !),
lead him off=down the lovely meandering path : –, –; –. –

Ruth (amused=reproachful) : "I mean Felix – –." Whereas I, roused to
serious dudgeon by that five=star idiot : "D'y' know what we definitely

have to reintroduce in Germany ? : THE NOBILITY. I'd say we're ripe for it :
just look at him go ! – There's millyuns of 'em. Just think how we could
reward ‹loyal civil servants›, ‹deserving offisirs›, even ‹parliamentaryans
of all parties› : they'd serve themselves t' death at the mere prospect. The
government could save a good third on salaries & perks; and/or the burden
on us tax=payers 'd be lifted by 1 third." "The latter's hardly likely," Felix
said, musing; "they'd have to ‹establish› a Ministry of Nobility first thing,
includin' baggage=boys & hair=olds, ‹Le Noir Fainéant›. – But you're
right o'coarse; that'd be the crowning 5= 7= or even 9=pointed tiara for the
Nobull Enterprise. Speakin' of ‹crowns› : might we not p'r'aps, in light of
our vickt'ry over the local forestry office ? a very teenyweeny 1, Ruth ? –";
(and sank pleading=adoring to his knees; finally putting their faces back at
equal height – and Ruth immediately scrunched hers in mistrust; given the
unwonted sight). / "Imean Felix. – How big's that ‹teenyweeny› of yours ?"
she inquired, not without asperity. (Asperity Aspermont Aspermatism.)
Whereupon I had to think of ‹Crater Helenae› o'coarse; and was coerced
into an explanation, in spite of Felix's horrified menacing face : "We
would, naturally, let *you* decide the measurement, Ruth," I cajoled. But
she, mocking : "Your mouth's like a wallet, with nothin' but phony fifties
in it : no way : here : here's your ‹Crater Helenae› –"; and pointed to her
own daughter, who, somber & black=striped towered beside her above the
primal glacial valley. And then we received 1 thimballfull, a very different
‹crater› than what we'd ordered. "T' your health !" Felix said venomously,
as I gloomily gazed into the corky cup – barely covered the bottom of the
birchbark tumbler ! – (and he would, more correctly, bear two names in the
future ‹Imean=Felix›). / "So, my child –" Ruth, businesslike : "'nd now
we'll indulge ourselves as well –". And poured some – and yet ‹some›
more – : many times more than our ration – : "Ruuuth !". To which she :
"Nono"; and, harder still : "Your nose alreddy looks like – like wine
yeast." : "Shoulda told me that 25 years ago : when I was wooing=you !",
Felix gnashed; and received the apt reply : "It didn't look like that then. –
Come : here, my daughter –". And Hel extended her arm by a yard, with
no trouble. Set the tumbler to her silent face; (and didn't pull an iconic
muscle : even though I had, with clever foresight, filled it with 100=
proof ! – "Good was thy drink, mother." she announced after a while.)
Then Ruth did likewise; kwott leet=set Juno; (and as it was stuck away,
my poor flasklet glinted, glassy & gloomy, at me : its faithful lord). Now,
however, with inconspicuous heavy significance, I laid my hand round the
telescope –; (and Felix nodded, more determined than grim Hagen : !).

"But please place the breadcrumbs, as a lectisternium, here : on this
sandy spot : The titmice want to live, too !" –

: "Whereas we shall separate now for a quarter hour – *must* separate –", I added, with sanctimonious regret. We made slight & catty bows, as if by prearrangement. And withdrew, almost immediately, through the midst of coniferred=armies. / ("Maybe we'll find some now," we could still hear Hel say. Turnaround : ? They were all=reddy moving up their water way. But were quietly groping before them – you could see it by the sightly=un-natural backward tilt of the upper=torsos – with their feet. Aha ! To Felix : "Fill in ‹pearl oysters›.").

7

‹No hay atajo sin trabajo.› –

"At least they're finally outa sight," Felix greedily replied : "C'mon; give us an honorific swig." : "You're allreddy practicin' for your job as ‹hair=old›, 's that it ?"; he added as well, for decency's sake : "Listen, they're never all *that* far away : 'nd y' can dance through these woods pretty damn fast. – Well; to baffoul the eevul chants –". / : !. – : ! ! "Ahhh –". / "A splendid region, actually !"; Felix, while we promen=aided more peppily through prickly shrubwork : a circular trooplet of mushrooms; 1 light-ninged tree, the bark peeled off in spirals, the sapwood, too : ‹The Land of Flints›. / Granted, there were also tank=tracks, (which, however, fortu-nately turned off from our path, to the west, where the sun was already hovering rather snugly above certain treetops.) : "Well, what sorta trees are they ?". But he, the wept of Ruth=Susanna, dodged cleverly : "I refuse to know trees that habitually allow tanks to drive into them." Not without dignity; somethin' to it. Ne'ertheless : "‹Ash, when green, is fire for a queen›". : "Why's that ?", he inquired after a pauselet; (over 50, and still thirsty for knowledge : but that's how it should be !). And I described for him the sweet fragrance of burning ashwood, (to the x=tent that one can paint a new=strange odor with words) : "But don't go felling any just for that ! Only if perchance some clodhopper 's already done miss=chaff with his ax : then y' fork over a mark, 'nd take your faggots." –

– : "Gettin' cooler, don't y' think ?". "Not excessively" I reposted with flippant pouty=lips; "All the same, your concern does you honor o'coarse : come the next crossin', we'll permit ourselves t' cover up the ladies' upper bodies a bit : *that was what you meant, wasn't it ? !*". And, before he could assure me of the sulky opposite, I had alredy led him sternly over to the bank; softer & slightly more menacing : "There; take a look at *that* – !" – For there they stood, not 30 primal=stream yards away, on a dam between 2 ponds; scratching & thinking on the dyke. – "Interlaken" a stirred Felix whispered; I, more censorious : "'sindeed : ‹Inverlochy›. If you can grasp my meaning. – C'mon. We'll join 'em." –

"You'll have difficullty ever masterin' the 250=foot contour line without Us," I announced gruffly; showed it to them, too, on the map page, drawn in black, thick & threatening : right across their path ! (And they were sweet; and played along; and hooked onto our steeled arms – enchanting in their need for support; all ‹weaker sex› : ‹Unmeke in his courage, the eyenstar of trowe deedes› ‹Yet was his herte gay›.) We, then, all heroic defiance; all black (fekete) regiment of the Hunyadi Matyjas; (1 eye, granted, always aimed at the=their convex and/or concave wonders, as heroes are wont to do – Ruth's plump shadow, however, was indeed a sight to behold; even Felix, who must have been, to put it mildly, accustomed to her attractions, pressed her forearm hot-hungrily to his nose.) / : "And now each of you will put on a jacket !". We tugged (quite clumsily to be sure) the soft=gaudy stuffings from their pouchlet. And went at it : this time it was ‹hands up !› for them. But held them high, so heart=felt & smiling at our tender care; (and we let ours glide, yea=slither down them, *sooo*. Felix, the pig, used the opportunity, while I was cloaking Hel's head, to lend Ruth ‹a hand›, of the sort that would have had FREUD's highest approval, ‹The Man Who Touched›. "Imeanfelix=pff –", Ruth starry=eyed. Then, to be sure, I perforce had to at=tend somewhat dilatorily to Hel, too; she stretched her arms, poor things, so stiff with X=stasis. A somewhat very long piece o' goodfortune. While that ewenuch beside me, his nostril hair quivering lecherously, was still pursuing his sordid handywork. And I smoothed the colorfull thing – at one time, in my day, they called those glad=rags ‹cassocks›; what they're called today I don't even want to know – down & downer her body – (a paucity of buttons as if she were the strictest mennonite : her hollow belly) – : "Felix : Hurryup.") –

"C'mon : We shall assist you to pass this so glummy pond – ‹gloomy + glum› in plain English. – 'd you find any pearls ? Or eels p'r'aps ?" : "Oh, there're eels here, *too* ?"; and at once I had to report further details to housewifely=nibblelusty Ruth, about the nightly catch of said critters : by torchlight; in the Lutter; equipt with hip=boots; "frightfull up='er= toonities for couples, let me tell y' ! : 10% of the locals owe their ex=istence to just=such amusements." But she simply rocked her unbiased pretty=thick head : "Fan=tastick nook here," she remarked matter-of-factly. And, striding=forward, (with the sheer=same words as Felix=previously) : "Y' know –" she confided to me; "we're considering whether : we ought not t' buy a little piece o' land, too ? At first we thought about SWITZERLAND –"; I inter=rupted her at this point : "When GOd created Switzerland, HE squandered all his gifts on nature till it's no longer beautiful –

and there was absolutely nothin' left for the people=there : nono=Ruth !
‹Flatland & Ref'rence books› ! *my* CREDO." (And responsibly skirt some
lovely heather; nor=walk in a deer=track; honor a fefferling's yello.) /
"*Quite* right" she replied with M=fasis : "You're somebody a person can
con=verse with : HEL & school ! : what *is* goin' t' become of HER –" – and
shook her head anew, keeping steady alongside the pond. "Well, a bookdealer surely; quite=organic"; (who'd ‹never need a ladder, even for the
highest bookcase›, I just managed to squelch it). "Ah, You=two and your
damned books !" she bristled self=controlled : "Hel is already intractable
enough : I haven't heard her really laugh now for months." / And keeping
steady alongside the pond. (‹An Israelite speedboat cruising the Sea of
Galilee› was the dainty=revealing report on the radio not long ago. Behind
us the laconic dawdles of father and daughter; beside me, in Ruth's knap-
sack, the chink of her garter-belt-snaps, ‹Phoebus, what a word !›). But the
wind was turning ever more obviously=gradually to the north, (a supersti-
tious alumnus would surely spell it ‹grad=U=ally›); and the sky, although
still half=clear, had begun to move.
  : Shhwrrr ! ! ! and all Three started back ! (Hel ‹instinctively› against
me; and I laid calming hands on both her hips, (as if I wanted to depants
her, (which p'r'aps I did, too) : what a good thing that my, let's call it,
‹arm› was already too weak to be able to carry out even a fracktion of my
notions !). And what a to=do, those three !) : "Poor ducks, ladies & gent. At
the marshy ends of these ponds, there they land & live & spawn : permit
'em their paltry standard of death." And away they flew, into the purple
hole of the sun. / Mystic regions ? : "You're simply not used to it, contour
lines with wild ducks above. And, ‹mystic›, Hel ? : We *are* not here for
Miss=Tick; we are in the country." She strummed a somber chord on her
own tummy; and then, as if by way of x=periment, turned my afforism
round : "‹Realism› ? We *are* not here for realism : we are in the country."
(Didn't sound half=bad, either.) –
  : "So. That's behind us." (To wit: that dangerous=aforesaid line.) Ruth
uttered her busynesslike "Safe." And even Hel offered me her thanks, by
means of handshakes & curtsies – "Forlorn maid; thou mockst thy aged
godfather ? !" – but she made winkie eyes, (1 at each side of her long face);
and inquired with malicious cunning : "Do you wish to apply the rod ?".
(And let her eyes rest on me, hungry & awaiting further tongue=works :
‹Corruption of elderly gentlemen by minors› : there should be punishment
for *that* !).
  "And so here – for 1 last time – you can wade in : not *much* can happen
to you now. Unless you nixies are contriving to be nickered !"; and a slight
raise of my cudgel, the junupper one, menacing. Hel nodded (‹I know !›);

obediently walked into the brook, and bent down over the stony cross-
bands; (Miss Bandaraneike. But the water around her stearin skin looked
all leaden now. And again the ramble & whissle of invisible pinions beating past us overhead : it was ‹high time›; in every sense of the term.) "We
shall bravely make our lateral pass. And in a quarter of an hour . . .", what
was with Ruth ? To make her point like that ? (*Another* house lot ? – But
no; it was much worse) :

   : "Lookathat, kids – : those tree roots ! Howbizarre ! –". We looked
around around us. Then at 1 another : except for a bank=ruppt fir stump,
like any of a hundred we'd met today, blackbrown with whitegreen lichen=
wicker (wicher=licken) we really couldn't . . . . . : "Yes, that's it; THAT 1 !".
/ And here came Felix, galantly bearing the snaggle. Laid it decoratively on
the needle=worsted; (and then we Three walked around & around, admiring it; like ninnies. In her grave manner, Hel watched us, five=sexths of
her torso towering above the water. – Be polite, and compare it to something; but quick, to what ?; oh, carefull now : 'd be awfully easy to make a
misstake !; better just nod at the thrill of it . . .).

   – : "Superb –"; Ruth, in a rapt whisper; then, more excited : "Like a
skate-ray, isn't it ? !" – –

   : "Say, we'll take it with us. – Put it on one o' the tables in the store. And
stack nothin' but STEFL editions of STIFTER around it : people'll be crazy
about it, Felix !"; she made enthused fists, and beamed from one to the
next. (The first folks to be driven crazy would doubtless be Us. Felix
made one last try; he said casually) : "Wouldn't be all that bad, p'r'aps –
I mean : *definitely* not !", he hastily corrected himself, under the influents
of Ruth's eye, making to express its dismay. But turned to me instead,
and said, full of perfidy & all intimate=businesslike : "Uhm=we'll make
a note of the spot, Franz – 'nd t'morrow One of Us 'll drive over – with a
car – –". (His ‹One of Us› was a real treat ! But I didn't have to pursue the
point; for Ruth had already interrupted) : "So that Somebody can get the
jump on us in the meantime, right ? Nono : heave to; it's not all that heavy."
Now with undisguised trenchancy : "You are men afterall !". (Hardly anymore; 2, 3 times a year.) But she wouldn't hear of it, and strode to the water
way; for the sweet sake of brevity. Over her shoulder : "If need be, you can
both take hold." (And then naught but cold shoulders.) –

   : ? – ? ?. : "Nono, Felix ! *You=two* want some crowning bit o' finery for
your murch'n'dice and/or établissement : later, 'ph=all else fails, changing
off. But on principle, no." He still seemed totally irresolute; (which is to
say, he knew of course to what he was dewty=bound). "Enough to make a
man want to rambottom his way through an oak=fence !" : "Damn fine,
Felix : where 'd you get *that execration* ? Just imagine it ill=lustrated !";

I put my hands to my flanks, and made a lusty din; (an occasion for yet another ‹GOd bless celibacy !›). "And STIFTER of all people," he said scathingly, "the ‹Satchel› or whatever that crap is titled. – Oh, that woman, if only the devil 'd finally . . .". (At this curse the sun went down, and the heaven gave a frown : "Doesn't have to, Felix." Also, to soothe him some more) : "In 10 minutes we're at our goal. Rest a little. – And it's only a coupla steps from there t' the village." (He already had the ‹skate-ray› in his hands as it was. We strode, long=legged.) –

: " 've y' thought of anything for my reprint=enter=prize ?"; he, grumbly. And I, (happy I could distrackt him) : "So not FOUQUÉ's ‹Parcival› then ?". "Nope ; no=way." he replyd caustickly. / "How about JEAN PAUL, ‹The Paper Kite› ? Not a soul knows it; cause it's not included in any collected edition." – "There y'see; now that's worth consid'ring –", he commended. / "The ‹Quinctius Heymeran of Flaming› by old LAFONTAINE ?" : "Never heard of it." ('s if that were a reason !). " 'd have to read it first." / S'lections by LEOPOLD SCHEFER ? : "Haven't y' got 'ny *more* unfamiliar names ?", he asked sarcastickly. Then testy : " 're these guys uncopyrited ?". All of 'em, totally. / "Apropos ‹total› –" he said nervously : "Is it really totally empty ?" Here, please : he was allowed to shake the tellascope sheath with his own 2 hands – ? : not the feeblest jiggletinkle togglejinkle shook a snuggly answer. "We're as good as there. Look : the first roof is in view." / : "Just down this path t' the left=here : 'nd there's the meadow; they'll be here any minute. – Well, give it t' me for a little, too, Felix –". (And the foolish fellow actually gave it to me, for the last 100 yards ! And soon Ruth and Hel would behold from afar how I was bearing their precious skate-ray; ‹voilà un homme› they'd indubitably have to conclude. Whereas, at the sight of those magnify=cent wading feet, all he could think was : "Just imagine 1 helleva printer's error : that set ‹cunt› for ‹cent› –; and everreddy gave it a try : "Ascent; indecent, lucent." "Not a red cent," I said coyly. But he was enthusiastically plunging ahead : "dead center : centrifugal force ! – Well ? !". "Fi donc" I ejaculated; (although somewhat mechanically : could I just leave her to some gross thickskinned ‹boss› ? . . .) –

: "Laydeez and Jennts : You see before you the fountain=head . . ." : "Leave us outa this," Ruth said; although not in the least impatient, (or even ‹angry› : so high did Felix tower above her new, barbarically splayed furniture. But I added fuel to her fire, too : "Say, the wood's still *quite* hard & firm : with a little care it'll last *fur=evver* ! – I could tell just from carryin' it." I added discreetly : modest=y'see.)

And offer valet=service. : Felix to his Ruth – : was I mistaken ? (I really had to turn around to them : ?). : "Ouh nouh," Ruth responded : "You're not

'n the least misstaken. / Lissen . . . . .."; and agreeably=nimbly waved
the cloth triangle up & down : . . . . . . : it crackled electrick=indeed ! THE
LADY WITH THE SPARKLING PANTIES what strength the woman must have ! /
Meantime, Hel was patiently doing splits above the fountainhead. "Hey,
c'mere : help me !". I reached under the scant vault of her armpits,
unfathomed caverns; helped her to the safe shore; (and abigailed for her,
piece by piece. – "I have my nicest frizzle skirt along. For 'mergencies.",
she indolently confided.) / And were really so close=to=town, that from up
on the high bank came the yapping of arfs. The cropped moon ventured. A
child watched us from not=faraway; (who had been setting fertilizer bags
on fire : red scraggly beards were still flapping from the soil. Strange sen-
sation, and I thumbed my=own silver=gray : silver=gray, another term for
pre=nocturno : all would soon be all=over ! –).

8

: "*What* time's the taxi s'posed t' come ?" : "Twenty-one hundred thirty
hours," Felix reported; and I involuntarily distilled that to "Nine-thirty,
then." (Hel noticed right off : 3 elderly syllables were juxtaposed against
8 hypermodern ones; and gave my elbows an enthusiastic squeeze – I
pulled the 5 (unlacquered) talons out, 1 by 1 : so was ‹in opposition› on
principle ?).
   What was this here ? : "Well, a tractor=ballroom; unmistakable." Because crude=beaded, rippled, retreaded, Conti=soled tracks intersected,
converged, ringwormed, waltzed over & across 1 another till it was hard to
explain in any more rational=reasonable way : "Just beyond midnight,
when the lumbering Northern Bear turns back, they move out : growly-
grummbullythump. Before those who pose=ess them, roused from the
fuddle of sleep as from a bog of stupidity, can perform husbandry. Steer
their way here, all on their own. Circle 1 another, un=tiring, on the SOIL
BANK : dun lop men ! 1 fieryred heavy COUNT INNENTAL, around a little yel-
lowgreen=skedaddler, Miss=shyling brand. – As women are wont to be." I
concluded bitterly : "‹Resulting›, presumably, in something like ‹electrick
centrifugal pumps›, ‹rotary=tool=cutters›, or at the out=side, a moped."
They nodded wistfully. (Perfectly believable, huh ? And the clouds ran a
race across the bright moon.)
   "Oh –" Ruth said, moved to delight : "I can already see that we really
are going to have to build a home here, Felix : the house=itself can be
quite small" – (which, by her lights, presumably meant a minimum of 8
rooms) – "but the lot as large as possible; with birches on it & heather.

Totally isolated : they'll just go crazy when they see it !". (In other words : visitors three times a month; motto TOTALLY ISOLATED; ‹Isolation Association›. Felix rebutted this, then, all on his own) : "Somethin' we can think about once Hel's taken over the shop. – By the by : isn't it getting t' be time for us to betake ourselves to the village, to the Federal Army highway ? Franz ?". I earnestly seconded the proposal; and we set ourselves in motion, couple-fashion, toward the East. / Before us, Ruth & Felix arm-in-arm. (The latter with the ignoble stride of a man whose underwear has burst its elastick : he who dares these deep woods must also brace himself for such. Ruth strapping & springy.) Their shadows had merged, and were marching along in silence, northwest of them. (Also in the same direction, a couple of starry bulwarks in the sky. Opposite, against a bluegreen background, just the semi=hemi=demi=moon.)

Who watched us rather malaplotly. In the manner of which I am specially fond : the egghead laid somewhat askew, the chin directed critically at me; (Hel, too, bridled and trotted off, making for the scrubby shadows). Where at once a dog set up a racket (ergo, a ‹larger breed›); but we all Four politely halted, too, and gave him a chance to prove his watchfulness. / "Isn't that singing, too ? –" Ruth, head turreting, full cheeks varnisht silver. – 'sindeed; a choir. And downright ‹adagio›. ‹Exult with us, ye Serroughim ! Give thanks to Him who Try=umphs !› : aha; KNAPP's ‹Spiritual Treasury of Song›, number 582, ruffly; in syngagyng a sangasongue. Whereas we were merely mutely try=ing, 'neath the startall of stars. (But just at this decisive moment, our shadows appeared to have suffered badly broken legs) : ‹For alarmed, my heart doth ever flee, beneath his magnet=minute=y.› – "A clockmaker convention, p'r'aps ?" Felix inquired excitedly : "‹Alarm› and ‹magnet=minute› – I don't think I misheard." "Gasbag. – Tosspot !", (Ruth, after some reflecktion; with resolution) : "*I* think it's romantic."; and held out a defiant palm to me : ?. "The *whole* of it, Yesruth"; (including the nocturnal landscape, that is : y' take some bad with the good. A lot, in fact.) / Still standing there : "I'm sure you=folks haven't any idea *how quickly* it can happen sometimes ! On the night between the 1st and 2nd of November 1960, the *leaves* met their *fall* instuntaneously : whole regions must've suddenly turned red." – "Like partsa the surface of Mars in the telescope sometimes," Felix remarked, a subsubscriber to CHAOS for many years now. / Likewise still standing there : the delicate tick of seconds ? "The battery for an electrick=fence. Counting the night away to itself." (‹The whole night›. We wandered chastely on; sequence as before.)

She was behaving more brambly again, (spurred me with her shoulder, too; but I was as deep as the Pole Star) : "Mommy claims –" I heard her grumble=flirting, while I practiced self-control : "that at my age y' don't need 'nything but hard soap & NIVEA=crème." (For once mommy was right. We stood, all=Five, facing the excessively ill=lumined bulletin board, safe behind its chickenwire.) :

1000.

MURDER !

On October 28th of this year, the body of an unknown female, presumably a servant girl of about 20 years of age, was found near Radenbeck, in the district of Lüneburg. The body revealed traces of a violent death. / Description of the deceased :

Height 4 feet, 4¹/₂ inches (Prussian); Body : well-nourished; face : round; nose : small; lips : projecting; eyes : light brown; hair : brunette or brown; eyebrows and eyelashes : ditto. / THE DECEASED WAS IN APPROX. THE FIFTH MONTH OF PREGNANCY. / Clothing : jacket of black orleans, trimmed with braids of black=white cotton, lined with gray dimity; dress of white-gray luster, lined with gray shirting, hooked from the front; bodice of linen with white dots, hooked from the front, lined with white dimity; coarse linen shirt, frequently mended, no markings; stockings blue at the bottom, black in the middle, grayish brown at the top, in good condition; 2 pieces of cloth for garters, apparently ripped from a kerchief, white with blue dots; old russet leather boots with laces, 10 Hanover inches long, repaired at the seam on both sides, wooden patches under the vamps and a row of nails under the heel, eyelets set with brass; hairnet of black silk with black beads and ¹/₄ inch rubber cord; small hat of black silk, trimmed along the front brim with black tulle lace, and above with artificial red roses, with black= silk ties and broad black=silk dangling ribbons with green dots, smaller white dots, white and green stripes; white=linen handkerchief with no markings; shawl of light gray or lilac, with brown hem and gray fringe; belt with one rose, of the same fabric as the dress; petticoat of linsey-woolsey with three red stripes and hemmed with blue and white striped linen; a second petticoat of black linsey-woolsey and hemmed with blue linen, still good; another like it, badly worn; a very old cotton quilt petticoat, blue above and striped with white, red and black below, hemmed with blue linen. / 1 key and 1 five groschen piece were found on the body. / The deceased was last seen on Monday evening, October 24th, in Bavendorf, district of Lüneburg; in the company of a man who declared that he and the woman were from the region near Hitzacker and were on their way to Gifhorn. The only other information concerning this man is that he spoke

Low German, was of medium height, and had a blond moustache, and wore a ring on his left hand. / OFFICIAL WARRANT : Information concerning the person of the deceased or her companion, including the last residence of the latter; the apprehension of the latter if that prove possible, and notification of the undersigned office concerning any and all ascertainments. / LÜNEBURG November 1st.

(Meaning still left from former year. And all written by hand; with ink that looked like bilberry juice. / So better just forget it.) I let go (as inconspicuously as possible) of Hel's forearm; (‹My father, the rogue, who eat me up› : nono. Leave me out.) She had already grown quite indistinct.

9

And stand. And wait. With skate-ray. / While it glared down on us from the highway, grew quickly, and passed like lightning. / "Confused pedestrian sinks," Felix suggested, "to his knees before the car : ‹SPARE ME› ! –". And laugh as loud & robust as possible : ! (And She, too, had dark tears running down her shadowed face : I could help Her wipe them away; but I could not help Her.)

NEW YEAR'S EVE ADVENTURES

1

(Snipping=snipping=snipping slips o' paper : if Somebody had sung me *that* lullaby at my clothes-basket, how at age 50 I'd be helping construct an index for a twelve-volume lexicon of saints . . . !. And glance at the things one more time from the idle corner of my eye : a thing with no guts, but only a spine; (and sometimes not even that : a book, a sick book, a terribly sick book); I took more & more exception to this ALBAN BUTLER !). –

: "I would address GOd with formal pronouns, just on principle; I don't get familiar with just anyone." "Didn't y' ever use familiar pronouns speakin' to your father ?", was his dignified censure; and snipped, (but also showed his teeth now as he adjusted the little metal stencil – $2^{15}/_{16}''$ by $2^{1}/_{16}''$ – and gave a mighty snap of his scissor-beak; though not the might of a strong man, just a nervous one). : "Hey, quite reluctantly ! I always liked how in old books the kids used formal pronouns to send their parents packing : distance=distance. Tell me where you're going; and I'll head off in the opposite direction !". He snipped. Irksomely muttered his "Holy Bembo –". : "Quite right, Jule : from the Italian ‹Bambino› meaning sweetbaby Jesus. You're always de rigueur." (rig her). –

: "Aren't there enuff *yet* ? !". – I first mustered the modest pile; then, somewhat longer, him; (and briefly the pile again : appeared my look had its effect; he even lowered his head. And snipped. Imploring) : "Don't ever lettem talk y' into another job like *this*, Jule : due January 5th ! And a ‹concise index› at that; meaning one that requires y' t' *think* : never seen the like; 400 marks split two=ways 'nd ‹think› besides ? Let the guy who translated this crap do the job!" (Granted, the remark was not original; I had now offered it several times over the course of the last few nights. And also knew his truly not in=valid rejoinder : how his publisher had discreetly coupled it with his next translation contract, aut BUTLER aut nihil; and then left him ‹the choice›, pff. 'Fonly y' had the time : in more idle hours, once you've done some honest work, there are indeed nonmoronic, cultural-historical reasons for reading Acta Sanctorum – but like this, when he had to be done by tomorrow morning !) : "Watch out : he'll make your next

contract conditional on you convertin' t' catholicism first." : "Dammit,
don't even mention the possibility !", he said, terrified. –
    – – : !. / – : !. / – – : !. / – – :
"Shall we take that hour's break ?" was his cutting question (with the scissors, that is) : "turn on the radio, I don't wanna miss the time=cue; my
watch never runs just right." (Hmyes; we had promised to reward ourselves
at the changing of the year. And then get back to work afterward. Tomorrow morning, the big index=file under his arm, he'd have to catch the
bus=back to Hanover : he was figuring 3 days to type it up clean, and at
24 hours a piece, pff. / –. – : "Well c'mon c'mon ! –", me, bent to the lemon
glow of the dial; (they'd be babbling boldly again in the Ox=ident, the
only nut=house run by its inmates; there's no government job so small it
doesn't deserve the gallows : wasn't that a soft junkling there now from
o'er the Seven Hills, the babble of Seven Mills, kiloheartsy & all Watt you
Wilt – ?). – Better adjust it a tad softer still –, – : okay.).
    "But by now, after all that ceaseless=snippling, you've learned the bliss
of repetition, right ?" : "I make a point of learning that by quite=different
activities", he replied peevishly; and eagerly directed his large ear to the
government=apparatus. / Where, predictably, there resounded the beloved
hodgepodge of bullschmaltz & observations by Leading Politicians, (all of
whom wished to ‹fight for peace› : to think they still have to use the demo-
bilized wartime phrases ! For fear of unnecessarily dampening the night's
spirits, there was as little mention of the robustly creeping rearmed=ruin-
ation of finances as of the imminent rise in postage rates). And more
‹Rhinelanders› in the prime of life. Episcopal words implied that, as is well
known, a good sheep lays down its life for the shepherd. (And we, collabo-
rators with BUTLER, weren't so much as permitted a quick illegal screw of
the face) : "'m tellin' y', Jule : next time" : ‹DITT=DITT=DITT !› –
    : "Eleven thirty pee emm : let's go Jule ! I can't listen t' anymorra this –";
he was already getting up, more than obedient. (And I took another interested look at his case for *two* sets of glasses : how practical ! He'll *have* to
bring me one the next time.) / Another peek at the stove – the little door
opened all on its own when, still a yard away, I stepped on the ‹'propriate›
floorboard : 500 times a day, roughly; now *that* could very well drive a man
crazy ! (Cold-shouldering : "I'm talking with the stove –".) He watched in
sympathy how, before putting them on, I first held my lined jackboots up
and twirled them round so the opening pointed downward. – : "Fetishistic
ceremony ?" : "Nah. Makin' sure no clothespins 're in 'em." Also, since his
expression seemed about to perturbate the more, (there is neither fantasy
nor logic left among men) : "Bosh, ‹monomania› ! Y' saw yourself 's
evenin', how the cats were playin' in the hallway : there've often been

clothespins in my runaround shoes. Or pingpong balls; and I'm not a man whose gonna let his metatarsus have the same accident twice." He contentedly hitched his am=mors wrapper round to morbleu, (drapery for the embrasure); nestled rheumassuaging at his lambskin collar, : "Once I get my neck warm, I feel warm all=over." And to top it off, his flat-black-round wizard's hat.

: "Flashlight ? – Superfluous : Oliver is in town. – But we could do *one* thing –"; (he, dean of all lazybones, was already standing, determined to take a break, outside the cottage; at the very edge of dappled night) – : "have a look at the chimney !". (And slip in & out). / – : ? – : ! : ! ! : "How bout that ! ?". For a splendid smoke=plume, long & curlywhite, arose from the house's somber gable bonnet; (and the twilit mask of the moon watched us with interest. – Explain : how I had tossed the worn-out rubber ball we found recently onto the blaze; and we could now admire the smoke to heart's content : "CLAUDIUS, ‹New Invention›; ‹Addenda & Sup'lements›.").

– : " 've you got the flask on y', too ?" – : "'re you suggestin' : we have another right *now* ?", I hesitantly inquired. But he, defiant, " 'sindeed ! –"; then, more dejected : "I gotta seize the moment, seeing as how SHE won't even let – –". (The sentence was left open at the rear; ‹By dark of night, a werewolf left wife & child behind›; fine; but) : "Not so much, Jule. We still have work to do." : "Oh; the night air'll keep us chipper," he claimed. Meanwhile I opened & closed the Bab el Mandeb Gate. And we turned up the footpath. Toward the 238´ 9½″ hill.

2

Treeable fields, countable stars, (navigable, marriageable, cashless). For the sallow moon (on a bristly felt pad) as good as dominated the Noble Enterprise. Otherwise, just 1 hand full of stars. And 2 lofty castles in the air, cloud=forts, silver=bulworx : one in the north; and we strode, con= fabulating, toward the other, in the east. He swung his infernal shinbone, and pointed with it : ?. (The orange star, just above the path ?) : "M'arse the godda war, o'coarse. For once ‹in opposition›."

For the distance of a hammer=throw, he kept sassy silence. Then claimed that my ‹walking ahead was obfuscating his view of the path›; played the more indignant; and demanded "Another !". : " 're you fixin' to go sighko ?". But he got an unimpeachable grip on the flask. Pounded his planked chest as he drank; and didn't choke on it; (There're guys who can do it : I once saw a guy in the milli tarry who spurted up the barrax steps while guzzling a bottla beer; in Sprottau. Prob'ly a mattera grace. : Now why were these ultramontane turnsa phrase constantly crossin' my mind ? ! Ahyes; BUTLER o'coarse.) He fockused on me – :

: "The *things* I've *done* for *her* –" he said (nay, ‹scanned›). Explained that he meant his ‹His Frigid One›; and followed up by calling it a case of hope crestfallen. : "Spell it with a ‹Ph›, Jule. – T' think you're still not innured to the axe=yumm : ‹Women have so little zeal for knowledge !›. And y' can tie a Great Federal Seal on that one." (Inasmuch, however, as I was unable to resist the well-known amused smile of the bachelor, though behind lids lowered with all my might, he swept away my demurrer with an English phrase that even=I had never heard before; (ahwell, 'twasn't in vain that he'd spent the last 2 years translating gangster novels, nothing but cathouses & drugdens, enabling him, 'zounds Romany & Shelta, to steal the march on me a bit); quite apart from the fact that, unlike myself, he truly loved polylingual lit, the kind you find on film=rolls; or carbon-paper boxes.) He spake his lamentacioun as we continued plumping uphill; ‹Man use crypt, faund in a buddle› :

: "All my life I've proved man enough to keep my wife from having to work for strangers : I kicked away the cumuli that ventured to form about her, and defended her soft-boiled breasts from every storm=front – without a care, she, my beyashmakt ever=jejune, praised the LOrd GOd whether for good sleep or the ghosts" – (and at that I ope'd my eyes to hear the better : I knew Lady Gertrude; false pearls at her neck & a real devil in her undies; she was everything a man could dream : but, woe, what=all she was *besides* !). "What is the body ?, if not a horse to convey the drunken rider through the knockturnall woods of this world; a contrivance to keep the thinking head at a distance from the ground ? – And if I should err, I surely err in the best of company !". And as he was provocatively taking my measure, I gave him my curt & worthy imprimatur : "Speak on, Jule; thou speakst well this day."

: "I early humbled myself for her sake. Said to asses of like=seniority ‹Ho, Camerade !›, and whispered behind superiors ‹Thou ninny ! →›. I alternated swallowtail words with thundering eructata; and no garbage breath escaped me that was not spiced to please her with OLD CHANCERY or Harz=cheesy ambers, with pinkee dillisks & thymey dumplets or shallots out of Arnheim. Her chambrett I bestank so to spunish furiosos; and all my life defrayed the costs of her feeding : her turlyhide I laded with sweetend potatums and plumped mil(k)t=rice in her do=o'day=numb . Her squat beauty I swathed in nightgowns of my breath, from HIDDENSÖE unto MONA, tuberosy & sylkyblack; and infallible periodskirtings, unlibertied of fringes; groinscrubbers, too, and talcum with wolvesfoot for her moister angles." (‹All angles are equal› : the claim may bring a mathe=muttician to rage, but nothing could be more plausible to a poor gillyflower=person. While he, EZEKIEL 16:7–14, schnappsodized on) :

: "Her room I fitted with red=earthen circle=gardens and intercablings of gutta-percha; everywhere gleamed most softpadded empire, and fountains brusselaced from Albrecht's wells. I taught Her total eclipses of the moon in their seasons, and spoke to Her of STRABO's chlamysed figure; I described for Her the seirim, and CHWOLSON's nodding terafim were not alien to her." (And with voice louder than nesussairy) : "I journeyed with curiosa, and did skald often enough myself. I couched her roundings; oil-clothed over for cohabitation; and set my oil=hat for South West, until I appeared like unto LETTOW=VORBECK downunder : Who will refresh me, ovawearied, decalorized by the massage of fire ! ?" (‹Who shall deliver me from death from bondage ?›; but he fouled & howled so vehemently over par that I handed him the glassy air=brick once again : ! He, mollified) : "Oh thou of uncircumsized eye, much there is that thou doest not yet discern."

All this spoken in a region everso desolate, in leafless time. We were walking now past frost-skirted young firs, (all between 12 & 15, when the beasts get coquette !); and scant-powdered birch shrubettes (there wasn't money enough for ‹more›); and pointy stars stabbed through even the sparsest branchlets. / – : a very distant=delicate ‹Bow ! : Bow !› ? : "Let's call it : a ‹pheasant=hound›. There was even ‹pheasant=haze› at one time, so says ADELUNG."; (Signed ‹Lord de la Lande›. You couldn't yet see the light that belonged to it; although, *I* knew well enough where it lived.) / And stand there. (‹With no sign of a life›. Apart from the tan oak leaves, obviously cut from expensive packing paper, still twitching from their claw=like branches.) Despite the hibernal reduction, an enormous number of details : no matter what, you always see more than you can put into words. –

And drink ice-chilled air; the evershading needlewood at our back. / : "Where are We ? !"; Jule. And I, right foot set with dick=tatorial gravity on the TP : "10 degrees; 21 minutes; 37 point onetwosixtwo (1262) secunts east of Grinnitch. : 52 degrees, 42 minutes; 25 point zeroninenineeight (25.0998) latitood north." Pause. "At 238 feet 9 inches above sea=level : ‹Vivat Jhaun Neighpor of Merchistoun› !". "Uh=long live," he said hastily. And pondered. With passion : "Couldn't you p'r'aps express the current= time somewhat more un=popularly, too ? – I dunno : the older I get, the more I'm averse to things poppular; strange." (Please; I had prepared myself) : "2 millyun 438 thousund 030, point hmlessay 99 : ‹Julianic Nights you'll never forgettem !›". "Which is bout the same as zero 31," he specified, with amazing discernment. With great e=motion : "Hey, ain't that a marv'lous pros=speckt ! –"

Oh yes, besnowed meadowy expanses, finely hatched with last year's grasses : "The ‹Lax Moor›." 1, 2 strapping birches 'pon it, (one unfortunately abused to serve as a hunting blind); the loveliest copse of alders in the whole township, with whom you could converse as with trees of age & experience. (‹A tree for habitual greeting› : ought to suggest that again to the Messers Granger; as in Hermann's days; (though I don't set so terribly much stock in him, Hermann). But probably best by employing folklorick omens : ‹So long as Mathberg Woods endure : so long holds Hillfeld firm & sure !›, (‹If snow doth fall on New Year's Eve, the old year soon will take its leave›.).) / "Ohyah : even the barn looks classy." While we, upon carpets of ermine, strode to the edge of the sand=pit, enough to phynully put you in an aëronautic mood; (and make the features of the aër yet more enthusiastic). / Now I pulled out my tasting=spoon, ‹lipto sum tea›, which I carry with me in winter on principle; (rugged aluminum; would be invaluable without the printing – but in this world of ours there's nothing left unprinted); ladled from the nearest tree stump. And sampled. – (So knowledgeable, so expert, that Jule at once turned curious, then envious. And demanded it as well. (Very tasty, by the by : more old columellow=stuff that has got mislaid for the most part – or better, mis=tasted, mis=tongued –, the ability to ascertain the tastes in rain & snow; and then conclude whatever can be concluded. There are beety sorts; and some that smell of dog; sometimes of soggy raw flesh; seemed new=trull today. And/or there was no way adequately to tip the tongue=scale, made sluggish by the savor of mountain=dew; but that can happen sometimes with any instrument.) And Jule shoveled, ‹my boozem rages Physuvian›.) : "But now let's draw some infurences ! – What sort=a snow is it ? : 's its origin the deeper air, from Lake Dümmer ? Does it come from the Harz, where spooks mount Brocking, Nehsing & Silverslogging ? Can you taste the ‹so-called GDR› ? Or would you guess the direction of Eydtkuhnen, if not indeed Alma Ata ? : speak up !"; (and meanwhile kept shoveling between whiles, till even the handle was coated with frostwork). – "I would say : the sorta snow that always comes from dead=a=head." And chilly silence (mine); and perplext pondering (his). / (Very distant, SSE, a car motor. P'r'aps a vet, helping some poor sow or other. Jule did not hear it; he was list'ning to a little . . . . .) :

: ‹Kss. – Kn=Knpp ! – Knn.› –

: ? ?; Jule's paleface; (I immediately barred my mouth with my finger, by way of example : !). ‹They are lightfingered, nor do they shy from the moon›; and point : a little to the righta the loathsome hunting=blind . . . : ? . . . : ! !. (A marten namely.) The slim horizontal=guy; with his white notch for a sweater=neck : "That's how you identify 'em." (Some demigranger or other had apparently dumped brandnew garbage; from a dilapidated blue tile oven, prams & chair detritus, to scarffed-up tin cans, and culled p'tatoes.) He cast 1 glance up at us, all ‹Hawkeye›; but nary a greeting, simply went on botanizing, most sedately, across the frozen disk of sand. – And we soon withdrew; respectfully, on tippytoes, on a straight slant across the straggly woods.

Stand there dumbfounded ? Sure : firs sproutin' like blades of grass; behind them the sallow moonsky, and – aha ! – mid all the ‹greensward›= grafix, jauntily flung about 30 feet into the air, a half duzzin bicycle=tires : trees with earrings, 't'sall; and that had flabber=ghasted the ignoramus ? : "Just a perfectly normal amusement of farm=boys. Can y' imagine how bored they must be ? : I once watcht for a good five minutes while two kids spreading manure, kept tossing the shit behind 'em, back over their heads. Outa pure desperation; just for variety's sake. Y' get that way in the country. – Call it ‹sirrealism›, so let's get out from under." / Or : "Noo=Jule : ‹Collectin'=Pinecones› is outa the question in the Federal Republic; ‹there's something rustin' in the stayta D=Mark›. – 'Tis said there's a law in world history that requires rack before the ruin," I concluded with equanimity. (But then did stop stockstill; and consider my sister's recent=silver anniversary, yonder in the GDR : in many respects, she'd seemed more congenial & ‹normal› to me, with her livin'=standard from the twennies & thirties. Far fewer cars, (very soothing !). Much cheaper rents. RECLAM= editions like in days of yore; and the new encyclopedia already had 8 volumes ! All broad=casters to the contrary, the laburnum was in bloom; 'nd I hadn't seen a single tank in either the kinder=gartens or the toy stores : *that* had pleased me right off !). "Wellnów. I wouldn't wanna be on the other=side either," he said nervously : "'ve you spotted somethin' else ?" (Because I had stopped beside the first tall birch. : Self=evident; where aren't there other sights to see ? Here, in fact, threefold) :

1.) A ‹natural› ice-bridge across the narrow ditch; and the pretty pattern of hare=pawlets on it. (And further, cross=country. But he smiled too refinedly my way, like a coil=potter. Whereupon I felt myself morally compelled to point out for him numero

2.) far less ornamental) : in the ploughland snow a teeny bunny, first shot and then dying of fever & hunger. "Notice the eyes : alreddy tidbittily picked out by crows." – : "That's GOd's affair; not mine", he tried to talk his way out. Then, indeed with greater shudder : "My, but you are a terribly upright charackter !". ('twas, granted, an insinuation – I am after all just 1 more poor bastard made in Germany – but even=I sensed an urgent need for needinganother.) – And so I accompanied him back to

3.) the same birch; and had him sight on past the trunk – : ? – : "No. To the right." – Till he had at last made out that 1 murky pointa light : "The only place in the whole districkt where y' can spot something like ‹the next village›." – (Since it seemed to disappoint him) : "O' course you gotta thinka somethin' else at the same time ! : ‹It was not long before they came to yet more deserted valleys. Only rarely was a cottage to be seen, with low-burning lamp behind its window-panes, or the dying glimmer of a hearth visible through the half-open door, where a family still waited, it seemed, for the master of the house to return, who might perhaps be wandering drunken across distant hills.›" (And offered it to him then & there – : –)

And wrested it back from his flummoxed talon hand. : "D'y' hear it ? ! –" – : ‹Pumm !› – : ‹Pummpumm=Pumm !›. (Nothin' but little pumms on the horizon : thus knocketh the New=Year at the gate !). – / : "Jule ? – !" : "G'rhard !". – / And *more* acusmata : and the lower=horizon was seized with charming lutescent spasms, greenish, too. And renewed mortarations : the west sides of our countenances promptly took on catchfly hues : "Jule – ?". And he, dignified, as is only proper at life's turning=points : "G'rhard."

– : ‹Pfshshsh – – : Pfff ! !› : *THAT 1* was *very* close ! – Right : not a half=mile ahead, the daintiest golden effervescings began to parabolate from the Parrot House, the sort I suppose one might meet in a goodly portion of earth's inhabited regions : pink & yellowygray; and dull seagreen & cinnamon brown; (the puppy we'd heard before now accompanied every deadeye=shot with enthusiastic upplouds.) While the hamlets glowwormed. The Mountain of the New Year, ‹Munsdeludo›, commenced rising before us. And we, aware of our response=abilities, strode village-ward, (where the canzonas of the canaille could be heard now), through kneehigh ramparts, thrown up by the snowplow. : "There're 7 by the way." (Birches. And he at once nodded judiciously : "Thus one speaks of ‹7 birchues & 7 sins›".). –

(But very cautiously now.) : "'Tis best we walk invisible." (The moon alongside; demure or odalisky pale.)

3

Close past the aurodrome of rustimusicality – it sounded like the heavenly militia practicing ! / Peek round the corner : the blue ice-cream flag waving lustily, not 100 feet away, above the burst-open tavern door; in which stood the Landlord, rigorously rattling his keep=keys, Granduke of the Granary,

Boondockers in Beer Heaven; Hopsfulls and Maltcontents. – : "Corambé ! Just like with Rascal=Henke recently."

Loden-trousered volunteers, triddlesnapping round self=made=widows in neat half-boots that made their strapping calves that much more visible; brewsing & ruminating. Able-bodied farmhands, all mustered out with a gonorrheal staff in their mars=shall pants, and roughkneed cleaning ladies, inflamed by hot, glowing with byooty and cruelty : he Homo Arraktus, she Chan=drép. Cockytic codgers, life-size monomedallists, with venerable cookie=dusters, and double-bedded grandwenches, fiery rings round their mouths and buttermilk in their hair; the snow cuntched underfoot, they fletched & stretched. To be sure, more urbane participants, too : he Tarzan by sartor's grace, she Miss Celle en gros, and both gummeryward subscribers. Inexcusably scanty-clad shop=helpmates, with chic gladhands, doing their dammdest to show what wasn't in stock; and ambijockular coughee salesmen, antsypantsy globalltrotters, (one might have taken them for highschool teachers, if their faces hadn't had such intelligent expressions). The ‹Raven & Sugarloaf› Inn. / : "Let's pull back, Jule. In the shadow of this shed."; (before he could even take his stand, allhell broke loose –) – :

: crouched down; lifted her shin drape; and – as quick as the dean of Badajoz – ‹whiz !› – ("Kee=rist, what black vulvet !", Jule, moved. As mud as she cud be. And, naturally, didn't look all that bad in her invisibles; inaudibly circumclinkt with garterbelt snaps. But : "Listen, avoid unnecessary invulvement : Rural Beauties usually suffer from gruesomasst ‹fluxes›. Because in winter, ruthless and merciless, they have to use ice-cold out=houses : keep your finger off."). / All the same, shear without pawse and despite the grimmy cold, couples appeared : lads, pollen=full, and moist ecstatic lasses, quivering on perlon=pipes; she his groundflor, he her furrstirry; enero S=Cape : "Vaginula blandula; ‹Concerning Kiss'n'itch Rites among the Erstwhile Wends›". (And within, the kettle-drum banged out the boarwarlike writhem; and the base=tube=a farted at every third fingarse=snap.) / Naturally, elderly aborigines ruptured the silence as well; some merely wanting to pass water, or stretch their legs. : "Play 'nuthuh round," they confided each to the other, (meaning ‹slut= machines›). : " 'nd t'morrer back t' the mudditch." The leaden smoke of their stogies vexed us like temporary nose-rings; (‹Punishment of Sniffers›). / But now she did appear : the most soilicited Athanasian of south Hillfeld, along with the most renowned beard-splitter from the northern halfa town – ("Well, Mister Threelegs ?"; for Jule was bending forward as if he'd have liked to toss this baby off with the bathwater sometime. And/or ‹be at loggerheads with her›. – But, faith, 'twas gettin' hottenheavy) : he stormtroopt the bearasst berserkette, her cuntenance cosmetickly wrencht, (and dubbledecker minutes of vow=alls); her thighs splayed wide; he shot her dextrassly between wind & water – and tried to raise up limpgroined and netherloindish, while depanted, she casually volleyed a 12=pounder from her muzzle. (Lilacking in the clouds; and the moon waited discreetly in his own Marble Arch, entrance to Hide Park. They had no words for their feelings, nor needed they any; instead prumptly retreated to the inn & out=house, in'n'out hose.) / : "No ! : Nothin' for *you,* Jule !". – / A subcivil=servant, who o'coarse had to fumball with his flashlight, illooming us as well, and consequently recognized me, and consequently greeted me – although, an obvious embarrassment, he alreddy had his Phallstaff in his Caesar – shyly accomplishing only a fraction of what he had intended here. Greeted again, quivering with rage; and with=drew. : "Converted fillinthrope; has never seen the sea. He works for the railroad; she can't stand low commotions." / A totally emaciated pair, (‹He hath besprayed her thrice with lotions soothing›); but she was urging him all the same yet again, big eyes on her prowd nose, all sortsa lips below : cachez ce sein ! But, LES FILLES SONT LIBRES; wounded, he staggered into the Jungfrau's col; (and Jule, sympathetic : "Chee=the mort's bite !". Inasmuch as I was only too familiar with the basseuse of his mauvais goût, I did not assume straightaway that he had felt the ‹sting of death› and therefore called upon his ‹mediator›. But rather, with musing shakes of the head, went on watching the deafmutual intercoarse.) Until the phellow finally suckseeded in giving her the last specimen from the bull's interior. (‹Now seeks he refreshment from cheese and from cod, CANITZ›.) / "Enuff studdy of Fortunatus' purse; and the nevergreens of our E=motions ?"; (and gave a try at a boobyprize smile : ?. He consented; with 1 somber nodd from the days when squires still received tributes in assay upon waiving their right to examine a birthday-suited bride. – And so into mid=lane, quick as lightning. Then, at a dignified stroll, on past the reigning beerocrats; who paid us – quite rightly so, from the viewpoint of nonprofitability – no special mind : " 'py nooyeah, Mistuh Crusius !".)

And unruffled, stride off to their right. With whompings behind us; softer pummpings; and, fading, bellsabubblings :

: ‹Sure the láss / es ar'eager / to pláy=now.
In the pár / lor & in / the sa=lóng . . .›

4

While tarbarreled night rolled on more muted behind us; and assininification yawned again, stretching out her leaden scepter over the EEC, (oh, peckish, peckish !); while from on our left, there where no farmsteadings were, came a 40% display of cooper moon=dainties, and while the repulsively high ‹gallows›, (ostensibly just for drying out the firemen's hoses) kept semaphoring its first candid ‹MORITURI› of the year, Gratis & Long – at just that moment, wouldn't y' know, the circum=hatted fellow came to a halt. He was mulling things over so intensely that his eyes started rolling; dandled for a moment with lips & teeth; and then began to grumble :

: "Nur wenig frommt's, daß ich, ein müß'ger Fürst, / am stillen Heerd hier, an dem kargen Strand, / bejahrtem Weib gesellt, dem rohen Pack / ein viel zu gutes Recht mit Würde sprech' / Das scharrt & schläft & frißt – und kennt mich nicht !›. – Okay, translate that ! And be equally masterful and instantaneous about it; or . . . !" (And behind him the Greek ‹pi›. – I decided 'twere better to make a stab at it; if only for practice : case one would ever end up again as a POW or in some other sorta concentration camp; and some megalomaniacal warden were to develop a taste for a court jester. So furrow brow; & soloic stammer) – :

: "‹It little profits →›" – (here he nodded, well-pleased; a noble word, ‹profits›, is it not ?) – "‹that an idle king /› (a supple bow : and I won some time while he vainly attempted to suppress a smile of deluded grandeur) – ‹by this still hearth, among these barren crags, / match'd with an aged wife, →›" (cautiously leer his=way : ? on the brow of his head, a battle between indignation at my presumed license and the thrill of the expert translator. The latter soon won out; in token of the serious vexation his Mem=Sahib must have caused him. And offered curt, though warning endorsement. I kissed, in my mind, the hem of his robe, (for he still had not had me put to death); and continued with submissively disgusting enthusiasm) : – "‹I mete and dole / unequal laws unto a savage race, / that hoard and sleep and feed and know not me !›". (Full of lofty disdain; so that King Yule needed only to underwrite the proper emotion with a gracious nod : ‹Executed at our Summer Palace in Novosibirsk› ! He was so full of himself that he was quite empty.)

: "What d' y' know –." (inspired to further strolling; invisibly accelerated by most duty-bound boredom) – "wasn't all:that: stupid."; (and never has an alphabet=scrubber gazed more superciliously upon a typewriter= oiler). "Okay, that's that, Jule ! Don't forget, I have in my hand the power t' weaken your Coffee Royal just as I please." "Yes o'course, sorry," he said contritely; "I merely meant that you could easily have 'em set your own name at the top of a translation sometime : d'y' wanna leave the world never havin' once been in print ?". (If possible, yes. While I prepared our ingress; and we ground our way over snow with ashes, oh cinnamon oh sugar.)

: "D'you always bang your feet like that ?"; me, pointedly & cold, (since he was about to clean his soles by knocking the edges of his shoes on my frontdoor; he apologized again). "Nono, Jule; you stay here for a seck. I'm gonna take a quick look at the fire. 'll be right back." ("What'm I s'posed t' do ?". I heard his crude & sulky quibbling behind me. / And hesitated yet once again at the stove before grabbing the thick oaken chunk : I always feel sorry for the wood. When I picture the farmers' annual winter slaughter of birches; just like last month; there oughta be laws. – But it was much too dark for scrabbling in the shed for briquettes.) –

: "Let's do somethin' for the New Year, too, okay ? !"; me, with severity; outside the house again. "Gladly=gladly," he replied filled with great hope. But then gazed at me in mighty disappointment when I merely pulled a boxa matches from my coat pocket; (a coupla days before I'd found an old Bengal light in a drawer, and really was curious). We now proceeded in procession to the ‹spruce nook›; and I coerced the sadsack to join me in a few preliminary ingenious conjectures concerning the color of flames we might expect. Turned around solemnly, making little polite bows to all four winds – "Captatio benevolentiae, Mr. Impulsive : so they don't blow it out !" – and then scraped across the scratching surface –; – ! – ? (nothin'; damn). "Give it to *me* –", Jule, whose interest had be=gun to be aroused afterall –; – ! – : ! ! ! : nothin'. – Till he was taken by the notion to ‹pre-warm› it with a regular match –, – : ! "Ahhh !", behold the sparkling= frazzled, pitchgreen=hissing hole in the night ! –

: "Forgiv'st, my LOrd, this witchery of flame ?". He did indeed lick his lips again=subcon'ly; but then shook his head in vigorous confirmation : "Charmingly done ! – It just occurred to me : uhm='ve y' ever noticed how when you're awakened by the alarm, – usually I get up a good deal earlier 'nd all by m'self – that the trill, be its sound ever so gentle, not only causes an acoustic interruption in the continuum of said dream – ‹so what's new› you may well mutter – but gives it a visual yank as well ? I've observed it now a good dozen times. The principle seems to be that quite suddenly, as sudden as it is apparently random, beautiful technicolor & richly articulated images emerge briefly. Then the ‹awakening› follows; and the material has vanished, while the trill of the alarm goes on." – "Best thing'd be t' give me an example, Jule."

: "A large sack sinks from above down into a very black space. Pointed at the top, open at the bottom – about 5′ 3″ tall" he anticipated my question; then : "The cone's exterior was a lovely brilliant lilac; with open fretwork, as if neatly carved with a vast number of ornaments – analogous to an over-sized shuttle=cock," he said impatiently, (since apparently a little ques-tion=hole had opened in my fancy & exemplary face; I hadn't even noticed) : "but much more elegant, finer & richer. Bright on the inside, tending to white; though even there an unmistakable pale lilac=shimmer; seemed to be illuminated, but the source of light was nowhere to be seen. The image – it was brandnew, I had just been a train station – sinks quickly, then, down through the black space; and comes to rest on a ‹concealed› floor. I watch, delighted – : and it's gone." (Hm; first let him go on.)

: "Or : in a dream with GRAY as the predominant color – was it some concrete metropolis ? – there suddenly emerged an elliptical=little lawn, seen sort of near & on a slant, the way it would appear to someone standing above it. The gray, which as noted had dominated until then, at once moved to the edges of my field of vision, where it became extraneous. The grass of a very rich darkgreen hue – much ‹more juicy & organic› than those flames just now; although they did remind me of it – the lovely tousleheaded blades ‹lay› gentle & soft : it occurred to me that it would be ‹hard to mow› !" (Since he voluntarily shook his head at himself, I spared myself the gesture. He continued, pointing, with his hands, at what he meant) : "And in the middle was a plump little island of tall yellow flowers, ‹butter-cups›; but with heads as big as dandelions. There might have been 20 to 30 in all. – This phenomenon's lifespan likewise very brief." / – / : "The first theory that comes to my mind, Jule –" (and here a responsible hesitation; was really quite int'resting) – "is m=thatthat, indeed equally ‹richly articu-lated›, pizzicato of the spluttering alarm could excite a parallel, radio=laric optical pattern : ‹nerve ticklers› in both spheres, huh ?". (Although he surely had already come up with this same, truly hardly remote notion him-self. He dismissed it, too. And, visibly ‹sobered›, merely provided a few catchphrases)

: "A wooden crate one time, about $1\frac{1}{2}$ by 2; which, while the alarm rang, filled up with brown logs – I intentionally gave 'em a thorough exam; 'nd I still recall that one of 'em had 1 blackbrown branch-knothole. / Or : a dis-tant darkgray hem of woods above nearby snowcover. Then ringing : and now, from left to right by the way, a pale gray plank fence, man=high, moves across : a polyarticulated wall of pickets. – ?" "Ripe for IMAGO, Jule," I lauded; (inappropriately curt, I know; he deserved more. But now, at one-thirty in the morning (and with 6 hours of reading-off index=entries in view !), I was no longer capable of much, except perhaps the all=lallic protests of the creature : contra creation & creator) : "C'mon, Jule, avanti. Have a bite. – 'nd after that it's back t' the galley=oars."

5

and an eggcup with a wizened jacketed potato in it, a leaden bottle, a large ringshaped loafa bread, (me, as landlord, courteously doing the slicing. And Stand & Eat.)

: "Gimme the bowl of whaddayacallit –". Well, I gave it to him; (but it was canned mushrooms, cooked in vinegar & oil, with nutmeg, cannel & gariofle, a masterpiece by my cleaning=lady !). He munched slowly & sadly, and let his sullen gaze wander here & there; from kitchen table to long desk, here cuttingboard of limba, yonder gilt librarities; (I, too, would've most preferred to stick my head and its shriveled eyes into a briefcase, there to take my ease). / Help him with his to & fro gawking : here a sacka raisins, ("Not for you, Jule : for blackbirds & pheasunts."), there the white Not of an uninscribed slippapaper, yesyes. Here ‹TUNA IN ASPIC›, ("Open the can from the bottom – : ? : !"; for, as axiomatic and customary in capitalistic lands : there were 2 splendid slices ontop; nothin' but smithereens below !), there the serrated ruler, beside my memory=ring (consisting of 3 interlinked rings; one of which you let Drop & Dangle, whenever you wanted to remember something : decidedly better, and more ‹cultivated› than the shabby=modern ‹knot in a handkerchief›) : "No ! I will *not* sell it to you, Jule. Suggest it to the folks in Forzheim : but patent it first yourself; y' could make a killing with it. And as you spurt by later on the Queen Merry, y' can toss me a phony fifty. – B'sides, it's an ol' fam'ly airloom." I concluded; (blushing inwardly, for the situation was about like at MARKTWAIN's. Jule just displayed mocking dentals, too.) / The wine bottle ? Give it here; (and pulled the cork right up through the tinfoil : y' could finish 5 index=cards while y' futsch around with it !). The sauce=pan clattered, the cass'rolette bejingled out of his hand, (and the poltroon blamed it on the poor lighting : "Thy lamp is gone out; give me of your oil," he pled, unsure of himself. I was wearing the red robe of anger in any case (a kind of knit=camisole; whereas the skimmilked fellow was wearin' a smock like a church pew) : "Listen, there's a good 100 watts ! Y' prob'ly wanna indulge in another YUNO by the light of YUPITER=lamps, 's that it ? – Whatcha lis'nin' to ?". Jule first blew into the mouth of the beerbottle before he drank from it; explaining that the little tube-shaped fog at the top bothered him : he was no fogeater; shoved it into his mouth then, and showed it off : –. Muffled & Long; (the muttering of the pot to the hotplate) : "What'sit say ?" : "That people ought to be mercy=hypodermicked : the men at 45; I'll let you make the de=cision 'bout the women." / Leave 1 ringlet o' sausage ? ! : "It'd just take fright, Jule. – Meanwhile I'll put the bread in its cubboard as it is"; (and a sidelong grin; for it was the sorta sausage he didn't like). He stomped and washed it down with beer; while I sipped at rum with milk; lending a spiteful ear to the cracking of knees in our moldy trousers, (and the belch from the half-digested afternoon coffee tasted exceeding unpleasant – p'r'aps the punishment for my unfairness. "Damn, 'd choke a crocodile !", he went on groaning. And we drank beer to wash it down : radiomagic Eye & Parrot=tongue; LEITZ Wetzlar above, chicken=feet below, in thick stockings, shamenraged, the skinny calves; 'zounds puny=tail & ox=skin : on the left 35 point 5 square feet of desktop, which, or so I was in the habit of assuring visitors, once served Prince Metternich; to the right, a potted Tree of Knowledge, on it a four-year-old walnut, which no man had ever yet cracked, and other uninsured utensils : yes now for ‹general guard-duty› ! (as We=privates in the 2nd, & not=the= last, World War had dared to call a good=sound sleep; if one weren't such a romantick, one would 've had the most blackmarketable inspirations long 'ere this !). / Sweet curiosity had meanwhile singed a coupla fingertips, and sighlindrical sucking thereon : "Grease it up, Jule, grease it up." Because he was dabbing round=at them, nimble-lipped and tongue-tipped – : "Wiff waff ? !" – "Take 1 droppa sweat from the left nipple of a pastry-cook's wife. Stir in the dust from the fore-edge of a THESAURUS LOGARITHMORUM, still unused after 99 years of hereditary lease . . .". At this point he finally hit on NIVEA : ? : "In the bathroom; as is only proper." Inclined his bibulous countenance to the earth; and groping johnwards, sniffed winterwindily; (use the pseudonym ‹PONTUS EUXINUS› maybe : 'ncase one ever should write something ?) The red rough sod of the littler throw=rug.

And alone in the haunted inkwell; (while He, randy as a gall, unremittingly abused the apparatuses within). / CATS: ‹GEDACHTEN OP SLAPLOSE NACHTEN› : not long ago, that ‹Tunisian Camel Saddle› in Hanover, (‹guaranteed to have covered 200,000 miles in the Sahara !›), fine=fine : if only, of a morning & on the left, my middle finger, plus those adjacent, wasn't stiff as cork, (the right was just starting slightly, the hand of oaths; I had presumably had to swear too many in my life, and who knows what these Bonnonians 'll come up with in that regard. Quick, spit out the window : the way the silvery muck spewed out of you a good five feet !). – From the sound of it, hyperuncircumcized Jule was pissing the toilet=bowl clean. (Something the ‹Other Sex›, the riders of the bidet, can presumably do only with great difficulty. That was my Locus classicus, whenever Someone started in with ‹chaste COOPER !›; I always had some fun reading him the passage with the inserted bookmark : ‹Balls and parties are no longer the high-light of my life; rather, I confine myself exclusively to discreet closet rooms, where lovers enjoy the most precious moments of tender intimacy› : Title ‹CONFESSIONS OF A POCKET HANDKERCHIEF›. A modern author wanting to get on in this world, and we do live in a highly cultivated just society, would have to blue-pencil (‹blew Pens all› diverse words : ah, Divine harassment of Justice ! (‹He hangs himself – behold, a tyrant just›, HAGEDORN.) And most likely He was rubbing my NIVEA round his glansing ring : ‹may it thrive & prosper !›. –)

: "Well, Jule ? – We ready to go ?". / But first he celebrated my ‹splendid can=lid› : plywood is indeed getting thinner & thinner and light as a feather ! I countered with the toilet=paper in the GDR, which only recently= yonder, on the occasion of the silver anniversary of my – "Know allabout it !" he snorted in disgust : "Hell, they were just decoratin', that's all." : "Oh, no, Jule; hey, you've never felt anything like it up your crack ! made y' just wanna sit there forever : y' could become addicted !"

: "And now let's cut the dawdlin' : c'mon !" –

6

He snipped. (His pocketwatch on the desk had fallen asleep, too.) While I, with protestant mouth, leafed through . . . ; . . . – : "Hey, listen t' this : ‹They, in their turn› Germanized as ‹One after the other› ! This guy, the translator, truly deserved to be beaten to death by a sophomore wielding an obsolete WEBSTER !"; (he didn't want to hear it; but 'twas true). And more poly=glosses, to bridge the lacunas in our languors. (I reached again for my unique ribbon=box, in which, purely by accident, I had stored mothballs : had turned the modern plastic soft as down ! : to think it could corrode plas=stix like that.)

: ? – (To wit: the nocturnal humming of the powerlines) : " 've noticed it several times this hard winter : the wires contract when temperatures drop below=zero. Not long ago, I couldn't sleep all night 'cause I thought someone 'd pulled up at the neighbors 'nd left his motor running : it was splutterin' that loud. – Today noon, by the way, there was a report that it was causing summa the mines to explode in the no-man's-land over toward the GDR : ‹'Twill be a cold night, old man Rudolph said !›" –

: ?. – : !. –

: "DIONYSIUS THE AREOPAGITE, Bishop of Athens; Ten=59 –" (and down the resta the page with the pointa my pencil, ganglia transformed into race=tracks . . . . . . / Turn the page : . . . . .) : "Jule, cut that out !"; (when a paper clip gapes like that, you better pay attention).

(Or pay ‹respects› ? Nah; no respect. But attention.)

CALIBAN UPON SETEBOS

*GEORG DÜSTERHENN entertaynd ze Myoosuz –
(tscheeper Bey ze Lump) – eetsch Wonn of
zemm re=worded him for hiss horsepitellittitie
wiz Sam Bladdy mad=Teariels.*

CLIO

: just get off ! (End of the road just ahead – after all, I had properly=prof-
fered my obolus .) –

   Halt !; here, make a note of the departure schedule. / Beneath the ocher=
moon of the bus stop (the wan green ‹H›ellipsed by its face); its typewritten
placard irksomely neck=high, aptly circumtinned, a cellofeign mug : and
here they were again, the 4 womenfolk circling me ! (The huntresses, that
is, from the bus) : All in coquette=hiheeled jackboots of patent leather;
plus breeches; jerkins of yellow, yellow, brown, musturd-brown shamey
(Velveton; guaranteed at 10 yards to look like suede, ‹escapade›); topped
by skimpy wide-awake hats, billiard green – their chatterboxing had got on
my nerves the whole way. More their shrill fourfold fidgety splutter behind
me, than the anecdotings themselves; ’m always glad to lend an ear, often a
source of useful stuff. Sure, mostly tidbitty tattle=tonguing bacchanded=
jobs on girlfriends. Specially the youngest, with her pale, puffy face, kept
harping, unflagging & jealous, at a ‹Rosel›, who had allegedly got herself
balled by a COLA de caballo driver in the scullery – hat=trick ? ; I didn’t
catch it all; ah luvsweetluv. Most unpleasant of all, the tall megaera on
my right=here, (almost a complete head taller than I ! Sure, I was no moren
a handvledgling m’self. All the same.); a med=student, who had told
about a ‹bone bazaar›, ’s if it were the most legintimate institution o’ the
roundirth : ‹Who stole my hand away ? !›. And took a deepurr breath, and
started in about the ‹toe=tag› that she claimed was habitually getting itself
thumbtacked onto the cadaver’s big toe – “Y’ dunno the half of it” was her
disparaging comment when the other Three at once clasped red tapered
talons to sucker=snoots with vampirocity, (and I my briefcase to my lap).
And then vocally pant o’mimed how ’pon a clinical night, in the course of
a learned vigil, there came, stiffly shuffling ’cross the lie Noliyum : a lady
presumed dead, but rising briefly again in total disregard of the duties incumbent upon her as per medical findings : “and her toe=tag rattled. –”.
(Only such natures can indeed ‹love the hunt›. In any case, it was She of all
people who now stood high above me, a reaping whipcord in hand; and

read along in nonchalant sotto voce from the bus schedulette.) All in a region so wild and 'neath the reeling dusk of the autumnal hour, (on the very postmeridian brink twixt late afternoon and early eve : 12:40 A.M., given as the last nocturnal departure; astounding traffick for 1=horse towns & this dead=zonal border area.) – Turn around ?

: and promptly you stood before the town=sign SCHADEWALDE. (Resigned nods : I already knew I'd be reminded of ‹linseed oil›, 1 of my (several) lifelong idées fixes from the First World War : that had been a melancholy holiday, when, by way of exception & after weeks of gray-brown turnips, ‹potatoes in linseed oil› had appeared; (sewn up in a package from our Liegnitz grandmother and addressed in smudgy ink : and now I saw the lump of salt at the chipped edge of the plate du jour !) – – so – fine; fine'n'good. Over & done with. Until the next town sign, that is.) On the far side of the road, a whitewashed milestone ‹1.6›; (but figured from ‹where› ?, not a clue : ‹Bugaboo›.) But now begin striding with all due dignity toward the hazy set of buildings nether near nor far : I'd been wrong to concern myself with those lassies, who surely only wanted to spend a m=eager, demi=vurge=inall weekend ‹in the country›, and do it as broad=gestured as possible, as is the wont of youth. (How d'y's'pose a ‹third party› would use *me* as a walk=on ? With tam-o'-shanter, grayhair & copperschnozz ? Green leather jacket & rough-nubbed knickers; (my sole excuse for the asinine sox, with their jumbo red patterns, was that I did not ‹choose› that sort on principull, but simply pulled 'em on : ‹Gray Hair›, and SHE'd be sure to have it, too (presuming she didn't ‹touch-up›, like most modern Last Roses) : ‹Hoses›. I looked forward to it as best I could : ? – hm; didn't amount to much; laden with too many harsh memories from my first 45 years.)).

Better just stride dignified : –, –, –,. Indolent smoke figures stood atop the roofs. (‹And her name was Fiete› : ‹and the rest at present ?› I didn't know; not METHE anymore, hardly likely. Always assuming, that ol' Adder, the drugdealer from Bautzen, who boasted he'd ‹banged› her in the park, ever married her . . . . . ?); but my road began to head downhill. (What's this ‹my› ?; *the* road acourse; I'd not yet advanced to road owner. Although DICKENS even had a tunnel.) Well, maybe it'll work out, what with the new ‹Collected Poems› my tax consultant had urgently recommended – I'd earned so much off my texts for pop tunes & marches of late that only a vanity=press book could save me from the revenuers; (‹Taxation no Tyranny› : that JOHNSON was another crazy coot !). The dusk threw a handful of pale tumbling doves high above the ribbon of tar. (‹First & Last Loves› – ‹doves=shoves› but y' can find that in HEINE – my how I'd gushed about Her back then ! At 18, when still Prince of Arcady was I : naturally, seen from *that* standpoint, today's enterprise was completely unrealistic; but all I really proposed was to get myself into an explicitly & irresistibly schmaltzy mood by glimpsing a youthful love : the German of 1964 wants sentimentality & parade marches; just like in 18= and 1764. And whoever still believes in stuff like ‹Change Future Progress› deserves a monthly income of 250 marks; and I mean gross !). How grandly infertile the antennae=figures. Each turned toward Mecca, automatically sifting out seven times seven unsavory dispatches, a most hammurabullistic piece o' cake : permitting one's folk to receive *only those* broadcasts that one has strewn ! (‹Croon swoon opportune›). I could still recall only too well those first months after the war, when the ‹Delirium Tremens› in Darmstadt published my ‹Ode to Defecation› : how speedily did I not abandon my adopting town & such unpopular thematics ! (Apropos ‹adopting town› : they had been able to provide me HER address post=haste merely on the basis of her maiden name. Must be whole agency-sized apparatuses; with thousands of employees who live from reconstructing no-longer-extant Silesian or Pomeranian municipalities ‹as if nothing had happened› – maybe one ought to regard it in fact, quite unemotionally, as a mere branch of local history ? All financed by our money of course. (That is, not from *mine* if possible : sooner do my volume with allround gilt=edged; on handmade paper thick as postcards; bound in skins of Patagonian virgins ! ‹Ear of rag able irrefragable ! – : Her rough raggable irrefragable›.)

But this brooklet=here – flowing on under the road so askew that its left railing picked up at the same level where its right 1=yonder left off – definitely had a stydgian look. (Which is to say, the faint=babbling waterway itself was mostly innocent of the impression. But tincans were rusting up from its narrow bed. Tufts of lopped-off alder kept fingering with displeasure : ‹measure for measure›.) I felt midstride for my PEREGRINUS SYNTAX : the most ancient of lyars, slovingly worn, was good enough for a TIMES=goûtlash of ecumenical councils & SKORZENY's memoirs : the man's a fool who wouldn't do his damndest to skim the rancid top from Arch de Bris ! –

(Ah, looka that : ‹The First Coxswain›. On terra firma, however; I left him more than enough time to finish. Then) : "Tell me – : what is the name of this brook ?". (Speaking very slowly; the way foreigners painfully employ their guidebook phrases : it's how I always speak with rural folk. And they with me, too, by the way.) The demitype, a patchwork of ligament, tendon & bone, looked up lemuroidully, an elm at his back, 2 paws still at his fly; (to 1 side a model=maple : quite marvelous crenated lady hands, 'proximittly ten thousand, lay about its trunk. Naturally=leafless its=self.) : "‹DUNGCRICK›" his loam-livid garron=profile answered; (‹laconic›, just as I thought – : but did I not now hear 8 hooves at my back again ? So make haste) : "How do I get to the inn ?". The fellow stomped the ground in the shallow ditch he appeared to be digging; (and pondered as he stomped : though I'd guarantee the destrier knew well enough; and a simple ‹dead-ahead› or the like would've fully satisfied me. I certainly did not intend to plead for a strand of the lockjawed crock's elflocks – yes, speak up !). He snorted heavily. – : "Well=suh –" he said, musing; : "theah's Tulp's, he'll take a body's money. Take mohren ten hahses t' get me in theah o' my own accohd. – A mighty landlohd; y' can't miss it." He pointed unruffled down the village road, his arm suggesting its curve; (and might have uttered still more, had not the huntresses been as good as on my heels !). He stubbornly tuned his mouth=works back to zero. The first called to the next : "Alex !". She then, named the third "Hermine"; (the fourth just stood there, puffy & randy. At least that was my impression; perhaps she was just *barely* still a virgin – " 'twixt'er toes" Roland (an acquaintance of mine) used to remark bitterly at every mention of the word.) She watched the mini=truck pass by, loaded with an eternity=box doing a rude dance; still empty from the sound of it; prob'ly on its way to fetch its contents; some guy who'd rolled a 7. – Great chance for me, to step well to 1 side, and then (dignified) on my way. –

Barn caves, their spermwhaley maws gaping at me – I tried casting them a simpleton's look, so that they'd take me for 1 of Their own and let me pass by unswallowed. (Should've fitted myself out with camouflage togs; a kind of LÖNS=hat and a green loden coat. But my whole life long I've lacked the requisite ‹ramrod back› and manly=sweaty jehoviality : funny, people've always & immediately taken me for a baseless intellectual – nowadays that's no recommendation ! ‹Intellectual› seems 'bout on a par with a medium=nasty curse for 90 years of every century; if you're lucky it can also connote a certain respect for 10 years or so. Which is then called ‹Weimar Republic›. Back when SHE was still named ‹Fiete›.) – I sighed. And in that same moment spotted the inevitable milkglass=baldachin.

EUTERPE

: and here came a dog roaring round the corner, of sullenest hue & of a size that would've scared the hell out of a less practiced traveler; (I was merely chthuneasy). But gave me an enthusiastic laugh; yowled in droll high tones, and drummed its forearms on the plank fence and set it rattling. Which diverted my attention to the narrow front yard, jutting out from the right side of the long half-timbered building; (uptop there appeared those same pallid deft doves from before – ‹a deaft dove› : maybe SHE couldn't hear anymore, who knows what=all awaits me here – landed (with muffled & elegant applause of their pinions), and then minced, with polite nods my way, down Gable Street). Gently weeded, autumnally=naked Mother Earth. Narcissi predominating, if I was not totally hoodwinked; (‹Marseilles tazettas› : last year, in the middla spleeny Emsland, I saw hyacinths & other bulbosities sprouting=budding=blooming from turnips, hollowed-out as ersatz vases, wiz korro=nets of mediyum saize, ovoid=ellipsoid= squeezed=double-edged). – : "Kirby ! – KIRBEE ! !" came the athletic bellow. And the brick of a dog actually managed, with the right half of its head, to gaze at *me* in infatuation; while airing its left floppy ear somewhat in the direction of the call of the inn door, (through which diverse sorts surely had come striding and/or staggering as well; for no less than the MAYOR'S OFFICE and the PUBLIC TELEPHONE were likewise located within, Congress of Public Communication Workers). And meandered full of pointless paths, so narrow only garden dwarves could use 'em, 'round a middleclass=oval central bed filled with wolf's bane for the nonce : the short thick, lernaeoid=flabby soil sausages of voles lay allabout. I dared to taper my left indexfinger, and amid steady=coaxings of "Billy Kirby Billy Kirby –" scratched the shortshorn fur of his brow –, – : and behold : he lowered (for him, identical with a mighty sinking of) his skull, friendly & dignified, to meet the taper of said member; (had only tossed on a pelt to keep from becoming human : Here shall I now find thee, Constanze ? –

– yesyes : Con= or Non=stanze; it was not all that easy.) Meanwhile ‹The Landlord›, unmistakably he, appeared at his door, (as only a man can appear at his own door) : broad, in an unpleasant way; the cap on the hulky head; in his hand a ring with (excessively large) keys; all potent landholder. Oral cavity very evident; the words, however, apparently hardly larger than English ones, and equally pompous=disjointed, the well-known deliberate monosyllabilism of high=rankers (who simultaneously pull up mentally somewhat short at the rear; eminently suitable for princely private archives); the tongue drumming slagly inside, (just like the famous tatoo beaten on taut manskin) : "Kerr=bee – – kerr=bee – –." (Now why had I come up with that added ‹Billy› as easy 's pie ? – Ohyes : KUPER's pie o' nears. But it could just as easily 've been ‹Marion›; much more applicable really : Topper Takes a Trip. – Well, c'mon, upper=gray matter; He was obviously waiting.)

– (‹Taprooms› of my life; and they knew no end ! Earlier, in my twens, stuck in a shreklekh job, I frequented ‹train station pubs› – from ‹*phren*etic› & ‹*quaint*› : rottin' helluva play onwards ! And now, once again, *thisspot* here.) / First the whaddyacallit entrancing : left, a small round table, onelegged=pegfooted, (though at the bottom it splayed into 3 sturdy roots – at which point the rhymes came to me, too : ‹sensing & fencing›). At the rear a stairway of medium width to the rite & up to chambers and souls. Next to the door, through which I was now bound to pass, a pompous sign, (full of glass mug=fragments of former passersby; something like a Nyooten=disking sighpher left behind just off center, which resulted, naturally, in the ever-popular mysterious out=of=bounts effect : ‹I want to become an impenetrability› ! Well f'rall I care : my nerves weren't quite as shot *yet* as KAFKA's, who filled his britches outside every closed door, 'cause there might well be something behind it : 7 years a clerk on the merchant cruiser ARGO, m' dear; the world's a *wee* bit more complicated 'n that; je m'en fous !).

Alone again alone; meaning, at a corner table (with my back covered, homage à KAFKA; to say nothing of the flanx) : and then the wallpaper alone ! Shrubwork, pine o'ertupped, with brownish deer, (2 hinds for every buck, as is only proper); riders in frockcoats blewed horny, (huntresses living from what their muskettes bagged); hairrier focksounds, (‹pointer flushes setter !›); a woodlet, jocund p'r'aps in kiddies' eyes – seen a good 300 times, however, just like=here, helm & hunter's horn, a bit *too* often, once you had your fifteenth year behind you, ‹Like Me›. Or the portrait across from me, half lifesize & twice as natural; (some sixteen-point stag or other : 'm also still sufficient mastera my nerves, thangod, that I don't have to take a second glants to know with whom I have the pleasure in such cases – let's just call it ‹Bismarck at Friedrichsruh›; hits it just about on the noggin, ou !). ‹Hagenau›, ‹The Nightingale of Hagenau› : I was ‹garrisoned› there for some months, too; and, post=humously inspired p'r'aps by the aforesaid REINMAR, had invented a new prose form, ‹PHAROS or the Power of Poets›. Evil chance had preserved the manuscript down to this day; I decided to commit the thing for good & all to my silent hearth come next winter. – But that ‹v. Hagenau› might provide a pseudonym, hm ?; 'cause my dapper volume had to appear pseudonymously, my tax consultant was right as rain there. Let alone, that aforefixing ‹Georg Düsterhenn› to leerick poems is quite impossible : folksy ?, means easily understood & sunny, merry ol' art. ‹v. Hagenau›, hm hm; Georg; round these parts they woulda called me ‹Jahtch›, along the Wall, the natives say ‹Orgy› : ‹Orgy von haargenau + Nite=in=gayl›; well at least make a note of it –)

– and, absentmindedly, fingering my protean PEREGRINUS, look up at him : ?. The fellow had splanted himself in fronta me, hands on tabletop; and asked brutally : "Beer or beer ? !". The sill (with heart decor) to the right & left of his shoulders; and above the TV, that horrozontally striped vase, modern & goofy. While outside the savage-hued bastard of car &

camper bountst by; (: so you, too, need some taming, amigo ? – I set my
eyes so piercing; and asked so quick & scathing) – : "What's all this
damned traffic here ? !"; (and 1 very curt energetic head=jerk to where the
vehicle had just passed : !. – Not a bad joke, really, his question, drolling,
but had prob'ly misspoke himself.) He lost a considerable portion of his
vulgar self-composure (to which he was not entitled); and informed me :
"– 't was the SEISMOS rig. – In the unduh ground blastin' bizness."

: "Might you still have a room for me for the night ? !"; me, lofty &
disgruntled; (all the same, since he now seemed sufficiently unsure of himself, the ‹still› implied an initial=tentative def'rence on my part : as if I
credited him with 500 rooms, and every=1 overbooked). – "Justasec –" he
said, respectful now; took his mitts from the table, turned head & shoulders around 90°, and bellowed at the room's third door : "Ol=she !". (This
again now in his previous fashion, spare of manners & words : Care=full,
friend ! – But 1 of the 9 sub=divisions would definitely have to be titled
‹Home Sweet Home› : 'fonly I can manage yet once again to be so veryvery
simple & gracefull ! I had 'ndeed knocked out a coupla splendid hits. The
one awarded the STRAUSS=prize that year, opposing conscientious objec-
tors, ‹to be sung at the mustering of the troops› :
"the sergeant laughed and snickered :
: ‹So you're no hero either ?
With heart not true nor Fed'ral ? –
Be gone, you lowly coward !› –")
But now the door he'd screamed at – damn, didn't that color tend toward
linseed again now, too ? – made ready to open – : and quite a young woman
still. Going by his oxygeny bawllowing I figured Her=Majesty for a two-
hundredweight pile-driver; with irongray mustaches, and a riding=mis-
tress rear. But this 1=here, slender & with a little sullen tilt forward, as if
dragging her faded zebra=apron; uptop a yellow=green headscarf; a dripping tallow-candle in her grubby fist – "Down 'n the cellah. Powuh's off
aggin.", her lean mouth said by way of 'xplanation – gave artless ear to her
god'n'spouse's question ‹if theah's still a room left ?›; (very nice of him,
adopting my ‹still›); but quickly realized the situation, (tho not quite
swiftly enough to keep his face from having to semafore a ‹Dammit=
woman, say yes !›). "Yah" she sulked. : "Tell Rieke t' change the sheets."
(Exit Madame Tulp.)

: "I'll have a small pilsner, please." (‹Me & my bottle together forever : glugglug, gluckgluck›; did wonderfully well at the time. Unfortunately I was still green & dumb in those days, and settled for a flat fee;
whereas royalties would've brought in a lot more – well, I wouldn't make
a slip like that again nowadays. And better quickly erase this ‹Orgy› I'd

automatically jotted down by mistake as well; (then blow a puff, flatulent=
cheeked tube=mouthed; then brush away the phibrous debris with the edge
of my hand : actually I was far less excited than desirable for lyricull production. Here he came oafing over with the damp glass.) – : "I'll pay now,
okay ?". –

   : "Thunderation ! – Why's that so *cold* ? !". (The change that is, that
he had brought me from my ten-mark bill. He visibly rejoiced behind his
facial flesh at this Little Tryumph; and I let him have some rope; then,
however, admonished him by rapping the table edge with the 1 five-
mark piece : ?). : "Comes outa the freezuh." he proudly retohted; "my wife
keeps a cigahbox o' change in : huh ice=box. – It's huh joke, but of'en
backfuhs". I let him get away with this for once. But now, with more
decamping mind, waved him off again. And then sat there to myself, of
furrowed & allegoric=ferment : didn't it seem as if ideas might be . . . . . ?
. . . – (?) – – : ! :

       : "The lights aglimmer . . . . ."
Nah; wryth=hum too short; ‹I sat, the lights aglimmer› – : ‹swimmer›. Still
too tacitean=terse, the silent man's exit : even the dustiest layerman can
mess=more with longer lines. And y' don't swim at home by lanternlight;
not unless you've got above-average water in your cellar : ‹dimmer› ?, but
that shoots the mood right off. ‹Trimmer›, tree=trimmer : what's my SYN-
TAX have to say ? Grimmer, skimmer, slimmer hymner. So, wrong again;
once a man's past fifty – as usual, there's some US=report or other about it,
not=KINSEY – he has fewer strokes o' genius. But it had a nice hopsy &
blackbrown taste, this cozy mugga beer. – : W=wait ! ‹beer !› –

   :"I sat all cozy drinking beer",
da-dámm da-dámm da-dámm da-dámm : ‹dear› ! :

      "here came my – – uhm – –"
nah; don't use ‹cozy› again) – –

      "here came my happy lad so=dear"
that's it, sure ! (And smile broadly, self=suggestively, 'spite Bismarck &
wallpaper, broader still, to get myself even more sentimental : now hit 'em
with the popular adverbs !) :

      "with arms –"
hm ‹arms› or ‹little arms› ? Can the people, our people, my people digest
yet *another* diminutive ? I would say – ‹yes›. So then run my Faber=point,
run :

      "with little arms to hug me tight."
So that made lines 1, 3 and 4. Which meant, however, that line 2 now
had to rhyme with ‹. . . ight›. – (Justasec. What 'd it all look like up t' this
point –) :

"I sat all cozy drinking beer,

....

here came my happy lad so dear

with little arms to hug me tight."

Logic demanded you supply a few details of time & place, kwommodo kwanndo – ‹my landlord just removed from sight›; but that wouldn't work 'cause it sounded like ‹Just› was the yokel's name : ‹Landlord Phil the flowing bowl !› – :

"just as the day eased into night"

?. (Better not; the commonfolk have pretty much lost touch with ‹ease› as a verb – or more correctly, lost tongue – ‹eased, changed, turned› : wonderful !) :

"just as the day turned into night=period."

Quite=tolerable; sort of ‹soft=warm twilight› ; ‹DÜSTERHENN's Dark Hour›. But then I had also anthologically plucked syllables of vintage=banality. And the contents were really the final hammerblow : I mean, if I don't succeed *this time* . . . . . fine, but now to proceed :

: what do the parents of such happy hugging little-armed children do ? 'twas not the custom of the house ‹At Our Ol' Homestead›; contrarissimo : Father A. Paul Düsterhenn & Mother Moosedear promised us kids ‹whuffer› for far slighter claims on their time & budget; (which in some dialect quite foreign to me, meant ‹smacks›; there was no mistaking it, our cheeks were treated to them all too often). A realist of ZOLA's stamp would therefore have greeted the happy lad in question with whuffers; fine, I'll make a note of it; (after all, upon the publication of my first experimental verses, my parents, too, had made clear & public, in a deposition bearing both their autographs, how truly ashamed – in fact ‹embarrassed›, (an expression, in their language, of a still stronger degree of the same emotion) – they must perforce feel, after the fackt, for ever having brought such a mooncalf into the world.) All fine & dandy; but what . . . . . ? . . . . . I gazed upon my fortunately & unwaveringly infertile lap; trying by sheer force to project a sweet=babbling boy : . . . . . ?. (And my girlfriends, Fairfat & Farty, had also proved clever at ovoiding the same : . . . . ?). What was that wisp o' light doing there at the narrow end of the counter ? – oh I see; the Landlord was about to make a little fire in the stove . . . and had a match . . . quite laudable given this allsoul's weather. Nono : ‹Vivat the Prophylaxis !›. And since the German People, toddling through 2000= years of history, had resolutely refused ever to have anything to do with reality : might not, at this point in the poem, some sorta little=uhm g'ardian=angel ? . . . . .

: "And o'er us brushed, no sunbeam this,"

(no sir, abs'lutely not; given this low from Iceland)
              "a ray of light, a matchless glow, –"
: it was all there : the ‹match› of the match; the gloomy day with a fleck of
light, ingeniously transformed : the streets are as good as paved with gold;
vats of gold where'er talent's eyes comes to rest : and let us not despise the
‹bliss› now ! I'm certainly no longer an intellectual, alla BENN, who on principle chose the rarer of 2 rhymes : hadn't ‹Salamis› already tried to insinu-
ate itself ? : Get thee hence, be=gone ! : :
              "and it, it seemed –"
Double ‹it› ?; doubt it. And by using the comma had I not introduced a
slightly ironical t=it=tering tone to that Twofold=It ? So it had to be removed posthaste; for The German, if he is anything, is not=ironic; (‹Irony›
has such a gallic=mediterranean feel about it.) So meditate gallically;
(‹mad uttering› at the door now, too; damn the disruption, right when the
religious punch line . . . . . – : Hell, the thing was gradually starting to
border on contemplative lirrick !) :
              "and it now filled me with its bliss :
              ‹His angel guarding here below !›" –
  – : Lookiethere, it was the hunting lasses again ! They laught & natterd,
infernervously : "Hello ! – Hello & Evoe !". Let tongue=pennants flatter
like hell, and carried on generally like a halfpounda uranium; apparently
known round here. : "Himister Tulp !". And He beamed broad favor :
"We=ell ? – A'reddy gotta day's wuhk b'hind y' ?". (I did not catch the
answer. On the 1 hand, because I was busy with a quick but critical review
of my first, and successful, one may presume, stanza – looked as if the
whole thing wanted to end up as a series of angelic epifunnies ? Well, fine
by me; was there anything more up-to-date in the news ! ? at most, rearma-
ment : nothin' in that; I was right on the mark. And on the other, because
all five of 'em were chattering at once; (‹Betty Martin was a huntress=
young› : according to Doctor JOHNSON, that comes from ‹Britomartis› –
what notions these lexico=graffers do come up with !).). There were checking out a map, so totally ‹meanwhile› that at 3 cable=lengths y' could spot
the sheer pretext of giving me a hungry once=over; ‹Is he from here ?›.
"Nope" the Landlord pronounced. Shared cig'retts. Went. & came. And
held out for Ev'ryone (me, too, sad to say) his coal shovel : stiff blackiron
(ire on blackstaff, linseed oil again on the handle !); and on it, a dead black-
birdy (by the tangeriney beak). (And only 1 small suitcase for 4 skirts ?
Sure; the modern lady can put her wardrobe in a nut; and still carry her
Meg'umportance with her.)
  Rise aloof. Notebook & HEMPEL into my costly small & light shammy=
leather case; (so once again unjust : my luggage was just as minuschool).

Meanwhile yonder : "Oh ! – inna *barn* aggin ? In the *heigh* ? ! – Well 'f it don't get too cold, at night : okay b' *me*." Turned anew to door number three; (and then the same ritual as with me before : first the wife; who was commissioned to give ‹Rieke› the word; somesorta fuck=totum it seemed). / : "And some supper for me, too, alright ?". And, since he apparently wanted to brag about his kitchen's prowess in specialties of the house : "Fine fine. As bountiful & punctual as you like; expense is no object. – uh : When ?". (To judge by which, another good, even very good, hour. So I can take a bit of a walk; I enjoy doing that by twilight. And in this case, if only to escape the 4 ask=me=snoots directed my way, ‹The Paradise of Vowels›, silkenred & moist. – My body betook itself & me with it from thence.)

– and then stopped stockstill in the vestibule – ‹And her name was Rieke› ! : Could it be possible that SHE lived right=here in the same house ? ! (‹Fiete=Rieke› : the wonder would have been no less remotely great were the Pléiade=edition of the ‹Recherche›, majestically criteaked, suddenly to appear in the GOETHE=SCHILLER correspondence. – Wonder if I could, if I should, dare probe still deeper into the edificialities now ? Pretext, the water clos...; Ninon de. Or better to let it ‹grow organically› ? – And since I had never lacked for a dearth of courage, I decided, after responsible deliberation, for the organic s'lution.) And walked into the open air.

CALLIOPE

The sun crashed and congealed behind an oaken column; Both bled. The gray canvas=overall, lacking in firmament and raggedy=patched, likewise betrayed much unpleasantness. As far as eye could see. In any case, the whole region desolate, and although clear, somehow foggered as well; (and dead=center me; with the lovely but not-all-that easy task of reaping optimistic details for my ‹Country Delights› subsection).

For the very first shanty looked good as deserted ! If it weren't for the flickering air above the chimney; and this Yeo=Man here, as plastered as he was brickred, (who swung out wide & manor=lordly before pulling in at his gate : obviously seasoned at tractoring; fellows so morbidly low-browed they ought to have numbers too; or drag harrows), I'd 've bet my precious SYNTAX against my Steputat, that Nobody was home. (Equally unwise and cumbersome, my antipathy, ineradicably infused in Weimar years, toward all draftable tauromorfs; because 'twas the order of our geopolite day to honor them per aversionem; and ‹Revival of Medieval

Ideals⟩ the mace & emblem by which we reliable men recognized one
another) : "What d'yóu know about Meier Helmbrecht ?". But the dark-
hued cat merely uttered an impatient cry of woe, while walking beside me
(though on the far side of the hedge); (nono : ⟨The best are as a brier, the
most upright is sharper than a thorn hedge⟩ – I tried flexing my elbows,
like that=fellow, as if so strong I couldn't crook 'em any farther, trying to
get myself in a similar mood; even strode straddle-legged a tenth of a fur=
long . . . . .) :
>   "Who strode there so proudly across the Soil bank ? :
>   : the farmer, the farmer !"
(but get ridda that capital ⟨S⟩ on ⟨soil⟩ !, 'twas thus that he stank, aeh, it's
all nonsense; what I clearly lack is the naive, intimate eye for detail, graffic
& elemental within the bounds of the seemly, pure & true.) And gave my
mouth another skeptical purse & my own shoe-tips a nod : ⟨pure & true⟩;
the dust they (humans) throw in their eyes their hole lifelong ! For if there
was ever an Either=Or, surely this was it right here; (well, let's move on
through the hamlet; I truly had better things to do than lift so much as 1
blinder from the eyes of the nations, free of charge – more precisely, at my
expense – when it's the knack we=finer=sorts live by.)

– Vileage hamlet : ⟨Hamlet spoilt by Man⟩. Could mean a) ⟨Danish
Prince undone by mankind⟩; b) ⟨1 man corrupts a burg⟩; a job you could
surely spare yourself 'mongst rural folk : even as kids they're smuttier by
far than students in the GDR; (an assertion ⟨secured by rhyme⟩, as I once
heard a German=proff lecture smugly : *They* of course are the greater
simpletons by a *good* 3 whacks !). Meanwhile from behind the ramrodding
war memorial, a fiery-red head-sized ball came bouncing broadly, which I
(veteran half=back) deftly stopped; and as lads & ladettes emerged, passed
it to the one x=hibiting the longest leg stilts – and the pea=cocky tribe at
once began its parade, now singly now tootinsomebull. One velocipeder
artisted more boldly on his way; another did curbside headstands; were
rewarded by fleeting maiden glances, (and more sprouting cockspurs,
growing tools, with boyish pride). The best developed lad stood ⟨offside⟩
now and tormented a long banana. Whereas the most theatrickalass – a
fluttering calico; her arms spread cunning= and constunst=ly my way :
quicunque vult ! – cut tight ellipses on murmuring rollerskates; first round
nix (and seemed her name was "Lulie !"), then round doublenix; and at last,
artfully breathless, merely threw herself up against a girlfriend's knit
sweater; (and kyckled jennysaucy).

A water pumper with bovine gams – (I squelcht a pilsified pere=grin :
when all's said'n'done, I don't pump money either) – who was swearing to
herself. Bataclán=Bataclán, ever more viggerous grew the scuffle with the

pump=handle & her bicker with her=Self, (which at the final=sub-conscious level was intended for lollygag me. And to avoid all danger of her repressing It, goodhearted fool that I am, I made my strides entic-ingly springy & smiled an asinine wanderlusting smile) : Hvérgelme= hvérgelme !). Though I was truly not even remotely in the mood : in fact the ‹Songs of a Wanderer› sexion was in such a state that ‹unsadistfactory› would've been a high mark. Originally I'd imagined I could interpolate RÜCKERT : but there wasn't *any*thing more to interpolate; (not to speak of ‹uriginally›). –

–. / Just small wood= & bushworks stood lonely in the broad flats; those, too, coated as if with fine mist. (I had by now in fact come to the edge of this town, though a different edge, true : on my left the multiple ‹Z› of a hi=tension pylon built a pyramid; 1 of the three-cord cables dangled bankruptured – right; ‹Powah's off›.) On my right, a no less insolvent ‹last garden›, its whitegraygreenblack fence defentsless; at its feet, herbs of the northern hemisfear, odiferous frayed whorlspikes, Piperita sylvestris acquatica, (from the sound of it, I'd venture ‹for tea›, grewsomely healthy or for the sistema urinario). And oval-heart-shaped ripple=toothed, Pulegium gentilis arvensis, common in wet fields on the southfaces of ditches; (: 'fonly writin' prose weren't so dangerous; there're times when I hanker to try it !). But best a turn to the right & back, stay close to town, I was afterall no explorer, neither Louis nor Clerk.

: pretty trimmed willows. (The grass=b'low, however, rather discolored lumps. Everywhere.) A watercourse it seemed way=yonder. But nix= Avernus, oh contraire, several crowcaws; (somewhat later they flew above my path; 7 of 'em; 1 by 1. While the grayting Oh=Zoon sloshed in my lungs.) And 1 asocial aldergroup after the other slowly shoved past, mistletoe=mistletough; (the loveliest, with 6 house-high stalks, sadly had a hunter's=l$_a$dd^{er} deadcenter. Too clear against today's milkglass sky.) / Or the almost=black disk of this treestump here : with long needle-fine blades o' grass sticking out in 4 places. It's some sort=a Law of N'tour; I'd seen it oftimes. They grow, in fact, not from *below,* ('twould be striking, I grant; as a tryumph of energy); but rather it's a mattera woodworm holes, into which first building=block=soil, then grasseed falls, blowbreezeblow – : and away we go !. / At some seasons the ditch might be a brooklet, (at the moment not a lisp to bid me halt); the water ‹stood› shy, and gazed ‹at› me as it were; a virgin=gloomy acqua=face in a mop of green hair; (how nice. I greeted her. And the two teen=poplars as well; and, along=side, the long mistyfigure on the liquid bile. / And always steady round to the right : I'd *have* to land back in Schadewalde.) Shoulda brought along some low= light=brown rubber boots. / ‹Put up your twigs !›. (Apparently the start of a pond; this little dam=here, huh ?). Quite rite. Shadows of sedge & fish. And this demi-drizzle was really not acceptable; I had, well&wisely, chosen a ‹high› for my trip. (Well, p'r'aps only an inditchenous=subspecies. But nary a boreas to chevy the clouds' heavy=scent. – And a little more to the right once more.)

Rite. (For if this wasn't the town=dump . . . ?. Yet another sight to which I always, if it's not all too phoulsmelling, pay some attention.) / 1 of Colonel Phall's wire=baskets, rough=meshed & squasht=flat as the FISCHER=Lexicon of Psychology. / 1 rusty scythe. / I felt sorry for buggy=baby wheels. / Someone=in=town was apparently a professional MAXWELL drinker. / And further oilycapers; kicked out of hell (ayee behind the stove) and up to heaven (ayee sandpitted freedom) : become ‹a fool›, and give up reason; (to save its seat). / And here came the 1st buildings=back into view.

(Although remarkably roomy for dwellings. And without the screech & cry of kids. – If it'd at least been pouring downrain; but like=this, feeble damp'ning of honest folk ! –). / And pulled up short at the foot of the chimney giant : 1 hall=mark ! ('fonly for hasty=surveyance. – Folk superstitions claiming these=things stood on a massive blocka copper (worth 20,000). Uptop, for a lightning=rod, a fingersturdy platinum pole (worth 6,000). But fine=still=mute=old=red all the same. In other words, a deserted brickworx. I walked right in.)

: desolate spare, wandering 'mid spars; (sparring partner; sparetime= spartan). Chthonic=charcoalies; (meaning=sure to be clay=pits in the vicinity, filled with water, nolens volens : cute centers of cuming camping= grounds.) Currently, however, cunsiderably more crematoriumlike; (but o'coarse I'll have my self cremated : the dead don't need to rob the living of exterior space, too !); ‹Hector's Cremation›, nothin' but bluing-ovens & iron oxydull; (‹The Sour Slave›, heroic=comic opera in 3 acts, text by Calza=beegy; ‹Molestation of the Dead through Gauzes›). / Empty the dry shelving, extinguisht the killn; (I took shelterer) : and how They had all whirled & bustled ! Whether by strike or frog – how such jargon sticks in your mind : schoolkids marched out on an excursion, almost 40 years ago, to a brickworks near Hamburg : *that*'s how I still knew it ! (And an essay ritten on it afterward, naturally. 'Twas probably my very special kismet : to have to write allabout it all; ‹Laugh=Song, ritten in a Lyme=killn›.) / In its silent fashion, the dusk began to turn flitter-mousy. (Ideal breeding=spot here for those black rubber triangles. And for the village youth no less. / Must really get very cozy, later at Hel's : I had never found intruding owl= hoots any more ‹eerie› than radio voices, or the breathy yowl of longdistant wee=hour trains; compendious theory of the compendiant.) / All the same, still a good half hour until suppé. And the air seemed to have gone all still

& darkgray again. / : ‹Well, c'mon, Orgy.› (‹Marching is healthy›, says the major; an article in the ‹Süddeutsche›, so it must be true. ‹Join the Wehrmacht and see the next world !›) –

And halted anew, prox'mutly only 300 yds further on, by the mild sheena the JACOBS COFFEE=sign – : even I had seldom been *so full* of half-formed=decisions ! For 'ncase I *should,* (as seemed to bid likely now), jot away several more necrow=proletic knockturnidays in the inditchynous zonal region . . . ? – Sucked deeper of the (mediochre tasting) air; (didn't know myself if sighing or=not). And entered the wildeast= store : . . . . :

. . . . . : a sem'nly mute sorta place, but in truth a terrubbly x=citing dollhouse world ! / Gaudiest ads madpackardized from a sector of at least 270° : I *had* to buy such'n'such a margarine, otherwise ! ! / The girl to my left was just pulling, METHO'Dick & Sly, the taowel from her phoamy face : and if I would perchass but 1 of those pineneedly tablets from the plasdick=boxlet rite where her knee began, she would, so the promise of her exspurt mouth – & she swore by her own goddass word – uttend frig-fancily to my wonts, guarunteed, well ? ! / But the roomlet, ten Bey ten, was in every sense ‹fulljammpackt›. For a while a lowcul frisked her boozernose round in the air closeby, (where=I was thumbing the cigarbox that held the postcards : and my most urgent mail, why 'ncase sure, I'd have to . . . . . lookathat; ‹Greetings from Schadewald›, 3 inphernally phalse fotos, 1 atop the other, from 1930 judging by the reproducktive teckneek : that was the right one. I held it tight in my hand; (: presuming I can also get the 'propriat stamps !). / Not x=orbitantly far from the flooral=wax, the kipper crate; comprom=eyes; (to think how ‹Henkel Düsseldorf› always engenders ‹Cock'll diddle=do› for me !) As good as soundless, the stallwart keroseen stove glimmerd in its corner. A camembeardy codger f'landering in some dead language or other with the plumpasst salesgirl, (‹Declaration of Love via Interpreter› : 'd surely have to snap a few of Amor's diverse pinions. Or – as is quite conceivable, if not 'nfackt natural – being an excitable youth, bring on a fitta hickups.) They hummed & hissed; (Omega Tau, Omega Tau; ‹had a cow, eeow=eeow›.) And had it all put on ‹accownt›, in little booklets; (with a shamey & smeary look on their faces : but I will let my alabasturd cash be a model unto you.) / Shadowfolk, both thought= & sense=less. The exersize of their tongues, a mech=anical ruppitition and cunt=inuation of gradeschool usages. Here a runnynose gazed into the midst of a deepcut liberteen=bosom; (and casually continued his mass in=vest=igation with her neighbor on the other side – where he spotted me, and did it ever unnerve me : I mean x=actly like an acquaintance dead (my God, these 30 years !); a semidemi=foe by the by.)

/ – : "Marc's wortha Chagalod –" / (Ah, my turn at last). : "Stamps too ? : Very good. – And then a piece o' this sausage here, please –"; (very cheap sort; I had, I know not why, thoughta Kirby). – : "Thanx alot."

–. – : Singing ? In Lowersacks'ny ? ! (Prob'ly some missed=ache : Frisia no can dat.) – Lis'nin' – ? – (2 shots, those o'coarse. Feeble & moist, like the cottonball packing the fox uses for its bath; (let's hope they didn't hit him). And ne'ertheless ! –) . . . . .

: ‹I go where'er my lantern goes. And my lantern, he goes with me.› : *that*'s a fish I'd like to snare yet ! / And now I saw, at little distunts, a coupla gentle balls o'light floating through the trees. And headed that way at once : *that*'d been a thrill for me as a young lad in Hamburg, too ! (Whence, p'r'aps, the decisive enhancement of my pref'rents for the moon & not-the-sun. The tertium, naturally, my congenital ‹bad eyes› : let's hope I find my new pre=scription reading glasses waiting for me at home. – Tho 'twas a bit late in the season for such equinoxialities.) –

– and it was only 4 of 'em. Not even ‹man high›; but rather 1 tall lass; 2 little girls; and finally 1, rather pintsize boy. Or put differently : 1 green-murkish shining concerteena; 1 redribbed sphere(h)oid'n; 1 mighty big moon, (twice as impressive 'cause of its little ponytailing bearer; kindly= sunflowery, domainic=demonic); the pintsize=bigjohn legged it eagerly alongside, in his hand the skewed old tincan; its bottom skillfully prickt 20 times, not by a round, but by a 4-sided ! nail, a wire for a handle, (so that the stump o'light burning within wouldn't grieve his hand too much : know it well; prob'ly did the same m'self. ‹La=bimmel La=bammel La= bumm.›). / ‹Canned stuff›, (via ‹unopend›) : a childhood=sweetheart had 1ce showed up with 1 with a well=etched & stock portrait of Kaiser Wilhelm II : and *how* We had whinnied ! (Had been a workers' neighbor-hood; Borstelmannsweg=Eiffestraße : Madness, thy name is electioneer-ing – I automatically had to picture one with portraits of those=involved. Definitely suggest it to CDU campain head=quarters : they had never come up with that; every suggestion is valuable. (‹Blindman's buff› ? : accordin' to WORM invented to mock JULIUS CAESAR's designs against the Nordic Peoples; another 1 of your bad professorryal=jokesters.)).

But touchingly=beautiful, these zealous battle-fatigued wee voices here, weary from p'tato digs. That managed mere fragments of songs : 14 days ago there were still 20, surely. / On past timber=work=walls. – (: "BuuHH !" roared some fledged rascal or other from behind the maple. And the little light-bearers shuddered in song.) – In villitches like this, one sometimes comes upon the obscurest magazines, fading in attic slopes, dank in cellar dank, whole JEWEL ISLES of kitsch, priceless for the creative plagiarist; or rare volumes of lexica, the very=first MEYER, brimfull of the most curiously skewed coproliths, (that you need only to soften & stir with verbal waters to reap an endless=rich harvest for little articles in provincial=rags : ‹education=wise› the Germ=Man lives at the kneevo of 1840. JOYCE never lived, ditto FREUD. Neither GAUSS nor CARROLL. For him PROUST is ‹queer› 'nd nothin' more; OKEN passé=crazy; and not a soul has never=ever hearda KRISTIAN HINRICH WOLKE; which to him – the G=man – awful to say, seems ‹reason 'nuff› !). / But here, too, before my eyes, were tokens of the approaching dia=spora, which even an optimist could not ignore : the tall=boned girl had already packed her moon home. And now the redribbed=ball (on an over=long fishing=rod) was booted into its goalgate; (behind which bicker & wrangle raged, like in an ol'folks home : nothin' beats an 85=year=oldster putting a quivering hold on the squabble throat of an 84=year=older. Or graynnies, droppin' long on the flabby, accusing each other of imp=potents.) / But the Last=Two went on singing. Wonder= full tim'rous & tough. ‹Düdic or Sassic Poesie, Didactix, Epi=taphies, Songes, Romances & Ball=ads› : thus strode the hun=braided lass beside the pintsizer unto where He dwelled. – : Slam=shut !. –

Alone & yet shining : she gazed a darksome while at that shut door. / Then turned hard on her heel. And, head stiffly lowered, she came slow & unstoppable down the street. (Me=always under cover of the aforesaid warrior memorial. – Held it – the lantern – no longer quite so expertly, o'coarse.) / *Singing* yet however; if only twixt her teeth, brave lass ! As she passed, I understood the words. – / : ‹Drunk t'day. 'nd drunk t'night. 'nd drunk=aggin=t'mórra !›. – Marched thusly, in (s)loveliest Illabaturorbis= mood, badness=buds contra crow=pie=broch, down between the barn shadows; irongray loden=caper. I saluted propeerly after her.

And then likewise disposed my powers to walk my right & true path.

ERATO

: But which 1 was that ? – Presumably this very=sandy 1 here. Spottily plastered with a 300 pound=mix of stones & tiniest taters, the ideal frenchfries, (latest Fedrepublican practice it appeared; and we still wonder p'r'aps : The way these guys skwander money from our pockits !). And now one of these masters who sleep with the roots passed me by; puffed on his windy throne, the yokel (behind him a galvanized vat of teardropping sullage); and he gave a rootabaggy whinny, for I was voluntairly commencing my side=step. (Bloated pale roundhead; globuluried smirk affixt upfront; ‹Silent Strength›, the sort I esteem so very highly. He surely didn't scratch chest & shoulders just for fun that often, (‹God bless the Duke of

Argyle !›).). But since ‹O. TULP› was written on his tumbrel, I followed this cheapo guide through Schadewalde, o=differant & at a not inconsiderable distance.

Voi là ! : there 100 yds ahead of me, he turned in now; (now I call that a sents of oh rien dayshun). And again retarded my already quite hesitant step : could she, the Sublime Goddess, Madam SAGA of the golden teeth, actually demand that I tag behind & creatively buckolicize ? (But then the devil of a notebook tryumft afterall; and I stepped, as steal=thily as possible (in the good sense) behind the tractorian's absolewtly unmistakable jet=stream, and into the driveway – after all, under the pretense of Mythological Themes, a certain Paulpotter was able to busy himself quite jauntily with reality; (if not, 'nfackt, was ‹allowed› to : ‹We› were almost that far-along again nowadays, when Anyone intending an honest sketch of what he's seen had to insert a j'ave with every third stroke, just by way of precaution). And so first 1 mental, hypocritical ben addicktus. Then eyes ears nostrils wide –) :

Goddamste twilight ! Above=memymineI, the stormtroops of wild clouds at work; (‹Pibroch of the Donuil=Dhu Pibroch of Donuil !› : the raging stutters of a motor, upset about something, be it only the human hand in its belly : ‹Pollpótter=Pollpótter=Pollpótter !›; (ah, had to conseed it itself). Then, more calmly, petering=out : ‹Père=Father Père Father. Père. – Father.› The ear mnemorizing this belly tongue for a good while.)

All gates open, keeping officious silence. / The cavern of the stall. (‹Cow=moo. Cow=moo.›) Hooded tartarusties; wheels hanged on the walls, starshapely crucifixees; 2= to 7=tined dung= & ditch=forks, a gristly sight; the Iron Mask of a pump. The stately plate=forms of dung, (from the toppa which, as usual, the head=cocks would practice their appeals to their people). / Mesh-shirted, he bellowed down the crooked courtyards. / Whereupon & after a time, another wetnursery shadow broke languidly loose from one of the limburgian labyrinths; and set the wrake aside: (‹Leave untended the herd; the flock without shelter. Leave the corpse uninterred, the bride at the altar : leave the deer, leave the steer, leave nets & barges !›). They disposed themselves, each to a different end – : – and, with apparent ease, lifted the vat off; hay=rodishes & the Spirit o' the Dung; (wouldn't 've been easy to award the Grand Prize of Strapperdumb : even in light of the terrestrial refraction, both had a truly felonious breadth of shoulder, whether male or fee=male, (Feire=Fiess & Uri=Pansa; and then there's air=male, too); and each appeared to have obtained a papal dispensation to carry the thick ends of his/her legs at the bottom (and weighed down with giant=rubberboots besides). – But were servants of at least one *other* divinity, as promptly became apparent.

– TWO HUMANS or de jure belly : he delubberately tousled hair with his left, while his right zoomed ab ovo downhill, and handycappt round at her breast. She first acted dewly ughrieved, cimmerantic cul. But then, so unwearying were the unicorn's dandles, began quite quickly to yield, and fondle his hunkness, (‹feeling fingers in Pole=land›, ‹without enter= rupting›). Finally, taking a seat on the shaft, lifted her peplos over her navul, ‹See the Machine !›); and he did a knee=trembler, not to be ridickculed ! (‹How she wallowed & wrecked revenge. Distorted and weakened him !›). / The nightjar brushed along over me now. And such a loud purring round my e'en=now gaudy=pied sox, I couldn't believe 'twas a cat at first, (sounded like a 100=pound porker : might 'nfackt be bred on *that* basis, too, the hon'rable Sirs & M'dames Kittycat; and then orga- nize purring=contests, in England : ‹In the Company of Humm=Tops›.) Matters yonder were still going glissato legato peezi=cato – (‹Gip, quoth Gilbert›; prob'ly a diaphragmal spasm) – animato=itchytato, worsen the perpetuum mobile. Rittardando : accelerando. – ? – wellfin'ly his herculean posteerior swelled, (‹the war pipe and pennon are at Inver=Lochy›); and the shaft twitcht in cockoffunny : Préstoprestopresstoh !

Then the beast that is not – let us call it the so-called cosmocomic eros – began to unscrew into its two main components : Zebra=Otto, of the furmented visage; and she, the nameless one, whom by now I had conclu- sive cause to consider his spouse at least. She silently set her over=all in order. Seized, then, her rake, tarrying most stiffly gainst the wall; and van- ished whence she came. / Whereass he, with trowsers good as sloughed, shuffled lamely across the courtyard; rather toward me, (without spot- ting me : an ass like a rasp !). Went into a squat next to the dungheap's elevated primal shore, prickly heat by the organ pipe, (cf. KEHREIN, ‹Hunt- ers' Jargon›. Of which the 4 huntresses would likewise make passionate use – I'll have to try to picture that, later on); groaning, laid 1 very large egg; (and had no need for grimacing at him=self – which, e.g., I always must do – though the odor was such you could have pointed at it with fingers, ilu mann=mann ! Ahwell; the workaday is 'ndeed elementary ex=istence.)

I squeezed my little bundla books more tightly; and my self out through the gate. (I had, years ago, heard a catholic professor lecture on the ‹Ad- vance of the Renaissance›, as if it were Mongol hordes – he could go on sleeping in peace : there was still no danger of *that* in Germany, not by a long shot !).

POLYHYMNIA

: "Good evenin'. – ?" (At least one of 'em nodded. Although without letting it stop him middrink.)

Some bustle already. While I took my table reserved in the corner; and
after some hesitation affixt my beret on the antlers. / Not far to my north-
east, three archetypes, Dall Damb & Aggli, were studying the Book of
Kings – 18 : 20; two=four; (chapter & verse it seemed; not that you could
've labeled them ‹bible scholars›) – Redchix from before was there too.
(And now, as long as no one's sitting op'sit, extend my – unfortunately
somewhat too short – legs; and stretch : on the 1 hand, a shame it wasn't
Saturn= Sun=day, & thus an opportunest chance to observe les fonctions
mentales dans les sociétés inférieures, à la *when* do they begin to sing; and,
if they do, *what* ? A colleague, a recent traveler in the Lüneburg Prairie
(i.e., at least a few hundred miles from here), was frequently prepared to
swear nothing could be heard more often than the ‹Horst=Wessel›=Song,
‹then all the sea=men drop silent›. Since, however, he earned his meager
living by playing the ‹Good Left Man›, not a soul believed him; to be sure,
for those few commissions that were offered him on rare occasion, he had
earned the name of ‹Anti-SCHMIDT›; but He would *never* manage the final=
crucial test of a villa in Lämmelberg !). ‹Drinking songs›, goes without
saying, had to be included, for tossing money round like billowaves, (they
had particularly laid that on our good=citizened hearts in their latest re-
fresher course : skim the cream off our buying power; and so delay the
inevitable inflation, if at all possible, for another six months. Ah well; the
revenues of my IBM had long since been invested in Real Property strate-
gically distributed across federal territory; and/or in gold bars, exactly sur-
veyed & buried, (the coordinates, inconspicuously=encoded in our books,
then set in print for safe-keeping) : ‹Come redheaded Lotti ! I'll have
another toddy !› – Well, we'll see what sorta useful noise these guys are
capable of offering a fellow.)

Spindle & Trencher; Hallclock & Ladle; Funnels (i.e. hats) & Cudgels
(equals bottles). / The Landlord, with his ashlar face, served up the soup;
(‹Glue with Bran›; at one point it chewed gristlemorfus, endomorfus
corpomorfus, a sinew & bone herm afrodite – well, dammit, slipslide !).
Then, as fundament to something still awaited, a dough of flour, cheese
& anchovies. Bywaya cumulating pleasures, he betook himself to the tee-
vee, gave it a few probing pokes in the teeth : . . . . . ; . . . . . : and away we
went ! The blue grayny shadows grinned & hissed; (and you really did taste
less, from the di=version). / And wouldn't you know, the infamous Channel 4 ! That's why He was so zagroisteruss. (On the announcer's breast, a

ribboned medal that looked like a comet.) – A brief, but surely important, dialog concerning immortality, a good 2%=verifiable now on the basis of HOFSTÄTTERian research. Between an atheist, (who uttered pure blasfummies & nonsense; a disgusting fellow, with a bareassed, jailbird skull, looked like 3 communists : the guy couldn't even speak good German !). And another solemnity, clad for business & patience, who neighsayed responsibly; a scroll from the Dead Sea in his hand, the mere display of which easily reduced Him to dead silence : PROOF !. The whole thing ended with a such a devastating moral for all those who were not=yet members of the CDU that even the Landlord looked up for 1 second; (‹The Underside of the Arketypal› : wouldn't it be fun sometime to use X=rays during debates like these ? So that it looks like 2 skulls arguing ? – Prob'ly too ‹literary›, huh; (and/or frivolous; which is considered identical by most). ‹Our chancellor loves his roses› : at his peak, *that* had yielded me a regular dungheap of money ! If only one knew precisely what the Foreign Secretary loves. Or BRENTANO. Because EHRHARDT wasn't going to get a chance at it anyway; let's not deceive ourselves there.) / The Landlord appeared meanwhile to have sacrificed a piglet, and came bearing the Black Pudding.

While I was still lifting my cutlery, fulla care, the door opened, and 1 new crofter stumbled o'er the bronze threshold; a lovely Me=Ander, (obviously already semi-inspired; ‹clos'd from the minutia he walk'd difficult›). But appeared to be somehow ‹well-regarded›; for yonder, the mighty aired themselves, seated : !, (you could positively smell it, the stinking=match from those fraternal=hemisferes); the doffing of his hat likewise took a goodly time; hey, take a loadoff. / For the ‹news› ? : 1 of my senses 'll suffice ! (I'm not all *that* senile yet, knockonwood, that I'd have to watch with wide-open mouth how that minx=up=front, a smirkmugging rightwinger, alternately looks at her typescript. And then tries ficksing *me* with piercing eyes; interrupted at best by shockingly false accounts of knaveries in reality long since outdated : I believe neither in your ‹wall›, friend – ‹caterwaul› : that I'm willing to spin out a droll & mighty chested song of it, is quite a differunt=matter; (in truth, if you really want to know, it was traded for Cuba umpteen months ago !) – nor in the protestations of 90=year=old Breslauers : who couldn't recall Silesia's ever having been Polish. – Nah : in light of the world situation & the state of Federal German affairs, ‹Bloodpudding with Laurels› was downrite symbolic fodder !).

– : HEY !, were things gettin' merry now ! The door practic'ly burst at its seams – (simultaneously behind me came the familiar ‹Mr. SANDERS Shares His Record Collection› : none sing so wildly well as the angel Israfel !) – Tulp beamed caesarian & lapid; (Piece o' cake; the pertest venatrix was now hanging askew at his neck) : "Liber, Pater" it's called; they indolently eyed the room's contents; (and not a few beamed shots grazed my way, from not a few oreyels). Repaired, then, to their supparé coven=table by the tiled stove, (to which they promptly turned spreadlegs; ‹warmin' up hubby's dinner›); "B'rometuh's climbin'" the Landlord remarked tout-sweet=amiably. With furrowed brow I nibbled from the aforemenshunder dough, (which in several spots seemed to conceal inclusions of bean flour; whence the origin of ‹carat› as word & concept : if only, at least on a few certain occasions, one didn't have to think anymore !). –

    And now 1 curious=better oldster came in; who demanded a 7=cent= stamp (uncanceled). Greeted Us=All; equally cheery and far=away. Then the Landlord announced the Pithoigia Fest : a new barrel was just being tapped in the cellar huh ? ! – (I'm anti on principle.) Likewise the hunt-resses; (the tall 1 now seemed to have taken on the name of ‹Lene›. Mean-ing you'd first have to address her as "Say, Lene." And then a real quick pumice. (O'coarse you didn't dare ‹think› there either; she had started in again now about how deer's bladders can freeze in winter : what notions ! Or f'rall I care, fackts.) / : *What* was my gnostic gnoshmate urging me ? : that I converse with him bout postage stamps ? (With oldage cunning, he had apparently picked up my scent right off as ‹somethin' diff'runt›.) All the same, it was remarkably difficult to come to terms with him – the mo-ment you started to speak, he was already waiting impatiently for the enda the sentence; then, in a kind of hasty echo=effect, repeated your last words; and was on to something else. Going by the dialect, from the Magdeburg area; ‹Where's his accusative ?›.) But the big 8=fold stamps from the GDR were really a great concept : space=hued background; plus the young couple, terra muy=cognita & selenissima luna; inbetween, the busts of the argonauts in diving helmets; and finally, tastefully placed, indeed ordered, the famous flying TV=antennae, the which are named Loo=Nix and Eggs= Plorer, draped with their precise launch=dates. – Nice idea; nothin' like it : they oughta go ahead 'nd give the East 2000 years of fairplay=please – just as X=ians have had, too – then, calm & cool, we'll compare the fruits. (‹Laissez=vous toucher par mes pleurs› : Sir X=of Billy balled; and the anascru, in her jaunty togs, laughed more stridulous.) I decided to be more tight-lipped; first, in order to suggest to the Old Gent that one ought not to speak upon a soup=eater in that fashion, (besides, I was sure to rejoice in some pimples in the days ahead, on my neck most likely; or behind my ear & on my scalp : this unwonted saltshock here was sure to have conse-quences); and then, too, because he, like all folks sitting opposite over the longhaul, appeared to have grown 1 paira legs too many, (and those longer than regulations allow). And nonetheless gave him my ear anew, for he

swore that thing was worth its ‹100 Michel=Marx› ! (Not that that GOEDEKE
of philatelist̀s could be said to be so very unknown to me; but the (unin-
tentional) dyspeptic poly=pun on the currency of the New Covenant was
truly high class. As a reward, I inquired of him what, in light of that, *my*
only postage stamp might be worth : a canceled Tristan=da=Cunha set of
four ?) –

Again the music fell so wildly well on the ear that horror struck all
present, and the Landlord filled the stove with more rattling anthracite.
Then, shovel in hand, he strode over to our table; and demanded to see ‹The
Russky Stamps› himself. – : "Could y' give my ass a quick kiss, o Tulp ?",
the learned codger remarked with nervous energy. Then eagerly asked
me anent the particulars. – : "Dunno nothin' bout it. – : Dunno nothin' bout
it." – Until I gave an, ex=asperated, shrug. (Should I eat 'nything else ? I
still had an appetite; in the general direction of ‹Frankfurter›, ‹cut my mustard›. Or like what the 4 vamps there were smacking at : somethin' banger-
like, filled with pork brains, (‹stag=gellied›, hm ?). – : "Dunno nothin' bout
it !"; (despite his age young enough, then, to consider that an objection). I
couldn't think of a reply.) / I had also had to observe now & then with 1
eye, how the box had been trying with might & main to explain the pictures
of a ‹well-known› painter who had apparently died a few hours before : all
of 'em done in popular modern brushwork; which is to say, the sort found
often & gratis in my day on the walls of public restrooms, (‹For Men›;
those of ‹Women› being less familiar) : PF !; these dabblers, who casually
snot out 6 oil paintings on an equal number of canvases every morning,
their impertinence was indeed worthy of envy ! The audience was challenged to find stirring titles for the final, still unnamed half-dozen – the
best 700 for each would be published in a monograf already in preparation – : ? – and I joined in watching, most unwillingly : ? : (‹'tis lowly
bushwork; perhaps for a hunter a counterfayt wrought›); always presuming he's holding it rightside up, my suggestion, 1 for all, would be : ‹Done
in a Hurry› ! / One really ought to work muchmuch faster. It was sadly
my curse to be ‹concrete›, ‹rien n'égale mon malheur›; and since ‹The
Church› had reasons for favoring the abstract, (and our dipol=plomacy
was at least half Church . . . . . : good thing ‹The Military›, if nothing else,
was at least concrete : I mean, what=all ‹turns & taxes› an artist nowadays
must mangage, in the sassiest senses of the word, the simple fella can't
even imagine !). And I automatically had to take a look=round at the
simple folk –

: Hotchpots of day-jobbers & nightmayors; uncrowned spoilers of the
lawn. (‹The Landlady with the Wurst=Box› – yet another heavy S=allu-
sion.) Card=exspurts, bo=opic & skat=ological; strong necks, blue backs,

white bellies, (or what passes for ‹white› : if at least they'd had bundles of ivory bristles instead of teeth, green ones. In the lassy nook twitteration & handelings of a degree to turn a man all porous). A jawnty nature (a shame he boozed, to judge by the odor, half Gas=stir half Poll=licks), who stood up to offer his contribution to the evening's amusements by passing round a copper penny, claiming Someone had engraved ‹The Whole Our Father› on its polished reverse : ? : ? – as the rarity was about to come my way, I languidly declined; (‹the relation of the highly=cultivated to ‹religion› must always be a source of puzzling=dismay to the commonfolk› : I could discern the accuracy of this maxim, of which we were re=minded during our last committee=meeting, from the several respectfull=confused side-long glances). Even the codger whose sole interest was immortality (where'er it might come from) shook his head in annoyance as the bright metallic Our Father came into view; (he collected stamps, period – another acquaintance of mine, a not half-bad sort, spent his free time calculating logarithms, ellipse=areas, quadratic=roots no less : quite right; it doesn't make a helluvalotta diffrunts ! (Though that 1 ‹it› takes in a great deal)). ‹And at his› (the codger's that is) ‹belly a cymbal hung›, in form of a pocketwatch : ‹O'er his heart a dream was strung›; (I also knew what about : thumbnail-sized, perfectly=perforated darlings : ‹and HER name was Ma Ritzyus› ! – : " 'm jist gonna have to –"); add ‹check it out›. He shook, by waya farewell, his white=high head at the eurynomic round=table : he didn't believe a word we said ! (Enviably=onesided. Once you have a ‹se-cure pension›, & be it everso small, then=that's the ideal ! Plus a houseboat in the stycks.)

I crossed, almost immediately thereafter, my arms; leaned back; and tried – defying the Radio Orcusstra of Hamburg, (which under the direction of Paul Burckhardt, now threatened to offer the ‹Moon-Ghost Ballet› from Jacques OFFENBACH's operetta ‹Journey to the Moon›) – to gawk maturely; world=eidetic=starbright & lukewarm, (‹And surely you remember it well, Fiete=Rieke ?›) / But this music made itself a rumpled bed inside my ear : over=weening loud twriplings; underscored with dragon=snorin'; (ah well; I was old=enuff to be prepared for the middle of the tastiest BACHian fugue to turn into a tri=bop –). / Someone blared, in soulfull bliss, a "bring on the SEAGRIMS !". And the Landlord gave his young=gaunt spouse – both busy putting their energies to work entering all=assembled in a very large ledger – an equally commandeering and condescending pinch in the butt, (at which She reared up, laughing=yelping); and declared, turning to Us=All : She truly had nothin' to complain about, afterall she'd ‹been to town only last spring›; right ? !. (While among the venetrixies at least 3 dozen bloody-red, scalpelick fingertips lay on the table; they wantonly bewhispered those wrinkle=free faces : ‹Noose from hell› – Nah; better act as if sending one's gaze out for a stroll . . . . .) . . . . .

: a gloomy paneling, as if of Virginian walnut; (more probably the local moor=oak, oaky anus & tight=ass). / The allside=board : with little zigar-boxed ziggurats, ‹White Cloud› and ‹Celle Thickstem›; something tiny= twisty, lemony=black there ? (I immediately guessed at a ‹Tuba Elmers›); a flabby plump booklet in 4°, (telefone book & map in one; I was formulat-ing, out of laziness, nothing but surmises. More correctly : overtaxed by the many=new travel=impressions). . . . . . : – and my gaze went very=fixt all the same : It really did look marvelous ! That glass jug=there. A squat sturdy belly; a short athletic neck; and even the handlet attached was only apparently dainty : in company with that over=sized cork the effect was wild & unified; esquiresque; (even the crazy wallpaper appeared less asi-nine in its proximity). *What* was written on it ? –; (I arose as art=fully & =lessly as possible; like unto a man of refinement who stretches without stretching : ?). And sink back again; (‹ONE GALLON› aha). –

– : ‹Wonn Gallun› ? ? – 't's pretty close to impossible ! (It looked way too small for just shy of 5 liters.) / And yet, a trustworthy sight; I automati-cally projected it onto my desk – : ? – sure – yes; fulla whizzky, downright cobblerbowly=plausible. For those months when 1 ton of water falls from heaven. – Murmurration had arisen beside the Landlord : filling the (lin-seed hued, naturally) doorframe, a figure in blue overalls. Stringy female face; incredibly broad, massy breast . . . . . only when my eyes slipped off again, did I recognize, from the whole deportment, the woman from before in the courtyard, (‹the bloom is off the rose now› ! Yesyes.) A drunken king bee tried to concentrate the rest of his available gristle, and approached her, in a kind of skin-dance, (Esow inside his skin), his Lethe bottle in his hand, raised for fingersnapping – ? : – she made 1 single motion of her arm; (which sufficed, however, to send him staggering against the tile stove – and at once there arose a hoot as if from naught but monkeys & billies in the Casa del Fauno). When, with pitiable slowness, a play of features be-gan on his face, expressing his wish to regain lost terrain, oh no, here I come now, her sole reply was a stony : "Beat it Gustaff !". And he obeyed implicitly; (his ‹Gustav› was no longer derived from ‹Hystaspes›; at best from ‹castrated›). I merely lifted my (sad to say, grown somewhat undeco-ratively crooked from much writing) indexfinger : ? –

In the direction of the bar : this time the Land=Lady came over; (and allowed herself eyes harder than any clodhopper is entitled to. So that I was forced to regard her – unfortunately : I am a jenntleman – as if she were standing a good 800 yards away; while saying hyperpolitely, but halt-ingly) : "Might I have a look at that jug up=there ? –". She was apparently expecting a larger order, and was about to flair both mouth & nostrils. But now I focused the large eye for 16 hundred; and let the middlefinger of His Majesty my Right drum so nice'n'slow on the tabletop : Going ? ! : Going . . . . . She had pulled it down now, face ascrewed. Let her gaze flick once back & forth between the jug and me. And had most likely gained the impression of a possible ‹deal›, nosed it out in fact; for she lifted the apron from her gaunt pelvis, and slowly stroked his (the jug's : 'twas an out-and-out personage; I'm not always the last to acknowledge that sorta thing) sturdy glassy belly –, – (had itS=value for her, this somehow ‹ungratified› stroking ? Yes; most likely; for her Landlord was really nothing moren a mere=rage.) – : "Thanx alot." –

(Well; I gladly presented my short=subject for the benefit of the poor Schadewalders – who wouldn't have much variety the whole year long.) / Left him (the jug : a figure like a famous baritone !) stand untouched beside me for a brief while; (though regarding him, but that goes without sayin', as if a wee bit mistrustfull, from time to time). Now I know, as is only proper, the widest span of my hand, from the tippa my Pinkie down to thata my Thumb (9 inches; for Whoever has to know precisely); picked it up consequently in my left, and measured decoratively : – –; : – – hm. (Diameter of the belly 6; height circa 8. Let's say 72 times pi. : makes 226 plus or minus 10%, at most. – And sank then into genuine meditation : ‹ONE GALLON› ! / OhIknow; but there was no way He was an ‹American› : this was old glass; and, above all, much too fine a shape.) While everyone intently plumbed his temple-bone. Even the Landlady used the cat, who was shyly peeking inside checking things out, as a pretext to squat down and gaze at me across the astounded animal; (‹a wife speaks one way to the cat, another to her husband› : I've long suspected that). / On the television a bockser was displaying 2 broad front=paws : these were the guarantees of vick=try ! (Well, leave it on : the technically accurate description of bruisings in HOMER, the jousts in ARIOSTO & FOUQUÉ, are ultimately the xact same thing. The refined types can death-rattle all they want : STIFTER's ‹Witiko› is & will remain a mean handbook for officer candidates. And the only worthy attitude for a thinking man is that of Doctor RABELAIS : VOLTAIRE plus STERNE divided by 2 ! – But y'don't dare say it nowadays.)

Justa : Mo : ment ! – – : has the English gallon *always* been 4¹/₂ liters ? A wee Lilienthalic voice within promptly replied, (from my most adolescent plains : had I not in=fackt once wanted to write a ‹SATASPES›; HERODOT 4.43 ? In Nibelung=verse; ah that too; just don't think about it !). I automatically nodded to my imposing Landlord : in 18 hundred 24, by my scant knowledge, the Great Britannic measures & weights were refixt, the gallon enlarged, right ? I allowed myself the license, and looked at Mister Jug's

bottom (by letting him hang from my pinkie) – ? : Ha ! : an ellipse; with a
rhombus inside; and next to it the year 1808. (And I *was* in the old Kingdom of Hanover here; and it *had been* in personal union with England until
1837. : Fits. Very nicely.) / The faces of the whole sircul had been watching dozy=politely; the players no longer reciting their mishmash of numbers & card=slang; in the Speaking Mirror, the floating impalpable pictures of dead men thronged, (as good as dead; the film must've been from
about 1931) : RICHARD TAUBER gave a greasy smile; and, as a man appointed
for raising hearts, entreated the huntresses, who listened up at him with
eager pale faces, (and gave him rather ex=pertessive nods : Four Yellow
Jerseys. Out of respect, I first let him finish – Had they ever made a killing, old LÉHAR=back then ! Or KARL MAY, too; eternal para=gones for us
strugglers for folksiness, y' can't honor 'em enough. Still *thinking* much-
toomuch : ‹dumb & horny›, that's the recipe for success. And a father who
holds his child dear won't let him learn *anything,* not 1 *damn thing* !). –
"Good Landlord=uhm ? –".

(What was the bizarrest offer ? – These big prosporous landowners were
definitely not in outright ‹need of money›; though always highly susceptible for cash.) I slowly pulled out my ‹dollar purse› of sand-colored
leather. Looked beyond him, while my thumb casually snapped open the
shutter. Undid the most secret buttonwork as well; and with a simple flip of
the wrist let it be visible : G O L D ! ! !. (Swiss francs naturally; Sons of
Mines & Mints; I had laid in a largish supply there . . . our currency . . .
well, be silent & safely still, my heart; none of 'em 'mounted to much anymore.) / "I would like to buy this jug here from you –" (while the first guilt
droplet fell upon the table, and dispersed to a jingle sum; the Landlord
waited impassively). : "Holds : 3 point 7 liters –" (just missed saying ‹8› by
a hair, unspeakably false tactix; for ‹seven› has always been the holy=
rounder number 'mong commonfolk; it (the folk) now wrenched its ears) :
"*My* suggestion – : gauge it with 6 bottles of ALLAN KARDEC –" (and wasn't
he pulling up erecter, the ‹master of gauges› ? Wasn't he starting to beam
all gracious=lawgiver ?) : "– and pour everybody as much as he wants.
Whoever wants a smoke, gets 3 GÜLDENSTUBBES, too : put it on my tab."
(And silence. Whether chieftain vassal or serf, peons & pashas.) Oddly
disposed faces 'mongst the huntrinyesses. And the folk in the mad=chic
mira=mirror whispered; (that all life has a soul, No One can pull that 1 over
on me, in viewa Redchix : didn't the fella on my right have just half an
ear ? ! But a cap with a bill o'coarse) : "I'll pay in gold –", I concluded,
emphatically simple; (6 times 7 fifty; plus a coupla stogies; round 50
marks, so 2 disklets let's say. Although I had let 10 be visible, naturally.) /
The mutteration of his cuss=tummers already bespoke a high degree of

enthusiasm. He began to nod; greasier even than RT=before. : And repaired to his bar=counter. / Gauntsmirkt the Landlady there. Produced a
funnel; (obviously ‹outa the kitchen›). Tulp uncorking=engauging,
'zounds Aether & Hyle. While silhouettes of the Messers Granger crowded
round his hands & the jug, (which I watched jealously : don't smithereen it
now at the last moment !). Now & again someone recalled the owenus of
gratitude, and gave a hasty nod my way : !; (finefine; don't mention it. He
alcornoqu'd impeccably; ‹Owed on a Greashn Earn›. – But) : "Don't drink
straight from the jug, please ! – Fill it into waterglasses." Said : done. And
now began

The Night=Life of the Guts ! (Which, however, within the briefest of
spaces, must be followed by the Twoi=let : the way these guys were tippin'
the peri=joos – better just pen that long=due postcard . . . .) / No gurgles
now, only the unpurest Manns=vile=pipings : they made the backa their
heads more declivitous, nothing but halffull glasses in flat-wedged hands;
they expounded & pounded; their cheeks reddend; (‹Mr. WALTER KREHNS›;
zip code 43). And turned lively : the voices cruder, the gait tumbler; one of
'em, no longer a man, merely a gin, took the risk now, and lifted his crater
to me, à la ‹here's lookin' atcha !› – and the intimate clangor just couldn't
find its way through his mangled teeth; still welking 'neath my abstract
gaze, he made a rustic rightface; (‹let them speak now unto you› – but
‹welk› : Now who was that again ? ‹Von Welck› . . . . . : I mean my
memory's truly past all & every help. – ‹Dear Krehns, in case anything
important comes up . . . . . my plan is to stay here in Sch. till Monday.›
Greetings=signature; allthough I wasn't feeling all that good about it :
double ‹all›.)

They consumed meanwhile the sweet gifts of god amid noises that
someone accomplishing the opposite would have had little difficulty pro-
ducing. And it gave such strength to the beast Redchix that it told the latest
'neck=dote 'bout Karon's missus : how she'd wondered why her cows
were forever miscarrying. Until her husband, after much Weighing &
Swaying, finally sought the advice of the vet; who flatly informed them
that it was merely a matter of their well=water – (at this point I mentally
stenograft the seequell report concerning the Pitt and the Penn=Julumm;
it contained so many good & useful items for a large rural thriller, like
the one I had once planned long ago, under the title ‹Open Pipe›. And the
others also contributed some semi=fine details from cesspits; about like
the way JOYCE reconstructed, a posteriori, a whole family history from its
dirty linen, ‹O tell me all›) – and what she, the missus, had indignantly
replied to the vet : her ancestors 1 & all had drunk exclusively from that
water; and she intended to do the same her whole life long ! – : "Ha=He=

Hi=Ho=Hu !" (But if that water really *should* have a contraceptive effect –
'twould indeed be a well of wonders, that you could publicize far & wide :
men would hie themselves hither with their girls, cheery lads with cheery
lasses, to the lustiest pillgrim=itch spot. You could arrange pilgrim x=cur-
sions; a hotel district, with lots & lots of little roomettes, to get that well
springing : you could bottle the stuff, and start up 1 helluva=maleorder=
business ! – I'll have to propose it to Roland sometime.) : "Quoi=quoi=
quoi=quoi=quoique !".

I arose. (While the cohort of blissfull damnees continued their unwearying drinking=contest. ‹Lethe=METHE : in case SHE was in the vicinity, she
was probably asleep by now.) Had the Landlord describe for me the path to
the mailbox – ("Put the jug up in my room then, allright ?") – and trod the
night.

URANIA

: wasn't all that dark. Although it – hf=hf; hf=hf – smelled of pastured earth
and rotting woodchips; of moldering, (‹at my molder's knee›). Goes without saying, that during the first few minutes a tree dammed my path now &
then, most of nasty shoulder=width, Labúrs u Lavie ! But since I moved my
head each time, (‹Nono; neither=nor›), they soon no longer made bold.
Very large cubes & triangles roundabout, as usual. / Above the sky was
stretched a bright gray, rather thick skim=mold; you could see precisely
where the light dispersed inside was coming from : from a round lantern;
an all=impic face on it, a cold cheek of connven=shun; (the stick on which
it surely had to be fixt – I had seen it just a while ago – as well as the child
who doubtless, though speechless, bore it could not be made out at the
moment. One calls such things infurence by anal=logy; for purposes of
proof.)

‹A little to the right› he had said – – I hesitated amid farmsteads, where
lights had long since been doused; and between which an unreasonably
large number of gray dead=ends gaped, (mostly just ‹entryways›, sure, into
‹Rural Inns of Court› in prospects, as per above); I decided the better
course was the main traffic artery, recognizable as such. / Personne. Not 1
breeze ‹moving›; just my own 2 soles tapping soft across the cobbles, ‹Hu
passes by zis roadsolait ?›, (Compagnon de la Majolaine naturally;
everandy). In=between, weary but dutybound, come to a halt and think
neit=thotts : halfnaked maples. The light slime above, in which clustered
strings were princip'ly stored, (‹The Power Company provides your city
with li=hight› : and by the by, a faultless singer's shadow, the 1 I cast

there !). In a nearby wall, the square of murky ruby, ‹Know you the land where ultrared hens brewd ?› : behold the eternal warming lamp burning there; (‹here's lookin' atcha›, in a 1000 visions : pity I had to squelch *that* dernyay cree; keeping up your reputation for being even a relatively upstanding man is a downright calamity !). / Onward, headshaking : thinking how dumb, how hopelessly backward it=all is; no future whatever in view for a long time. (Not to mention how the past stank !). But Rhein with its ‹PSI› wasn't any better either : the smallest shortwave station put them to irredeemable shame when it came to range & dependability of function. Why, anytime I want, I can pick up the voice of a Comanche 4000 miles away : ‹common cheese, you co=man, from the Cross=Hatch=Age, the Upper Alluvium›, (inbetween 1 com=ma, comical !).

– but did I ever jerk back from that deep road ditch : outa here ! (From which I had been greeted by grunts & how ? : Damn, that must be a 7=hundred pound boar !). I first wanted to make my rear=treat; but then insinuated to myself that I was a man after all, right ? – : KRRRR ! – CHCHCHchchch . . . – (Calm; calm'n'cool.) – (Damn, so alone on this moonworn road; it was & remained tee=toe=tall=emp=tee : was that perhaps HACKELNBERG with retinue appearing now ? To issue me the notarized bill for my free=spiriting notions ?) – For *that* was more than obvious : I was *no* match for a zoo=morfuss foe of 700 pounds ! (Screw=war-experience & non-intervention medal with crossed dinner forks ! I had afterall been simply a writer & reckoner.) / And did manage to pull myself together – : the worst thing that can happen to me is that I'll dine with JOYCE this evenin' yet. (And/or, wait upon HIM.) / I strode, with firm as possible stepp=stepp=stepp, to the aforesaid unpleasantly deepdug ditch on my right – the settler on the far shore (cirka 36 inches away), had reared a thuja to treeform on 1 stycky corner of his property; most lovely=diversion. And then looked brassy=pompom= bereted, down in : ! – : ? – : ? ? – : and it was *empty* ! (‹Calm'n'cool, Orgy›; Rest in peace & freedom : no real magic left these days; and the swine's end is the sausage's beginning.) Just snortle away, you; *now* I shall let reason rule; (me, cappedtally bebasquet; ‹There, where the week has 3 days›). Calm'n'cool. –

Beautiful cloud gauze above. (And supp=terranean grunz below; sure.) But why was this teeny=water pissing like that ? My logic obediently informed me : ‹Caws 1 pype is seeping=thru under the road.› Well bong. But why's it grunting ? : ‹Caws 1 X=hundredwait boar is botanizing for potato peels & veggies at the drain=grate covering it.› – Oh : merely the nightsong of a hungry soul ? I stepped, most erectly, to the other side of the road, and eyeballed across that plank=fents there : ? (: ‹Why not at once go, Doctor Raisono ?; back to=whence you came.›) : KRR=CHCHCh. All the same I

spoke to him as a friend : "Out so late ?". That barely raised the rams-
head; but rather, went on hitchhogging trufflumphantly, his whole body
awaddle. – : "D'yóu know where the mail=box is ?" : "Krrr=chchch." (In
other words, he neither.) –

This clarified, I wandered more loftily on my way. (Maybe I really
ought to procure myself a donkey ? I rejoiced afterall in a goodhalf=acre of
land. – Granted, if he were then to begobble my young larches & rowan=
trees ?) / Ah here=the bridge : ergo I was tolerably correct afterall; for it
had been mentioned somehow. I leaned 'gainst the iron parapet, with what
looked like a green coata paint in the moonlight, gazed at the poly=glazed
water; (and the dam poly=glotted in muffled water=frenzy : ergo, actually
ought to be called ‹The Glotter›. That flows from the region where the
dead=languages are stored : an excursion in the region where words reside.
The owner of the bankrupted mill would then be the ‹Glotter=Miller›,
MOLINE.) In time its sound came to me so bleak & sans foam. And the superfluous water diffused to a very=small pond, gray=dyed at this hour – (one
really ought to map it out; on a leaf of bearberryleaves : outline bridge
sole=alders : sure; one ought) – and SULLA was truly deader than NAPO-
LEON; (though He, too, was pretty much at nill. I sneezed. – : ‹Neezy bene,
Orgy !›. Meaning, then, that here the Nisi flowed. – To bizniss :)

: where was that let'er bocks now ? I just kept walking on; along the
rarified moonlight. / A train rumbling chiliometers away ?; (at once I laid
my hands behind my ears – – ? – whereupon it rumbled more loudly
o'coarse, but it didn't add *much*). – In general, the edificials seemed determined to hold back at road's edge; only one, mighty=x=tant barn still accompanied me for a=while on the right; (but I x=presst my thanks to it, too;
by walking round it once; crediting it with ‹a mailbox› as it were). –

– Hmyes. / Resumée : ‹lost› ! (At smaller vexations, you should simply
turn your beltbuckle around : 'nd send it on its way. I decided, as an addi-
tional measure, to wander a bit farther. To give nice'n'full expression to
my disdain for a creation without mailboxes : ‹Go to, Orgy !›.) / The moon,
ovful & white as an owl egg, allowed but few stars to rise up beside it.
(Among which, then, there was no longer any union at all, not even spiritual : very refreshing ! I'm against ‹unions›.) I once read – if 'm not mistaken it was even by an astro=number financed by the cath'licks – that
there are loner=suns in space that spend their whole lives in splendid desolation between galaxies; (the ‹misanthropes› 'mong Them speak, I s'pose,
of ‹galactic=rabble› !) : so that (presuming you had such goodluck) you'd
see *only* moon & a coupla planets. In a narrow, cello=feign band; a few
gaudies, fr'all I care, scattered cross The=air sky. Not a word 'bout ‹constellations›; the way they crouch of an evenin' along all our=horizons,

skinny teenettes & whippersnappies; (‹untoweled=down› crossed my mind, astral swimmingpooly : really must be awefully beautiful, on a SITARA like that ! Strictest tri=angles of light 'd be possible there : MOON I = CORONA DÜSTERHENN = PLANET ‹ORGY› : The end ! –).

The moon, it too hung in nice'n'tidy card=anic suspension, ladled casein across the sandpath : is there no constellation called ‹Riding Club› ? (Nah : the nabobs hadn't even had energuts enough to adopt new 1s every 700 years.) And/or to leave at most 1 dozen old ones, outa piety; and constantly see the rest with a jaunty=new eye : here the ‹Bicycle›; here the ‹Typewriter›. There the ‹Bower›; there ‹KÖHLERS Logarithm Handbook›, (with which, granted, I have reckoned much; although there are far better). (The ‹constant dozen›, need I say, with no national or religious connotations; more the happy=humankindly images of allways interesting organs, like ‹HANS CARVEL's Ring› : no PRIOR could have anything against that.) / At the fork in the path, a hiphigh mono=lith; inscription no longer legible; (well, let's assume : ‹Bootpoint, turning linked›.) – Crazy 1.8 miles ! Although that 1 gusta=wind had just let out a splendid=disagreeable rustle : an oaklet; no taller than my hand (provided I held it over my head. Every leaf defiant=sturdy : the others were already at work lettin' their foliage fly. (So that this Young Thing would stand like this the whole, presumably very=juicy (cause cyclic=) winter. Produce its bit of quailing wispy= music. The lovely leaves=all turning pale yellower & drier : sha=moá, chamois.) A foliage=transpanner; & a snub to transiency.) – I automatically cut 1 now, too (most aversely; and terrified, looked about, a man handycappt by convention – ?) : but only the treelet rustled; (in half virgenial half peequed upprobe=ation); and the nor'easter cut starker in the stone : All we want is fysic, fysic, fysic !. –

In any event, look=round snug as possible, (‹Inspite, inspite› ! : Should I turn my belt round a*gain* ?). / Nogo ! Concentratin' on BIOGRAPHIA BOREALIS : the moon, that colloid critter, bemonogled me from above=&=behind. 3 lites wayin the distance; stuck together, (for they held out longer than I), meaning the ‹next village› : the 1=single arc lamp that it (the village) could manage; the forgotten & unswitcht yardlight of farmer QUASIGROCH; the little lamp of a self=maid=widow. (Or, let's be humane as possible : f'rall I care 1 child up in a bleak garret – I know about that ! – at lonely & deft play with its building=blox : *I do not favor ‹unions› !* / Neither US=neighborly co=opperayshn; nor GDR=ish NAW=spadework after work; 'nd they can slice me up in little pieces !). / ‹Klee=wit› ? – Sure was; although, having strayed *very* far over Vandemonsland, it sounded like the feeble ‹YAHOO› of a drunk. – : "Welll ? – Kiki=pupu ?". (That seemed quite correct; for it came intimately closer. Made a couple more curious gestures into the middlegray

air; gave a brief laugh, like a wicked man; then sat down cross from me in
a birch and did rev'runts with head & body) : "Kriwit, good colleague."
(To be such a fool as to beat such merry folk with a hawthorn switch ! The
way ‹The GRIMMS› loved to see it.) But I guess he didn't have much time,
either. For he gave a few tipps with his beak; and then, holding close to the
skywall, a Lord in gray on gray – : swept away. / So fine the pale moonshine sand. / Here, at this spot, Somebody seemed to have fallen on his
face, that's how the print looked. (Like a seal. Or an intaggly=o. Or the
negratif of a death=mask. / In truth, surely just another farmer who'd forgotten to wipe his shoe across it. I wouldn't 've done it in his shoes either :
that, if you please, is the wind's job. Combined with rain, f'rall I care : so
that, in 100 millyun years then, they'll dis=cover the petrified mug of an
ugriculturalist from the ADENAUERIAN.) – I'd prefer to sit me down on this
stone=here, and write poetry . . . . .

and so – – hm; p'r'aps proceeding accordin' to the law of cont=rarities
'd be *just* the thing ? (And since I was squatting here, surrounded by shal-
low=plowed fields, – a downright offense to the backside . . . . .) :
     : " 'Twas in the woods." Period.
Ha=ha ! / Since Missy Oakie was trying to share a few lively messages :
     "The trees they were asleeping" 'nother period.
The lunar eggskull in southern=sallows ? Pert=skewed; a real contre-
taunser ? Come to me, do, tuck=tuck, in my poem :

> " 'Twas in the woods. The trees they were asleeping.
> The moon did smile and listened to their dream.
> Derúmm=derúmm=dumm SHADOWS dumm=dumm DEEP'NING.
> And silent waves did kiss the pond agleam."

(Since in ev'ry respect I was comin' up dry : ‹Your ass froze to the stone it
doth so seem›.) / But why'd I squinted and written so poorly at the end ? –
did a car, of all things & at this nightsleepy hour, have to come bountsing
up the road=here ? ! –. –

– and the tinshark even stopped. And peered curiously at me with
hypergarish kraken=eyes; (but lowered them decorously once forced to
perceive that I went on sitting, proppt calm & large against the bright night,
writing folk=poetry : What a Nebbochant !). On pneumatic=flapps; hovering images, oscilla, before its glassy brow; its protruded belly growled.
And even began to climb out ? ! (I sensed an unruly urge to feign frightful
stupidity !).
     : Gray; all in gray; great & bloated. The head as good as bald; (even the
face tacked on upfront had a pastyd effect at close range; the honorable

Pustet, esquire). Now he began to twaddle politely at me in a high impotent voice, à la "What is it *you*'re doing here ?". – "Did you think I'd lost my way and was preparing my last will'n'testament by waya precaution ?", I asked in return, in my most jingling Federal German, (‹brusque› was the word they would've used in an old-fashioned novel; but since he did not seem to be the worst sort, I added more tractably) : "Actually I'm lookin' for a mailbox." He sniggered, sans energy and barely audible, (strangely high brow) : "Obegyupardn –" he said, equally approbatory and abstracted, "just looked so co=mical eleven at night 'nd some guy's sittin' on a mile-stone & writin' by the lighta the moon – name's H. Levy by the way 'f it's just a postcard givvit t' me 'nd I'll mailit seein' as I'm headin' toward Habighorst –." And *what* a sound on such an already heavily neutralistic night, that completely=accentfree, murky eunuch=tenor; (and had barely looked at me during his entire soft parboiled babble. – But ‹Habighorst› ?; didn't that have some sorta litterary market value, too ?). Well so what; he'd wanted to be helpfull at any rate. "I am a writer," I abruptly declared ; "and I've been jottin' down a few=uhm – moonlit moods." "Ah –" he said, and his gaze wandered 1ce around my neck regions, (apparently doesn't want to look Anyone in the face anymore; somethin' I can often under-stand) : "Don' find that very offen roundere. – Would y' have 'ny objection 'f I siddown here for a minute 'nd smoke a cigarette gotta a whole night aheada me trav'ling round 'nd checkin' the machines betchu're not from roundere either –". He grabbed a seat now; and since the banks of paths are equally mile-long and free, there wasn't much I could do; (Mainthing's he's not out'n'out queer; ‹calaïscalaïscalaïs› the motor ruminated away). And it was too much for him, too, it seemed; for he got up again, and turned it off : me 'pon my staene, my arms crossed indignity, (cause my hands 'd started to chill). He gray & gibbous : a man from whom smoke came now'n'then. –

The washed-out milk face above gazed musing upon us; (comparing us p'r'aps with the pen & ink of Phiz to Boz, ‹Pickwick› caput 29). – : "What sorta machines ?", I inquired at last; (since silence, too, knows its time; gets silly after that) : " 're you some sorta civil=servant ?" : "God forbid" he replied scornfully, "no condom machines I've got the li sunts for=four counties didn't wanta take it on at first the machines cost a helluva lotta money but then my brothern law put up a little 'nvestment capital 'nd now I can't hardly keep up with it had t' buy m'self a faster car now that was a topnotch tip –" he pointed with his other, cigaretteless hand at the expen-sive vehicle model ‹Exchequer's Vexation› : luxury=liner up front pull=man car at the rear (camouflaged as cargo space). I didn't need to ask further=questions; he went on monotone & sorta self=propelled : "ev'ry village gets a machine – can show y' one of 'em lateron gotta replacement with me – 'nd then I drive round the Promisst Land like a madman 'nd all I have t' do is pull the money out b'low stick the new stock in uptop y' wouldn't b'lieve the 'mounta stuff gets used –"; he dragged smoke in deep; while I digested the information. "Course we knowa coupla tríx too" the capotaine capon singsang on : "y' gotta give the machines a smart dabba paint if y' wanna diddle the grangers 'nd we hired a sykolla=jest t' work up the name for us x=tra call it BEARMETTLE so they All feel strong as a bear 'nd fulla mettle 'nd a metal mark a package somehow seems like a logicull price –"; (the tool of success; but there was prob'ly 1 question yet to clear up) : ?. – : "Nah 'lmost never in villages witha church," he said, "the rev'runds obstruct 'em there but then They get their per=cent for makin' babies 'fonly they'd admit it out in the open noway that'd mean public scandal even tho They're the ones who love t' do it mostev all" to be on the safeside, I interrupted this particular stream of consciousness (for his sake; though he was quite right when it came to these costumed clerix; all the same *he* rejoiced in his far thicker=coarser foreskin=ersatz=complex !) : ?. – "Three in each," he said defensively; "but we givvem somethin' for their money : as a mattera policy one's black the girls go crazy when He brings out a tool like a nigger's hardly a woman what can with=stand it 'nd if it makes for some fun there's really far too many people in the world like to see Anybody 'ncluding X 'mself refute me wouldn't y' say I'm right – ?"; (I shall surpress the High Name that escaped him here. But ‹right› naturally; only a prophyssional idiot could argue with him there. We sat a while downright pensive in the infertile light : yesyes, the question of humanity.)

The sky cover seemed to get thicker & rubberier drop by drop; (the Virgin Oak just barely petticoaketting now; and you had to listen for a long time; and only then, sympathetic, join in her frou=fru=shivers.) And now 2 pointsa light chased across the distant horizontality, side=loopy star= shooty – – : "The road to Endewold" he remarkt, (and they were gone). / But the moon was really leering from the heavenly underweir like a rolled= up condom, no arguing with that, (‹The Power of Patterns›; the pattern has power : He powers the pattern; he laughed listlessly from the right=arched corner of his mouth, sending a slovenly knot of smoke packing at the same time) : "– mostly in the car 't's alleather 'polstered 'nd the sleepin' bag's a bloomin' mollycoddle no compar'son t' cons'ntration camps you're completely inde=pendant peacef'ly eatin' your cornbeef & mazzah 'nd 'ncase they ever should drop a plutonyum=bomm on us y' can turnround slip in behind the wheel & kiss it goodbye –"; he shook his head, dead= & prob'ly also live=sure of himself, till you could clearly see the wobble of his pudding=face – (is there such a thing as gray pudding ?) : "Y' mean to say they might condemm us to a war ?" I asked him, (more for smalltalk than to procure his opinion). He gave an unbiased shrug of one fleshy shoulder : "Ah yunno I dunno –"; and for the first time since I'd known him, he made a little pause, (thus honoring the topic with more total attention); gave the same one another shrug; and went on with a certain sublime devilmaycare (which, to be sure, I've frequently encountered on Federal German earth'n'soil, may well be the rule) : "makes me no diff'rents how it turns out even if they skin me alive mamma never cookt for us when we were kids. We didn't re'lize at the time how that was a kinda school for life we were happy t' have a little dry bread & cheese in the house – course y' ended up fartin' like meshugga y' may well laugh but my papa's last word was ‹boomerang› –" : and at that I turned to him, much more curious now; (you hear the wildest things when it comes to ‹Last Words›, from ‹Morelight› to ‹Merdealors›, (from Rangoon to Mandalay), from ‹Children, love one another› –) : "Say that's not bad –" he said, pondering; but before I could flatter myself for having shifted his interest from the Tall Mud to the Good Buck, he was already proceeding : "Specially that ‹one 'nother›. Have t' make a note of it for our ads'. – No it was like this," he picked up the thread of his earlier tale with more verve : "the last time they took him t' the hospittle the nurse shoved a commode up next t' the oldman's bed 'nd he used it too 'nd from all that unaccustomed good & reg'lar food it'd came out looking like a ‹boomerang› he said & demonstrated. And then he spread his arms a little more & kippt over right then'n'there. – Hmyes." He got up, on the 1 hand elefantesque on the other balloonlite; thrust a Lunula into the sand with his heel, and carefully buried his butt, (: cigarro tras cigarro el tiempo apura. Colilla tras colilla al hoyo lanza. Per el aroma pierdese en el cielo; which I, for my part, doubt). "I've gotta go by waya the inn anyways," he said, "you can c'mon on back with me it's alot simpler put your postcard in with my mail=there" – (he pointed to the glove compartment) – "it'll automatickly get sent right along no way I can f'get gotta send a telegram anyway –". We were seated now.

He reached in a semi-languid fashion for the various knobbs, so that the motor noticed that its mas'ser couldn't give a hoot whether it functioned right off or 30 seconds later, so did it rightoff. The gray shelter of the night began slowly to unroll its skin past us. (Presumably the fello was such a brilliant driver simply because he had too little interest in anything else to get nervous (or nasty for that matter).) Strong & quiet the motor, too : so we silently drove down the gray sandy stream in our tincanoe; a through trans=sit. (Offer a bill in the Bundestag : all ‹through› express= trains be equipt with bibles; they'd take it under advisement like that ! And then send it on to committee for study; title ‹Boom in Parliaments›.)

– "Pf=Tulp – –" he began, after 20 seconds of time transformed into space :
"he's 'nother one a my crank customers the richest man in these parts a
staff like y' never ev'rybody up to their ears in debt to him 'nd he's nothin'
but a stale ol'Nazi who woulda loved to butcher ev'rything well he had t'
go 'nd get married in his oldage 'nd that young wife gives him proper
what=for –" (the objection I raised here on the basis of my own observations was heard patiently, true; but then shoved aside with a shake of the
head) : "Suresure he makes a showa bossin' her round 'nd she lets him do it
too she's no dummy but just giver 'er a chance 'nd she'll take him round
Cape Horn three times a day –" : ‹WHUPP› rumm bulled the bridge, tossing
us elastickly in the saddle, (‹The daughters of the Kongdom of Moab shall
be at the fords of Arnon› – I leaned back more reservoirdly, and shut my
mouth : to think I was still *such* a poor judge of men ! Granted, I hadn't
paid but nominal amounts of my attention to that incongruous pair; all the
same.) / Desolate this bit of (geometrick) intersection; ‹the shadows
napped in pent-up darkness deep'ning› – voilà ! and it compliantly appeared all on its own, the missing line; (with the x=ception of ‹pen=tupp›;
the ladies can't bide that – altho the connoisseur would immediately be
re=minded of ‹Pen=tackle Pain & Hexagramm› : maybe a special edition ?
In a small printing, cum foot=notes, pro sapientibus ? OhmonDjöhnie !
‹Posthumously› at best; and not even then; we put the last 200 yards behind
us even more wordlessly.) –
    : "Thanxalot !" (Ténaronténaronténaron). He shook his head in fare-
well : "Don' mention it. – I gotta come back thru town=here inna hour'na
half *again* anyway once 'm done with my loop round Habighorst providin'
o'coarse some wild gannef hasn't tried to crack my machines. – : a poet –"
I heard him muse & recapitulate yet again. Then the door of the meat=safe
(no not ‹Methe› : but ‹meet› ?) shut, pulled by his hand (once again, I hadn't
slammed it energetically enough) into its snap=lock. (: ‹Korrókorrókorró !› –
    : ‹Karátsche Karátsche Ka . . . . . ›

MELPOMENE

. . . . . & castiglionecoglionicoglioni moonish dying echomix. While I,
nervousmanly, (‹Who knows what will happen to me ?› !), bangmaneu-
vered across the concrete squares, neath the xtinguished baldachin (‹On the
History of the Baldachin› : based on a Kaiser's word). But ne'ertheless was
capable of breaking open the door with unarmed hand. (To think I needed
to give m'self such shots of verball courrage. Just cause of some very distant menaseeming possibilité of investing a corposant fifty-year-old; with

my ex=isled self mayhap mostly mine. – I tried twice, stern & imperious, to think Bassan ma nelka, arrogant as Herr Windbrecher von Tausendmort in persona grata . . . . . and pulled up short : could it be possible, that old GRYPHIUS had flung a punderbolt on ‹to break wind› and ‹thousand morts› ? Quite probably : those old slysters were gen'rally more than we thought of 'em. I quickly gave my self the sobriquet of Literastic Poltron, and was then able to approach with greater composure : 'twas indeed something to me, wasn't there ? –) –. –

– : ‹THE TILL=CHECK›; comic epick in a 'propriate number of cantos. Tulp, that is, herotic at the bar raleng (behind him the indefatigable wallpaper; I was slowly coming to estimate the number of riders at legion), his mighty left hand stuck in the poopdeck of his spouse, (who, pressing a gnarled bummerang of superannuated peat to her breast, apparently did not even notice the POPEry, not to mention feel it : has Anyone ever actually demon= strated that his ‹rape of the lock› could mean (indeed, intend !) something appreciably different from the customary=homogenized ‹theft of hair› ?). He first gazed at me in forcefull princely fashion – : ? ! But since my 2 peeps met him straightaway cold & gay, (well=drained from negotiations with countless pirate captains of press & broadcasting), he broke off his excursion in clutter; (for Orgy's got the GOLD, how it rolled & bowled, every Leopold I'll hold and fold, though told he's bold, old & cold, mani- fold scold & uncontrolled !).

: "The bill ?" the Landlord, magnannymus; (I had explained that it was my habit to settle my debts with the world each evening : a man sleeps better that way, in the hours twixt moon and milkman – a maxim that obvi- ously impressed him; (nor was it meant to accomplish any more than that). So on with it : ‹Merchant contra Kauffmann›). He totaled with a pensil= scepter, thick as my ringfinger but three times as long. Leaking minutes passed by overhead; inter=whispurrd with merry falsehoods from the glass visage; (she had, in response to his majestick gesture, turned it ‹down›, rather successfully deaf muting the mummies; (tho you almost had to look at it even more often now to figure out *what* Liga Grisha was fingerfidget- ing & panto=mouthering ?) –).

: "Int'restin' progrim y'know," he proclaimed vig'rously, with two understrokes of the total – (I had long since decifered it, and merely pro forma, for the good ring of it, jiggled my purse the while) – he provided the diejest, in the wellknown alalic=hash of the folk. And I really did listen=up too :

AT THE BOTTOM OF THE ELBE NEAR LAUENBURG ! :

: "They've figguhd out – thru somesohta magnedick=rays –" (cyrcle- ceasing : GOUÉ !) – "that wheah the bohdah a the zone crosses th' Elbe,

theuh's some right lively traffick goin' on in the rivah=bed : speshull
a=gints !". (‹Jinnts›; in rubber=diversuits.) "'nd not jist from the Othahside
t' heah. Pankovia was quick t' broadcast some wisdom of its own, too : that
Bonn was slippin' foemuh Ess=Ess=men thru, too. In th'op'site d'reck-
tion." And looked at me ex=spectantly : ?. I nodheaded mutely. / (Crazy
scene, o'coarse, groping along float harn=assed & cocklemussly in the
poor=pall opfusscation, steered by rough=raidar, sighn=eyed capsalls
tuckt in their cheex. And stop-watched at every grope, breastshield to
breastshield with muteyouall collisions : Bmmm ! – But it was too much
for me; I can't concern myself with everything; I shuddered a little even
now at the prospect of my Dreams Tonight !). – : ? –
  : "Rieke put it up in yoah room" (the glass jug that is) : "I pouhed in what
was left from bottle six foah y'." (Meaning, an honest man.) / (‹You're an
Artist, Too !› seemed to be the progrim's name, announced by the lackher
doll, a stereotyped smirk about those eleusisweet lips : but 'm no longer
green enuff for tulip=gorges like yours, my womannequin. – Better to pay
up.)
  And checkt him with the palma my hand : not another word about medicine & husbondry : "Just be glad I'm not payin' in ‹Michel=marx›." He
laught a=loud across his whole frontline : "He showd up heah aggín. I'm
s'posed t' tell you, ‹That was a goddam lie : theah ain't no sitch thing !› –".
I decoratively lifted only my (wellgroomed=bristly) right eyebrown; and
profile=actorly put away my pursa=gold : ! – then with equanimity : "And
Who – in your opinion – is right in this instunts ?". "No question o' that
whatevuh," he said pompassly : "He ain't got nothin'." I just gave a measured nod; (since we were manifestly dealing with a decision in my favor;
you could always betray 1 or 2 principles in that case). She had nudged her
way closer, and regarded the Deadly Dust; which He strove to mannipulate
in sov'reign fashion; (although y' could see the frank dabbly lust of both,
guinea=hen and gin=i=cock). But he really had to tallony up that much
moolagio in his book (‹HAWTHORN=Pudding is always speciel›; wine-red-
dish on pulp paper). "Shut the dooah to, man –" she gently reminded her, at
the very least dubble=crowned, Louis d'or. I, millerisible hidalgo, waited
gallantly – she noticed at once, and displayed mo'whoric teeth : "I had
fresh sheets put on. – Aeh, 'm gonna go lei down, Tulp." Noticed, ostensibly only now (: I don't believe a word, my little duckat !) the proposition so
easily drawn by coupling such trains o' thought; and withdrew in sweet
confusion. (So he was right, my Levy=pettifogg'ray. – Recently an acquaintance o' mine, his head shaking in ever greater frustration, was studying RÜCKERT's poem ‹The Adulterer› in my large edition; till I pointed out
that title was to be read, much more correctly, as ‹The Idol Tour›.) – "Y'

have 'nything like a church in town here ?". He was finished with con=
verting it into marks, and first relished repeating the tally once more, puffing his dubbloned=florined cheeks. Then, in cold defiants (left over from
Verden) : "All we need." (Meaning, no. I hadn't seen one, true; but then
‹preyer=chapels› can be set up inconspicuously most anywhere, even
where y' least suspect it) : "Good. – Very good."

"Good. – That's that.", he decreed with finality. Pulled himself up even
more king o' the heathy; partook of a pint of genuine=hanoverian air –
(making him broader still; I braced myself, butted gainst a genuine cyc=
lopsider (from ‹butt›)) – and then bellowed like the famous brazen bull :

: "RIE : KAH ! ! !" – –

: and did my heart ever land me a blo : ! (And then came, mercilessly,
innumerable little punchlets, so fast 1aftertheother that I had to wrench my
mouth for air – which he, as a matter of course and with eye proud & glassy
(from the x=ertion) attributed to his vocal prowess.) Damn, what a moment !;
after thirtiplus years to see HER again ! I mean if *that,*, so my babbling
thoughts, didn't benefit my lyrieks : amo amas amat. (Ammó=amáss : I lofft
a lass & she vas tall ant slender. I heard the door go, and for a few cowardly
fractions closed my round eyes. Heard the Landlord's ordnance : "Show
the gen'lman his rumm." Upplied some strength to bite my chincheex apart.
To be man again. Opened . . . . . ?)

: . . . . . ? !

: . . . . . ! ! !

– and gazed right
into a broad rott=iron face . . . . . : I'd had *that* honor several times today
already ! ? / My eyes must doubtless have stood out somewhat from my
head; for the Landlord observed me closely. But then presumably ascribed
my fixt gaze to the pumpherknickersly desire (known to him p'r'aps from
litteratour) of Great Men for a little v'ryety in diet now & then. Smirkt
contentedly; (did a ruff estimate I s'pose of the number of days by which
my visit might well be x=tended). At once whispered something to her in a
dialect (a dead one, p'r'aps ?) that, given my momentary state of soul, I
found incomprehensible. And then, pregnant with good wishes for sleep,
extended a right hand that a normal Creator could have used for making
two : –. –

–. – / – – –. – –

and alone with the Rose of Schadewalde. / (‹Ze misstick Roaz› : my confusion so great I would never have thought it possible at my age ! I just kept
staring at HER) / : the way She stood there, in her blue linen dress – (hadn't
the members of a certain ‹Louise=League› worn them in my youth ?) – the
bed=rolly'em lamp in her left meanial hand : the ringshaped flamelet, (call

it fifteen watt d'y'say ?), waited, likewise skwisshed by fate, (dependent), in its (too narrow) glassy house. – I'll be damnd, 'twas undeniably the kneetly=trembled Lass from before ! ! ! – / (And what a vainglorious brat she *was* back then ! (Her father a druggist ?) : I had not ventured so much as to speak to her even 1ce !). But this was really going a bit too far, that I should play the sharecropper & dam=tender of a stinking bumpkin, stunk-rotten to the roots ? (And/or sheered=ender & dam=cropper : amáss=aMát, I laid her flat); She was still waiting at the halfopen (naturally another lin-seed-hued) door. –

: ‹The Deaft=Dove on Far-off Terebinths›; (I gradually recognized Her; piece by piece, with difficulty, slow & sure : swan-neck belly breast & chinelas : why do I weep so ? / Just pull my raffish worldly self together : ‹Rafn the Skald›. Take another gulp; so –) :

: "Uhm= . . . : would you show it to me please –". – / (: damn, those were the very first words I had ever exchanged with Her ! And naturally had to be of choice ambi=gooity); and her answer was likewise merely noncom-mittal. "Oh –". Turned her back on me; and maid to stride ponderously ahead. / Past the portrait; (and the portrait couldn't hurt me; couldn't lift its crutch – so 'nfackt more a variant on Old Fritz, huh ?; 'nany case I gave the fello in question a patronizing nod) : the *voice* still seemed to resemble hers, too; the 'xact same jagged alto She'd used to converse with her girlfriends in the ol'days (and to give me a tricksy once-over now & then). It was my=turn today to give a once-over to her wrestler's back, (the rear of which had more old oakleaves than either wind or probability theory allowed : anyway, the Landlord was cocksure I'd shag her down to her cambium.) Sure, if I hadn't seen her a while ago . . . . . then Aman mite p'r'aps . . . . I really made ev'ry effort to generate some kinda steatopiggyan lust within me . . . . . : but given the anteseedent sircum=stances I most assuredly couldn't manitch it ! – She was steadily climbing the stairs aheada me; and prezenntid zumm epperishns to me : the blue-cruciform cuirass; below it 1 rearend, double mass, (‹al manach› the place where the camels kneel; and one add=ores. – Nah : guess you better Count Me Out –) –

: "Here. –" / She corporally boxed the door open. Proppt herself side-ways on the jam; (and had a bosom, this woman, that I could barely nudge past : as a lad longago I woulda dis=puted that she was in possession of such; so greatly did I etherialize Her à la ‹Boyish POE=it luvv› : what a jackass *I* must've been ! : Boorish Po=luter, that'd be more the size of it !). I now=only needed to sink a gracious hand into her commodious cleavage and fish for pearls until I quivered down to my blissfull end. (Above=Us a mouse began to gallop. And the night at once did its acustick dewty;

sounded as if it weighed 10 pounds & was tipptapp dancing across a drum : damnstright; didn't absolewtly take a 1st=class ticket to Schadewalde for me to get a dose of the clap ! I strode even *more* indecisively.) Toward a table, century=old & worm=holed, (shoved against the wall by waya precaution; all the same, looked as if it was having trouble keeping its legs); and sluggishly laid my SINTAX=satchel beside my newest jug : which SHE had brought up=stairs for me . . . . .

Cast me a cold eye now, too – (not anything like ‹watcht me›; she probably didn't get that invulved on principle) – gave me 1=short nod : ? ! – When I still could find nary a word, she turned around and started to m'arsch off. / I was almost sick from pure insertitude ! I ran to the door; I wanted to call her back, to the effeckt of ‹'sn't thErinny remembrance of me – ?› – She had heard me. She turned, in midstairway now, yet once again : ? –

– (my, what a Blue Angel ! – Nah. –) / B'sides, she'd surely be dead tired, (the humendacious babbling inside me began : she had quite alot behind her afterall, the laybors of the day & such, Nahnah). I took my tongue firmly in both hands, so to speak. I uttered in broken (tho fluent) high German : "Wake me please. At sex ay em." She hearkend for a moment to the sound of the ciphers, (‹the 6 is the bawd of the multuplication= table›; or the whore); then gave a businesslike nod. Turnd away. Then that goddamste lowsy lantern put her outline in hyperfock=us. Pro=visioned her as well with a (ridiculously short) shadow=train; that juggled along behind her, (‹Maiden jug=jug=jug›) : I lost HER, she lost her way, down the (linseed-hued) stairs : ! .; , – . . . . .

A mirrormirror on the wall ? I took a step toward me; and carefully observed the mask of (well not just ‹dub›=iety more like) tri=biety. Besides, the damn shard was so fulla waves & streaks that you could easily 've demanded money for a look=see – I wrencht a mouth in disgust, at the bloated goat=there : ! (whose ‹face›, however, took on such a quasi=muddy look at that point, that I voluntairly left the field to him : tat twam asi, alas'n'alack !). / Next to the sleepin' box; alone as the seven o' Spades : I stroked it mindlessly. – A pillow stufft with moss, ‹Our Lady of Bedstraw› : I attempted, without much sucksess, to project the wild beauty on it : ? (No luck as a hole body; ze yoony=versl hevvn is in ze shayp uv a SWEDNBORG says mann.) Or several lovely wilder=nesses ? (Can one read pornografy in the future, and, at the uppropriate passage, let the book drop & think of HER ? – – : NIX ! He gave not a thought to unwrinkling.)

PFFF : this then the last word of the Sentimental Journey ? (And yet another wondering that befell myself : sure; a stupid wife is an afflicktion; (altho an ‹intellectual› must be downrite unbearable); but *her* kind of all things – stop jigglin' your feet, mousey ! – I guarantee anyone with *her* ‹round his neck› for any amounta time would stand a 100 rounds of grog just to be rid of her again ! Why was I grinning now ? – Ahyes. Had come to me how clever soldiers in Norway, at the starta the Occupation, had hustled with the inflation=money from 1922 : ‹1000 marks for 1 night !› ?; hardly a maid who could resis . . . : hadn't *that* phrase, *too,* already oc-curred 1ce today ?).

Well 'tanyrate : I'd be able to brag in the future that I'd seen her navel. (Mutter=practice – certainly my face 'd take on a Grand=Seigneurick x=pression; but *I* was not voluntarily returning to *that* mirror ! – and so all blasé, half John half Tenor uhm : ‹I've seen that navel of *Hers* before, too›). The ‹answer of the deep› did not fail : it moaned from somewhere, (had the devil had his way, it mighta come from *my* mouth !); but as I have no affection for the deep, (‹aquaria› yes; that's something for Us), I did not respond; but rather simply felt, blue & amused in one, how my baseless-ness was still steadily increasing today. But a) is probably typical for the traveler; and b) everything gets smaller=cruder with ageitation.

In the jug, won=gallon – : that too sheerest deep thought, ‹wonder + gall›; was I, me in the primalife, feeling like the Old Man in ‹Immensee› ? – just a little puddel of fluidel ? Libethric=pimpallish. I beseized it with my calm=firm owner's hand, (‹Drunk t'day, & Drunk t'morra›) : No !; no point in it, THE WHOLEDAM THING. In other, clearer words : 1 large swig. (And here's to HER, the ‹strange daughter Jovis› !; and at once I nodded a hoarse ‹Alaaf› to her against the wooden chamber wall.) Goes without saying that age is increasingly a soliloquy in a dilapidated brickworx, a mono= mime before a wavy mirror, (I intentionally did not invent the third meta-phor : I had carefully trained myself to cede that tri=pulsion to my ac-quaintances. Nor was there any reason for me to write elegeez 'pon the sweating window.) A gummy=nasty non-obligement, most welcome in my situation, appeared to want to establish contact with me ? – "My pleasure; Düsterhenn."

I bent low over the table, (‹Horsetrader with lantern› occurred to me : so murky was its glimmer); I wrote a little slippa paper full – wait !; but o' course, in our antiquated jagged gradeschool gothic; (which, as I had just recently realized to my astonishment, youngstirs could no longer decode : I had appeared hopelessly passé to them, a contemporary of the ‹KNITTER›; well, that's life) – :

FOR RIEKE

1 corner folded=under, (I always use the upper=rite), and lay 1 golden 20=franc=piece beneath : which she would then be sure to find, at 6 o'clock in the morning (after

having first bent in tender=vain over the empty bed). I have to com=
pensate her for bringin' the jug up; I thought slyly. (How strange : ‹No=
Love› left; not even at 5th or 6th sight ! –.) Till it fin'ly occurred to me, at
my current advanced age : that ‹love› had had nothing whatever to do with
it back then ! As little as with POE's definition : prettified mind-games, and
nothing more; oxidentally affickst to eggsidentals; (tho acoarse somehow=
lewdicrously de terre mined : ‹The EMG is more important than what
occasions it›; mania sirmise came to me now . . . . .). / : ‹Nother swig,
Orgy ?› – : sure; nother swig. The aforesaid ‹occasion› was indeed cause
enuff. (All the same, careful, don't let con=cretions & per=ceptions start
their minuit=minuet.)

The slippa paper lifted off again – : there the thing lay; 1 goldround
chryse=isle in the wrinkled wooden=sea; mundus not particularly intel-
ligibilis. (A man'd have to be pretty far gone to pick ‹PONTUS EUXINUS› for a
pseudonym – welll, p'r'aps I'll go that far yet. / Headshaking, & cover it up
again; carefully.)

Nah : better to wander the night through, if need be. Hope it doesn't
come to downrite rain; and my bill with this part of the world had been
demonstrably settled. Even if only to the next village. (Whose inn one
would hope still stood open; which is to say : He who pays in gold may
make bold to knock most=Anyone awake.) And had been a long time since
I'd pilgrimed & notated my way through such a special mix of autumnal
night & milkglass sky – : how enterprising this Orgy was; I hardly recognized him; (if he wasn't just scared). / But first another visit to the can : so
I can stride forth daughty & unimpeded for the first half hour at least. (Un-
dignified, fishing it out from under the bed !). – And stand there; and wait;
(‹The head large & dull, the mouth agape›); an excoriated enamel=hollo in
my right hand; a flimsy hornlet at my belly, it reeked, (‹The Book of
EZREEKIEL›); bifurkations of veins, goosebeeried, (Above me the mouse),
and 1ce again, no end to it : I'd hadn't had all that much . . .   . :
hf=hf=uh, hf=hf=uh : did the crap ever *stink* ! – Damn I'manidiot : She'd
find that t'morro morning *too* ! I was shamed to absurdity. (And to improve
the aroma at least, hit upon adding a shot of schnapps : – ? – whereupon the
odor, I mean spontaneously, grew so infernal that it bountst my head back.
– Just shove it away with a shudder !). –

 : did I have it all ? : Beret on; jug in hand; satchel clampt under the same
arm. – Ohyes, that piece o' sausage yet; case Kirby's prowling round outside, let him have that. (But was really a pretty crazy outfit for a nightwalk;
specially since to have my righthand free for the banister, I'd have to im-
provise by stickin' the sausage in my mouth – well, man's an artist, that's
all.) I opened the door, softly . . . . . ? –

In the deeps of the house the zero hour began to toll in the most repulsive fashion. Which I, old tactician, (and at the moment a sadder end a viser man b'sides), very promptly used to camouflage my tapparture. / Below : I didn't even bother to approach the large frontdoor, (was sure to be lockt); but instead, the nearest vestibule=window. Before cranking it up, 1 last look=back – : Pff !; Madness, thine is the vickt'ry. (Wonder if, outa sheer meanness, I ought to leave a scentmark behind for that braggart, the Landlord ? I could easily 've hoisted a lovely one. But then, a bit more soberly, I checkt out the much too roomy vestibule : no yuice. Firstly, it'd fritter away by morning; and secondly their noses were much too numb.) I decided instead to swing across my own rear, and out the window : how comely & sweet thy first love for to meet.

: did I have firm footing ? – I did. (And first close my eyes to get 'em used to the night : Above all, if there be no more marriages !). –

TERPSICHORE

The second of my senses to report in, as I was almost certain it would, was my nose. I, as a layman, differentiated merely between cowdung and rotting beets; meanwhile, however, so as not to be totally indolent, presst the casements somewhat more tightly with my back. / Then eyes open : –; – : the road (for which I had ditto braced myself) it was not. The black out= & sidelines of the edificialities were too close for that; ergo a courtyard. I began to stride very slowly forward, but *not,* for the best of reasons, following my nose : the sky turned paler with sheerly every step, (and consequently, in this case, more friendly : right; the moon'd be busy rompin' about somewhere, albeit somewhat lower now). And now I smelled the 10 yd-long sugarbeet=marblecake, on my left, and not just that; I also recognized the straw=tips with which they had ornamented the top. As I was skirting it, an archéd portal cut through the high shadowall : into the open. And at once, goes without saying, I steppt in under it, and peered – ? Then turnaround – : Damn, it was the same courtyard from before ! Where the farmhand had oculated her on her sleeping eye; (wasn't there a hort=i=culous ‹grafting of the fork›, too, trembling unsayable evernew ? S=top, nothin' there : a great thought=traveler (‹Traveler in Thotland›) that yes; but no more globedrotter, please.) Now I knew x=actly where I was : down left, round left. And then dead ahead; 3=fold noteworthy spirited stride.

Hesitate a bit yet; and enjoy the mood of farewell. (I could afford it now, this once, having committed myself to the night anyway; and besides, it all just grew clearer and clearer, even for the lowlying eye : 'twas indeed already damned wild & wintery !). Hm. – Was it not p'r'aps expedient, prior to my final departure from this devil's thrashingfloor, merely to taste (or, better, to exaggerate) the autumnal night, to have a prophylactic last wee swallow ? To said end, and ashamed as always, I stepped back a bit into the courtyard. Lifted the jug, circumspectly borne topsy earthturvy, wearily to my balladeer's mouth – (yet another attitude worthy of old Mr. SHANDY : my SYNTAX clammpt under my left arm; 3 fingers of my right hand laboring to do the same with 1 foota sausage; in the middle a gallony= slave, approached by most fattened flatfooted fetor : ‹Setter down Orgy.›) And as I fixt the cork there ensued not far from me (not so much out of cunning, but rather all en passant) a cracka=light; narrow but very dis- tinkt : ! I had to syghe; for doubtless here again something wanted to be noted; (and what's a singer good for really if not to simulstenografize the uni= sive perversum ? An offense to all, a true joy to none. I groaned yet again; and betook myself then, ‹cunscious of dewty› in the direction of the shining crack). Which was not all that easy, and my approach more a scramble : apparently a larger number of pinelogs had been stored here; and then, by the silent hearth in wintertime, to be brutally chased up the former – I bescaled the rubbleworx, dole= & softfull as possible, by dint of the standard toil such long=roundings represent for our no longer prehen- sile feet. Brought my, now spicy, balladeer=breath under control. And bed- ded my great eye . . . . .

. . . . . : Madonna mia Cara !

: Huntresses, unlike a ny saluted ere now; (‹'tis true I swear : a mas- turbating soul ? !›). If anyone was ever in the wrong, in this case it was Ben Akiba; (quite unlike him, I leaned light & slitskinned against the planx . . . . . : mi follere canzon, what a terrortory was this=here !). –

The interior of a (badly lit) gyants=barn : Irish curtains wavered; straws bundled; round MEG with the fetal cuntenance. / LENE, the snakelady, kneel- ing over an aluminum tub, her moist teeth shimm'ring gold at some dangle of incidents or other; (and yet between her shoulderblades a plethora of pomp & prodigy.) / Yon HERMINE, all rock=&=roll=hams, let her choplets abound. / And finally the last one, who was called ALEX, with blond-brown hair down to her godgifted shoulders. – Her three-quarter length fawnskin, the garb of the consuckrated, (like that of those who transport people to the hardly unbrocken mount in WILSEDE), hung from a thick stanchion; (and beside it a pityfull tiniest=rabbit, merry & lively till just moments ago : I stomped my mental feet & cursed this cruel=flexible folk !).

Rising vertic'ly from the hardpounded clay, a high pintle-shaped flash- light (3 stacked batteries, at least). Small, daintily flesht hands in the little suitcase; high-insteppt tootsies on camelhair blankets (‹from northern

Chinese beasts› : Well-nigh decockooned cockuettes atop verytubble imperishabbylities). / One's leopardy blouse still hung open; (otherwise, granted, she had nothing else on; a buttery smooth CANOVA). – Reciprositations; (‹The Mime of Me, Her & the Maggies›), they tossled one another's beards : here a titt=anic mop, bi=cheeky acrobadicks. There an aural os=culation, plus babytalk of lovers, (and much greasy gapings : they hastily oiled down with jellies, seemengly wanting to belong to themselves.) LENE DE LONG had fetched the fullsome plastick bung from her carry=all ('parently the cache for the holy utensils); strewed it with some mixture (let'say ‹salt ashes & pepper› ?), strappt it on upfront with fibula hands and feeble=eyes; approached, in wrentched third gear, her hrosyred mewing AMEGA (so she's the novice ?). They kisst their way up 1 another; and taking the peak of the hill, stamped something dreadfull; fooled around in greased furbelows, beaded – and then she Polished her agathodemoanal cuntessa, (an amalgum of diverse techniques, by the by; a real hairringboniest itch) – sunk she=in=she up over the motherapearled knee.

But these=here too, ALEX atop HERMIONE, lavisht each other : mi sur le do they drummed with holloverberating ditchits, bellypallid subtribaddick sloebellied, hersute contra hersute, (STRECKFUZZY assay at love), zounds tittsian & tittoretto, giorgion=headed & bellyni=shafted. Legs ringariding (little aluminumb=spurs on their blooming fuchsia heels), frigstressed poly=rodding in nauseaching middledoms, overvaulted by high backarch, chloeretic minnesackers & slackasses. Where words once were, only cackles, minyasmas & gluckles now dwellt, sweet mouthings along Riekin' peepworks (oh, let me not think on *that* !). / But the happenising was clearcut : whether the blondsteeled ALEX, or LENE's wellkempt leannass : the bulless with the silver horn; (and switcht now; and the young quainties simulcroaked & quackled, fundybayed=greasygoosed) : and the new mingleman, mort on mort, got bowsprit and rudder no less mixt, a most human wrythm. (1 hollow tooth, 1 hollow mountin'; eachin ev'ry her own ruttspause.)

But the shadows knobberated, handlactive, before my overtaxed eyes, be she sinderella be she mahogunny girl, the wooded mounts the vale, (even short hair really ought to be able to rise mountin'high : if you lived in a truly Free State, ‹Hymnals for Lesbians› 'd surely be possible, for lamias goatleapers incubesses & necromammies). / Given what this LENE here was pricktising, sweatsupply, sauscey & sassy, (and the jowls of her subalturn slippered & quickslavered; tally=li tally=lo – suddenly that wallpaper hunt came to me again : 'fonly I'd known the name of the manufackturer; I'd definitely do *one* room with it, to spite refined visitors !). / Her belly began to spittle, the way she did the Diana=dip ! And was the other dyke beside=

her ever copullulating, too, so that li'l dappullridden HERMINE had be=gun
to whinny, (allround calves, everhard or slottery, eitherway, depending on
aggregate mass), the wet fixture, hiphornily swanging through odifurous
culdesax, chevvied ahead, hoofs to butt, bride o' the wind, she c'unt 've
sludged it better, layin' it on at a tempo till the echoes stutt'ring off the
sills couldn't keep up. (Once, with a shake of the head, as I took to my
jug – sometimes the imp=pression comes over me – the wall complained;
and they stupped short : ? – but then chalked it up, deaftly, to heaven's
plaything.) Although soon there=after they all got up sirsumcordally,
(: 4 deepcloven pale moons illoomed there in the shed). / : "Didn't hurt
diddit ?", LENE inquired ? And MEG gave an enthusiastic shudder : au
countraire : ‹More=Mère !› (They were puffing bellies again now.)

   But my ‹position›, too, might've been termed complicated, with no ex-
aggeration : secured at only 3 points, right foot, left foot, left shoulder, (I
had just turned the right as far from the wall as possible to execute a
philosofical swiglet – a man in the standing state of dissolution, allegory
of the intensive present – let's hope the legs weren't all too resiny, ‹Swan
of Schadewalde, hold fast› : you're reeky, I'd soon have a coupla tics to
pull, too; (let's hope not on my glans, as once in my twens; had been most
onannoying). And as regards venrubble precocious bysexuality, I wasn't
even vaguely an exspurt. 'Tanyrate these poor things seemed to be havin' 1
helluvalotta fun.

   ? But why ‹poor› really ? : ‹If lying can mean standing, then things stood
well with them›. Yeesswhýý?: I didn't know m'self. / But, savvey, that
woulda been 1 for Master Roland; he constantly had his pen at work on
something of that ilk; allevem illustrated, so that a flippa the page could
turn any fairly idealistically inclined lad into an atheist, for the 20 years of
life he had left ! These doctors have opportunities of which the normal
earthworm, with 3 ‹lll›, can't so much as dream, (and/or if he does dream,
then not even vaguely like the truth : skillets with no handles, oval wrinkly
hairy, yearning for eggs; and half a score of them of the foulest sort off to
one side; then another most bluest flowera knighthood, and so it went, all
in color if possible=pff). Whereas when it came to the active side, he
(Roland) wasn't half so bad – our ability to celebrate Black Masses is,
thanx to Mother Nature, wryther limited – but p'r'aps the mere term ‹infra-
red› ought to give us pause ? The bombylophormous singsong of the 8=
mm camera is not merely eagerly accepted (so he had explained to us, as
well as demon=strated od oculus) as a lab'oratorial=ravishing mille=lieu=
sound, but it also has a hyp=notickly relaxing effect : the patient's hand
automatic'ly saunters down her body. In especially tight-clencht cases, the
nurse=assistant, armed in masculine white, half knighta the grail, half

angelic presence, serves up a harmless swig of ether; (‹The Book of
ETHER› : he now knew how the soul is constructed, he would calmly explain
of late: and pass round a cross=sexion of the thing that set allpresent shuddering; and by the by, FREUD was the man; and JUNG, peevy & unclear, not
much moren a step backward). And what They had lacked in statistic'ly=
thousandfolderol material, he could deliver in an abundance that woulda
surprised even Them, the ‹Xray=Bus›, MEGAanthrophilandering from village to village, ivorytowering shingly bussybosomed – once at an intimate
gathering, far past midnight, bottle at hand, he had alluded to : how you get
the most int'resting phorms to step back a bit – : ‹Lock you hands behind
your neck, please. – Deep breath : *and* holdit –› – meanwhile tireless tape
recorders, (the microfone outside, near the gangway), recorded the conversations of the villagers, chilly & randy : which were then given to folk-
lorists for evaluation, and/or to Germanists from the editorial staff of the
slang=lexicon, (‹once heard in salva terra Perilous sweet refrain›; one of
the first corollary findings, needless to say carefully guarded & pigeon=
holed, consisted in the awareness of the ridiculous unrealism of all previous literature). And as must be quite obvious, pollsters and various parties
had, at exorbitant rates, subscribed to extracts, (that was how They then
financed ‹further sectors› of their self=sacrificing scientific endeavors);
but when 1 government (which he did not wish to identify more closely)
along with its ancillary secret organizations likewise decided to get involved gratis, the researchers – with unfeigned indignation, as is only
proper for an upstanding scientist – tortured those bullying bepistoled em-
issaries out in the reception room by subjecting them to rays that they felt
down to their ultraviolet ends, until they spontaneously begged his pardon;
(but one could have done without the ‹Drug=Dose› or that ‹Thrice Holy
Light›). And had to giggle inwardly : everything surrounding these guys
had, in some perfectly organic way, turned slightly meshugga : Roland had,
as a special rarity, *2 queer tomcats* ! He had, quite naturally, reported about
this ‹Instance of Homoeroticism in the Animal Kingdom› in his scientific
journal, ‹with illustrations›, of course; yes, at the start even mentioning the
full names of the two parties involved – from which, only with great difficulty, we were able to dissuade him; (it's simply not proper; in the end,
though under constant protest, he had agreed to ‹Hodge› and ‹Hidigeigei›).
It may sound quite incredible, but there is still no detailed, un=biased description of, let's call it ‹pencil sharpening›; not to speak of Xrayed
bussems. One *could* do it, to be *sure;* and not under some shock title like
‹Pants down !›, but rather in a fashion appropriate both to high=art & powerful instinct; but not only would the attempt, with unseemly certainty, be
defamed on our shores (under the motto ‹private wine, public water›, but it

would also be punished forthwith : if governments hate any 1 sort of artist in particular, then it is the ‹naturalist›. I once heard, with my very own ears, a ‹leading politician› declare with total conviction : ‹There's really no need for art› – quite understandable from his standpoint; for ‹art› implies ‹observation› of the world, and that in turn implies ‹an eye for facts› : and *that* is just about the greatest of superfluities in the eyes of the governing; (at least among the governed : the greater the range of the artillery, the more near-sighted the cannoneer may be.) / Better cut this short; dangerous trains o' thought, which above all were not only bootless for my lyrical projects of the moment, but also might very well untune my lyre – and decided to set my eye again to . . . . . : ?

They were now sticking fruit. Into the mouth : a pallid wide paunch, hot MEG, neath rasp=barey=tipps. Teaspooned a half grapefruit out of its own rind. LENE's sexportaled lizardagility, a genius of the loins. Musing girdles on unsooted wall. HERMINE's midriff proustested the PALPable night=mare, behold an unheard-of pale brider. From over my shoulder, veiled to the eyes, a sort of moon never seen in the settlements. The most bawdily fitt still seemd to be this ALEX, (a type that prob'ly every=man has turned to look arear at; and this time too she stretcht her stern toward me; and what had come to me so often before seemed to be coming for me anew). They x= changed a few maiden growlscouting passwords; hastily rubbed their pulse (leguminous fruit) with balsam. And then began the Great GORMAGON !

: ‹Gomorrha t' you !› : ‹And t' you a Sodom !› : and so they rowtated in Higher MALTHUSiasm, and shaddows nodded applaudicks, (in human gullies wild & mazy), a lap around ventres à terre. Allala=coustix were approaching bit by bit on rollerskates; or along beeways : LENto loins flingered round menny elflockt grottoes, gropantic mitties scritching woolyhandily, flammingo arms hugged rammed groins, occasional unfathomed swellings bounst in place, chaokoontic, j'Allah & inj'allabared : tufties clotted midriff swellings twatledovey teeter betotter hiphopt kisses bellow dangle skinny straddle lilies muscle iris=ship of honeywedging self=devouring coddlegaudy arshyblonder in Sahaira : a cotytittic hornpipe, with obligatoed furtbellows, (whose duodecial sounds, granted, you would not 've been able to imitate with the most eager=manic mouth : no mortal Howth hath them engendered !). / All the same 'twas getting palpably cooler here by me. And boring, too. (Not that I was of a mind to slander life en bloc : *I* know only too well how to discern if the whole cosmos is diminishing, or merely me=myself; but mostev it was really rather stupid. Naturally there's a successful spot in the universe now & then; but the majoritia the products of that sete boss was bungleworx, quick & slipshod, like those of an old= rude plumber's helper : if it were a book, the author 'd sure be told a thing or two. But as it is, they all cowtowed.) – I once again took some more measures 'gainst the chill; (don't worry; I know my limits). And began a last espyonage=series; (before departing) :

: enough of lovestock enough of bareall ! / LENE – (: an*other* medico, just like Roland : *that* 'd have to produce quite a brood !) – was now powdering all excess=able armpitts; (if *I* might make a suggestion : with deedytea; debug the premises : ‹prebug de misses›). She warbled the while, phalse & hoarsey, a long song; (the wurst of 'em, so Roland claimed at least, are said to have been tattooed with a secret=symball – I could indeed supply it, and the rite spot no less; but there's a court in Karlsruhe for that). / Cacklations ruttled : a MEGatrull. / ALEX, all proud=prudent heroine pro, (naive lights would 've glibly included her as a ‹Kneeling Figure› in an anthromug-grafick photo=album. And then prob'ly 've been dreadfully amazed), was hiding the bunging aprons and the broncobusting towels in the tabertackle box. / While HERMINY, red as a carbuncle, was still beJoying the false=staff; and lifted it, her I=doll, to the light, and let it ‹run down›, thyrzarrely long & thick, (& dry=off & aband=on). / They dressed, the huntresses; one an-other, for the preponderant part, while diligently off'ring compliments; (not however with Jaeger ‹hunting›=shirts, ‹My System› : that was another queer duck, that p'tickular Gustav, who discovered his soul, better late than never, by the way of his nose !). Nono : here was a darkgreen back, (the belly, however, polkadotted hi=yello & black : tongue smooth, hands wan). Here a violet pajama, striped in medium brown, (crazy combunation !). There the breeziest dressingown I've ever met, all gray & silky. And LENE naturally in tightest leo=tards and a ditto pullover, coalblack like a preying womantis from the deeps. (Their paddles birches scourges lashes leaned sociably round a stud. That lost itself above in the twilit fabric of beams.) / Crouch & ‹make their faces›; (as if they'd had none before !). They coated their eyes with Puk; and evesdroppt each others most perspurated body-parts. They named the salves that they rubbed on the right spots, in xact doses, and in hi Cosmetic; i.e. a lingua franca invented (& spoken) by hi schoolers, Chná, use it freely : they shook their bottlettes like bar tend'rasses, quaint colors quainter forms; they murmured of Bess BOG and Ruben Stein; they knellt more informally, and let their rosigills be admired. / Gnasht nourishment too; (these ‹nuts› are truly splendid formats : the brains of the Walloons, the sweeteyes of the Hazels, the moons of the Paras; paradise & peri). They spooned crème de la crème and treacles; with rough halfsinged lips, (that must've tasted of Senoussi's : I've never really had a smoker laydy; prob'ly cause I don't myself). Foamy sips from cokeamammy bottles (‹The paws that refresh !›); and they shone all too fair; round midnight. / LENE had rustled up a long red thread; knotted it, smiling craftily, into a great=circle : ! Whereupon her MEG, with porc'lain doll-headed drabrapture, knellt over her wayer; they lifted kundrolling hands, to a twofold 10=finger=system – – then laid out a cat's cradle, setting even me to wonder; (sure, our mother taught us=kids such ‹casting= off›, too; but the play of these=two with their thread beat anything I'd ever seen by a pornarchaic mile – ! – Just the way they angled their heads a bit at the troublesome spots) : "Hatchoo ! !" – dammit, I had sneezed ! And right in the crack. – : ? – let's hope –. But they didn't seem to have heard a thing. (Tho LENE did angle her head a little more acutely. HERMINE lookt up from her driver's manual, memmorizing something. And ALEX apparently had a more copious task; she briefly excused herself.) / ‹Auto ex=pressions›; wouldn't y' know : the whole language seems sexually superfetid somehow ! Just listening to the way She was stagewhisp'ring again now about a ‹lube job› – and the others nodded her encouragement – about ‹mufflers› and ‹spark plugs›; all squeezed through a ‹throttled choke›; ‹gave gas› to some sorta ‹cam shaft›, new to me; and their 6 ‹clutch=pedals› stepped on it, rumblestiffer . . . . .

: ! ! ! – :

: and staggered behind me, as if stabbed by a tribade : I've never taken an INVERTED RIGHT like that in all my life ! – Hyena hopt to the left : I stared into ALEX's racy profile; its blonde hair a bout to serpentine : she laughed=tears of rage at the site of me; meanwhile howling away like the Bohras in person – I immidiotely lost my head ! The pinelogs under my footing began to roll, (I promptly felt as if something were wounding my foot !); thankGOd she first had to dodge the pinchdevil raft, too : ‹The Phall of the Singer› . . . . .

. . . . . Rundammit ! Runforrit : . . . . . ! / . . . . . : ! ! wasn't the hole barny space starting to mumble, then to rage ? . . . . . : ! ! !

THALIA

: oxensized dog barks ? ! – In my confusion (and probably also because the dangle of the gallon, in my free right arm, discomfited me), I had run a little toward the sandpath on my right. But was wide awake now; turned me round on my heel, and began to decamp in earnest : *this* was *not* a game anymore ! For my aging halfwelterweight, 2 of those elasticians would presumably have more than sufficed . . . . . : run dammit ! : if not just LENE alone; these medici know just the painful spots to make a man go to pieces. Not to mention 4 such focksy ladies *plus* Kirby : I fled & flit, setting even me to wonder ! (Andrew O'Phlegeton, you really make haste to fly !).

: "GETT'IM ! GETT'IM ! ! !" – Wedges of shrieking, and : "Sic, Kirby, sic ! ! !" : ándaándaánda=hóptohóptohópto my synthetic soles sounded like castanets : GOspodin pomilui They definitely wouldn't take wergild ! If only I didn't have to clamp my left arm like this – : "HAZZA ! VITE=VITE ! ! !", and a growlation rang out behind me, so bassheavy the dog must've been galloping soundlessly e're this, such was his joy that he had me now, just 2 leaps & I'd be dining . . . . . . and/or serving at his round table of 12 apuzzlementors – 'parently that High Name automatically enlightened me willynilly, for my left hand let the piece asausage dangle wretchedly back behind me – : ? – he seemed to have grabbed it in midspring (and to be passably bribable; for I no longer felt his hot breath blowing directly on my nape) : but *mine* was sure piston=pumping –

: "CHITO=CHITO ! ! !" venumous high & strident : *so near* now the para= diddle of *those* hard hooves, the air adhearing to me already whissling with whipplashes – I felt the bast peeled from my heels How on my rite & on my left flew cititowns & hamlets ! I sprinted along neath the moonz bluddy gallows, instinktively I hung my supplycant panting tongue out for him, and while allahcharonjunior I drumcudgled across the bridgelet deddy= mummy deddy=mummy it got me : !

: an initial crossblow from the left, a skullgrazer, that felt as if my scalp had flown off with my montero : that sailglided batlike across the railing & into the Crick (and would now doubtless drift down it for good'n'all) : 4 pitch'em=after laughs wreckem=penst me so shrilly in both ears : if I let myself be sir rounded now, I was a goner : Shass oh Poet !

: *I had to have my left arm free ! !* With bleeding heart I droppt my precious SYNTAX alongwith satchel : it slappt as if meeting midair with the blow really intended for me (what a faithful servant of his master : were They, to judge by the hardbreaking sound of it, slugging with their cypripores ? ! : ‹EMASCULATED BY TEETH !› I could letter'ly see the headlines, in a thermofaxy blur, as if in a newsweak magazine a good thing there wasn't much left of me to emasculate all the same I would've preferred to leave *that* hair in place : if They hadn't been so severely sapped from be- fore I'd give up I –

– : ? : ! ! ! and recognized the deliv'ry van the lugzury liner ! From earlier . . . . . Second Wind ! . . . . . I did a death-rattled pike-dive at the passing gray . . . . . strait into the midsta condom boxes . . . . . rattl : ‹GO !› – . . . . .

*　　*

*

(Stopping three thousand yards later.)

He, schooled to quickest=cleverest reactions by a concentrated camp-life, had leapt behind the shud'ring=rumbling wheel without any great question; and had hopelessly outdistanced the Wild Chase for now. Now he came around, and regarded me with shaking head; (he had simply left the murkylit trunk, with me mid=ship, wide=open). "Thank you," I heard him say. (My lungs & heart were still going so strong I felt as if I consisted of nothing but those two.) – : "Thank you –" he repeated more sternly, and stared at me. (I was feeling queasy to a degree such I've not known since the military when dive=bombers 'd chase us cross the meadows.) He'd been about to turn away with a shrug. But apparently only now did he realize just *how gone* I was. He laid a hand on my shoulder; he said anxiously : "Wellnow – pittisake; don't go fallin' asleep right here in my car."; but he clearly meant the *brother* of sleep. (And sit there; & pant. –. –)

Very slowly. the night took on shapes again. / Left a bitta woods. A black loom of trees, dark & silent (: but *beautifully* silent !). Gaspin'. – Fields open and free on the right : ‹free› ! Wonderful. –. –. –

"You coulda really put NURMI 'mself to shame," he said; more relieved once he noticed I was starting to survive at last. (Ohyes : I should've thanked him long before this o'course ! – But I wasn't even capable of it myself just yet, my voice flagged so in the dust. I preferred just to sit, wondering if once again I'd collideorscaped my coronary. ?) He gave another shake of his ashen-hued head; he pointed to my lap : "Whaddja bring along with y' *there* ?", he inquired with curiosity. – And I lookt down at it too – ?

: WON GALLON ! Totally unharmed. 'sindeed, with something still *inside* : I raised it to my mouth with two limpy hands; I upended it, I drank & drank; (till he took fright, and pulled it away from my mouth – there, in resisting, I noticed for the first time the fine=slicing pain in my right ankle : all I needed ! Now I'd be able to nurse a solembloody contusion for the next 4 weeks.) / I hid it in my lap : *something at least* ! From here on out I'd fill it with noble whisky 1ce a month. And then I could empty it, brooding, for the dance of the thousand hours; 'twould breathe a blaze e'en from the ashes still. (‹Red nose, a phase of maturity›.) He waited patiently for me to start my account. And between whiles helped me up front; beside him; in the ‹suicide seat›; (well so what : with a respectable man it's only the head that still lives at the end !). –

A Note on the Texts

The stories in this volume first appeared as follows:

Tales from Island Street (Aus der Inselstrasse)

"Drummer for the Czar" ("Trommler beim Zaren"), *Süddeutsche Zeitung*, 26 September 1959.

"Trading Keys" ("Schlüsseltausch"), *Frankfurter Allgemeine Zeitung*, 3 May 1957 (under the title "Schlüsseltausch mit einer Sammlerin").

"The Day the Cactus Bloomed" ("Der Tag der Kaktusblüte"), *Süddeutsche Zeitung*, 21 July 1956.

"Neighbor, Death and Solidus" ("Nachbarin, Tod und Solidus"), *Die Andere Zeitung*, 16 February 1956.

"Hurrah for the Gypsy Life" ("Lustig ist das Zigeunerleben"), *Nürnberger Nachrichten*, 27 July 1955.

"Cautious People" ("Die Vorsichtigen"), *Süddeutsche Zeitung*, 27 July 1957 (under the title "Nur ein Schritt vor die Türe").

"Strange Days" ("Seltsame Tage"). *Süddeutsche Zeitung*, 20 October 1956 (under the title "An solchen Tagen").

"Rolling Night" ("Rollende Nacht"). *Die Andere Zeitung*, 21 November 1957.

"What Shall I Do?" ("Was soll Ich Tun?"). *Frankfurter Allgemeine Zeitung*, 12 January 1957.

"Rivals" ("Rivalen"). *Frankfurter Allgemeine Zeitung*, 26 August 1958.

"At the Telescope" ("Am Fernrohr"). Südwestfunk, Landesstudio Rheinland-Pfalz, broadcast 9 January 1958.

"Tales from the Isle of Man" ("Geschichten von der Insel Man"). *Frankfurter Allgemeine Zeitung*, 6 April 1957.

"Field Trip" ("Schulausflug"). Südwestfunk, Landesstudio Rheinland-Pfalz, broadcast 23 October 1958.

"Song of the Meter" ("Zählergesang"). Südwestfunk, Landesstudio Rheinland-Pfalz, broadcast 11 July 1957.

"Moondog and Pink Eyes" ("Nebenmond mit Rosa Augen"). *konkret*, September 1962.

"Prone-Told Tale" ("Auf dem Rücken Erzählt"). *Süddeutsche Zeitung*, 12 May 1956.

Stürenburg Stories (Stürenburg-Geschichten)

"An Advance on Life" ("Ein Leben im Voraus"). *Hannoversche Presse,* 9 June 1956.
"The Howling House" ("Das Heulende Haus"). *Hannoversche Presse,* 3 September 1955.
"Summer Meteor" ("Sommermeteor"). *Auf den Spuren der Zeit. Junge deutsche Prosa.* Edited by Rolf Schoers. Munich: List, 1959.
"Guerrilla War" ("Kleiner Krieg"). *Hannoversche Presse,* 27/28 October 1956 (under the title "Bericht vom kleinen Krieg").
"The Water Lily" ("Die Wasserlilie"). *Hannoversche Presse,* 23/24 March 1957 (under the title "Das Kind mit der Wasserlilie").
"He Looked Too Much Like Him" ("Er war ihm zu Ähnlich"). *Fuldaer Volkszeitung,* 14 December 1956.
"Black Hair" ("Schwarze Haare"). *Hannoversche Presse,* 15/16 September 1956.
"Tall Grete" ("Die Lange Grete"). *Kölner Stadt-Anzeiger,* 15 May 1956.
"Little Gray Mouse" ("Kleine Graue Maus"). *Tagesspiegel* (Berlin), 19 December 1956 (under the title "Große Herren wissen manches nicht").

Country Matters (Ländliche Erzählungen)

"Windmills" ("Windmühlen"). *konkret,* November 1960.
"Sunward . . ." ("Die Sonn' Entgegen . . ."). *konkret,* June 1961.
"Tails" ("Schwänze"). *konkret,* September 1961.
"Cows in Half Mourning" ("Kühe in Halbtrauer"). *konkret,* December 1961.
"Great Cain" ("Grosser Kain"). *konkret,* May 1962.
"Piporakemes !" ("Piporakemes !"). *konkret,* October 1962.
"New Year's Eve Adventures" ("Die Abenteuer der Sylvesternacht"). Hessischer Rundfunk, broadcast 23 August 1964 (under the title "Abenteuer eines Philologen in der Sylvester Nacht").
"Tools by Kunde" ("Kundisches Geschirr"), "The Waterway" ("Die Wasserstrasse"), and "Caliban upon Setebos" ("Caliban über Setebos") first appeared in Schmidt's *Kühe in Halbtrauer.* Karlsruhe: Stahlberg, 1964.

The present translations were made from volume 6 of the *Das Erzählerische Werk* (Haffmans Verlag, 1985) and volume 3 of the *Bargfelder Ausgabe, Wekgruppe 1* (Haffmans Verlag, 1987).